Song of My Heart

**Center Point
Large Print**

Also by Kim Vogel Sawyer and available from Center Point Large Print:

A Hopeful Heart
Courting Miss Amsel

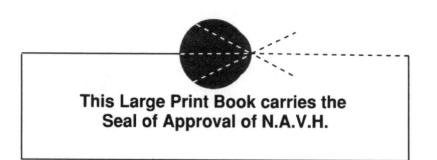

**This Large Print Book carries the
Seal of Approval of N.A.V.H.**

Song of My Heart

Kim Vogel Sawyer

CENTER POINT LARGE PRINT
THORNDIKE, MAINE

This Center Point Large Print edition is published
in the year 2012 by arrangement with
Bethany House Publishers,
a division of Baker Publishing Group.

The text of this Large Print edition is unabridged.
In other aspects, this book may
vary from the original edition.
Printed in the United States of America
on permanent paper.
Set in 16-point Times New Roman type.

ISBN: 978-1-61173-287-0

Library of Congress Cataloging-in-Publication Data

Sawyer, Kim Vogel.
  Song of my heart / Kim Vogel Sawyer.
    p. cm.
  ISBN 978-1-61173-287-0 (library binding : alk. paper)
  1. Large type books. I. Title.
PS3619.A97S68 2012b
813′.6—dc23

                                    2011041034

For *Kristian,*
my little songbird.
May your songs always proclaim
the faithfulness of the Lord.

"I will sing of the mercies of the Lord for ever: with my mouth will I make known thy faithfulness to all generations."

Psalm 89:1 (KJV)

1

DALTON, INDIANA
MID-MAY 1895

Sadie Wagner let out a squeal of delight. A tufted titmouse shot from the budding bush nearby with an indignant flutter of gray-feathered wings. On an ordinary afternoon, Sadie would regret frightening away a bird that offered such an enchanting melody, but today she was too excited to pause for regret. Gathering her tattered calico skirts in one hand, she clutched the letter from her cousin Sid in the other and dashed for the house.

Bursting through the door, left open to allow in the sweet breath of spring, she cried, "Mama! Mama!"

Her younger sister, Effie, turned from the dry sink, a dripping cloth in her hand. Her brown eyes widened in concern. "What is it, Sadie?"

Sadie waved the letter. "Good news! Come!" Catching Effie's wet hand, she tugged her sister through the doorway to Mama and Papa's small bedroom. Their feet beat a staccato rhythm on the pine floorboards, matching the rapid tempo of Sadie's pulse. She released Effie and fell on her knees beside Papa's bed. As always, the sight of his drawn, pain-riddled face raised an ache in the center of her chest. But surely the opportunity presented in the letter would ease some of Papa's burden.

Mama, seated on a chair beside Papa's bed with a half-empty bowl of potato-and-onion soup in her hands, sent Sadie a troubled look. The lines of worry etched into Mama's brow had aged her. She set the bowl aside and touched Sadie's heaving shoulder. "Goodness, child, why are you in such a dither?"

A gleeful giggle spilled from Sadie's throat. She held out the letter, showing it to both of her parents. "Look! From Sid. Remember he promised to write once he got settled in Kansas? He's there now . . . all settled in . . . and—" She paused to catch her breath. The dash across the yard had winded her more than she'd realized.

Effie danced in place, wringing her hands. "What does he say, Sadie?"

"He says there is a job for me in Goldtree!"

Mama's jaw dropped. Papa sucked in a sharp breath. Effie clapped both hands over her mouth and stared at Sadie with shocked eyes.

Sadie's confused gaze bounced from one family member to another. Why did they appear distraught rather than elated? Didn't they—like she—see Sid's letter as an answer to their prayers? For weeks they'd been asking God to provide a job for Sadie. She waited for someone to say something, but they sat in stunned silence.

Sadie released a huff of frustration. "Didn't you hear what I said? A job!" She flipped the letter around and smiled at her cousin's scribbled text. "As a clerk in Baxters' Mercantile. For"—she squinted, trying to decipher Sid's penmanship— "sisters Melva and Shelva Baxter." She smiled at her mother. "*Honest* work, Mama." Unlike the only jobs available in Dalton. "With a fair wage."

Mama still didn't respond, so Sadie turned her attention to Papa. "Sid says the owners wanted to employ a young woman since they are woman proprietors. They'll provide me with a room and meals in addition to a monthly salary, so I'll be able to send nearly every penny back to you." She deliberately avoided mentioning the other part of Sid's letter—the part that made her heart twist in eager desire. Pointing it out could seem selfish. "God answered my prayers, don't you see?" *All of them . . .*

Tears flooded Mama's eyes. She blinked them away and reached for the letter. "But in Kansas, Sadie? It's so far away."

In her excitement, Sadie hadn't considered the distance. Her elation faltered. But then she squared her shoulders. "It won't be forever. Only until Papa recovers from the accident and can work again." No matter what the doctor said, Papa *would* get better someday. She took Mama's hand and spoke softly, soothingly, the way she'd comfort one of her little brothers if he awakened from a bad dream. "There's nothing here in Dalton, Mama. And somebody has to work. . . ."

Mama worried her lower lip between her teeth. Sympathy swelled in Sadie's breast. Mama wanted so much to take care of everyone—Papa, the children, the house. She knew Mama wanted to be the one to meet the needs of their large family. But cleaning houses—the only decent job available for a woman her age—couldn't bring in enough money. If both Mama and Sadie could do house-cleaning, then perhaps there'd be enough, but someone had to see to Papa and the younger children. This job in Kansas would solve all their problems, if only Mama and Papa would let her go.

Papa cleared his throat. He lifted a thin, vein-lined hand and plucked the letter from Mama's lap. "Sadie-girl, you and Effie leave your mama an' me alone. We need to talk this out."

Sadie started to ask to be included in the discussion, but Papa's brown eyes, faded from their weeks of pain and worry, begged her not to argue. She wouldn't grieve the dear man. With a nod, she pushed to her feet. "Of course, Papa." She gave his grizzled cheek a kiss, took up the discarded bowl and spoon, and ushered Effie back to the front room of the house.

"Close the door," Mama called after them.

Effie clicked it closed, then whirled on Sadie.

"Whaddaya think they'll say? Will they let you go, do you think?" Her whisper quavered with excitement.

Sadie moved to the dry sink and resumed the task Effie had abandoned. The wash water had turned cool during their time away, but only a few dishes remained. She chose not to waste their precious coal supply to heat more water. Scrubbing hard at Papa's bowl, she replied, "I don't see how they can refuse. Somebody has to provide for the family, and as the oldest, it makes sense for me to be the one."

Effie's lips formed a pout. "I could help, too, y'know. I'm thirteen already."

"You won't be thirteen for four more months," Sadie said, "and you're still a schoolgirl."

"But summer's comin'." Effie tossed her head, making her brown braids flop. "Only two more weeks, an' I'll be home all day. Least I could help during the summer."

"Just what kind of job do you think you'd find?" Sadie hadn't meant to snap, but she couldn't encourage Effie to consider taking a job. Her sister wanted to grow up too fast. Childhood was precious—Effie shouldn't wish it away. Sadie softened her tone. "Besides, you'll have a job. Mama will need you here to help with the boys."

The four dark-haired stairsteps—Matthew, Mark, Luke, and John—had always kept Mama hopping. Now that Papa lay confined to his bed, needing almost constant care, responsibility for the boys often fell to Sadie and Effie.

Effie sighed and scuffed to Sadie's side. She picked up a length of toweling, but instead of drying dishes she swished the bleached cloth against her skirt. "I get tired of doing housework an' chasing our brothers." Effie's tone picked up a hint of defiance. "Sometimes I can't wait 'til I'm all grown up an' I can just do what I want to 'stead of cooking an' cleaning an' tending the boys."

Sadie raised one eyebrow. "I don't know of any woman who just does as she pleases." Sadie, at twenty-two, was considered a woman, but she still hadn't found the freedom to do what she wanted most.

Effie tipped her head and sent Sadie a pensive look. "Do you really want to work in a mercantile?"

Sadie pinched her lips closed. If she were honest, working in a mercantile held little appeal. But after everything Papa had done for her— giving her a secure home, loving her as his own —she wouldn't let him down now that he needed her. "It's honest work. I don't mind it."

"If you were a boy," Effie mused, "you could just work in the mines, like Papa did. Then you wouldn't have to go away."

"God didn't make me a boy," Sadie replied, pushing aside a brief pinch of regret. Papa loved her—she knew that without a doubt, even though she wasn't a boy and wasn't really his—but if she were a boy, she'd have endless job possibilities. Then she could provide for the family and relieve everyone's worry.

She plopped the clean bowl into Effie's hands. "Put that dish towel to work." Reaching for the spoons, she added, "Anyway, you know Papa's always said he wanted better than the mines for his children. He has dreams of college for Matt, Mark, Luke, and John. So even if I was a boy, he wouldn't want me to—"

"Sadie?" Mama's voice carried from behind the closed bedroom door.

Effie grasped Sadie's arm. "Reckon they've decided already?"

Sadie gently disengaged Effie's hold and then dried her hands on her apron. Her heart thudded hard against her ribs, both eager and apprehensive. "I guess I'll find out."

Effie gulped. She wadded the toweling in her hands. "Should I come, too?"

Sadie hid her smile. Effie hated to be left out of anything. "Mama only called for me." She took Effie's shoulder and turned her toward the front door. "Go check on the boys—see how much of that ground they've readied for Mama's garden seeds." If she knew her brothers, they'd done more playing than working, yet she couldn't drum up even a smidgen of criticism. She adored the entire freckle-faced lot.

Effie's face puckered in disappointment.

Sadie gave one of her sister's dark braids a light tug. "If the folks want you, I'll give a holler." She waited until Effie skittered out the door, then hurried to her parents' bedroom. Forcing herself to stay calm, she offered a quick prayer. *God, I want Your will most of all, so if they say no, let me accept it.* But even as the plea silently rose, she realized the depth of her longing to travel to Kansas. To take the job. And fulfill the dream that resided within her heart.

She opened the door and stepped in. Twining her fingers together, she searched her parents' faces. Their burden-weary expressions offered no hint of what they had decided. Mama pointed silently to the foot of the bed, and Sadie quickly sat.

"Sadie-girl . . ."

Tears immediately sprang into Sadie's eyes at the sound of Papa's weak, raspy voice so different from the boisterous, booming voice he'd had before the tunnel collapse that had nearly killed him.

"The idea of lettin' you go so far away is a mighty tough thing." Papa heaved a huge sigh. Mama dabbed at her eyes, and Papa took her hand before continuing. "But after reading the letter an' praying together, we think—"

Sadie held her breath.

"—this job is a true answer to prayer."

"Y-you mean, you're giving me permission to go?" Sadie hardly dared believe it.

Papa closed his eyes for a moment. When he opened them again, the love shining in the velvety depths sent Sadie scuttling around the iron footboard to perch at his hip, where she could clasp his hand. He said, "We're giving permission . . . an' thanking you for being so willing to help your family." He grimaced. "I hate being so beholden . . ."

Sadie lifted Papa's hand to her lips and pressed a kiss to his knuckles. "It's not your fault, Papa. Don't blame yourself."

"Man oughtta provide for his own." He sucked in a big breath and blew it out. "Soon as I'm up again, we won't need you working to support us. You'll be able to keep your earnings. But for now, we're thankful you're willing to help, an' thankful there's a job available."

Sadie shook her head, still reeling. She was going to Kansas! She'd earn a wage that would help her family. And—her heart tried to wing its way right out of her chest—she'd finally be able to satisfy her desire to sing on a stage. Caught up in her thoughts, she almost missed Mama's quiet voice.

"You're a woman now—time to be stepping into your own life."

Sadie met Mama's gaze. Tears glittered in her mother's eyes, and even though her lips quivered, she offered a tender smile.

"You've got a gift, Sadie. It's time to share it." Mama lifted the letter and pointed to the final paragraph—the one Sadie had tried to ignore to protect herself in case they said no. "When your papa and I saw this . . ." She read Sid's message aloud. " 'There's a new opera house opening right here in Goldtree. Man in charge is looking for a singer. I told him about you and how good you are. He wants to talk to you about performing.' "

Sadie thrilled at Sid's confidence in her abilities. Hadn't Mama and Papa always told her she had the voice of a songbird? They'd encouraged her to use her talent, too, claiming God never wanted any of His children to waste their gifts.

Mama lowered the letter. "We can't be selfish with you, holding you here just because it makes us sad to be apart. A job *and* the chance to sing. God's opening a door, and we want you to march right on through it."

Sadie bustled around the bed and launched herself into Mama's arms. Clinging to her mother's neck, she whispered, "I'll make you proud, Mama." Shifting her face, she beamed at Papa. "You too." Memories welled up and spilled over—of this man welcoming her into his heart, always treating her as his own child even after he and Mama had a brood of their own. "I'll remember everything you taught me, Papa. I'll work hard for my employer. I'll read my Bible every day and pray." She swallowed the lump that filled her throat. "And I'll do my best to reflect Jesus, the same way you always do."

Papa stretched out his hand, and Sadie clasped it. She kept her other arm wrapped around Mama, joining the three of them. Papa smiled—a sad, wistful smile. "You've always made me proud, Sadie-girl." He squeezed her hand. "Now close your eyes. I want to pray."

Sadie bowed her head and closed her eyes for prayer, just as she'd done thousands of times before. She listened while Papa thanked God for His provision and asked Him to keep Sadie safe from harm during travel. While he prayed, warmth surrounded Sadie, a feeling of security and peace. How she'd miss her papa when she went away.

Tears stung behind her nose, and she sniffed. The opportunities waiting in Goldtree were an answer to prayer, but for the first time Sadie considered how hard it would be to walk away from her little house in Dalton and the dear ones residing beneath its cedar-shake roof.

2

GOLDTREE, KANSAS
LATE MAY 1895

Thaddeus McKane slipped the latch into place, securing the wagon hatch, and then gave the wood a solid whack. "That's it, Sid. Thanks."

The young man on the wagon's high seat touched the brim of his hat in reply and then slapped down the reins onto the horses' tawny rumps. With a creaking of wheels, the wagon rolled away, leaving Thad in the middle of the dusty street beside his pile of belongings. A meager pile, he noted. For a man of twenty-eight years, he sure didn't have much to call his own. But it did make moving from place to place a heap easier. *But I wouldn't be upset, God, if You finally saw fit to let me settle somewhere.*

He squinted up and down the street, taking in his new place of residence. Businesses were scarce, especially when compared to Kansas City, but he couldn't help but admire the neat appearance of every building. Whitewashed clapboard siding beamed in the afternoon sun, with splashes of green, yellow, red, and blue gingerbread trim giving the buildings a festive appearance. Folks obviously took pride in their town. Thad liked that.

A tired old nag clopped toward him, pulling a ramshackle buckboard. Thad grabbed the handle of his threadbare carpet bag and swung it out of the way of the buckboard's wheels. The man on the seat stared at Thad, his somber expression curious but not unfriendly. Thad tipped his brand-new Stetson. The man gave a hesitant nod, then turned his focus forward.

Thad chuckled. Mr. Hanaman had warned him folks might take their time warming up to him, and it appeared he'd been right. But Thad wouldn't complain. He'd just do what his Bible instructed—treat them the way he wanted to be treated—and they'd come around.

He returned his attention to the town, seeking the bank building. The letter from the town's mayor had instructed him to go directly to the bank upon his arrival in Goldtree—but not be too obvious about it. Thad had puzzled over the strange warning, but never one to disregard a direction, he'd instructed the young man who'd delivered him to town to let him off near the mercantile rather than the bank. He'd understand Hanaman's reasons soon enough.

Stacking the carpetbag on top of his wooden trunk, he grabbed the trunk's leather handles and braced himself to heft his belongings.

"Young man!" A strident voice intruded.

Thad peeked over the carpetbag and spotted a tall, reed-thin woman on the porch of the mercantile. The porch's roof shadowed her from the waist up, but even in the shade, her hair glowed as white as snow on a sunny afternoon. She wore her gleaming hair slicked back so tight it raised her bushy eyebrows a notch. He bolted upright and snatched off his hat. "Yes, ma'am?"

She frowned at his trunk and bag as if they were litter cluttering her street. "Was you fixin' to cart them things somewhere?"

Thad scratched his head. Did she think he ought to leave them in the middle of the road? "Why, yes, ma'am."

The woman rolled her eyes heavenward. "Youngsters. Why're they never endowed with good sense?"

A grin twitched at Thad's cheek. It'd been a long while since anyone referred to him as a youngster. Despite the woman's grumbling, Thad took an instant liking to her. She had spunk.

Fixing her frown on him again, she shook her head. "Good way to strain your back, carryin' boxes to an' fro." She jabbed a bony finger toward the corner of the building. "Got a wheel-barrow around back. Ain't mine, mind you now —belongs to Asa. But you're free to use it. Oughtta make things a mite easier for you."

Thad smiled. "Thank you, ma'am."

"Just make sure you bring it right back when you're done." She tapped her forehead above her right eye. "I never forget a face, an' I'll know just who to send Asa after if it don't come back."

Thad had no idea who Asa was, but based on the way the woman drew his name like a gun, Thad decided it would be best not to annoy the man. "You can assure Asa I'll bring it right back, ma'am. I promise."

She balled her hands on her hips. "I'll be countin' on that." She spun, her gray skirts swirling, and headed for the door. Her muttered voice trailed behind her. "Youngsters . . . need a heap more sense, to my way o' thinkin' . . ."

Chuckling, Thad jogged through the narrow gap between the mercantile and what had to be a restaurant judging by the good smells drifting from the open door. A wooden wheelbarrow rested upside down beside the mercantile's back stoop. He whistled as he easily toted his trunk and bag to the bank, a stately brick building located on the corner of Goldtree Avenue and Main Street. After a moment's thought, he left the wheelbarrow, with his belongings in the bed, parked right outside the carved wood double doors. The empty streets—was every Wednesday afternoon this quiet in Goldtree?—offered no hint of trouble.

He took a moment to brush as much travel dust from his trousers as possible, then closed the top button of his best shirt. The tight neck-band made drawing a deep breath uncomfortable, but he could manage for a short meeting. He removed his hat and ran his hand through his dark hair, smoothing it into place as best he could without the use of a comb or mirror. Then, satisfied he'd done all he could to make himself presentable, he stepped over the entryway that proclaimed the date "1874" in six-sided blue tiles on a background of yellow and white.

A neatly dressed man peered out at Thad from behind a row of four iron bars. He straightened the ribbon tie beneath his chin and said, "Good afternoon." His voice came out croaky, as if he hadn't used it for a while. "May I help you?"

Thad clomped to the narrow counter and angled his head to peek between bars. "Yes, sir. I was told to meet—"

"McKane!"

A portly gentleman with salt-and-pepper hair and a thick gray mustache strode toward Thad, his hand extended. The fruity essence of pomade traveled with him. His three-piece suit and black silk tie left Thad feeling more than a mite under-dressed, but he reached to shake hands. "Mr. Hanaman?"

The man nodded, his broad smile nearly buried beneath the mustache. Thad kept his own mustache neatly trimmed above his lip, but he let the thick dark side whiskers grow a bit wider on his cheek. He had his reasons.

The banker beamed at Thad. "That's right—I'm Roscoe Hanaman. Glad you've finally arrived in our fair town." He released Thad's hand and stepped back, giving Thad a head-to-toes look-over. "You appear to be just as strong and able as your uncle promised me."

Thad felt like a horse on an auction block. He tried not to squirm.

Curling one hand over Thad's shoulder, Hanaman swung his smile on the teller, who continued to stare from behind the bars like a monkey Thad had once seen in a circus cage. "Rupert Waller, meet Thaddeus McKane, newest resident of Goldtree. I hope to talk him into serving as foreman on my ranch."

Thad sent the man a startled glance. "I thought—"

Hanaman's jovial chuckle covered Thad's protest. "Well, come along now, McKane, to my office"—he propelled Thad across the gleaming marble floor—"and let's get better acquainted." He ushered Thad into his wood-paneled office and closed the door with a crisp snap. His shoulders seemed to collapse for a moment, but then he drew a breath and they squared again. He gestured with his thumb toward the bank's lobby. "You're no doubt wondering about my comment to Waller about you being my foreman."

Thad nodded. "Sure am." He slipped his hand into his trouser pocket and rested his weight on one hip. If Hanaman had something unethical in mind, he'd turn tail and head right back to Kansas City, even if the man and his uncle were longtime friends.

"Have a seat there," Hanaman said, flapping his palm at a wooden chair facing his massive desk. He settled his bulk in a leather-upholstered, wheeled chair on the far side of the desk and waited until Thad eased into the smooth wood seat. Then he propped his elbows on the desk and gave Thad a serious look. "I apologize for my little falsehood—"

Thad frowned. Was there such a thing as a *little* falsehood? According to the Bible, lying was just plain wrong.

"—but we need to have a certain level of secrecy as to your true purpose for being here."

Thad's frown deepened. "My uncle told me you wanted law enforcement. Since I worked for a while as a deputy in Clay County, he thought I'd be qualified to help. But I have to be honest, Mr. Hanaman—you're starting to make me wonder if I shouldn't have come. I'm not one to involve myself in underhanded dealings."

Hanaman waved both hands, his expression frantic. "No, no, what your uncle told you is right! We do need law enforcement. But . . ." He glanced toward the door, as if ascertaining no one held an ear on the other side. In a much softer tone, he continued. "The town can't know *why* we need it."

Thad shook his head, thoroughly confused.

"Hear me out." Linking his hands together, Hanaman leaned forward and held Thad captive with his serious tone. "Goldtree is a fine little town, filled with God-fearing, honest folk. With the verdant grasslands covering rolling hills, ample water supply, and temperate seasons, it has all the right qualities to grow into a successful city."

Thad covered his lips with one finger to hide a smile. He'd never heard a more convincing sales pitch.

"As serving mayor of Goldtree, I want to see my town achieve its full potential."

Thad surmised an influx of folks to Goldtree wouldn't hurt Mr. Hanaman the banker, either.

"It is imperative no negative dealings mar the town's stellar reputation. Do you understand what I'm saying, Mr. McKane?"

"Thad, please," Thad said automatically. Then he released a rueful chuckle. "No, sir. To be honest, I'm not sure I follow you."

Hanaman's brows pulled into a fierce V. "You mentioned underhanded dealings. . . . I suspect, Thad, that someone might be making and distributing liquor."

Thad slumped in the chair. When his uncle had

indicated the town wanted to hire a lawman, he'd never expected he'd be called on to handle something so immoral—and personal. "But liquor's been outlawed in Kansas—we're a dry state."

"A law is only as good as the men who abide by it."

Thad recognized the sad truth of the man's statement. He flung his arms outward. "So why bring in an outsider? You're the mayor. If you suspect this's going on, why not call a town meeting an'—"

Hanaman came half out of his chair. "We can't tell the town! Oh my, no, the worst thing would be to tell the town!"

Thad crunched his brow.

Blowing out a huge breath, Hanaman flopped back into his seat. The chair springs twanged in protest. "Please, you must understand, this is a very sensitive situation. I have printed handbills ready to send to every city of importance in the eastern states, inviting hardworking, moral people to consider making Goldtree their new home. If word of this spreads . . . why, I'll be doomed!"

The man smoothed his hand over his heavily greased hair and angled his body toward Thad again. "I have high hopes that Goldtree might replace Clay Centre as the county seat."

Thad raised one eyebrow. "Without it being a railroad town?"

Hanaman waved his hand, dismissing Thad's comment. "But why would our fellow Kansans look upon Five Creeks Township with favor if illegal dealings took place in one of its communities? No, no, your true purpose here in Goldtree must be kept between you, me, and the four other men serving on our town council."

Thad chewed the inside of his lip and considered this information. Could he knowingly take part in a deception? *God, help me out here. Give me some of that sense the lady on the mercantile porch said I needed.*

Hanaman sighed, rubbing his thumb on a dark blob of ink marring the desk's polished top. "Your uncle assured me you were an upstanding man who followed the Good Book and was willing to fight on the side of right. I thought you'd see the importance of breaking up this ring before it does real harm to the citizens of Goldtree and our surrounding communities. But if you're—"

Before it does real harm . . . Hanaman's words echoed in Thad's head. He leaped to his feet. "I'll do it."

Hanaman's jaw dropped. He staggered upright. "Yes? You'll take the job?"

"I'll take the job."

The man let out an undignified whoop. Then he blustered and regained control of himself. "And you'll uphold the vow of secrecy?"

Thad folded his arms over his chest. "I don't feel good about letting people think I'm just a worker on your ranch. They'll need to be told up front I'm here to maintain order. They don't need to know the particulars—I'm fine with trying to sneak up on the lawbreakers an' bring 'em to justice—but I'm not willing to outright lie to the citizens of Goldtree."

Hanaman worked his lips back and forth, making his thick mustache twitch. Thad waited, letting the man make up his mind. Finally Hanaman stuck out his hand, and Thad gave it a firm shake of agreement.

"Very well, Thaddeus McKane. Or rather, *Sheriff* McKane." A smile crept up the man's jowled cheek. "With the town growing, and the frequent visits by cowboys moving cattle to market, it only makes sense we'd benefit from a full-time lawman. The townspeople shouldn't question it."

He strode from behind his desk with deliberate steps. "I'll call a meeting of the entire town council this evening. You're invited, too, of course. It will give us a chance to discuss all of the particulars of your new job. There's a private room on the second floor of the bank—use the outside stairwell since the bank itself shall be locked. We'll meet at, let's say, eight o'clock. That should provide you sufficient time to get settled and"—his gaze flicked over Thad again—"cleaned up. Do you have any questions?"

"Just one." Thad rocked on his worn bootheels. "Where am I to settle myself?"

"I suppose that's a necessary detail, isn't it, Sheriff?"

Sheriff. The title would take some getting used to, but Thad kind of liked the sound of it. For now. Until he had the chance to swap it for Preacher. His stomach knotted.

"I'd originally envisioned you calling the bunkhouse at my ranch home for the duration of your service here, but now . . ." He pinched his chin, his eyes narrowing. Then he snapped his fingers. "I own the building next to the mercantile. A druggist rents the entire upper story for his living quarters as well as half of the main floor, which serves as his business. The other half of the main floor is currently unoccupied, so it could serve as your office. As for living accommodations—"

"If I can lay my hands on some lumber, I can portion off some of the space for a sleeping room. I'm handy with a hammer an' nails." Thad shrugged. "I won't need anything fancy—just a bunk for sleeping and a dry sink for washing. I'm not much of a cook, so I'll take my meals at the local café . . . that is, if you've got one."

"Oh, we've got one!" Hanaman patted his ample stomach. "And it's a fine one, too. You plan on taking your meals there and charging them to your expense account. The councilmen and I will see that Cora's paid." The man's face puckered, his brows low. "But I think we might be wise to find you a little house to rent. A sleeping room in the back of the store hardly seems——"

Thad didn't want to get too comfortable. He had plans beyond Goldtree. "Most likely, I'll spend a goodly part of the day wandering the streets, getting to know folks, sniffing things out. So I can make do with little." He scratched his head. "But I might have need of some sort of jail cell."

Hanaman formed a fist and bounced it off the corner of his desk. "There's a cellar underneath the building—nothing much, just a storm shelter in case a twister comes in our direction. But it could be used as a holding cell."

"That'll do," Thad said.

"Fine! Fine! Everything is falling into place splendidly." Hanaman dug a key out of his desk drawer and pressed it into Thad's hand. Then he slung his arm around Thad's shoulders and escorted him to the lobby. "The building is catty-corner across the street from the bank. As I recall, the previous tenant left a few items behind. Feel free to make use of anything you find, or toss them out in the back and I'll have someone haul them away. There's a pump in the yard behind the building, as well as an—*harrumph*—outhouse. Anything else you need, just go into Baxters' Mercantile and charge it to my account."

The man's generosity knew no bounds. He

must really want these criminals caught. Thad slapped his hat on his head. "Thank you very much, Mr. Hanaman."

"Roscoe," the man corrected, his booming voice jovial. "We'll be working closely together, so we might as well be on a first-name basis." He ambled alongside Thad as they stepped out into the afternoon sunshine. "Get settled in your new office, grab some supper at Cora's"—he pointed to the white building with red trim down the street that Thad had guessed was a restaurant— "and be back here at eight o'clock. I'm sure the other councilmen will be proud to make your acquaintance."

Then, without warning, his friendly expression faded to a look of worry. "Thank you again, Thad. I know I'm throwing quite a burden at your feet, but after your uncle told me"—his face shifted sideways, as if he was ashamed to meet Thad's eyes—"about your father, I felt certain you were the man we needed to set things to right in Goldtree."

Thad's chest grew so tight it hurt to draw a breath. The mayor knew about his father? Did the rest of the town know, too?

As quickly as he'd sobered, Hanaman brightened again. He gave Thad's shoulder a clap. "Go on now. Make yourself at home. And let me be the first to say, welcome to Goldtree."

31

3

Thad pushed the wheelbarrow across the street to the building he'd call home for the next few weeks. Or months, depending on how things went. False-fronted, painted white with yellow trim, the building was long and narrow. Two doors with see-through squares on the upper half faced the street. The door on the right sported an arc of gold-painted letters on its window: *Spencer Thornton, Druggist.* So Thad put his key into the lock on the left-hand door. The wood had swelled, and he had to plant his shoulder on the door to force it open, but that didn't bother him. A few swipes with a planer would fix it.

Dust rose when Thad dropped the trunk and bag on the wide-planked floor. He sneezed twice, then squinted around the shadowy room. A pile of mouse-eaten blankets filled one corner, and a metal bed frame leaned against the far wall. He spotted a few gray shapes lurking in the far end, but he couldn't determine what they were in the meager light. But once he opened the shutters on the north side of the building and gave the front window a good scrubbing, it'd be a heap brighter.

He wanted to explore his new room, but the

mercantile lady had told him to bring the wheelbarrow right back. Asa might need it. So he locked the door behind him and wheeled the empty wooden cart next door to the mercantile. Before he could take it around back and return it to its spot by the back door, the same woman who'd spoken to him earlier dashed out on the wooden walkway and waved her bony hands over her head.

"You there! You!"

Thad came to a startled halt. "Me?"

"Yes, you! What do you think you're doing?"

Baffled by her accusatory tone, he pointed to the wheelbarrow. "I'm putting this back."

She planted her fists on her skinny hips and glared at him with enough ferocity to drill a hole through his head. "And just what're you doin' with Asa's wheelbarrow?"

Was the woman senile? Thad yanked off his hat and scratched his head. "Well, ma'am, you told me to use it."

"I . . . what?" She jolted upright. "So! Not only are you a thief, you're a liar, as well."

"But, ma'am—"

"Thief! Thief!" The woman's shrill voice filled the street. "I'm tellin' you, he's a thief!"

Folks stuck their heads out of the nearby places of business and stared at Thad in disapproval. His face felt scorched. "Ma'am, don't you remember? Just a little while ago, I—"

A second, equally shrill voice exploded from inside the mercantile. "Melva, what's all this caterwaulin'?" Another woman—tall, thin, with snow-white hair pulled into a bun—charged out onto the boardwalk to stand beside the one accusing Thad of thievery.

Thad blinked several times—sun must be in his eyes, making him see things—but when he looked again, he still saw double. "There are *two* of you." He finally noticed the one hollering at him wore a brown dress, while the other wore gray. But in every other way—right down to their matching scowls—they were identical.

The gray-dressed woman snorted. "Yes, there's two of us. An' I can tell you right now *she's* the hysterical one." She whirled on her sister. "I gave the young man permission to borrow Asa's wheelbarrow, Sister. The fella was a-tryin' to tote a trunk just usin' his arms! Good way to hurt hisself." Her glance zipped to the wheelbarrow. "An' he's brung it back, just like he promised." She waved toward the corner. "Go on now, young man, an' ignore Melva." She grabbed her sister's elbow and escorted her back inside. Their combined voices continued to rail, but at least they were yelling at each other instead of at him.

Thad scuttled between the buildings, eager to escape the curious gawks of his new neighbors. What a way to introduce himself to the town! He turned the wheelbarrow upside down on the flattened grass, exactly where he'd found it. Then, instead of returning to the street, he jogged behind the buildings and made his way back to his new home.

He paused for a moment before letting himself inside. The building's position at the intersection of the town's two main streets made it a perfect spot for a sheriff's office. He'd be close to all of the businesses if someone needed him to come in a hurry—he suspected the woman named Melva might demand more than her fair share of attention—and he could easily oversee much of the town just by standing on the boardwalk. Not that he intended to spend his time standing still. He had an illegal operation to uncover and bring to an end.

But first, he should get settled and cleaned up so he didn't miss his meeting with Mr. Hanaman and the town council members.

Inside, he unlatched the shutters on the north wall and folded them back. Lacy spider webs, dotted with dead bugs, decorated the corners of the windows. Grimacing, he grabbed up a rag from the pile in the corner and slapped at the sticky strings. The stirred dust made him sneeze so he abandoned the task until he could locate a bucket for water.

With the shutters open, weak shafts of waning sunlight slanted across the floor, revealing a bureau with a missing drawer, a scarred table and two chairs—one of which needed its legs tightened—and a crate containing a dented coffee-pot, three mismatched tin cups, four spoons, two forks, and a lantern with a cracked but usable globe. Thad thanked the Lord for the provisions. He'd use everything, and gladly.

His nose continued to tickle, so he opened both the front and back doors to clear out the musty smell. The cross breeze didn't carry any of the accumulated dust out, though—he needed a broom. The mercantile surely sold them, but he didn't care to encounter Melva and her matching sister again. " 'Least not 'til after I've put a good meal in my belly," he muttered to the empty room. His stomach rumbled in response to his statement.

He looked toward the front door, remembering Mr. Hanaman had said he could charge his meals. His stomach growled again, pinching with hunger. Breakfast had been only cold biscuits and some dried beef far too long ago. "Yep, a hot supper'll make me feel a heap better." Before he entered the café, though, he should clean up. Then he'd be ready for the meeting.

Fresh shirts and trousers waited in his carpet-bag, but where could he change? He could close the shutters again, but the front window had no curtains. After a moment's thought, he took one of the discarded blankets outside and shook it good, dislodging enough dust for the Almighty to build a full-sized man. By wedging the corners of the blanket into cracks between the wide wooden slats that formed the walls, he created a triangular-shaped makeshift dressing room. Before changing, however, he visited the backyard pump and gave his face and hands a thorough wash.

Clean and freshly clothed, Thad felt ready to head to the café and order a meal. He hoped Mercantile Melva wouldn't come after him with a frying pan. Thad made use of his wide stride and hurried on past the mercantile windows. But only because he was hungry.

Sadie took hold of the stage driver's hand and allowed him to assist her from the coach. For a moment, she wavered, her legs reluctant to hold her upright. The stage ride had been short—only three hours from the train depot in Clay Centre to the town of Macyville—but the ride had jounced her so badly, every muscle in her body ached from straining to hold her position on the wooden seat. She drew in several deep drafts of the clear air, relieved that the stilled wheels were no longer stirring up clouds of dust.

"Thank you, sir." Revived, she removed her hand from the driver's steadying grasp and reached to straighten her hat, pulled loose from its moorings by the jolting ride.

The driver tipped his sweat-stained hat and offered a wide smile. "You're welcome, miss. Lemme get yer bags." He clambered onto the stage's flat top, grunting a bit with the effort of hoisting himself up the iron bars serving as a ladder. "You say you got someone comin' fer ya here? Wouldn't wanna leave ya stranded, but I got a schedule to keep."

Even though she'd only met the man a few hours earlier, he was the only person she knew in Kansas, and she wasn't eager to see him leave. "My cousin is to retrieve me." Sadie reached to pluck her carpetbag from the man's hand. She hoped he wouldn't expect her to take her trunks in the same manner. They'd certainly land on her head and squash her flat. She was fairly strong—for a girl—but the trunks were heavy.

In addition to all of Sadie's wardrobe, Mama had insisted on sending two hand-pieced quilts, framed photographs of the family, as well as some other keepsakes, all intentioned to stave off homesickness. Sadie's stomach had ached the entire journey. Maybe setting her things from home around her in her new place would eliminate the aching loneliness for her family.

Thoughts of family led her to Sid. Where was he? He'd promised to be here. Placing her hand above her eyes—the little brim of her favorite flowered hat did little to protect her face from the bright sun—she scanned the street. No sign of her cousin.

"Heave ho!"

Sadie squealed and jumped back as the

stagecoach driver shoved one of her trunks over the edge and let it fall to the ground. It landed with a resounding thud, but to Sadie's relief it didn't pop open. She hoped the things inside hadn't been damaged. The man poised to give the second trunk the same treatment.

"Driver! Wait up!" The authoritative call stilled the driver's hands.

Sadie spun at the familiar voice, relief and joy igniting in her breast. Her cousin drove a buckboard down the middle of the street. She smiled at Sid's lazy pose, elbows propped on knees and hands curled loosely around trailing reins. Apparently Kansas hadn't changed him. Even as a child, Sid had always been easygoing —it was one of the things Sadie liked best about him.

Sid drew his wagon alongside the stagecoach. He set the brake and hopped over the seat into the bed. "Hand that to me, mister, and be careful this time. Might be breakables in them trunks, y'know." Although Sid was half the driver's age, the man followed his directions without hesitation.

To Sadie's relief, the second trunk passed safely from hands to hands and Sid set it in the wagon's bed with a gentle plop. Then he leaped over the wagon's low side and scooped up the trunk the driver had dropped. He sent the man an innocent look. "I reckon the stage line'll be accountable for damaged goods if Miss Wagner discovers somethin' broke inside o' here?"

The man scratched his grizzled chin. "Dunno. Nobody ever complained afore."

Sid raised one eyebrow. "Huh. That so?" He marched to the rear of the wagon and slid the trunk into the open bed. He placed her carpetbag next to it, as carefully as someone might lay a baby in a cradle. Then, her belongings secure, he held out his arms and offered Sadie a smile. "You made it!"

Sadie dashed into his welcoming hug. "I made it!" She pulled back, giggling. "And I probably smell musty."

Sid grinned, his matching dimples sneaking out of hiding. "No worse'n ol' Rudy here." He gave the horse standing within the traces a light smack on the rump.

Sadie delivered a playful punch on his arm, the way she'd done dozens of times when they were children. She and Sid, being close in age, had always enjoyed an easy relationship, more like brother and sister than cousins. Not that they really were cousins by blood. But all of Papa's family had accepted her as readily as Papa had.

The stagecoach driver climbed back into his seat and raised the reins. Before he could slap them down, Sid called in a friendly tone, "I'll be sendin' a telegram to the line's main office if any of Miss Wagner's belongings were damaged."

The driver snorted and brought down the reins. The coach jolted forward and rolled down the street, dust billowing behind it once again.

After waving her hand in front of her face to clear the dust, Sadie slipped her hand through Sid's elbow. "I'm eager to begin my new job"— and begin sending money home to Papa and Mama—"but the journey tuckered me more than I thought it would. How can sitting in a train make someone so tired?"

Sid turned her toward the wagon. "I don't reckon it was the ridin' that tuckered you as much as the havin' to say good-bye." Grasping her waist, he lifted her aboard.

She settled on the far side of the wooden seat, wincing. His comment had been far too truthful. Her heart ached anew.

He swung up beside her and offered another bright grin as he released the brake and flicked the reins. "So . . . your ma didn't fuss about you comin' all the way to Kansas? To be honest, I figured Uncle Len an' Aunt Esther would wanna keep you close to home."

Sadie sighed. "It wasn't a matter of want, Sid, but rather of necessity. The folks need the money I can make." Recalling her good-bye at the train depot in Dalton, unshed tears made her throat hurt. Papa, bedridden, hadn't been able to see her off, but Mama and all the children had come, even though it was a school day. Sadie would forever remember the image of Mama's face, smiling through tears. She'd never suffered a more painful farewell. But the job was a blessing, and she would celebrate the opportunity to help her family. "I appreciate you letting us know about it. It's a real answer to prayer."

Sid shifted his gaze forward, and Sadie did likewise, taking in the countryside. The landscape reminded her of Indiana, except there were fewer trees. Small hills covered in green grass and decorated by clumps of brush stretched out in both directions. She memorized the picture so she could describe it for her family in a letter. She'd promised to write every week, but she would probably write every day. At least until she felt settled in.

"Won't deny a bit of selfishness in bringin' you here," Sid said. He sounded sheepish.

Sadie sent him a curious look. "Selfish?"

"Well, sure. Me bein' the only one out here, no family around . . ." His dimpled grin landed on her again, giving her heart a lift. "Good to have my favorite cousin close by."

Sadie leaned briefly against his shoulder, then sat upright. Turning slightly in the seat, she gave him her full attention. "Tell me about Goldtree. All I know is it has a mercantile where I'm to work as a clerk and an opera house where I might be able to sing." Eagerness swelled within her. Would she perform once a month? Once a week?

Maybe more? For years she'd dreamed of entertaining audiences with song. Now the dream could see fruition. She wriggled on the seat. Couldn't Sid hurry the horse a bit?

Sid chuckled. "It's pretty small, far as towns go, but the mayor has hopes of it growin'. The man openin' the opera house—his name's Asa Baxter, an' he's the one I work for, pickin' up goods from the railroad an' deliverin' things to folks in nearby towns—thinks it'll bring business to Goldtree. Maybe even new settlers. So he's hankerin' to get a good singer on the stage. I told him you were the best."

Sadie clasped her hands in her lap, delight almost making her giddy. "How often is the opera house open?"

"How often?" Sid fiddled with the brim of his straw hat. "Well, it's just gettin' goin', Sadie. But I reckon now that you're here, Mr. Baxter'll be advertisin' programs on a regular basis. Like I said, he's eager to bring folks in, an' the whole town council's approved it."

Spinning to face forward again, Sadie braced her hands on her knees and stuck out her chin. "I'll do my best to please his customers. And I'll work hard at the mercantile, too. They won't be sorry they hired me. I promise."

Sid grinned. "I don't reckon anybody'll be sorry you came. I'm thinkin' this is gonna work out real good for all of us."

4

Sid slowly pulled back on the reins, drawing Rudy to a halt outside the Baxters' Mercantile. It wasn't easy, making Rudy stop with such gentle motions—the old horse responded better to a firm jerk. But he couldn't jerk on the reins without disturbing Sadie. She dozed against his shoulder, her hat all askew and one strand of sunlight-colored hair falling across her cheek. She'd never looked sweeter.

Holding his right arm, which served as her pillow, as still as possible, he set the brake with his left hand and then reached up to brush her face with his fingertips. Her skin felt as soft as silk, raising a yearning in the center of his chest. He watched her slowly waken. Her eyelashes fluttered and then her mouth opened in an unladylike yawn. As the yawn ended, she sat upright and looked around groggily.

"Oh. It's dark."

Sid chuckled at her observation. During the ride, dusk had fallen. With so many trees on the west side of town—rumor had it the founding men had arrived in fall, when the cottonwoods were at their goldest, and had vowed the trees would stay standing for the next generations—it seemed evening fell earlier in Goldtree than in other places.

"It's only an hour past suppertime," Sid said, climbing down from the seat and then reaching to help Sadie. "Are you hungry? Cora's café is right next door, an' she serves clear up 'til seven-thirty. There's time to grab a bite."

Sadie shook her head, the wisp of hair swishing along her cheek. She pushed it behind her ear before Sid could do it for her. "I'm too tired to chew." She laughed, a soft, rueful sound that made Sid smile in reply. "I think I'd rather get settled, if you don't mind."

"Then let's take you around back and ring the buzzer so the Misses Baxter'll let us in."

Sadie sleepily glanced into the back of the wagon. "What about my things?"

"I'll get 'em. Don't worry about it." Sid guided Sadie to the rear of the mercantile, his steps light from having her at his side. He wished he was bold enough to tell her he'd do anything for her. Ever since his pa's brother had married Sadie's ma and brought his new wife and stepdaughter to visit, Sid had been fascinated by Sadie. At nine years old, he'd fallen headlong in love at first sight. With hair as shiny and yellow as rays of sunlight bursting from clouds and eyes as blue as a deep lake, she'd been a beautiful little girl.

And she'd grown into the loveliest of ladies.

Sid stopped on the back stoop and gave the brass key a firm twist. It buzzed, alerting the mercantile owners to their presence. Sadie swayed, nearly asleep on her feet. He curved his arm around her waist and she leaned against him, offering a weary smile. He had to squelch the urge to brush a kiss on her forehead. If he kissed her now, he'd probably scare her.

Footsteps sounded on the other side of the door, then the curtain shielding the window lifted. Sid raised his hand in a silent hello to one of the Baxter twins—even after three months in the town, he still couldn't tell them apart. The curtain dropped back into place, the door swung wide, and the woman greeted in a loud, cheerful tone, "Come in, come in!"

Sadie drew back, apparently startled by Miss Baxter's volume. Sid had learned the twins were always loud no matter if they were happy, sad, mad, or indifferent. He suspected poor hearing was the culprit. Sadie would have to get used to their penchant for hollering. He gave her a slight nudge on the back, and she stumbled across the threshold. Sid followed her.

"Miss Baxter, this is—" Sid started.

The woman took hold of Sadie's hand and gave it a shake. "This must be our new clerk. Sadie Wagner, if I'm rememberin' correctly," she bellowed. She towered over Sadie—no woman in town came close to the Baxter twins in height.

"You look like you've had a rough trip, young lady. I'm thinkin' we need to fill the washtub for you."

Sid gulped. He didn't need Miss Baxter putting pictures in his head. Backing through the open door, he gestured toward the front of the store. "I'll fetch Sadie's things. She has a bag and two trunks. Is Mr. Baxter around? I could use his help."

Miss Baxter shook her head. "Tell you what— just run on down to the corner an' tap on Sheriff McKane's door. Remember how he stood up Sunday mornin' in church an' vowed he was here to help?" A sly smile curved her thin lips. "Well, he might as well be earnin' his keep. Heaven knows there ain't no crime in Goldtree to keep him busy."

She threw her bony arm across Sadie's shoulders. "I'll take this gal on up to her room— first door on the right as you go up the stairs, Sid. Just come on in."

Sadie sent a panicked look over her shoulder as Miss Baxter ushered her toward the enclosed staircase just inside the door. Sid gave Sadie an encouraging wink before turning on his heel and dashing for the corner building where Thaddeus McKane had set up shop. He puzzled over the mayor's sudden decision to hire a lawman. As Miss Baxter had said, Goldtree was a sleepy little town, although he'd heard tell it got pretty boisterous when the cattle drives came through. Still, it seemed odd to hire a full-time sheriff when the cowboys didn't visit but once or twice a year.

Sid banged his fist a couple of times on the doorframe, then peeked through the glass window. McKane unfolded himself from a table tucked beneath one of the north-facing windows and hustled across the floor. He opened the door and greeted Sid with a half smile, his gaze zinging into the street as if searching for trouble. "Howdy. Sid, right?"

Sid nodded, impressed that the man remembered his name. He must've met a good four dozen people on Sunday at the Congregationalist church. 'Course, they'd had that ride from Macyville to Goldtree together when Sid fetched him from the stage stop. Sid did more transporting than anybody in town. "That's right. Miss Baxter sent me over—asked if you'd be willin' to help me tote a couple of trunks. The mercantile's new clerk's arrived." Something fluttered in his chest, just speaking of Sadie. He'd enjoyed transporting her more than anything or anybody else.

"Sure I'll help." Sheriff McKane plucked his Stetson from a hook beside the door and plopped it over his short-cropped hair. If it hadn't been for the shadow on his cheeks, Sid would have thought the man had just left a barber's chair. He'd never seen a fellow sport a neater haircut.

"Stuff's in the buckboard," Sid said as he and

McKane ambled side by side toward the waiting wagon. "We just need to carry her things around back and on upstairs."

The sheriff rubbed his hand on the rounded top of Sadie's largest trunk and emitted a low chuckle. "I'm not against hard work, but I've spent a good portion of the past couple days building a wall to separate my working space from my living space. My arms are a little tired from swinging a hammer." He moved to the board-walk. "Why don'tcha drive the buckboard on around to the back, an' I'll meet you there." He set off for the narrow gap between the mercantile and the café without waiting for Sid's agreement.

Sid bristled. Even though the idea was a good one—it'd be a lot easier than carrying trunks from the front of the mercantile to the back and then up the stairs—it rankled that the sheriff had taken charge. He climbed into the wagon seat and brought down the reins harder than necessary. Rudy jerked forward, giving the wagon a sharp jolt that raised Sid's feet a few inches from the floorboard. "Rudy, you cut that out!" he groused even as he realized it wasn't the horse's fault.

Sheriff McKane was waiting on the back stoop as he'd promised, with one of the Baxter sisters standing guard over him. Sid swallowed a chortle. He knew a couple of folks in town the sheriff wouldn't be able to boss around. He guided Rudy as close to the door as possible, then hopped down, meeting the sheriff at the back of the wagon in time to grab one side of the biggest trunk.

"This way, this way," Miss Baxter directed, flapping her hands the way a hen shooed her chicks. "Mind them stairs—don't be trippin'. You'll bang my plaster walls all to pieces if you drop that trunk." The woman harangued them all the way to the top and around the bend.

"First room on the right," Sid advised between puffs. The sheriff had led, going backward, which had left Sid bearing most of the weight of the trunk. He'd make sure they reversed it for the second trunk.

McKane glanced over his shoulder and wriggled around when he reached the doorway, where lantern light flowed out into the hallway from the open door.

"Put it down careful," the Miss Baxter following them shrieked. "Don't scratch the wood floor!"

The other Miss Baxter, who stood beside the bed with Sadie still tucked under her arm, added, "Careful, fellas, careful."

Sid and the sheriff bent in unison and managed to place the trunk flat so none of its corners scuffed the stained but unpolished white pine floorboards. Sid started for the door, but the sheriff paused to tip his hat at Sadie.

"Evening, miss. I'm Thaddeus McKane, the town's sheriff. Welcome to Goldtree."

Sid gritted his teeth. The sheriff had been in

town—what?—less than a week? But suddenly he was the one to greet newcomers?

Sadie's lips quivered into a shy smile. "H-hello, Sheriff. I'm Sadie Wagner. It's nice to be here."

The sheriff gave a slow nod, slipping one hand into his trouser pocket. "Miss Wagner, I understand you're to clerk here at the mercantile with Miss Melva an' Miss Shelva." His gaze flicked from one twin to the other as he stated their names. Had he already figured out who was who? Sid's resentment toward the man rose another notch.

"That's right." Sadie stood stiff as a telegraph pole as the twin beside her—Miss Shelva, if the sheriff had been right—gave her shoulder several light whacks. "I-I'm so pleased they were willing to give me the job."

"They're good people," McKane said. "They'll take real good care of you, I'm sure."

Both women tittered, their cheeks mottling pink. Sid resisted rolling his eyes. Seemed the sheriff had the spinster twins besotted with him.

"But if you have need of anything—anything at all," McKane continued, removing his hand from his pocket and extending it toward Sadie as if offering her a gift, "you just come by my office. It's right on the corner, building north of the mercantile. I'm here to serve."

Sadie murmured a polite thank-you and ducked her head. Sid cleared his throat. Loudly.

51

The others turned to look at him. He scuffed the toe of his boot against the floor, earning a disapproving gasp from the Baxter twin closest to him. "Shouldn't we be gettin' that other trunk? Miss Sadie's had a long day. She needs her rest."

"Sure thing." McKane tipped his hat once more and swung toward the door. Sid clopped along behind him, with Miss Melva on his heels, advising them on the best way to carry the trunk to keep from straining their backs. After they'd delivered the second trunk, Sid assured the sheriff he could handle the carpetbag by himself, and the man raised his hand in farewell before heading toward his office.

Sid watched him go, irritated but not completely sure why. A sheriff *should* have a take-charge attitude. A sheriff *should* welcome folks to Goldtree. McKane hadn't done anything wrong. But Sid was still irked.

As he toted the carpetbag up the stairs, he finally identified the source of his aggravation. *He* wanted to be the one to make Sadie feel at home. *He* wanted to help her with whatever she needed. He wanted her dependent on *him*. So maybe, just maybe, she'd stop seeing him as her adopted cousin and start viewing him as—

He reached the door. Sadie sat at the end of the bed, an open trunk at her feet and her hairbrush in hand, smoothing her buttery locks across her shoulder. His mouth went dry.

"There's your carpetbag now," Miss Shelva announced, spotting Sid. "Bring it on in, an' then you skedaddle."

Miss Melva added, "Our new clerk's plumb wore out. We'll be tuckin' her into bed just as soon as we've filled the—"

Miss Shelva screeched, "Sister, ain't polite to talk bathin' to a man!" She flapped both hands at Sid. "You git. You can check in on Miss Sadie tomorrow." She closed the door in his face. The sound of scuffling rose from behind the door, and he envisioned the spinster pair descending on Sadie like a couple of crows on a pile of corn kernels.

He clopped down the stairs, flinging glances over his shoulder every few steps. He regretted not being able to say good night to Sadie. She'd looked so pretty with her hair down. Swinging himself into the buckboard, he took up the reins and lifted his face to the night sky, where a few brave stars winked against a nickel-colored background. He'd been wishing on the stars for years about Sadie. And now, surely those wishes would come true.

He'd found her a job that would support her family until Uncle Len could work again. He'd opened the door for her to sing on a stage—something she'd mooned over for as long as he could remember. And he had her here in Kansas, away from anybody else she knew, so she'd be looking to him—only him—for companionship. After all he'd done for her, she was beholden to him. Not that he wanted her to love him out of gratitude. But gratitude was a start.

He gave the reins a little flick. "All right, Rudy, let's get you settled in for the night. An' tomorrow mornin', first thing, I'll be fetchin' Sadie an' treatin' her to breakfast." He clicked his tongue on his teeth to hurry the animal. Morning couldn't come soon enough to suit him.

5

Thump! Thump! Thump!

What was that? Sadie sat bolt upright in bed and looked around the gray-shadowed room in confusion. Where was she?

Thump! Thump! "Sadie? You awake?" A piercing yell came through the closed door.

Realization flooded Sadie. She was in Goldtree, in her room at the mercantile, and one of the Baxter sisters wanted in.

"I got your breakfast out here, Sadie!" the woman on the other side of the door blared.

Sadie winced at the shrill voice. She'd heard more pleasant sounds when Papa pulled nails from old boards. Tossing aside the covers, she swung her bare feet to the floor and padded to the door. She opened it and nearly got her nose bopped by Miss Baxter's fist, which was descending for another rap.

The woman's thin face broke into a wide smile. "Are you awake?"

Sadie rubbed her bleary eyes. "Yes, ma'am."

Miss Baxter thrust a tray at Sadie. "Didn't want your breakfast to get cold. Me an' Sister've already et. Sister's gone down to open the store an' I need to be helpin' 'er, but we don't expect to see you down there today. You put your things away, get yourself all settled in, an' you can start your duties first thing t'morrah."

Sadie took the tray, nearly staggering beneath its weight. She stared in amazement at the well-filled plate. Fried eggs butted against a pink slab of ham, crisp-fried potatoes spilled over the edge of the ham, and a towering stack of toasted bread dripping with butter balanced on top of it all. Did they truly expect her to eat all of this? And would she be treated to such an abrupt wake-up call each morning?

"You hear everything I said, Sadie?" Miss Baxter bellowed.

Sadie nodded. Of course she'd heard. She'd never been around noisier women. Her ears had rung for an hour after the pair left her room following yesterday evening's bath. "Yes, ma'am, I hear you. I appreciate having today to settle in, and I'll be ready to start work first thing in the morning."

"Good. Startin' on a Saturday'll throw ya right into the fray o' things, but that's the best way to learn, huh? An' it'll be followed by a day o' rest, so you'll be fresh for Monday." She beamed. "Your arrival in Goldtree is just about as close to perfect as perfect gets, Sadie. God must've had His hand on you."

Sadie's frustration faded with the woman's reference to God's hand. It was something Papa might have said.

The woman spun and charged toward the stairway, calling over her shoulder. "When you're done with that food, you just cart the tray an' dishes to the washin' sink—follow the hallway to the west an' you'll run right into the kitchen— then put things to right in your room. Sister or me'll check on you at lunchtime. Have a good mornin', Sadie!"

Miss Baxter disappeared from view, and silence fell, much like the calm after a storm. Sadie bumped the door closed with her nightgown-covered hip and sank onto the edge of the bed, placing the tray in her lap. As she closed her eyes to offer a blessing for the food, a wave of homesickness hit so hard her body began to tremble.

She set aside the tray and crossed to the window. Pulling back the lacy curtain, she looked out at another clapboard building set very close to the mercantile. The windows, covered with muslin curtains, offered no glimpse inside, but the simple curtains were similar to ones hanging in the windows of her home. Sadie imagined a family seated around a table, eating bowls of cornmeal mush flavored with brown sugar or molasses, laughing together—the way her little brothers, sister, and mother must be doing at this very hour back in Dalton.

Tears flooded her eyes, distorting her vision. She dropped the curtain back into place and returned to the bed. The plate of food beckoned. Miss Baxter was so kind to prepare the tray—Sadie should at least try to eat.

A knock at the door—much softer than the one that had interrupted her sleep—intruded. Her new employers must have decided they needed her after all. She bustled to the door and flung it open. "Yes?"

Sid stood in the hallway, his dimpled grin in place. "Sorry to bother you so early, but the Misses Baxter said you were awake. I'll be leavin' for work soon, an' . . ." He held out a paper-wrapped bundle. "I brought you some breakfast. A cherry-filled pastry from Cora's."

Sadie suddenly realized she was still dressed in her nightclothes. Although the heavy cotton gown covered her from neckline to toes, she automatically folded one arm across her bodice

57

and took the pastry with her free hand, releasing a self-conscious laugh. "Thank you for thinking of me, but as you can see, I've already been served breakfast." She bounced her chin toward the tray on the bed. "Enough food for both of us."

She skittered to the end of the bed and added the pastry to the tray. Then she snatched up her robe, jamming her arms in and then tying the sash as quickly as possible. She turned to find Sid scowling at the tray of food.

He pointed. "Who brung you all that?"

Surprised by the resentment in his tone, Sadie remained at the foot of the bed rather than approaching him. "Miss Baxter." She forced a light laugh as his expression cleared. "I wish I knew which Miss Baxter. All last night, they referred to each other as 'Sister,' giving me no clue as to who is Melva and who is Shelva. How do you tell them apart?"

Sid shrugged. "I don't. They're as matched as two factory-carved spindles. So I just call 'em both Miss Baxter an' leave it at that." An impish light sparked in his eyes. "Wait 'til you meet their brother, Asa."

The opera house owner! Sadie's heart skipped a beat. She scooted around the end of the bed. "Will I meet him today?"

"Dunno. Maybe. He's a busy man—in an' out all the time." Sid's gaze drifted to the breakfast tray. "Did you mean it when you said there was enough food there for both of us?"

Sadie retrieved the tray and held it to Sid. "Of course. Help yourself."

Sid took the ham and placed it between two slices of toast. "I already ate breakfast, but this'll make a fine lunch."

Sadie blew out a little breath, relieved the food wouldn't go to waste. "Take whatever you want."

"This'll be fine." Sid pulled a handkerchief from his pocket and wrapped it around the sandwich. He whisked a glance toward the stairway, where the muffled sounds of the Baxter twins' voices and various clanks and bumps drifted from below. "You gonna work today?"

"No. They told me to use today to get everything settled. I'll start tomorrow." She looked at her trunks, remembering Mama's hands carefully packing. Loneliness rose again. She turned back to Sid and offered a pleading look. "Can you come by later, maybe at lunchtime"—if the Baxter sisters cooked as abundantly at noon as they had this morning, she'd have plenty to share—"and just . . . talk?"

Sid's face twisted with regret. "I'm sorry, Sadie, but I gotta take a wagonload to Macyville today. If there's nobody at the other end to help me unload, I might not be back 'til close to suppertime." He reached out and grazed the sleeve of her robe—a light, brotherly touch that eased Sadie's homesickness a smidgen. "But I'll come by this evenin'. We can take a walk around town—let you see all of it before you start work tomorrow. All right?"

Evening? An empty day stretched before her. Sadie forced herself to smile, although disappointment weighed heavily in her breast. "Of course. I look forward to it. But I better let you go now—don't want to make you late to work and have the Baxters wish they hadn't sent for me."

Sid inched into the hallway, waving the sandwich. "Thanks again for my lunch. Get yourself settled, an' I'll come fetch ya as soon as I'm back in town." He paused and his expression softened, his eyes igniting in a way Sadie hadn't seen before. "I'm glad you're here, Sadie. *Real* glad."

Sadie hugged herself. "I'm glad you're here, too, Sid." Otherwise, she'd be completely alone.

He winked, then spun on his heel and hurried off. She closed the door, slumping against the sturdy wood with a sigh. Her trunks waited at the foot of the bed, open but still filled with her belongings.

Determinedly, she pushed herself from the door and marched to the breakfast tray. "Well, Sadie, this is home now. So eat your breakfast, get dressed, and then let's make this room *feel* like home."

By midmorning, Sadie had shed a few lonely

tears, but she'd arranged her belongings to give the room as much of a homelike essence as possible. Only one thing remained—the framed print of her family, taken just two weeks before Papa's accident. She gazed at the photograph, tears pricking at the sight of Papa standing tall and proud with Mama on one side, Sadie on the other, and the younger children arranged from Effie down to little John in front of them. Dressed in their Sunday clothes, with the boys' cowlicks neatly slicked down with oil, and a ribbon the size of half a loaf of bread holding Effie's dark curly hair in a tail, they made a handsome picture—one that reminded Sadie of happy times.

"I miss you," she whispered. She blinked rapidly and set her jaw. No more tears! She surveyed the room, choosing the best location for this special item. She decided to place it on the corner of the little stand beside the bed so she would see the photograph first thing upon awakening. She set it just so on the wooden top next to her Bible, then paused in the center of the room to admire her handiwork.

The white wrought-iron bed looked grand wearing Mama's Jacob's Ladder quilt done in navy, cranberry, and cream. *"It'll give you good dreams, darlin',"* Mama had said as she'd folded it and laid it in the bottom of the trunk. Sadie pushed the memory away before it brought a fresh round of tears. The second quilt—a scrappy nine-patch in all the colors of the rainbow—hung over the footboard in case the nights grew chilly. She stroked the bright squares as she examined the rest of the room.

Across from the bed, the wardrobe doors stood open, displaying her dresses—including the new fashionable cinnamon twill with leg-o'-mutton sleeves and a creamy lace jabot, a dress Papa had insisted she purchase for singing on the opera-house stage. She crossed to the wardrobe and fingered one sleeve, running her thumb over the braid trim that graced the wrist. She wished Papa could be in the audience the first time she performed in Goldtree.

Determined not to descend into melancholy, she turned her attention to her small selection of hats on the upper shelf of the wardrobe. She shifted the position of the velvet sage so it aligned perfectly with the ones sitting on either side of it. The straw hat with its ring of silk daisies had gotten squashed during its ride in the trunk, but Sadie had stuffed three rolled pairs of stockings into the crown in hopes that it would regain its former shape.

Snapping shut the wardrobe doors, she turned, and her gaze fell upon the small framed prints of each of her siblings that clustered on the corner of the writing table beneath the north window. Her supply of writing paper, pen, and an inkpot rested on the opposite corner, ready for her use.

She pinched her lower lip between her teeth. She'd been so tired last night she hadn't penned a letter to her family. But—she whisked a glance at the little brass clock on top of the bureau—lunch was still an hour away. She could do it now.

Humming, she seated herself, took up the pen and a fresh sheet of paper, and began to write. She filled the first page front and back with the details of her travels. On the second page, she shared her impressions of her new employers. She giggled a time or two as she related her first evening with the twins, finding humor in the way they'd insisted they help Sadie with her bath and then screeched instructions to one another over her head as if she weren't there. She described her room, adding, *It's rather strange, having a room all to myself, but it's kind of nice, too. No Effie shoes lying at the foot of the bed to trip me on my way to the outhouse.* She smiled, imagining Effie's indignant response to her statement.

Midway through the third page, footsteps alerted her to someone's approach, and she braced herself for the—

Thump! Thump! Thump!

Setting the pen aside, she scurried to the door. One of the Miss Baxters stood in the hallway. "Sister said one of us'd check on you at dinner-time, so here I am."

Sadie wished the woman would introduce herself. She supposed she could follow Sid's lead and simply address each as Miss Baxter, but it would be nice to know who was who.

The woman fiddled with the strap of her full-fronted apron and peeked past Sadie. "Got yerself all settled?" Without waiting for an answer, she pushed past Sadie and charged to the desk. Sadie followed her, watching as the woman touched each photograph, moving them from the careful positioning Sadie had created so she could see each face. "These your brothers an' sisters?"

Sadie nodded, a lump filling her throat again. "Yes, ma'am. This is Effie, Matthew, Mark, Luke, and John." She pointed to each by turn, her heart wrenching with longing to be with them in person.

"Fine-lookin' youngsters." Miss Baxter tapped the top edge of Luke's frame with one spindly finger. "Neither me nor Sister married. Nor Asa. So there haven't been young'uns in our family for a heap o' years." She sent a pooched-lip squint in Sadie's direction. "Miss 'em?"

Sadie swallowed the lump. "Yes, ma'am, I do."

Unexpectedly, the woman threw her arm across Sadie's shoulders and gave her several solid whacks. "Well, Sister an' me'll pray for you. Good Lord gives us comfort for any hurt, y'know." Abruptly, she dropped her arm and marched to the door. "I'm fixin' some lunch while Sister minds the store. Bean soup an' biscuits fine with you?"

Sadie nodded.

"We mostly eat simple 'round here," the woman said, folding her arms over her chest and staring sternly at Sadie as if daring her to complain.

"Simple is fine. May I help you?"

Miss Baxter shook her head. "Room an' board come with your pay. That don't include cookin' or cleanin'." She released a soft snort. "Leastways, no cleanin' except in the store. So you just finish your letter over there—"

Sadie's face filled with heat. Had Miss Baxter seen what she'd written about her first evening and the bath-assisting incident?

"—an' I'll holler when lunch is ready." She stormed off with her arms pumping.

Sadie closed the door, relieved. Miss Baxter was far from shy—if she'd seen her name in print, she surely would have said something. But Sadie needed to finish the letter and get it posted. She sat back at the table and completed the letter, signing it with a series of Xs and Os, wishing she could bestow those hugs and kisses in person. She folded the pages and slipped them in an envelope, which she addressed in her flowing script. After lunch, she'd find the post office. And when Sid returned, she'd explore the whole town and sneak a peek inside the opera house.

Her heart fluttered. She hugged the letter to her chest. "I'll make the most of my time here, Papa and Mama. I'll make you proud of me—I promise."

6

Thad stepped out of the café and released a satisfied sigh. Roscoe Hanaman had proclaimed Cora was a fine cook, and Thad couldn't argue. Every meal so far at the homey little restaurant had pleased Thad's taste buds and sufficiently filled his belly. He gave his midsection a contemplative pat. No difference yet, but he'd best watch himself. If he kept indulging in Miss Cora's pies both noon and evening, he'd outgrow his britches.

At that moment, two men ambled out of the café, each grunting a little as they gave their waistbands a tug. Thad offered a nod of greeting, hiding his smile. They shuffled down the boardwalk, their swaying gait indicating discomfort. Thad chuckled. Yep, that pie would certainly add girth. But he couldn't afford girth. It would slow him down, and a slowed-down lawman was a useless lawman.

Tugging the brim of his Stetson a titch lower on his forehead, he turned and began moseying up the boardwalk. He'd walk to the far end of Main Street and then come back on the other side —the midday routine he'd established to make himself seen and available. Over the past week, folks had gotten friendly, lifting their heads from work to wave as he passed by. Sometimes they even came out and chatted for a minute or two.

Their acceptance increased Thad's confidence that he could be of service in the town. Of course, so far his services had been more on the handyman side, but he didn't mind. Every time he lent a helping hand, he built relationships. If folks trusted him, they'd open up to him, which made it more likely he'd eventually stumble upon that liquor-making operation the mayor suspected operated somewhere in Goldtree.

Without warning, a voice blasted in Thad's memory. *"Thad? You best answer me, boy! Where'd you hide my bottle? When I find you, I'm gonna—"* He winced.

"Afternoon, Sheriff."

Thad gave a start, realizing two women stood on the boardwalk in front of him. He tipped his hat. "Afternoon, ladies."

They smiled and entered the mercantile. The women's warm smiles and words of greeting erased the remaining vestiges of the unpleasant memory. *Thank You, Lord.* He started to move on, but a young woman shot out of the mercantile's door. "Whoa, there!" he cried, taking a stumbling backward step to avoid being run over.

She came to a halt and slapped her hand over her mouth. Wide, blue eyes stared at him in horror beneath the brim of a lopsided straw hat all decorated with daisies. Despite the start he'd been given, Thad couldn't hold back a laugh. When he'd met the young lady—she'd said her name was Sadie Wagner—after helping deliver her trunks last night, he'd viewed her as pretty but bashful. He wouldn't have imagined her being bold enough to dash around like an angry cat released from a crate.

She dropped her hand and pressed it to the unadorned bodice of her yellow floral dress. "P-please excuse me, Sheriff. I didn't see you." She held up an envelope. "I wanted to post my letter before the mail coach arrives. Miss Baxter and . . . Miss Baxter said the coach generally arrives at the postal office by one-thirty, so . . ." Her voice faded away as if she'd run out of steam.

"No harm done." Thad tried to keep his gaze on her face, but the little wisps of hair lifting in the spring-scented breeze and dancing across her shoulders distracted him. He'd never seen such yellow hair. It almost matched the centers on the hat's daisies. With effort, he pulled his attention away from the delightful coils. "You being new in town, do you know where the postal office is located?"

"Miss Baxter and . . . and Miss Baxter . . ." Miss Wagner gave her head a shake and pinched her brow. "I feel as though I'm stuttering every time I say their names."

"Then call 'em Miss Melva and Miss Shelva, the way I do," Thad suggested.

Her brow remained set in a perturbed crease. "I would if I could fathom which was Melva and which was Shelva." She sent a quick glance over her shoulder, then sighed. "They look so very much alike. . . ."

Thad smoothed his mustache, hoping she wouldn't see his amused grin. Did she have any idea how charming she appeared in her misshapen hat with sunshine-colored strands of hair spiraling along her slender neck? "Yes, they do look alike." He lowered his voice to a conspiratorial level. "But would you like to know how to tell them apart?"

She nodded, making the petals of the daisies flutter.

"They each have a mole at the outer corner of their mouths. But Miss Melva's is on the left and Miss Shelva's is on the right."

Miss Wagner's blue eyes lit. "Truly?"

Thad chuckled. "Yep. It's how I tell them apart." He gave a one-shouldered shrug. " 'Course, looking at 'em face-on, you've got to reverse it, which takes a little thinking, but it'll solve your wondering who's who if you can remember it."

"Why, I'd noticed the mole, of course—it's quite obvious—but not the reverse locations." She closed her eyes and tapped her upper lip, first on the right and then on the left, nodding to herself.

Thad watched, transfixed.

Her eyes popped open, and she gifted him with a beautiful smile. "Thank you! I won't need to trip over 'Miss Baxter and Miss Baxter' anymore."

"You're welcome." He needed to move on, but he didn't want to leave her presence just yet. She was a pleasure to look upon. He stuck out his elbow. "Let me escort you over to the postal office. Then you can get back to work."

She took his arm. He walked her across the street—slowly, prolonging the too-short journey. Her flowered skirts swirled, brushing his pant leg. He made no effort to distance himself.

"Thank you for your assistance, but I don't need to go back to work. At least not today." She had a lilting voice, musical in quality. "Miss Shelva and Miss Melva said I'll start working tomorrow. Today I'm to get acquainted with the town."

Thad's heart gave a happy flip as an idea formed. "Well, then, how about this? You post your letter, and then you can join me on my rounds. I'll point out everything I've discovered so far in Goldtree. In no time at all, you'll feel right at home."

Her face lifted to his, her expression surprised. "You have time to show me the town?"

He coughed to cover his chortle. Being new, she didn't realize how little time it would take. "I have time, and it'll be my pleasure." He opened the screened door and gestured for her to enter the post office. "Post your letter. I'll wait out here."

Thad paced back and forth, peering up and down the street. He slipped his hands in his pockets. Pretended to admire the clouds. Nodded at male passersby and tipped his hat to the ladies. Whistled a tuneless melody. Dropped his gaze and tapped his toe on a knothole in one of the boardwalk's planks.

A sweet trickle of laughter carried from inside the post office. Thad flicked a glance at the gingerbread-bedecked screen door. Jealousy tightened his chest. What had the postmaster said to make Miss Wagner laugh? And how long did it take to buy a two-cent stamp and affix it to an envelope, anyway?

Finally Miss Wagner emerged, empty-handed and smiling. "Mr. Rahn assigned me the use of a postal box—box number one forty-three. He's a very kind man with a delightful sense of humor."

Thad had met Mr. Rahn—at his meeting with the town council on his first evening in Goldtree. But the man hadn't cracked a smile the whole evening, let alone said anything funny.

She released an airy sigh. "With my own postal box, I feel as though I'm truly a citizen of Goldtree." For a moment, her smile dimmed, but then she clasped her hands together and aimed a sweet look in his direction. "I'm ready to see the town now." She glanced around, seeming to drink in her surroundings. "It is a lovely day for a walk."

The loveliest ever, Thad thought, but he kept the words inside. Had he ever felt so drawn to a woman?

Her gaze settled on him again. "Are you sure I'm not keeping you from your duties?"

"My only duty right now," he said, offering his arm again and wishing he could think of something humorous to say so he'd be treated to her trickling laughter, "is to help you feel at ease in Goldtree. So come along, Miss Wagner." He set a much slower pace than usual for his rounds. The white-painted Congregationalist church sat next to the post office, facing Main Street. Thad nodded toward it. "I attended there last Sunday. But I'll go to one of the other churches day after tomorrow."

"You didn't enjoy the service?" Her hands linked lightly over the bend of his arm, her steps matching his perfectly.

"Oh no, I enjoyed it very much. Reverend Wise is a fine preacher. But I figure, as sheriff, I oughtta spread myself out a bit—be seen in all the churches."

They turned west at the corner and headed for Washington Street. Miss Wagner asked, "How many churches are there in Goldtree?"

"Three. Congregationalist, Methodist, and Episcopalian." He slowed his steps, pointing to a large, iron-fence-enclosed area that stretched over half a block behind the Congregationalist church. "But all three bury their dead in one common cemetery."

Miss Wagner shivered, and her fingers tightened. "It's nice, I suppose, that they don't feel the need to separate themselves in death, but . . ." She sped her steps, and Thad had no choice but to follow suit. "Cemeteries are cheerless places to me."

He heard the sadness in her voice, and he wished he'd chosen a different route. But it was too late now. He tucked her hand against his ribs and ushered her as quickly as possible past the large cemetery. Still, he couldn't resist posing a question. "You do know, don'tcha, that a cemetery's just a resting place for a person's shell? That the soul's not there?"

"Of course I do." She sounded a bit tart, surprising him. She blinked several times, making him wonder if the sharp tone was meant to cover another emotion. "But the headstone is a reminder that the person is no longer here . . . on earth. And that makes me sad."

Thad considered her reply. He'd never spent much time at his mother's graveside, and he realized it was for the same reason she'd stated. They reached the far edge of the cemetery, and he deliberately slowed his steps until he drew her to a stop in front of the Episcopal church. She might consider him forward, seeing as how they'd just met, but curiosity overcame propriety.

With a little jiggle of his elbow, he asked, "Who's no longer with you?"

Miss Wagner ducked her head, showing him the lopsided top of her straw hat. "My father." Her face lifted, both sadness and a strange defiance showing in her eyes. "I hardly knew him. He died when I was four. But I still miss him."

"Why, sure you do." Thad missed his mother, even though she'd died birthing him. He missed knowing how it felt to have a ma. But he didn't miss Pa. He hoped God would forgive his dark thoughts, but he figured it was better to be honest than lie about it. His pa had never given Thad any reason to miss him. "Did your father know the Lord?" His gut twisted, knowing the answer where Pa was concerned.

Miss Wagner nodded, the little daisies waving their petals in agreement. "Yes. Mama said he knew Jesus."

"Then he's in Heaven." Thad tipped his head. "And will you be goin' there one day, too?"

A soft smile lifted the corners of her lips. "Jesus is my Savior, so I'll go to Heaven one day. And Mama says my father will be part of my welcome-home party."

Thad imagined his mother waiting at the pearly gates for him. He liked the idea. Just as soon as he'd thanked his Savior for erasing all his sins, he'd get acquainted with her at last. "Well, you just think of your pa living joyous an' at peace in Heaven instead of underneath an old gray tombstone, and it ought to perk you right up." Her smile broadened, warming him even more than the sun beaming overhead. He put his feet in motion. "Let's get goin'," he suggested, "before the day gets away from us."

He took her all the way to the edge of town, where the red schoolhouse with its bell tower marked the town line for Goldtree. School had let out the week before, and the place seemed lonely without children, so they didn't linger. They worked their way south on Main Street, where Thad pointed out the feed and seed, the blacksmith shop, the bank, and the Methodist church—"The only church in town with a steeple," she observed. They reached the corner where his office sat, butted up next to the druggist's shop, and Thad paused.

"This here is my office." He chuckled. "An' my home."

She cupped her hands and peered through the window. "You live here, too? It's very small." Dropping her hands, she faced him. "But I suppose, since you live alone, it's adequate."

Her comment, although empty of criticism, left Thad wishing he had a grand house instead of one small room at the back of a store. What woman would consider sharing such a cramped space? And just what was he doing, thinking about sharing the space anyway? He gave himself a shake. "Let's see the rest of the town."

He escorted her along the boardwalk, pointing to the community center and little grassy park across the street where, he informed her, he'd been told the townsfolk had picnics in the summertime. The mercantile porch roof loomed over them, so they stopped, and Thad threw his arms wide. "Except for Cora's café and the barbershop, which're right on past the mercantile, that's the whole town." He shrugged. "Well, the whole of the businesses anyway."

Miss Wagner's face puckered. "But it can't be."

He chuckled. "It's a small town, Miss Wagner, but from what I hear, it's growing."

She skittered to the edge of the boardwalk and looked right and left, her actions almost frantic.

He stepped to her side. "What is it?"

"My cousin Sid . . . he wrote to me . . . and he said there was an opera house in Goldtree. Th-that's why I came. To sing. In the opera house."

Thad scratched his chin. "Opera house?" He looked up and down the street, too. Had he missed something? His eyes found the community building next door to the post office. "Maybe Sid meant you'd be singing at the community get-togethers. The mayor told me the town comes together on holidays, after harvest, and for celebrations like weddings or births."

Miss Wagner shook her head, wringing her hands.

"No, Sid specifically mentioned an opera house. He said his employer needed a good singer."

Thad's eyebrows shot up. "Asa Baxter?"

"That's right."

Thad smoothed his mustache with one finger. "I suppose it's possible. I did hear that Asa's put in an order for a load of timbers from the mill in Concordia. Maybe he's fixing to build an opera house here in Goldtree."

Miss Wagner worried her lip between her teeth. He couldn't imagine why the opera house was of such importance to her. Still, he wished he could offer some assurance. He settled on the first thing that came to mind. "If you like to sing, though, the Congregationalist church has a choir. I'm sure they'd be pleased to have you join them."

"Certainly. I'd love to sing in the choir." She still looked sad.

Thad cleared his throat. "Well, Miss Wagner, I better head to my office now." He wished their afternoon hadn't ended on a sour note. "If you need anything else—trunks moved, questions answered—just come see me, will you?" He almost held his breath as he awaited her answer. He wanted to see her again. And again.

"I will." She held out her hand, and he took it. Compared to his big paw, her fingers looked fragile and delicate. He took care not to squeeze too hard. "Thank you for showing me the town, Sheriff. I appreciate it."

He opened his mouth to tell her he'd thoroughly enjoyed the afternoon and to ask her to just call him Thad. But before he could speak, a fractious voice intruded.

"Sadie, what're you doing?"

7

Sid hopped out of the wagon and stomped onto the boardwalk, making no effort to hide his irritation. He'd nearly worn himself out, unloading that wagon in record time and then hurrying the horses more than good sense dictated so he could get back and spend a goodly portion of the day with Sadie. Only to arrive and be told by the Baxter twins that she was out gallivanting around town. He'd spent the past hour searching, and now he'd finally found her . . . holding hands with the sheriff!

Sadie spun toward Sid. Her hand jerked loose of McKane's, which suited Sid fine. Sadie took a step toward him. "Sid! You're back early."

He tried not to scowl, but it took every bit of control he had. "Yep. Finished quick so we'd have plenty of time to explore the town before suppertime." He sent a withering glance in the sheriff's direction. Why didn't the man move on?

"I still got to put away the team—been usin' the wagon to hunt for you." Even though he'd meant to be nice, accusation colored his tone. "But soon as that's done, we can take that walk I promised you."

Sadie's face flooded with pink. "Oh, Sid, I'm so sorry. Sheriff McKane"—she sent a quick smile over her shoulder at the man who stood like a sentry less than a yard behind her—"gave me a tour of the town. I . . ." She ducked her head. "I forgot you planned to take me around."

Sid gritted his teeth. She *forgot* about him? Him, the one responsible for bringing her to town? He jammed his balled fists into his trouser pockets. Odd how quickly his temper flared. He couldn't ever remember battling a temper before. Of course, he'd never had competition for Sadie's attention before. Drawing a deep breath, he forced himself to use a light tone. "Well, least-ways, we can go to supper together, right?"

"Of course."

Sheriff McKane stepped forward. "I showed Miss Wagner the north edge of town. She might like walking to the south—and then over to First Street so she knows how to find the doctor an' the laundress."

Sid bristled. Why'd the sheriff think he needed to tell Sid what to do?

Sadie looked up at Sid with a hopeful smile. "I would like to know the location of the town's

79

doctor." She looked so sweet it took the edge off Sid's anger. "But can we take the wagon?" She laughed lightly, steepling her hands beneath her chin. "My feet are tired from walking around town with Sheriff McKane."

Sid needed to return the team and wagon to Asa's barn—he wasn't supposed to use it for anything besides business—but he didn't want to refuse Sadie's request.

"Sure. Let's go." He caught her elbow and propelled her toward the wagon. Grabbing her waist, he hoisted her aboard and then clambered up after her, nearly trampling her skirts.

"Sid!" She flopped into the seat, giving him a puzzled look. "What is your hurry?" Sliding over a bit, she adjusted her skirts beneath her and then checked her hat.

Sid flicked the reins. "Thought you were eager to see the doctor's house."

She huffed. "Not that eager." She turned backward on the seat, and her elbow bumped him as she waved. "Bye, Sheriff McKane! Thank you again for showing me the town."

"Giddap!" Sid smacked down the reins, and the horses obediently lurched forward.

Sadie grabbed the raised edge of the seat with both hands. "Sid Wagner!"

He ignored her indignant exclamation. "On the way, I'll show you my place. Got me a little house on Second Street, not far from the business part of town." He drove straight through the first two junctures without pausing to see if another wagon might be coming from the cross streets. Foolhardy maybe, but he wanted as much distance as possible between himself and Sheriff McKane.

When the horses reached the intersection of Main Street and Cottonwood Street, he guided the team east. After one block, he guided the horses to angle back south. The wagon frame creaked in protest at the rapid turn. "This here is the residential district of Goldtree. Not many fancy houses—mostly just regular, hardworkin' folk in town. 'Cept for the banker, of course, an' the doc." Asa Baxter had a big, fancy house, too, but since it was well outside of town, he didn't mention it.

He pointed. "See that big one with a porch both top an' bottom an' all the windows? That's the doctor's house. His office is the door on the south side. An' he answers it anytime, day or night, so if you ever have need of 'im, he's available."

Sadie didn't answer. She still gripped the seat as if she was afraid he'd bounce her out. If he wanted her to enjoy her time with him, he'd better behave himself. Besides, they'd left the sheriff behind. There was no need to rush anymore. He drew back on the reins, slowing the team to a plodding *clop-clop*. She drew in a breath and blew it out. Slowly, she moved her hands to her lap and wove her fingers together, as if she needed to hold on to something. He wished she'd hold on to him the way she'd been holding the sheriff's hand.

He tightened his fists on the reins. "Do you wanna see where I live?"

No answer.

Sid glanced in her direction. "Sadie?"

Although she didn't reply, she nodded. Her lips were set tight, and she looked straight ahead. Sid knew the signs of irritation, and he knew he'd caused them. But she'd aggravated him, too. Why couldn't she have waited for him?

He turned his attention to the horses to keep himself from asking the question. "C'mon there, Rudy and Hec, take 'er easy now." He tugged the reins, instructing the animals to go east, and he drew the wagon to a stop in front of his house. "This here is home."

Sadie leaned forward slightly to peer past him, but he couldn't tell from her expression what she thought. He knew it wasn't much—just a little clapboard house with a square stoop instead of a porch and three rooms arranged shotgun style. It wasn't even really his. He was only renting it from his boss. Asa had told him after six months he could consider his rent payments a house payment if he was of a mind to buy the place. But that depended on how things went with Sadie. He'd want something a lot nicer if he was going to bring home a bride.

"I rent it from Asa Baxter," Sid told her, watching her face for any sign of softening. "He owns a half dozen houses in town an' rents 'em out." Asa had his fingers in lots of businesses—landlord, drayman, mercantile owner, and farmer. If you could call a man who harvested grapes and hops a farmer. Swallowing, Sid dared to hint at his future hopes. "It's pretty small, but just fine for me now. But . . . later . . . I know I'll want somethin' bigger. An' nicer."

Sadie sat upright and turned her intent gaze on Sid. "It's a fine house, Sid. But would you take me to the opera house now? I'd really like to see it."

Sid jolted. "O-opera house?"

Her brows came down. "Yes. Opera house. The one you wrote to me about in the letter."

"Oh, of course, the one I wrote about in the letter . . ."

Sadie bopped him on the arm. Hard. "Sid, did you fib to me? Because if you did, I—"

He raised one hand in defeat. "No, Sadie, honest! Asa Baxter wants to talk to you about singin'. This mornin' he told me he'd be comin' into the mercantile tonight to talk to you an' take a listen to your voice."

She sucked in a sharp breath. "Tonight? An audition?"

Sid nodded, grateful the mad look had left her face. "Sure enough. An' if he likes what he hears, you might be able to start singin'—and gettin' paid—next week already."

Sadie's eyes grew wide, eagerness lighting her features. He got so caught up in how pretty she looked—face all aglow with little strands of golden hair swishing alongside her rosy cheeks —that when she spoke, he didn't catch what she'd said. He gulped. "Huh?"

She pursed her lips briefly. "Sid, where is the opera house? Sheriff McKane said he didn't know of one in town. And he's walked the streets of Goldtree from front to back and side to side."

McKane again. Sid snorted. "Well, that's his trouble. He's been stayin' on the streets."

"What?"

Sid wasn't about to explain his meaning. He'd scare her off before she had a chance to see the truth. "I'll show you. I don't think Asa'll mind, since he was gonna take you there himself tonight anyway." He gave the reins a flick. "Giddap there, Rudy an' Hec."

Sadie shook her head in confusion when Sid drew the wagon in front of the mercantile and set the brake. "Sid, what—"

"Just stop talkin' for a minute an' lemme show you." He climbed down and then helped her to the ground. He battled the urge to keep hold of her hand. Once she saw the opera house, she might want to turn tail and run. But she couldn't, he reminded himself. She needed the job. He released her and gestured to the mercantile doors. "This way."

The Baxter twins looked up—one from behind the counter, the other from the table of dress goods —as Sid led Sadie toward the storage room at the back corner of the store. The twin behind the counter called, "Asa was here a bit ago, Sid, lookin' for you."

The other added, "He said for us to tell you to stay put if you showed up."

Sid acknowledged them with a nod.

The twin at the dress goods slapped a bolt of fabric into place and screeched, "Where you goin' now?"

Sid pretended he hadn't heard her and put his hand on the small of Sadie's back, hurrying her through the curtained doorway. The room was a maze of boxes and barrels, but he led her to a doorway in the far corner, this one bearing a wood-planked, latched door rather than a curtain. He removed the key from a nail pounded in the doorjamb and unlocked the door, revealing a dark stairwell.

Sadie peeked into the space, then jerked back. "That's a cellar."

"I know it looks like a cellar from up here, but trust me. Go on down."

She didn't budge. "It's *dark* down there, Sid."

He sighed. "Lemme get a lantern." Both a lantern and a small box of matches sat on a nearby shelf.

He lit the wick, then took Sadie's elbow. "C'mon. We'll be able to see just fine now."

Sadie shivered, but she descended the wooden stairs at his side. Their feet echoed eerily in the narrow stairwell. The stairs made a turn near the bottom, and a long earthen hallway greeted them. A dank odor hung in the space, and the air felt clammy. Sadie hugged herself. "I don't like it down here. It's creepy."

Sid had felt the same way the first time Asa had brought him down. But he knew Sadie would be as surprised as he'd been when they finally reached the main part of the basement. Holding the lantern well in front of them, he guided Sadie down the hallway and around a sharp corner that led to yet another door, this one solid oak with a decorative pattern of leaves and swirls carved into the wood. Sadie sent him a curious glance as he opened the door, then she gasped.

The lantern's glow bounced off the polished tin squares covering both the walls and the ceiling of a small room—what Asa had called the foyer, the brightness almost blinding after the shadows of the dirt hallway. She skittered forward a few feet, her gaze lifting to a crystal chandelier overhead. She stretched one hand upward, touching the bottom tip of one glistening prism. "Oh! It's lovely!"

And she hadn't seen anything yet.

Smiling, Sid gestured to a pair of carved double

doors on the other side of the room. "This way."

Sadie didn't hesitate, scurrying along beside him with her hands clasped in front of her. He turned the brass knob on the right-hand door and pushed. The hinges released a soft groan as the door swung open. He angled the lantern into the room, and Sadie poked her head inside.

"Oh my . . ." Her voice held wonder. She stepped into the cavernous room, moving so slowly across the painted concrete floor that she appeared to float. He watched her examine the rows of seats, pausing to run her fingers across the top edge of one red velvet cushion. Her gaze drifted along the side walls, and she seemed to count the brass gas sconces secured on a background of flocked gold wallpaper.

He hurried to the front of the room, the glow of the lantern leading the way. "Look here, Sadie." He waited until she reached his side, then he caught her hand and drew her between two columns of stained oak and up onto a raised platform. Their feet echoed on the highly polished oak floorboards. Sadie turned a slow circle, her eyes taking in the lush velvet curtains falling from floor to ceiling at the back of the stage, the gleaming upright piano in the corner, and the pair of chandeliers overhead.

At last she faced him. He read both awe and confusion in her expression. "Sid . . . *this* is the opera house?"

8

Asa Baxter sat square-shouldered in the heavily tasseled saddle atop his black Percheron stallion, his head held high. He trotted the animal right down the center of Goldtree's main street. As always, folks paused on the boardwalk to admire the horse. Asa didn't give the gawkers so much as a glance, but inwardly he smiled. Nobody in Goldtree—or anyplace else in Kansas, he guessed—had a horse that could hold a candle to his Percival.

He reined in at the mercantile and sat scowling at the high-sided wagon standing in the street. Rudy and Hec, two of his workhorses, lazed in the traces. What was the wagon doing here instead of in his barn, where it belonged? Sid knew to put the wagon and horses away as soon as he returned from making a delivery. The kid might just need a good talking-to. Asa adjusted his ten-gallon hat, puffing his chest as he contemplated the dressing-down he'd deliver. But first he needed to dismount.

On his ranch, he always brought Percival alongside a fence so he could climb down without hurting himself. But there was no fence in front of the mercantile. Just a long way to the ground.

He sucked in a big breath and swung his leg over the horse's glossy rump.

The force of his sole hitting the ground nudged a grunt from his throat. His other foot, still caught in the stirrup, held him like a mouse with its tail in a trap. It took some doing to work his boot loose of the silver stirrup, what with his knee nearly under his chin. Percival was a tall horse and Asa was not a tall man. Asa hoped the townsfolk had gone on about their business rather than witness his clumsy display. Last thing he wanted was to listen to disparaging titters. He'd had enough of that to last him two lifetimes.

His foot popped free, throwing him off-balance. He grabbed for support, and his hand captured one of the thick tassels of black leather that dangled from the saddle's seat. He'd bought the saddle because of its ornamental beauty. The tassels, held by bold silver conchos, always attracted attention. Lovely to look at. And they'd come in handy more than once.

"Whoa there, whoa," Asa muttered to Percival. The big horse planted his hooves and held steady until Asa got both feet under him. His balance secure, Asa made a show of straightening his silk tie as he ambled around to the horse's head and looped the reins through an iron ring embedded in a limestone pillar next to the boardwalk.

He smoothed his hands up and down the horse's

sleek neck. "Good boy, Percival." Percival bobbed his head, nickering in response. With a clap on Percival's broad shoulder, Asa hiked himself onto the boardwalk in his typical sway-legged gait and headed for the mercantile doors. The moment he stepped over the threshold, Melva careened around a display of work boots with a huge smile on her face.

"Asa, thought you was headin' back to your ranch. Did'ja decide to eat supper with us after all?" Her long arms tangled around his neck, dislodging his hat. With his face buried in the abundance of ruffles hiding her flat chest, he couldn't reply.

From across the room, Shelva's piercing voice reached his ears. "Sid's in the storeroom."

Melva released her stranglehold and beamed down at Asa. After fifty-five years of looking up at his sisters, he ought to be used to it. But he still resented the twist of fate that had made his sisters tall and thin like their father and him short and stout like their mother. Broomsticks and a butterball—that's what the town's kids had called them.

Melva said, "New clerk's with him, so—"

"—you'll get to meet her," Shelva put in.

The pair was so entwined in each other's lives, they couldn't even deliver an entire sentence without the other's help. Asa swung around and headed for the storeroom.

"Asa, you gonna eat with us?" Melva called after him.

"Roasted chicken with carrots, taters, an' onions," Shelva added. "Your favorite!"

Asa waved his hand over his head as he charged through the doorway. Like a couple of pecking hens, they were. But he'd stay and eat their supper. Save him the cost of a meal at Cora's or the trouble of cooking something for himself at home. He stopped inside the storeroom, his scowling gaze swinging from one corner to another. Had Sid sneaked off without Melva and Shelva seeing him? No, the wagon was still outside, so he had to be around here somewhere.

"Sid? Where'n tarnation are you, boy?" Asa spoke softly. So softly it wouldn't carry beyond the curtained doorway behind him. The way he always spoke so folks had to lean in to hear him, bringing them down to his level.

No one answered. Asa started to repeat his question, but then he noticed the cellar door standing ajar. Melva and Shelva never went down there—they'd always been terribly afraid of the underground—so Sid must've left it open when he took the new clerk down to show her the singin' room. A smile crept up Asa's cheek, and he poked his finger against his lips to draw it back down. He was supposed to be aggravated with Sid—couldn't smile yet. But he'd have a big smile ready to cast on the new clerk if she proved as talented as Sid had proclaimed.

Asa bounded down the stairs as quickly as his short legs would allow. He thumped his booted heels—special-made a half inch higher than standard bootheels—deliberately alerting Sid and the young clerk to his approach. When he stepped into the large, decorated room designed for singing performances, both of them had their eyes trained in his direction. He battled another smile. Such pleasure in being the center of attention.

Ignoring Sid, he moved straight toward the little blond stranger. Sid had said his cousin was comely, and the boy had spoken truth. Even in a simple calico frock with a funny-shaped straw hat on her head, the girl was fine to look upon. If Asa'd been thirty years younger—and a foot taller—he'd consider courting the girl. But since that wasn't possible, he'd just make sure she sang as good as she looked.

"Asa Baxter," he said by way of introduction. "An' you must be Sadie Wagner, fresh from Indiana."

A slight smile tipped the corner of the girl's mouth. Shy. Innocent. Yep, the folks of Goldtree wouldn't find any reason to complain about her appearance. She held out a slim hand to Asa. The moment he gripped it, she said, "It's very nice to meet you, Mr. Baxter. I hope you don't mind Sid showing me the . . . er . . . opera house. I was eager to see it."

Asa released his best jovial laugh, although he wanted to wring Sid's neck. Hadn't he told the boy he'd show the girl the singing room? "Not at all, not at all." He stepped away and threw his arms wide, gesturing to the grand space. "And whaddaya think of it? Pretty fancy, huh?"

Miss Wagner nodded, but Asa sensed hesitance. He whirled on her again. "You change your mind about wantin' to sing?" Her blue eyes flew wide. She shook her head wildly. The actions bespoke eagerness, and Asa swallowed another chortle. "Well, then, since we're all down here, how 'bout you sing a little somethin' for me?"

He sauntered to the piano and grabbed the three-legged stool. "Sid, come hold this thing steady."

Sid scurried to Asa and knelt, catching hold of the stool. Some men might balk, but Sid had the sense to follow directions. Maybe he wouldn't be too hard on the boy about the wagon.

Bracing his hand on Sid's shoulder, Asa stepped onto the stool. He wavered a bit but held his balance and dug a match from his shirt pocket. With one hand, he turned the little knob that would start the gas flow, and with the other he flicked the match on his thumbnail—a feat he'd practiced until he could do it without burning his fingers—and tucked the lit end inside the nearest glass bowl.

The chandelier flickered to life, sending out a bright glow that illuminated half of the stage.

Asa hopped down. "Put that stool away, Sid." He crooked one finger at the girl. "C'mon over here, Miss Wagner, right in the light." He waited until she moved directly beneath the chandelier. The yellow glow lit her hair, giving her the appearance of an angel. She'd do fine—just fine—as far as looks. How he hoped she could sing.

"I'm gonna sit myself there on the first row. You just sing any song you like." Asa stomped off the stage and wriggled his bulky frame into one of the seats. He noted Sid perched himself on the stool back in the shadows rather than taking one of the cushiony seats. That suited Asa. Now the girl would sing to him, and him only.

She linked her fingers together and bent her arms, bringing her hands to waist height. Her face lifted, and she opened her mouth. " 'There is a safe and secret place,' " she began, her tone clear and sweet. The song poured forth, and Asa found himself mesmerized not only by the beauty of the melody but by the sweetness with which it was delivered. He held his breath, afraid the slightest sound might spoil the effect of the song. When she finished with a demure bowing of her head, his breath whooshed out in a rush.

He bounced to his feet, applauding so hard his palms stung. He scooted to the edge of the stage and reached for her hands. Tossing aside his normally soft voice, he boomed, "Lovely,

Miss Wagner. That was purely lovely. And just what was that you were singin'?"

"It's a song from the hymnbook we used in our church in Dalton. It was written by William Cowper, and it's one of my papa's favorite songs."

Asa gripped the girl's hands. "Lovely, lovely," he repeated, unable to find the words he wanted to describe her performance. "Hymns're fine, 'specially if there're ladies in the audience. But fellas like things a sight more lively. So I'd want'cha to sing more'n just church music. Do you know other songs, too?"

"Some." She whisked a glance over her shoulder toward Sid. As if she was a magnet and he a nail, he hurried right over. "Back home in Dalton," she continued, "Mama let me attend the local opera house. I'm sure I could replicate several of the songs I heard."

"Good, good." Asa gave her hands a final squeeze and then folded his arms across his chest. "So you got any questions?"

She sent another funny little look in Sid's direction. She bit down on her lower lip, ducked her head, then shifted her blue-eyed gaze to him. "May I ask . . . why do you have your opera house down here?" She glanced around. "It's really very pretty—one of the nicest rooms I've ever seen—"

Asa smirked, imagining how impressed she'd be with the room built farther back, the one accessible only through the tunnel from his ranch. Soon as he finished bolstering the walls with timbers, he'd be putting that tunnel to use.

"—but it's a . . . a cellar. There aren't even any windows to let in some sunlight."

Asa exploded with his best laugh—deep, rumbling, boisterous. "I can tell, Miss Wagner, you're as wise as you are beautiful, recognizin' this place as a cellar first of all."

She lowered her head again, sucking in her lips. "Do you gotta have sunlight to sing?"

With her head tucked down, he couldn't see her face. But he heard her quiet reply. "Birds sing better in the sunlight."

Asa poked a little fun at the girl. "You part bird, Miss Wagner?"

She looked at him. "No, sir. I'm just surprised you went to such trouble to build an opera house . . . under the ground."

Asa slipped his thumbs into the slanted pockets of his vest and let his gaze roam the room, admiring his own handiwork. "You see, Miss Wagner, takes money to build a proper opera house. I wanna make one of stone blocks—even fancier'n the bank buildin' Hanaman put up. But as yet . . ." He scuffed the sole of his boot on the painted floor, hoping he presented a sheepish picture. "I don't quite got the funds."

He tipped his head, peeking at her. "It was a heap less expensive to set things up in a building

I already own. Figure once I start drawin' an audience here, bringin' in money, it'll be no time at all 'til I can put up the fine buildin' with marble floors an' maybe even a balcony so's folks can sit up above an' look down on the singers while they're performin'."

Her eyes slipped shut, and Asa knew she was imagining herself on the stage he'd described. While he had her caught up in his plans, he added, "Shouldn't take more'n a year—maybe two." Yes, two years at most. But he didn't intend to use the funds for an opera house in a nothin' town like Goldtree, Kansas.

She opened her eyes and gaped at him. "Two years?"

Her dismayed tone worried Asa. He couldn't lose her now. "But this stage'll be ready for you a week from next Friday night." That is, if he managed to get the outside entrance built at the back of the store like he planned. The sisters would fuss about the noise, but they'd fuss even worse if he had folks traipsing through the mercantile and storeroom to get to the opera house. He added, "Assumin' you've a mind to use it."

Miss Wagner gave another furtive look at the cellar. "I . . . I would like the chance to sing. . . ."

"Then let's give ya that chance." Asa stepped back, deliberately looking her up and down. " 'Course, you'll wanna leave off the hat. Maybe let your hair hang loose. An' wear a fancier dress when you're performin'. I'd like to do shows on both Friday an' Saturday nights, but we'll see how your voice holds up." Very casually, he tossed out, "Pay is a flat three dollars per performance."

The girl gasped. "Th-three dollars?"

He recognized the meaning of her astounded expression, but he folded his arms over his chest and squared his jaw, as if staving off an argument. "I gotta be firm on that. You bein' a new performer an' all, I'm takin' a chance. Won't do no negotiatin' on the pay."

Miss Wagner clapped her hands to her cheeks. "Three dollars is . . . is more than enough, Mr. Baxter!"

Asa turned his face to the side so she wouldn't see his satisfied grin. He knew he'd snag her once he offered the money. Sid had said she needed to support her family. How could she refuse the chance to earn up to six dollars a week? And once she started taking his money—more money than she could make anywhere else— she'd be in his back pocket. Right where he needed her.

Asa faced her again, offering a brazen wink. He hooked his thumbs on his vest's slanted front pockets. "You excited, Miss Baxter, gettin' your first singin' job?"

"Oh yes." She lowered her hands, revealing rose-splashed cheeks.

Asa chuckled, congratulating himself. Voice

like an angel, sweet-faced and innocent—why, Miss Sadie Wagner was perfect. Nobody'd pay attention to anything else while she was standing on that stage filling the room with song. Yes, just perfect.

9

Sadie preceded Sid to the main floor of the mercantile. Stepping from the crystal, velvet, and varnished-wood "singing room," as Mr. Baxter called it, through the earthen walkway and then into the clutter of the storeroom was like walking from one world into another. The effect was nearly dizzying.

When she and Sid moved through the curtained doorway into the mercantile, the Baxter twins turned in unison from hanging their work aprons on hooks. Their bony arms descended in precise harmonization, and they each plunked their fists on their narrow hips. Standing with arms akimbo and with matching scowls on their faces, they reminded Sadie of a pair of statues she'd once seen stationed at opposite sides of a garden gate. She bit the end of her tongue to keep from giggling.

"Where's Asa?" Miss Shelva asked.

"We need to know if we're to set four plates

or three on the table," Miss Melva added.

Sid leaned past Sadie and answered. "He said he needed to check something in the cellar. He'll be up in a few minutes."

The twins looked at each other and clicked their tongues—three times, in exact timing with each other. Miss Shelva sighed. "He's been spendin' a heap o' time in that cellar of late."

"Can't be good for his lungs," Miss Melva lamented.

Sadie could imagine how much time it had taken to construct that beautiful room. Although the earthen hallway had felt damp and musty, the singing room itself seemed dry, and the air carried no foul odor. If Mr. Baxter went to such extravagant means for a cellar opera house, the one he intended to construct above ground would be glorious indeed. And she would be able to perform on its stage. She hugged herself to hold the wonder inside.

Tipping her head toward the open doorway, Sadie asked, "Miss Melva and Miss Shelva, have you been down there?"

The twins' eyebrows shot high. They chorused, "Of course I ain't!" They looked at each other, and Melva flipped her palm to Shelva, giving her the go-ahead to speak. "Sister an' me never go into the hidey-hole. If Asa feels the need to store things down there, he takes 'em down an' brings 'em back up."

"We're not much for closed spaces," Melva contributed.

They'd obviously never seen the expanse beneath the mercantile, Sadie decided, or they'd have a different opinion of the cellar. She opened her mouth to tell them what she'd seen, but Sid curled his hand around her upper arm and gave a light squeeze.

"Sadie, let's head over to the café now. Get some supper."

The Baxter twins skittered forward several inches. "Café?" Miss Melva blasted. "But, Sadie—"

Miss Shelva interrupted, "We planned a special welcome-to-Goldtree supper for you."

"We invited Asa, too, so's the two o' you could talk singin'," Miss Melva said.

"You ain't goin' to the café, are ya?" Miss Shelva looked very offended.

Sadie gave Sid a helpless look. She hated abandoning him after she'd taken that lengthy walk with the sheriff. She hadn't dared admit to Sid how much she'd enjoyed the sheriff's company. Even though her cousin hadn't said so, she knew he'd been upset about her letting someone else show her the town. And now yet another person wanted to treat her to supper. What should she do?

Sid shrugged. "Go ahead an' eat with the Baxters. I gotta get those horses put away anyway." His shoulders slumped. He looked so defeated, it made Sadie sad. "I'll . . . come getcha for supper tomorrow, all right? Little celebration for finishin' your first day at your new job."

Sadie nodded and gave him a look she hoped he understood meant she was sorry. He offered a quick nod, then strode out of the store. The moment the door slammed behind him, Miss Melva whirled on Miss Shelva.

"Sister, we was rude. We shoulda asked Sid to dinner, too."

Miss Shelva pursed her lips. "You know we already asked Asa, an' one puny chicken ain't enough to feed more'n four."

Miss Melva tittered. " 'Specially not when one o' the four is Asa."

Picturing the Baxter twins' very short, very portly brother, Sadie stifled a laugh. How on earth could such different-looking children come from the same set of parents? Her heart panged as she recalled a woman from the church in Dalton asking Mama the same question while looking at Sadie next to her younger sister and brothers. Sadie's blond hair had always made her stand out next to her half siblings' dark heads. Were Asa and the twins half siblings, too? She wouldn't ask—the question was too intrusive and impolite—but she pondered the idea nonetheless.

"Well, Sadie . . ." Miss Melva tossed her arm across Sadie's shoulders and aimed her for the stairs. "Let's you an' me head upstairs while Sister fetches Asa from the—"

"I ain't goin' down there!" Miss Shelva screeched.

"—cellar," Miss Melva continued as if her sister hadn't made a sound. "I'll get to settin' the table, an' you can tell me what you think of our little town o' Goldtree."

Miss Melva insisted Sadie sit in the corner and stay out of the way while she smacked plates, cutlery, and thick mugs for the stout brew she and her sister seemed to prefer onto the drop-leaf table in the middle of the little kitchen. The woman raced around, huffing with exertion. Sadie battled tiredness just watching her. Would Miss Melva and Miss Shelva expect her to work at such an exuberant pace? If so, she'd do it—Papa and Mama would be disappointed if she did less than her employers desired. And if she spent her days in such a state of busyness, she'd certainly earn her wage!

As Miss Melva pulled the well-browned chicken from the oven, the clatter of feet alerted Sadie to Miss Shelva's and Mr. Baxter's arrival. Miss Shelva ushered Mr. Baxter straight to the table and yanked out a chair. "Sit, Asa. Be comfortable. Me an' Sister'll have things ready in no time."

"Almost got it all ready now," Miss Melva said. "Just get the coffee, Sister."

Miss Shelva spotted Sadie huddling in the corner. "C'mon over here, Sadie. You ain't no wallflower, so no need to hide." Sadie slipped into the chair across from Mr. Baxter and tried to make herself as small as possible while the sisters completed supper preparations amid a steady stream of high-pitched banter.

At last they plopped into the remaining two chairs and promptly folded their hands. In unison, they ordered, "Asa, bless the food."

Sadie bowed her head. She assumed Asa offered a blessing for the meal, but she couldn't be sure. His low voice and mumbled words sounded more like a bee's drone. But he ended with a hearty, "Amen." He stretched his hands toward the platter. "Let me cut that bird. Looks real good, sisters."

Miss Shelva handed Asa a carving knife. Asa stood and angled his elbows high, brandishing the knife like a spear.

As her brother whacked the beautifully browned chicken into chunks, Miss Shelva asked, "So did Sadie sing somethin' for ya, Asa?"

Miss Melva boomed, "You gonna let her be your opry house singer?"

"She did. An' I am." In comparison to his sisters' thundering voices, Mr. Baxter's words fell like gentle raindrops. Using the knife as a serving fork, he flipped a piece of chicken onto Sadie's plate, grinning widely. "There you are, Miss Wagner. Enjoy."

Sadie waited until he'd served his sisters each a wing section and placed the entire breast on his own plate before she picked up her fork. Despite Asa's poor carving job, the chicken tasted wonderful, well seasoned with sage and other herbs Sadie didn't immediately recognize. She might miss Mama, but if Miss Melva and Miss Shelva treated her to meals like those she'd enjoyed today, she wouldn't need to miss Mama's good cooking.

"Miss Wagner?" Mr. Baxter spoke out of the corner of his mouth while chewing. "Before the openin' performance, I need you to put together a repertoire of songs an' show them to me so I know for sure what you'll be singin'." He jammed another bite in his mouth.

Sadie swallowed and set her fork on the table before replying. She wouldn't shame Mama and Papa by ignoring her manners, no matter how her tablemates approached the meal. "How long should the program be?"

"Oh . . ." He crunched his forehead. "Let's start with an hour. Maybe build to two, if you're able."

Although Sadie had sung in her church choir and for school programs since she was a little girl, she'd never sung all on her own for an entire hour. Her heart began to pound in trepidation. "I know at least two dozen hymns by memory, as well as several patriotic tunes. Would . . . would those be suitable for a . . . a repertoire?" She sampled the sound of the fancy word. Real singers had repertoires.

Mr. Baxter used his finger to work a bit of meat loose from a front tooth. "Well, as I said earlier, hymns an' such'll be fine for startin' out, but we'll need a little somethin' more eventually." He squinted at her. "You happen to know 'The Foggy, Foggy Dew' or 'Oh No, John'?'"

Sadie pressed her memory. Neither sounded familiar. She shook her head.

Mr. Baxter sighed. "Well, I'm gonna order up some sheet music for you." He jabbed his fork tines into the mound of roasted vegetables on his plate. "No worry, though. We got time. You start with songs you already know, an' we'll just keep addin' new ones until we've put together a program that'll rival anything a big city'd offer."

Miss Melva and Miss Shelva beamed at Sadie. "You jest wait, Sadie," Miss Shelva said.

Miss Melva patted Sadie's wrist. "Our brother'll bring fame to you yet."

Roscoe Hanaman leaned across the little table and lowered his voice. "I'm telling you, Sheriff, if you don't find those bootleggers soon, they're going to bring ruination upon Goldtree."

Thad pretended great interest in carving off a bite-sized chunk of his pan-fried steak. He wished he could eat in peace. The food was good, but the company was giving him indigestion.

"I've only been in town a week, Roscoe." He sent an unconcerned look across the table, hoping to pacify the mayor. "As they say, Rome wasn't built in a day."

"Maybe not." Hanaman used his fork to chop his green beans into tiny bits. "But I bet it came tumbling down a lot faster than it went up. And I don't want to see the same thing happen here." He smacked his fork onto the table and sagged in his chair, fixing Thad with a worried glare. "Goldtree was founded by my father and two of his best friends. They had high hopes for this community, and I don't intend to let their dreams die. But no town can stand strong when there's evil running through it." He pointed at Thad, his brows low. "You've got to find the lawbreakers, and find them soon."

Thad set his fork and knife aside to give the man his full attention. Seated in the middle of a half-filled café wasn't the best place for a private conversation, but the mayor had started it. Thad would finish it. Keeping his voice even, he said, "What you have to understand is you don't catch a fox by running wild. Foxes are wily. They're always on the lookout. You got to get a fox feelin' comfortable, like there's no need for him to fear, an' then you can bait the trap. That might take a little time."

Hanaman frowned, but he didn't argue.

Thad ate a bite of collard greens before

continuing. "It would help if you had some inkling of who's responsible."

Hanaman snorted. "If I knew that, I wouldn't have needed you. I would've just run the perpetrators out of town on a rail on my own."

Yet Hanaman—who was familiar with the town, its inhabitants, and its habits—expected a newcomer to uncover the ring and break it up in a week. Thad inwardly petitioned the Lord for patience. "Mayor, I give you my solemn oath, I'll do my best to catch these men an' bring their operation to an end." A too-familiar band wrapped around his chest, hindering his breathing. "From what I've seen so far, most of the men here in Goldtree are family men."

He'd been called to a house midweek by a boy whose father had stumbled through the door and collapsed. When Thad roused the man with cold water, the fellow claimed he'd taken too many doses of a traveling medicine man's snake oil. Thad had confiscated the bottle so the fellow couldn't repeat the incident. The worried look on the boy's face still haunted him. "I know what kind of suffering is brought on when a man squanders his pay on drink. I'm not inclined to sit around an' watch men destroy their families without doing something to help."

And once he'd busted up this operation, he'd hand in his badge, take his pay, and turn his sights to helping in a different way. He'd finally be able to pay for his schooling to become a preacher. The sooner he found the lawbreakers in Goldtree, the sooner he could finally replace the ugly mar his father had placed on his family name. But Goldtree's fine mayor didn't realize Thad had a strong reason to locate the bootleggers, too.

Hanaman released a long sigh. He propped his elbows on the table and linked his hands. "It's not that I think you're ignoring anything, McKane. I know you're trying." He grimaced. "I'm just thinking about the money spent on those handbills. I'm wanting to get them distributed in time for folks to get packed over the winter and make their way here next spring. Why, I'll be a laughingstock, bringing new folks into a town that's been overrun by drunkards!"

Although Thad hadn't discounted the idea of illegal happenings somewhere in or near Goldtree, he hadn't uncovered so much as a shred of evidence of the town being overrun by bootleggers. As a whole, the town appeared peopled by moral, godly folk. Hanaman's hysteria seemed overdone, but Thad would stay alert. If there was someone in Goldtree encouraging men to indulge in wickedness, he'd find them. He set his jaw. *As the Lord is my witness, I'll find 'em.*

10

By midmorning on Saturday, Sadie was ready to run upstairs, pack her bags, and talk the driver of the first passing wagon into taking her to the train depot. The Baxter twins' method of "showing her the ropes," as the women had put it at breakfast, consisted of screeching at her to "Come over here an' see what I'm doin' so you'll know how it's done!" She'd run back and forth so many times, she had a blister on the heel of her right foot, and her neatly formed twist of hair had worked loose of the pins and flopped across her left shoulder. She'd suffered less exhaustion after a full day of play with her four rowdy little brothers. And the day wasn't half over yet.

"See here, Sadie?" Miss Melva whammed canned goods into rows on pine shelves. "You gotta stack 'em three high, four deep, an' six across. That makes the best use o' shelf space. Do ya see?"

Sadie nodded wearily. "Yes, ma'am. I see."

"Sadie!" Miss Shelva bellowed from the opposite side of the large store. "Do ya remember how to add up an' record purchases in the charge book?"

Sadie stood on tiptoe and peeked over the shelves. "Yes, ma'am, I remember."

"Then see to the sheriff! I gotta get this flour measured for Mrs. Rahn."

Heat rose in Sadie's cheeks. When had the sheriff entered the mercantile? Her first command of the morning had been to greet every customer coming through the door so they'd feel at home. Somehow she'd missed Sheriff McKane's entrance. She tried to straighten her hair as she skittered across the wide-planked floor and stepped behind the counter. One squiggly black pin bounced from her shoulder, hit the wooden countertop, and landed on the back of his tanned hand. Sadie reached to retrieve it and encountered his fingers. She jerked back, mortified. "Please excuse me."

He pinched the pin between two long, blunt-tipped fingers and offered it to Sadie. "There you go." He angled his head to the side, seeming to examine her hair. "Looks like you've had a rough start to the day."

The kind understanding in his tone soothed the edges of Sadie's fractured nerves. She sagged against the counter. "The morning has been quite . . ." She sought a word that would describe it without sounding like a complaint. "Frenzied."

He glanced around. Half a dozen shoppers browsed the aisles or picked at the fabric table. In the background, Miss Melva and Miss Shelva dashed here and there, arms flying in every direction, tongues wagging. When he turned back to Sadie, a grin creased his face. "I'm thinking it's not the morning that's frenzied, but more like some folks are just a tetch overwrought."

His bland description—understated yet accurate —in combination with his teasing grin brought a giggle from Sadie's throat. She coughed to cover it—she shouldn't poke fun at her employers—but she didn't fool him. His eyes twinkled, and he leaned one elbow on the counter to bring his face near hers.

"Y'know, Miss Wagner, just because the Baxter twins enjoy runnin' around like a pair of wingless geese with a fox in pursuit doesn't mean you need to. I suspect you're no stranger to hard work. Am I right?"

Although it might be construed as self-pride, Sadie said, "I'm the oldest of six children. I've been my mother's helper for many years, and I always enjoyed helping her keep the house nice, work in the garden, and entertain the younger ones."

"That so?" He seemed pleased by her response. Then he gave his head a little shake. "Then you've seen how a person can get things done without—"

Miss Melva whizzed by, her apron flying like a sheet in the wind.

Sheriff McKane watched her until the storeroom door's curtain settled into place behind her. ". . . runnin' yourself ragged."

Sadie considered his statement. Mama had always been busy, yet she'd never appeared frantic as she went about her duties.

"Well, then," the sheriff said, straightening, "as long as you get your work done, you don't need to frazzle yourself. Remember that."

She appreciated his candor and common sense. "Thank you, Sheriff. I'll remember."

"An' something else you can remember . . ." He leaned in again, his mustache twitching. "My name."

Sadie drew back in surprise. "W-what?"

His friendly green-eyed gaze held her captive. "Would you consider calling me Thad instead of Sheriff McKane? You and me are the newest ones in town, and I think it'd be nice if we could be friends. Would'ja mind?"

Sadie contemplated his request. Mama had taught her a lady never called a gentleman by anything other than his surname. But Mama called the men who worked with Papa, as well as men from the church—husbands of the women she considered her friends—by their given names. Maybe the rule was different for friends.

Other than Sid, she didn't have any friends in Goldtree. The thought of being friends with the sheriff made her feel warm and comfortable inside. Especially since she knew he was a

Christian man—he'd made that clear when they walked together yesterday. Surely Mama wouldn't disapprove.

Her decision made, she offered a quick nod. "Thank you. I'd like to call you . . . Thad." The name felt right on her tongue. She added, "And you may call me Sadie."

A full smile grew on his face, bringing out a little fan of lines at the outer corners of his eyes. "All right, then. And now, Sadie, would you tally up my purchases here so I can get back to work?"

Miss Melva burst from the storeroom, waving something stiff and white over her head. "Sister, I found that corset in the size you was wantin'!"

Sadie and Thad shared a look that turned into a guffaw. He whisked his hand across his mustache, erasing his smile, and Sadie ducked her head to bring herself under control. Friends or not, she was on duty and needed to be professional. She added up his purchases and recorded the amount in the black ledger Miss Shelva had shown her earlier. Then she stacked the items in a small crate he'd brought along.

She slid the crate across the counter. "There you are, Sher—Thad."

He touched the brim of his hat, giving a nod. "Thank you. Have a good day, Sadie." An impish gleam shone in his eyes. "Don't get overwrought now, y'hear?"

She giggled as she watched him amble out the

door, his easygoing manner such a contrast to the Baxters' frenzy. Her gaze on the doorway where Thad had disappeared, she allowed her thoughts to drift for a moment. Such a nice man. Mama and Papa would like him, she was sure. She wished she could introduce them—it would mean a lot for her parents to meet the man who wanted to be her friend.

Another thought flitted through her mind, and she slapped the countertop in frustration. Why hadn't she asked the sheriff to come to the opera house for her first performance? It would be nice to have a familiar face or two in the audience. Sid would surely come, but even so—

"Sadie!"

Sadie's heart leaped into her throat. She jolted and spun toward the voice. "Yes?"

Miss Shelva waggled her hand, inviting Sadie to join her in the corner where the ready-made clothing hung.

"Coming!" She lifted her skirt and started to run, but then she remembered Thad's advice. Dropping her skirt, she drew in a breath and moved quickly but without undue haste to her employer's side. "Yes, ma'am. What do you need?"

At half past six, Sid turned the brass key for the buzzer on the mercantile's back door and then stepped off the stoop, watching the door for

Sadie's arrival. He smoothed his hand over the front of his shirt, making sure it was still neatly tucked. He'd changed clothes after work, putting on one of his church shirts and a ribbon tie, although he'd left his jacket at his house. The pleasant early-summer evening didn't require a jacket, and he didn't want to look too formal. He wasn't courting Sadie. Leastwise, not yet. But he hoped she'd be pleased with his fresh clothes and his clean-shaved cheeks, which he'd splashed with bay rum.

The patter of footsteps sounded behind the door, followed by the creak of the doorknob, and Sadie stepped onto the stoop. He'd peeked in the window before heading to work, catching a glimpse of her green-checked dress covered by a full-front muslin apron. She'd looked very prim and official—the way a clerk ought to. He looked her up and down in the evening light, and disappointment settled like a rock in his gut. She'd cast off the apron, but she hadn't changed her dress.

She swept her hand across her forehead, pushing a stray wisp of hair into place. "Hello, Sid. Are you ready for supper?" She stepped off the stoop and caught his elbow. "You might have to pinch me to keep me awake. I'm nearly asleep standing up."

He gave her hair a quick glance. "Did you take a little nap after the store closed?"

She shot him a funny look. "I didn't have time. We locked the doors at six, but then I had to sweep up. I barely made it to my room before I heard the buzzer."

That explained things. She obviously hadn't looked in a mirror. The Sadie he knew wouldn't step out in public with her hair awry and her dress rumpled. He touched his own tie. "If you need to straighten up some—you know, comb your hair or whatnot—I can wait."

She wrinkled her nose. "Can't we just go? I'm hungry." She gave his arm a little tug, propelling him around the corner of the mercantile. "Miss Melva left a pot of ham and beans simmering all afternoon. The smell came down the stairs and nearly drove me mad. I hope the cook at the café fixed ham and beans, too. With corn bread."

They stepped onto the boardwalk, encountering other townsfolk also heading for the café. Sid cringed. Saturday night. Lots of people enjoyed Cora's cooking on Saturday night. Every table would be filled. When Sadie got up to her room later and got a look at her tousled appearance, she'd be too embarrassed to set foot in church tomorrow.

He drew her back into the shadows between the mercantile and the café. "Listen, Sadie, you might wanna—"

"You there—who's back there?"

Both Sid and Sadie jumped at the stern,

masculine voice. Instinctively, Sid curled his arm around Sadie's waist. Her hair tickled his chin. "It's Sid Wagner."

"And Sadie Wagner," Sadie added.

A man stepped into the narrow walkway, his Stetson identifying him, even though his face was hidden by shadows. The sheriff swept the hat from his head when he reached them. "What're you two doin' back here? I thought you might be tryin' to break into the mercantile."

Sid bristled—most everyone he knew used this shortcut to get to the back side of the mercantile. Would the new sheriff be accusing half the town of burglary for it? And couldn't a person have a moment's privacy?

Sadie laughed. "You don't need to worry, Thad."

Sid jerked his head to gape at her. *Thad?*

"We're on our way to the café for supper."

"Well, then, let's get you a table." Sheriff McKane turned and headed for the boardwalk.

Sid dug in his heels. So now the sheriff seated folks for dinner, too?

Sadie started to follow, then looked back at Sid. She frowned and scurried to his side. "Come on." She caught his hand and pulled him onto the boardwalk, where the sheriff stood waiting. She smiled up at the man. "Were you heading to the café, too?"

"Yes. I eat all my meals at Cora's, since I don't have a kitchen."

Sadie's face puckered. "What do you do on Sundays, then? Cora's is closed on Sunday."

The man shrugged—a slow, careless gesture. "Well, last Sunday the mayor and his wife invited me over after church. But I can always eat hard tack and get by."

Sid nearly rolled his eyes at Sadie's expression of sympathy. Why'd she care so much about the sheriff and his stomach anyway? He gave her a little nudge. "Let's head in, Sadie. I thought you were hungry."

She gave him a dark look, which he chose to ignore. With his hand on her back, he hustled her through the door. The sheriff followed on Sid's heels. Wonderful aromas greeted them. As did noise. Townsfolk chatted and laughed, their voices combining with the clanks of forks on plates. Sid scanned the room, looking for an empty table. He'd never seen the café so crowded.

Sadie pointed. "Look—nobody's sitting at the table in the corner." She frowned, her fine brows pinching together. "But that's the only open table."

"Then we better take it." Sid started in that direction, but her hands curled around his arm, holding him in place. Her face lifted to the sheriff's.

"Thad, it looks as if you'll have to sit with us."

11

" 'O sing unto the Lord a new song; for he hath done marvelous things . . .' "

Sadie sat with her Bible open to the Ninety-eighth Psalm, following along as the minister read. His choice of Scripture sent a chill up her spine—surely this was the Lord's way of confirming she'd done the right thing by coming to Goldtree. Beside her, Sid sat straight and attentive, but the stern frown he'd adopted last night at supper seemed permanently etched on his face. How could he frown so in church while a minister shared from God's Holy Book?

She whisked a glance over her shoulder, seeking the sheriff, who'd saved the evening by keeping up a stream of friendly chatter despite Sid's moody silence. Although she didn't expect to see him—he'd mentioned he planned to attend a different church this morning—she still experienced a prick of disappointment. In a very short time, she'd come to appreciate his cheerful outlook and ready smile. But as much as she enjoyed Thad's company, Sid seemed to resent it. She wished she could understand why. The two men were close in age. Couldn't they be friends?

Turning her focus forward again, she listened to the minister's simple but straightforward message on the importance of a joyful countenance. She caught herself nodding in agreement at certain phrases and crinkling her brow as she tucked away others for further contemplation later. Mama had told her to choose a church home where she'd be spiritually fed, and by the time the minister offered his final thoughts, she believed she'd already located the perfect place for growth.

Reverend Wise set aside his big black Bible and boomed from the pulpit, "We have the pleasure of a visitor today—a brand-new resident to Goldtree. Miss Sadie Wagner, would you please stand?"

Heat flooded Sadie's face, but she obediently rose under the curious gazes of several dozen congregants.

"Some of you might've met Miss Wagner in the mercantile yesterday, where she's clerking for Miss Melva and Miss Shelva Baxter. But if you haven't introduced yourself yet," the minister instructed in a bright, non-abrasive manner, "take the time to give her a greeting today and help her feel at home." He lifted his hands. "Now, everyone rise for our closing benediction."

The moment the final amen rumbled, folks swarmed Sadie. She shook hands, smiled hello, and declined nearly a dozen invitations to Sunday dinner, since she'd already made plans. When the crowd finally cleared away, she slipped her hand through the bend of Sid's arm and they strolled east, heading toward his house.

"Goldtree is a very nice town," Sadie said, waving at a family rolling past in their wagon.

Sid didn't reply.

Sadie offered, "I can see why you like it here."

He continued onward in silence.

"Everyone is so friendly."

A small grunt escaped his lips.

The pleasure of the morning's worship and the warm welcome from the community fled. Sadie forgot the minister's admonition to maintain a cheerful outlook. She came to a halt and gave her cousin's arm a sharp yank that forced him to stop, too.

Sid glowered at her, his brows pinched in irritation. "What's wrong with you?"

Hugging her Bible to her chest with one hand, she plunked her other fist on her hip and glared at him. "What's wrong with *you?* It's Sunday— the Lord's day! The sun is shining, we've just heard an inspiring sermon, and you're being a complete grouch."

He turned his face to the side and set his jaw in a stubborn line.

"Sid!"

The muscles in his jaw twitched, but he still wouldn't look at her.

Not once in all of their growing-up years had

she witnessed such churlish behavior from her favorite cousin. Aggravation rose up and exploded in a disgruntled huff. "Fine. Be taciturn and muleheaded, if that's what you want to be. But you can be that way alone." She whirled and took one step toward Main Street.

He caught her arm. "But we were gonna have lunch together. I've got bread and cheese for sandwiches and a whole peach pie I bought from a neighbor lady."

Sadie loved peach pie. Her mouth watered, thinking about sinking her fork through flaky crust into sweet, moist peaches. But then she looked into Sid's stormy face. Her hunger disappeared in an instant. She pulled her arm free of his grasp. "Eat it by yourself. I have no desire to stay in your company when you won't talk or smile or act like the Sid I remember from Indiana." Just two days ago, she'd been so happy to see him. Now all she wanted to do was flee his presence. Tears stung.

In a much kinder tone, she repeated her earlier question. "What's wrong with you?"

He shook his head, looking down. "Nothin'."

Sadie sighed. "I don't believe you, but I'm not in the mood to placate you. So go on home, Sid. When you're ready to talk, you know where to find me." She stomped off toward Main Street. He called her name, but he didn't come after her, so she kept her head low and scurried onward.

Hopefully, Miss Melva and Miss Shelva would have some leftovers from their dinner they wouldn't mind sharing.

She rounded the corner and moved quickly past the barber shop and Cora's café, eager to reach the mercantile. Just as she turned to move through the gap between the mercantile and café, she heard a masculine voice call her name. Her heart lifted, and she looked backward, hoping to see Sid coming after her with a smile and an apology. But no one followed behind her.

"Sadie!"

The voice called again, from the opposite direction. Sadie turned her gaze and found the sheriff striding toward her. His wide, friendly grin juxtaposed Sid's surly expression. Without effort, Sadie answered his smile with one of her own. "Hello, Thad."

He leaned his shoulder on a porch post, a casual pose that put Sadie completely at ease. "Did you enjoy the Sunday service with Reverend Wise?"

"Oh yes. Very much. You were right—he's a fine speaker." She hugged her Bible with both arms to give her hands something to do. "Did you enjoy the service at the Episcopal church?"

He pursed his lips for a moment. "I'm glad I went. Always good to worship with like-minded folks. But I think I liked Reverend Wise's ways of presenting the gospel a little bit better." He shifted slightly, his boots shuffling against the planked boards beneath their feet. "With me rotating through the churches, though, I'll be able to get a taste of Reverend Wise's teaching on a regular basis. Be nice to just join one, but I think being seen in all of them's a better idea for me."

Sadie nodded, but she'd already made up her mind to attend the Congregationalist church.

"Well . . ." He pushed off the post, lifting his hand to adjust his Stetson. Most of the men around town wore cowboy-style hats, but for some reason the hat better suited the sheriff than anyone else. "I best let you get on inside an' grab your dinner. Reckon it's growing cold."

Sadie sighed. "I hope there's something left for me. I told Miss Melva and Miss Shelva not to expect me, so they might have eaten it all by now."

He puckered his brow, as if thinking deeply. "You were going to eat dinner with Sid—I recall he invited you yesterday as we were leaving the café. So what happened? Did he burn the pot roast?"

Sadie had been embarrassed when Sid asked her to dinner in front of the sheriff but hadn't included the sheriff in the invitation. Her discomfiture returned as she admitted, "We had a little . . . falling out, and I refused to eat with him. So now I need to find my own lunch."

Thad jammed his thumb toward his office. "You're more than welcome to eat with me. Just crackers, cheese, an' some tinned ham. Oh, an' canned peaches." A boyish grin appeared on his tanned face. "I'm partial to peaches—always have been."

Sadie's heart skipped a beat. "Are . . . are you sure you have enough?"

"Dunno. How much do you eat?"

Sadie couldn't hold back a surprised giggle. He managed to look so serious as he asked the teasing question. She caught herself teasing back. "I'm guilty of gluttony when it comes to peaches."

"Hmm. I better open two cans."

She laughed again, pleased by his answer. Then propriety beckoned. Tipping her head, she asked, "Are you sure it's all right, though? For me to eat with you . . . alone . . . ?"

He sobered. "I sure wouldn't want to do anything that might be considered unseemly. An' you're right—being alone in my office isn't a good idea."

Sadie nodded, disappointed. She enjoyed his company. He made her laugh. He reminded her a lot of Papa—the before-accident Papa: strong, steadfast, prone to good-natured teasing. And handsome to boot.

He snapped his fingers. "I have an idea. It's such a pretty day. We'll have us a picnic on the boardwalk, right under the town's nose. Nobody can complain if we're out where they can all see, right?"

Her spirits immediately lifted. "A picnic sounds like great fun."

"Good!" He poked out his elbow. "C'mon. I'll throw an old blanket on the boardwalk. You can tell me about Reverend Wise's sermon while we eat. I'm just sure he said something worth repeating."

Her cheerful countenance restored, Sadie accompanied the sheriff up the street.

Thad spread the musty old blanket in the grass at the park area across the street from his office. With the sun directly overhead and no porch overhang to provide shade, he'd suggested they sit beneath the single cottonwood next to the community center. To his delight, Sadie had agreed. She stood nearby with the crate of food cradled in her arms, waiting for him to get the blanket arranged just so. He couldn't stop smiling. What a pleasure, enjoying a simple lunch with this lovely young woman.

The blanket as smooth as he could make it, he reached for the crate. "Lemme take that. Sit yourself down an' I'll get everything out."

"I can help," she said, kneeling on the blanket.

"No, now, you're my guest today. Just sit there an' let me take care of things."

"Very well, then. Thank you."

Her appreciative smile did something funny to his insides. He got busy digging in the crate. The battered tin plates that served him just fine didn't seem good enough to put in front of

Sadie, but she didn't produce so much as a grimace when he knelt across the blanket from her and laid them out.

While he emptied the crate, she lifted her gaze skyward, releasing a sweet little sigh. "It's so beautiful. Is the weather always this pleasant in Kansas?"

Thad chuckled. "No, not always. Kansas tends to be unpredictable." He peeled back the lid on the ham and poked a fork into the tender pink meat. "Sometimes the coolness of spring stretches clear on into June. Other times it's hot an' dry. Been dry so far this year, but not so hot." He glanced at the sky, too, noting the puffy clouds floating overhead. The tree limbs swayed with the gentle breeze. His nose detected the scents of earth, grass, and something else that reminded him of lemons. Maybe Sadie's toilet water? "You're right, though, about it being pleasant." He admired the turn of her delicate jaw as she continued to survey the blue skies. "Real pleasant . . ."

She caught him looking at her, and her cheeks splotched with pink. She began fiddling with a blade of grass, giving him a view of the top of her little felt hat. He preferred seeing her face. So he plunked the cracker tin in the middle of the blanket and said, "Let me say grace, an' then we can eat."

He kept his prayer short and simple, then he

gestured for her to fill her plate first. She did so, without hesitation, pleasing him with her lack of inhibition. The few times he'd taken a woman out for dinner, he'd observed females tended to pick at food, almost as if eating was something to be endured rather than enjoyed. But Sadie stacked the ham and cheese on crackers and ate without embarrassment. Although she minded her manners —no talking while chewing or putting too much in her mouth at once—she appeared to enjoy herself. When she picked up a can of peaches, stabbed a pinkish-orange wedge with her fork, and carried it directly to her mouth, Thad nearly cheered. Finally, a girl who could be *real* instead of putting on airs.

A stronger gust of wind deposited a few bits of brown grass in Sadie's lap. She brushed them away, unconcerned, before reaching for another cracker. "The wind reminds me of home," she said. "When I left, Mama was just getting her garden seeds in the ground. I hope they've had some rain to make the seeds grow."

Thad carved off another sliver of cheese with his pocket knife and popped it in his mouth. He chewed and swallowed. "Do you like gardening?"

Her face lit. "Oh yes. I enjoy watching the little shoots push through the soil, and then seeing the leaves unfurl. Of course, knowing the plants will provide my family with the food we need to carry us through the winter is also gratifying."

"You said you come from a large family?" Thad pushed his plate aside and stretched out on his side, leaning on his elbow. Assuming the lazy pose might communicate his intention to stay for a while, but Sadie didn't appear offended. She flashed a smile in reply to his question.

"One sister and four brothers—four active brothers." She sighed, lifting her gaze to the tree for a moment. "I miss them. And my folks."

"So you're close, then." He didn't ask, he stated. Her sigh and the melancholy droop to her lips let him know how lonely she felt, being away from her family.

"Very," she confirmed. Shifting to look at him again, she said, "And you? Are you close to your family?"

Had Thad ever really been part of a family? It'd been him and pa, two people residing under the same roof. But family should mean the people cared for one another, looked out for one another, and took joy in being together. In that respect, he'd never been part of a family. But he didn't want to say all that to Sadie. "It's just me now," he said by way of an answer, allowing her to draw her own conclusions.

Her heart-shaped face puckered in sympathy. "I'm sorry. It's hard to be alone." Another sigh escaped her lips, but it was not light and airy like the last one. She pushed crumbs around her plate with the tip of her finger.

"Guess you'd know," Thad said, "since you're kind of alone, too, being so far from Indiana." The wind flipped the corner of the blanket over his plate. Thad flattened it back out and held it down with his elbow. "But you came to sing. So singing's important to you?"

Her wistful gaze drifted to the tree branches overhead where a bird chirped from its perch. "I've always loved singing. So when Sid wrote and said I could work at the mercantile and also sing in Goldtree's opera house, Mama and Papa said I should go—to use the gift God had given me." The bird flew away, and Sadie turned her attention to Thad. "I know I'm meant to be here. My folks and I prayed and prayed for me to find a decent job, and God answered. But it's very difficult to be so far away from Papa, Mama, Effie, and the boys."

Thad kept his voice light, even though his heart had suddenly decided to set up a fierce *boom-boom* inside his chest. "Are you hoping to have a big family of your own someday?"

"Of course! Big and boisterous." She laughed, the sound like creek water tripping over rocks. "I can't imagine family being any other way." She reached for the peach can and poked out the last wedge from the bottom, popping it into her mouth with a guileless smile that sent Thad's heart into his throat.

Thad slowly sat upright, his limbs quivery. He'd

never been a whimsical man, but in that moment he felt as though someone had pushed him over the edge of a cliff and he was soaring in the clouds. In that moment, he lost his heart to Miss Sadie Wagner. And he had no idea how to snatch it back.

12

"Asa, we already got one back door. Why'n the name o' all that's sensible do you gotta put in a second one?"

Asa sucked in a mighty breath and held it, waiting for the extra oxygen to calm his jangled nerves. Why couldn't the Almighty have given him brothers instead of a pair of harping, pestering, smothering sisters? When he could speak without snapping, he faced his sister. "As I already told you, Melva, if folks're gonna be able to get to the singin' room without walkin' clean through the mercantile, we got to have another door back here."

Melva's thin lips pursed into a tight scowl. "Well, Sister 'n' me're both just about tetched from all the bangin'. First all the bangin' you done for weeks on end underneath us, an' now all the bangin' behind us. If we come outta this without our hair fallin' out an' our teeth turnin' green, it'll be two winks shy of a miracle, an' that's a fact."

Asa allowed himself a moment to imagine his sisters with bald heads and green teeth. The thought made him smile. But he hid all humor from his tone as he responded to Melva's diatribe. "Never heard of nobody's teeth turnin' green from listenin' to somebody build a doorway. Scoot on back inside an' let me work. I still got lots to get done before Friday."

Melva let out a loud huff, but she stormed for the door. Just before she stepped inside, Asa thought of something and called, "Sister!" She paused and glared at him, but he ignored the searing look. "Send your clerk out here for a minute."

Melva's thick eyebrows rose. "You gonna make her swing a hammer?"

The ridiculous question didn't warrant a response. "Just send 'er."

With another blast of breath, Melva stomped away. Moments later, Miss Wagner scurried into the backyard. "Yes, Mr. Baxter?"

Asa tried not to give the girl a head-to-toes-to-head-again look-see, but she sure tempted a man. The Creator did some mighty fine work when he put Sadie Wagner together. "Just wantin' you to know, I been talkin' up the program all over town. Got lots of folks eager to come on Friday for the opera house's openin'."

The girl's cheeks flushed, and she tangled her hands in her apron. "Truly?"

Asa chuckled. Her fresh eagerness never ceased to please him. "Oh, you betcha. You been gettin' in some practice?"

"Yes, sir! Every evening after supper I've gone through my . . . repertoire." The pink in her cheeks blossomed into a deeper hue. "I have enough songs to fill a full hour." Her brow pinched. "Is—is that sufficient?"

Asa gave a blunt nod. "For now." But it'd need to grow to a heap longer before he could get the second part of his business in full swing. "Don't want'cha overdoin' at first, so stick to an hour for the first couple weeks. But you'll need to build. After all, if we want folks comin' back again an' again, we gotta give 'em somethin' more each time."

Miss Wagner nodded thoughtfully.

"I ordered a good dozen tunes. Soon as they're in, you can start workin' 'em into your repertoire." He liked the way her face turned all dreamy when he used the word *repertoire*. So he repeated it. "Yep, gotta build that repertoire."

"Yes, sir. I will."

He also liked how she called him "sir." He puffed out his chest. "Well, I gotta finish up this doorway now, so you head on back inside. Maybe after supper tonight we can go to the singin' room, an' you can practice on the stage. Would'ja like that?"

"Yes, sir!"

Asa laughed. A genuine laugh. The sound startled him. Suddenly uncertain what to do, he bobbed the hammer at the other doorway. "Go on now."

The girl flashed a smile before slipping through the doorway. Asa stared after her, the hammer forgotten in his hand. He couldn't recall the last time he'd spontaneously laughed. He often conjured a chortle. Sometimes it was required. But this one had blasted from his throat without forethought. He shook his head, trying to rein in his confusion. The girl had a strange effect on him. He'd better be careful.

"Hello there, Asa."

The jovial voice came from behind Asa, startling him anew. He swung around and spotted Roscoe Hanaman just a few feet behind him, thumbs caught in the little pockets of his brocade vest. Heat rose from Asa's middle. Had the man seen him moonin' over Miss Wagner?

"Hey there, Roscoe. What you doin' back here?" Asa hoped he didn't sound as resentful as he felt. Wouldn't do to make an enemy of the town's mayor.

Roscoe strode forward and propped one polished black shoe on the edge of the high wooden porch floor. "I was passing by on my way to sip a cup of Cora's coffee and heard the banging. There's been quite a lot of that over the past several days. So I thought I'd come see what you were making back here." His gaze roved over the newly cut doorframe made of crisp white oak.

Asa swung the hammer, assuming a casual pose. "Just a door, as you can see." But not just any door—a door with a half-circle window up above, fronted by a six-by-six-foot porch with a roof, carved pillars, and a spindled railing. A fancy entryway. "Needed it so's folks could go straight on down to the opera house." He grimaced. "Wouldn't do, y'know, to bring folks through the mercantile an' its storeroom. Undignified. Plus, havin' a separate door'll let my sisters secure the mercantile at night." One less reason for them to be fussin'.

"Good thinking, Asa. Good thinking." Hanaman nodded his graying head.

Asa smiled, feigning appreciation of the man's approval. But he didn't need it. He already knew it was good thinking. "Gonna have our first show this Friday night." Three more days and his long-held plans would finally be set in motion. "You plannin' to come? Miss Wagner's a real good singer."

"The missus and I wouldn't miss it," Roscoe said. "Miriam's excited that culture has finally arrived in Goldtree. But . . ." Hanaman's round face creased. "She's wondering, kind of like the rest of the town, why you aren't just using the community center for these shows."

"An' have everybody sittin' on hard, backless benches?" Asa injected as much shock in his tone as he could manage. "Might be all right for a town meetin' or a short program, but Miss Wagner's got a whole collection of songs ready to go. Folks're gonna wanna settle in, get comfortable, an' relish every minute of the show."

Hanaman's mustache twitched. "You're a fine salesman, Asa. You've piqued my interest."

Asa broke out in gooseflesh as an idea crept through his brain. Having the support of the mayor and banker would be just the boost he needed to ensure that all of Goldtree's residents put their money in his coffer. His pulse sped as if he'd just run a footrace. "Would'ja—" He sounded breathless. He sucked a lungful of air and tried again. "Would'ja like a sample performance? Gonna have Miss Wagner practice on the stage tonight after supper. Come on down, take a look at the singin' room, an' listen in." A sly grin teased the corners of Asa's mouth. "I think you'll like what'cha see an' hear."

Roscoe backed up a step, his smile wide. "Why, thank you, Asa. I just might do that." He lifted his hand in a wave and ambled around the corner of the building.

Asa pulled a nail from his pocket and positioned it against the smooth oak, but he didn't bring down the hammer. There was somebody else in town he needed on his side. Somebody even more powerful than Hanaman. His eyes flicked over the unfinished doorframe. There was much to do—a porch roof, pillars, railings—and steps so old ladies wouldn't have to heft themselves onto the stoop. But he still had two days. If he worked hard and put Sid to work on it, too, it'd get done. This errand was more important.

He dropped the hammer onto the wooden floor with a clatter and took off at a clumsy trot around the building.

Sadie stood between the richly stained pillars, the toes of her shoes aligned with a little mark Mr. Baxter had made so she'd be seen from every row of seats. He'd lit both chandeliers and all of the wall sconces, bathing the entire room in a yellow glow that turned the crystals dangling from the elaborate chandeliers into glittering diamonds. She hadn't realized her practice would be attended by more than Mr. Baxter. Her stomach trembled, and she pressed her linked hands more firmly against her waist as she looked across the trio of men seated in the first row.

"Anytime you're ready, Miss Wagner," Mr. Baxter called from his spot between the mayor and Thad McKane.

Sadie swallowed, sending up a silent prayer for strength. If she survived this practice—a practice that now had the feel of a performance—then surely it would indicate she was ready for a full audience. She drew in a deep breath, closed her eyes to fully focus on the music, and began. " 'Eternal Father, strong to save, Whose arm has bound the restless wave . . .' "

Although she'd intended to insert the relatively new hymn in the middle of the repertoire, she chose to sing it first for this small audience. She sensed they would find it more pleasing than her original choice, "Abide With Me." As she sang through all four verses, her voice gained strength, her confidence building. The joy of singing carried her to another plane. She forgot about the three pairs of eyes aimed in her direction, forgot about her nervousness, forgot everything except the bliss of bringing forth song.

On the closing phrase, she slowed the pace, increasing in volume and climbing one octave higher than the composer had penned. " 'Thus ever let there rise to Thee glad hymns of praise from land and sea!' " The words echoed from the rafters. She held the final note, giving freedom to her natural vibrato. The moment she ended with a demure bowing of her head, applause erupted. Her eyes popped open, and joy flooded her frame. Both the mayor and Thad had leaped up, and both enthusiastically pounded their palms together.

The mayor dashed forward and captured her hand. "My dear, that was splendid. The most amazing vocal performance I've ever heard!"

Still holding her hand, he spun toward Mr. Baxter. "Asa, it was genius to bring this girl to Goldtree. Why, her abilities will draw people from all of the neighboring communities. Goldtree will soon be hailed as the cultural center of Clay County. Genius, purely genius."

Mr. Baxter's chest expanded, his face set in a knowing smirk. "So you like Miss Wagner's singin', do ya?"

"Like it?" Mayor Hanaman's eyebrows rose so high they touched his slicked-back hairline. "I'm in awe."

Mr. Baxter slid a look in Thad's direction. "What about you, Sheriff? You think this girl's got any talent?"

Sadie held her breath. Thad's exuberant clapping spoke of his approval, but she wanted to *hear* his praise. He moved forward slowly, as if slogging through a sea of cornmeal mush, his eyes pinned on her face. Sadie's pulse tripped ever faster as he closed the gap between them. He didn't reach for her the way the mayor had. Instead, he anchored his fingers in the pockets of his tan trousers, his movements so slow she might have imagined them. And then, he opened his mouth to speak.

"Real fine, Miss Sadie. Your singing's real fine."

Simple words. Yet delivered with such sincerity and adoration Sadie's heart fluttered like a butterfly lifting on a summer breeze. She beamed in response, a giggle of pure delight spilling from her lips. "Th-thank you, Sheriff."

Mr. Hanaman raised Sadie's hand and planted a kiss on its back. "Miss Wagner, I could listen to you sing all night. But I think my time will be better spent alerting the fine citizens of Goldtree to the wonderful treat they have in store this coming Friday evening." He kissed her knuckles a second time, his mustache prickly against her skin. Then he released her and charged for the double doors at the rear of the room. "Asa, genius . . . purely genius . . ." His footsteps receded.

Mr. Baxter planted his hands on the armrests of his chair and pushed to his feet. He sidled to the stage and stopped beside Thad, who continued to gaze into Sadie's face with such rapture she marveled that she hadn't melted from delight. The man cleared his throat, and both Thad and Sadie jumped.

"So, Sheriff, ya gonna stay an' listen in on the rest of Miss Wagner's practice?"

Thad shook his head, regret tingeing his features. "I'd like to. As Mr. Hanaman said, I'd be content to listen all night. But I need to make my evening rounds."

Disappointment twined through Sadie's middle. She asked, "Y-you'll come Friday night, though, won't you? For the whole performance?"

His mustache quirked with his charming grin.

"You can count on it, Miss Sadie. Wouldn't miss it."

"Good! Good!" Mr. Baxter pounded Thad on the back with a pudgy hand. He chuckled, an odd burble of humor that almost sounded rusty. "Promises to be a fine performance, an' I reckon the entire town'll come. That means nobody'll be out an' about causin' mischief."

For a moment Thad's brow wrinkled, as if he were puzzling over something. "Reckon you're right, Mr. Baxter. Can't imagine anybody wanting to stay away." He inched backward, his gaze lingering on Sadie's face. "Thank you for letting me sit in on your practice, Miss Sadie. I look forward to hearing your whole program on Friday."

As Thad thumped off, Mr. Baxter waved his hands at Sadie. "All right, all right, let's hear your other songs."

Sadie experienced a sense of loss with Thad's departure, but within minutes she once again lost herself in the joy of singing. She moved flawlessly from one piece to another, and Mr. Baxter sat quietly and attentively through the entire repertoire. When she'd completed the final number, she gave a complete bow, holding the bent-low position for a count of ten before rising. Then she hugged herself and said, "Will . . . will that be sufficient?"

Mr. Baxter worked his jaw back and forth, his

forehead set in such tight crinkles it looked painful. Finally he let out a loud sigh. "I reckon it'll have to do."

His halfhearted statement wasn't the affirmation Sadie had hoped for. She stepped off the stage. "Is something wrong? I realize the program is entirely hymns, but—"

"No, no, I told'ja to start with hymns." He sounded cranky. "An' judgin' by the way Hanaman an' McKane went all soft, hymns'll probably suit most of the audience. But . . ." He paced back and forth, scuffing his heels, his chin pinched between his thumb and index finger. He stopped and pointed at her. "We need somethin' . . . more. Got that piano back there. Planned on havin' some-body playin' afore you start to sing—sort of a prelude, y'know."

Sadie nodded, even though she wasn't completely sure what he intended.

"I'll have the pianist here to accompany all your songs, too. Bigger sound." He waved his arms, a smile growing on his jowly face. "More hullabaloo."

"H-hullabaloo?"

"Why, sure! Your voice mixed with the poundin' of the piano." He leaped onto the stage in a clumsy hop and lifted the keyboard cover. He brought down both hands on the ivory keys. One inharmonious chord hung in the air. He laughed and slapped the cover back into position, making the strings *whang*. "That'll do it. That'll do it for sure."

Sadie stepped back as he charged toward the far corner of the stage and retrieved the crate he'd used as a stepstool when lighting the lamps. He crawled up again and turned the little dials on the chandeliers. Their bright lights flickered and died. Marching toward the wall sconces, he called over his shoulder, "That'll do for tonight, Miss Wagner. Head on up an' get a good night's rest. Big performance on Friday. Yes, sir, it's gonna be big!"

Sadie headed for the doors as he'd directed. His unusual chortle rumbled behind her. Suddenly, for reasons she little understood, the anticipation of performing faded into a lump of uncertainty.

13

Sid swiped at the dribble of sweat that tickled his temple. His eyes stung from squinting against the sun, but he placed another shingle into position and whacked down two nails, securing it in place. Sitting back on his haunches, he tugged his hat brim a little lower to shield his eyes and examined the remaining patch of unprotected porch roof. Just a few more shingles, and he could climb down, find some shade and a jug of water, and enjoy a little rest.

When Asa Baxter had told him he'd be doing carpentry work at the mercantile instead of serving as a drayman for a couple of days, he'd thought it sounded like a welcome change. The man had nearly run him ragged for the past two weeks, sending him back and forth between Concordia to collect enough timbers to construct a barn. But then he'd said, "Finish the porch."

Sid liked the idea of being in close proximity to Sadie. And porch building sounded a lot less strenuous than loading and unloading lumber. But he hadn't bargained on having to shingle and paint the railed porch in only two days. Sadie might be only a few yards away, but who had time to speak to her?

He had to admit, though, as he climbed down the ladder and stepped back to admire his handi-work, the porch for the new entry to the opera house looked mighty fine. Asa had insisted on a four-color scheme—white with green, red, and gold trim. At first Sid had thought the man was batty and the porch would resemble a circus wagon. But now that he'd finished, he liked the way the posts and spindles looked, the different turnings set off by bold color. Maybe he'd paint his own porch in a similar fashion someday.

That is, if he managed to convince Sadie to marry him.

He lifted the jug he'd left in the shade between the mercantile and drugstore and took a lengthy swig, his gaze lifting to the window of Sadie's room. Wouldn't she rather have a whole house to call her own? Sure she would. Every woman wanted her own place, a husband, and a family. And he was willing to give it to her, if only she'd stop fluttering her eyelashes at the sheriff and look at Sid.

The water soured in his stomach, and he whapped the cork back into the jug's opening hard enough to sink it below the rim. He'd have a time digging it out later, but he didn't care. He had more important things to consider.

What was it about Sheriff McKane that held Sadie's attention? Two Sundays ago, after their disagreement, he'd gone looking for her to apologize for his surly behavior and tell her why he'd been upset. But when he'd rounded the corner, he'd spotted her crossing the street with McKane. Looking up at him. Smiling. Laughing. The sight had sent him scuttling back to his house to brood for hours.

Being on the road so much, he'd had few opportunities to talk to Sadie, but over the past two days, he'd approached her three different times, hoping to apologize. Twice she whispered she was on duty and shouldn't fraternize. The third time he'd waited until the mercantile sign showed "Closed," but then she'd been in a rush to practice for her opening performance and didn't have time to talk. So he'd left, frustrated and heartsore.

Just that morning, he'd come around the building to find Sadie sweeping the front porch. Before he could catch her attention, though, the sheriff had clomped up and greeted her. Sid had expected her to send the man on, since she was working, but instead she'd leaned on the broom and beamed a welcome. McKane had slipped one hand in his pocket, the picture of relaxation, and they'd chatted for several minutes.

The image of the two of them—smiling and at ease with each other—would be burned in Sid's memory forever. What all had gone on between them while he'd collected Asa's lumber? Sadie obviously had time for the sheriff, but not for him. Couldn't she see she was breaking his heart?

But he had a plan to capture her attention tonight. By the end of the day, she'd be looking at him with that moony expression she'd aimed at the sheriff.

He grabbed an empty crate from the shed and began cleaning up the leftover shingles, tools, and paint brushes, weary but smiling. The one time he'd visited an opera house, the singer had been given a bouquet of roses at the end of the performance. He might not be able to find roses in Goldtree, but there were wild flowers sprouting in the field beside Asa's house. Just yesterday, he'd seen a good dozen clusters of foot-high stems bearing purple flowers with yellow centers.

As soon as he finished up here, he intended to ride out and pick a big bundle of those purple flowers, tie their stems together with a length of yellow ribbon he'd purchased a month ago because the color had reminded him of Sadie's shining hair, and he'd hand 'em right over in front of everybody tonight when she finished her final song. His heart set up a double beat just thinking about how she'd blush pink and give him her special smile.

Then, while she was smiling and feeling appreciative, he'd take her aside and set her straight on how he felt about her and how much her paying attention to the sheriff hurt him. He and Sadie had a relationship years in the making. She'd only known the sheriff a few weeks. She'd pick him over McKane. He just knew it.

The yard clean, Sid plopped the crate back in the shed. He paused for a moment to massage his aching back. Another yawn stretched his jaw so wide it popped. Mercy, he was tired. He peeked out the shed door at the sun, which had drifted toward the western horizon but still hung fairly high. Would he have time for a nap? He'd sure earned one after his long hours of finishing that fancy porch.

Then he got a whiff of his own body. No time for napping. He had flowers to pick, and then he needed to clean himself up good before heading to the opera house tonight. He aimed his feet toward his little rental house, whistling. He might not've gotten time with Sadie earlier in the week, but he'd make up for it tonight. How could Sadie refuse a clean-smelling man in his best suit bearing an armload of flowers? She couldn't. She was as good as his already.

Miss Melva poked Miss Shelva on the shoulder and pointed as Sadie entered the kitchen for supper. "Well, now, lookit our Sadie in her Sunday go-to-meetin' dress an' her hair all hangin' down her back."

Miss Shelva jumped up and rushed at Sadie, her hands outstretched. "Oh my," she crooned at full volume. "You're just as purty as a picture, Sadie. Never seen nobody look so purty before."

Sadie fingered the strand of hair that lay across the bodice of her newest dress. She hadn't worn her hair down except for bed since she was a little girl, and leaving the locks unfettered made her feel half-dressed and exposed. "Are you sure I look . . . decent?" Surely no lady would be seen in public with her hair unbound, but Mr. Baxter had insisted she shouldn't twist it into a knot.

Yesterday evening, after she'd practiced with the pianist, Mr. Baxter had said, "Them lights'll be shinin' on your yellow hair, makin' you look like you got a halo. You just do as I say, Miss Wagner.

Earn your keep." Recalling his comment brought a fresh rush of heat to Sadie's face. She appreciated the generous wage she would receive for singing, but she wasn't sure she liked the proprietary way he eyed her when she stood on the stage.

Miss Melva bounced up from the table and joined her sister in circling Sadie, admiring her from every angle. "You remind me of a picture in a Bible storybook I had when I was a young'un. 'Member that storybook, Sister? Ma read to us from it afore we went to sleep at night."

Miss Shelva bobbed her head. "I 'member."

"Picture of a angel sittin' on a rock outside the Lord's tomb—"

"—with yellow, wavy hair a-flowin' over his shoulders. Yep." Miss Shelva completed Miss Melva's sentence. She stroked her hand down Sadie's waist-length tresses, her thin face softened by a smile of wonder. "Your hair's just as yellow an' flowin' as an angel's hair."

"Downright beautiful," Miss Melva confirmed.

Sadie hunched her shoulders, embarrassed by their open admiration. She hustled to the table and sat, but she didn't reach for the serving bowls. Her stomach was too nervous to hold food. The twins plunked back into their chairs and resumed eating.

Sadie clasped her hands in her lap to control their shaking. "Are you coming tonight?"

"Don't got tickets," Miss Shelva said around a bite of breaded tomatoes.

Sadie blinked in surprise. Mr. Baxter had bragged about how many tickets he'd sold—seemed most of the town of Goldtree planned to be in attendance. She'd assumed, since the opera house was a part of the mercantile, Miss Melva and Miss Shelva would have no need to purchase tickets. "Mr. Baxter didn't give you any?"

"Didn't ask for none," Miss Melva replied. She wiped her mouth with the back of her hand. "Sister an' me never go in the cellar."

"Not even if a tornado was a-comin' could you get me down there," her twin said with a solemn bob of her head.

"Y-you won't be there, then?" Disappointment sat heavily in Sadie's breast. Although the sisters were her employers, they were familiar faces. Not friends, perhaps, but not strangers, either, as were most of the townsfolk. She'd counted on being able to look at them when she got nervous.

"Spiders. Rats. Who knows what all else is scurryin' around down there." Miss Melva shuddered.

Miss Shelva patted Sadie's hand. "When Asa gets the above-ground opera house built, like he's plannin', then we'll get our tickets like ever'body else. But we ain't goin' in no cellar."

"But if you'd only come down, you'd see—"

"Ain't goin' in no cellar," Miss Shelva repeated, even louder than the first time.

Sadie hung her head. "Very well." She pushed

away from the table. "I believe I'll go on down and sing through a few scales—warm up my voice."

"You ain't gonna eat?" Miss Melva gawked at her. "You gotta eat."

Sadie backed away. "I'm not hungry. I'll find something later." Both sisters raised a protest, but Sadie hurried to the stairway and clattered down the stairs, pretending not to hear. She didn't know how to turn on the gaslights, so she grabbed the lantern from the shelf in the storeroom and lit it before taking the stairs to the singing room.

Her feet echoed eerily as she made her way up the aisle to the stage. The coolness of the room touched her limbs and she shivered. Or maybe the emptiness of the space—all shadowed and silent as a tomb—made her shiver. *Spiders. Rats. Who knows what all else is scurryin' around down there."* Miss Melva's comment echoed in Sadie's mind, and her gaze zipped around the dark room, expecting little creatures to skitter from the corners.

"Stop being a ninny," she told herself. How foolish to adopt the Baxter twins' fears. To take her mind off the women's wary suppositions, she stepped onto the stage, held the lantern high, and examined the rows of velvet-covered seats. Tonight they would all be filled with people who'd come to hear her sing. Another shiver climbed her spine, this one of nervous anticipation.

"I've waited my whole life for this moment, Lord," she whispered, lifting her face to the stamped tin ceiling. "Thank You for giving me the opportunity to sing. Let me praise You in song, just as King David did so long ago." A tiny bit of her nervousness melted away with the prayer.

She moved to the piano, set the lantern on its glossy top, and opened the cover. She touched keys one at a time, singing a scale to match each pitch. She started softly, gently, exercising her vocal cords the way Papa used to swing a bat to limber up before playing a baseball game with his mining buddies. Only when she'd finished the scales did she remember she'd neglected to bring a glass of water down with her. She'd need to sip between songs if she didn't want to strain her voice.

She started for the hallway to go upstairs, but a sound captured her attention. A steady *drip, drip, drip*. Might Mr. Baxter have a spigoted water barrel down here for the attendees to satisfy their thirst during a break? If so, she wouldn't have to go out to the pump.

Holding the lantern to light the way, she headed toward the sound. Floor-to-ceiling curtains lined the south wall, and the dripping seemed to echo from somewhere beyond them. Sadie pawed at the thick velvet, searching for a seam. She finally located one, slightly off-center to the wall, and pushed the heavy drape aside. A solid wood door hid behind the shielding draperies. The dripping was louder, so she knew she was close to the source. She twisted the door's handle, but it didn't budge.

Listening to the drip made her throat feel even drier. She set the lantern on the floor and wrapped both hands around the brass handle. She twisted with all her might. The handle refused to turn. Frustrated, she leaned her full weight into the door.

"Miss Wagner!"

Although very softly spoken, Mr. Baxter's voice startled Sadie so badly she gasped. She jumped away from the door and whirled to face the opera house's frowning owner.

"What're you tryin' to do?"

"I heard water dripping, and I was thirsty," Sadie said.

The man snatched up the lantern with one hand and grabbed Sadie's elbow with the other. He escorted her back to the performance area, then released her with a rough shove that sent her scrambling to regain her balance. She rubbed her arm and stared at him, her pulse galloping in apprehension.

"Miss Wagner, I'm gonna say this once an' once only." The man spoke so softly Sadie had to strain to hear him. "The only doors you're to use are the ones that lead outside or into the mercantile storeroom. That door over there? It's for me an' me alone. You understand?"

He didn't raise his voice. She'd never heard him raise his voice. But the harsh tone he now used made the fine hairs on Sadie's neck prickle. She offered a quick nod. "Yes, sir. I understand."

A smile crept across his face, but his eyes remained slits of warning. "Good girl. Now, if you're needin' a drink, I'll just go up an' fetch you a glass of water. Maybe even bring a pitcher down. Would you like that?"

Sadie's tongue stuck to the roof of her parched mouth, but something more than a desire for water created the uncomfortable dryness. She tasted fear. "Y-yes, sir. Thank you."

He handed her the lantern, then turned to leave. But as he reached the doors, he paused and peered over his shoulder at her. "Oh . . . an' Miss Wagner?"

"Yes?"

"About that door behind the curtains . . ." Another smile—a friendly, guileless smile— transformed his face. "You don't need to be tellin' nobody about that. You know how goosey my sisters are. It'd only upset 'em, wonderin' what's back there."

What *is* back there? The question quivered on Sadie's lips, but she held it inside.

Mr. Baxter continued in the same affable tone.

"If you wanna keep singin' here, earnin' that three dollars a night, it's best you keep it our little secret. All right?" Without waiting for a reply, he clomped around the corner and disappeared from view.

14

Sadie performed Friday and Saturday night. Both nights, every seat was filled and a few men—including Thad on Friday night—stood along the side wall. Every time she glanced in his direction, his smiling face, illuminated by the wall sconces, gave her a boost of encouragement. Both nights she received riotous applause, whistles, and calls for an encore. By all means of measurement, the evenings were a success. But as Sadie sat at the desk in her room on Sunday afternoon, pen in hand, she didn't know what to tell her parents.

The ivory sheet of paper stared at her, the salutation lonely at the top of the page. How she wanted to share everything about the evening— her initial nervousness, her joy as music overtook her soul and carried her from the watching crowd to planes of bliss, her desire to dissolve into tears in response to the exuberant ovation and the wilted bouquet of flowers Sid shyly thrust at her at the end of Friday's performance. But if she were to share all, she'd have to tell them about the hidden door and Mr. Baxter's warning.

Slapping down the pen, she rose and paced the little room. "Perhaps 'warning' is too strong a word." She consoled herself, a feeble attempt to escape the fingers of unease that crept up and down her spine. "After all, he didn't *threaten* me." Her feet came to a halt as she recalled his friendly smile, coupled with the casually voiced, *"If you wanna keep singin' . . ."* She wrapped her arms around her middle and shivered. He *had* threatened her. He'd threatened her in the worst possible way, because he knew how much she needed that money to send home to Mama and Papa.

No, she couldn't tell anyone about the door.

Too restless to sit and write, she headed out of her room. Perhaps a walk would help her clear her mind. She tiptoed down the hallway, aware that her employers dozed in their bedrooms. Miss Shelva had informed Sadie that she and her sister napped every Sunday afternoon and Sadie should only disturb them if the mercantile caught on fire. She eased down the stairs, mindful of the fourth and fifth risers, which always squeaked, and let herself out the back door.

The bright sun hit her full in the face, and she lifted her hand to shield her eyes. In her haste, she'd left her bonnet behind. She considered returning for it, but unwilling to risk disturbing the sleeping sisters, she decided to remain bare-headed. She'd simply find a shady spot to sit. Immediately, the tree in the side yard of the community building came to mind, so she headed in that direction.

The streets were empty, everyone closed in their own houses for a quiet Sunday afternoon. For a moment, loneliness attacked, but Sadie resolutely pushed the feeling aside. At church that morning, Reverend Wise had advised the congregants on the importance of being content regardless of one's circumstances. Even the choir, which Sadie had joined last week, shared a song that encouraged a contented spirit. As she made her way across the street, she hummed "It Is Well With My Soul," finding herself smiling as the words played through her mind.

She might be far from her family, but she had much for which to be grateful. She seated herself beneath the tree, tucking her legs to the side and smoothing her skirts over her ankles. A soft breeze teased her skin, and she sighed, content. After the past weeks' frenetic pace—learning everything about clerking in the mercantile, practicing for performances, and finally singing —it felt amazingly good to simply sit and do nothing. She'd enjoy a time of rest, then she'd finish her letter so she could send her parents the money Mr. Baxter had given her last night after every-one had left. Wouldn't they be pleased to find such a substantial sum in the envelope?

Sadie frowned, envisioning the rows of seats in the opera house. Two sections of six seats across by eight rows deep provided seats for ninety-six attendees. Both Friday and Saturday, at least a dozen people stood along the north wall, bringing the number to over a hundred. Mr. Baxter charged a half dollar per ticket, which meant each night he'd taken in at least fifty dollars.

She gasped, her mind racing. If he collected a similar amount every week, four weeks a month, and twelve months a year, even after paying her and purchasing coal oil for the lights, he'd earn a tidy sum. The man would be rich in no time! Surely he'd have the funds to build his elaborate opera house—maybe like the one in Dalton that was constructed of carved rock with a spindled balcony and a curved stage—in less than two years.

"Just think . . ." Sadie hunched her shoulders, an excited giggle building in her throat. "In no time at all, I'll be singing on a real opera house's stage instead of in a basement singing room."

"What's that you said?"

Sadie yelped, slapping her hand over her racing heart. She whirled toward the intruding voice, and she nearly collapsed in relief when she spotted Sid at the edge of the shade cast by the tree's waving limbs. "Oh my, Sid, you nearly scared me out of a year's growth."

He grinned sheepishly and ambled close. "Sorry. Didn't mean to scare you. Was takin' a walk— thinkin' some—an' saw you. Can . . ." He gulped, streaks of red decorating his tanned cheeks. "Can I join you?"

She scooted over a bit and patted the ground beside her. "Of course." She disliked the wariness that assaulted her in Sid's presence. After their years of comfortable camaraderie, his recent churlishness had cast a pall on their friendship. Her heart had warmed, however, with his gift of flowers—sad-looking, droopy things tied with a bright yellow ribbon—Friday night. She'd tossed away the flowers, but she'd placed the rumpled ribbon next to her family photograph as a reminder of her once-close relationship with her cousin.

Sid plopped down, knees bent and legs spread wide. He leaned against the tree and sent an uncertain glance in Sadie's direction. "Nice out here. Not too hot yet. But now that June's here, it'll get a lot hotter in no time."

The weather was a topic for strangers. Sadie jumped to a more personal topic. "You weren't in church this morning." She watched his face for signs of irritation.

He sighed, staring outward. "Yep. Slept in. Purely tuckered after all that buildin' I did on the new porch an' then stayin' up late for your performances."

Sadie had stayed up late, too, but she'd managed to get up for church. She nudged him with her elbow. "Your folks wouldn't be pleased to have you sleeping through services."

A brief scowl pinched his brow. "Only one Sunday, Sadie. I'm not likely to turn heathen just by missin' one service."

She shifted slightly to face him. "No, probably not, but *something* has changed you. And I wish I knew what it was."

Although he didn't move, she sensed him pulling away. "Whaddaya mean?"

"I've never known you to snap at me, or act high and mighty." Would he bluster in anger? His jaw tightened, but his eyes didn't snap. She continued in a soft tone. "But more than once since I arrived in Goldtree, you've behaved boorishly with me."

His Adam's apple bobbed. He still didn't look at her.

"Sid?" She placed her hand on his arm. He jumped as if she'd pinched him, but he didn't pull away. "Have I done something to offend you? Because if I have, I'd like to make things right. You and I have been friends for too long to have this antagonism between us. Will you tell me what's wrong so we can go back to how we used to be?"

Sid jerked his arms forward, propping his elbows on his knees. "I don't wanna go back to how we used to be."

His vehemence, as well as his strange statement, dismayed Sadie. "You don't want to be my friend anymore?"

He shook his head.

Sadie looked down, blinking back tears. His rejection hurt more than she could understand. "Oh."

He wheeled on the seat of his pants, taking her chin in his hand and lifting her face. His eyes smoldered with deep emotion. "I wanna be more."

Sadie sucked in a sharp breath. "M-more?"

Sid gazed directly into her face, his fingers possessive on her jaw. "I wanna be your beau, Sadie."

"Sid!" Sadie pulled back, out of his reach, but his hand hovered in the air in front of her face. She inched sideways, putting a little more space between them. "You can't be my *beau*."

The dark scowl of days past returned, giving him a stern appearance. "Why not?"

She held out her hands. "We're cousins!"

"Not by blood." He rolled to his knees, anchoring her skirts to the ground with his weight. Then he leaned in, like a cat cornering a mouse. "You ain't really a Wagner. Oh, sure, you call Uncle Len Papa, but he's not your real pa. So that means we aren't real cousins."

Sadie's heart raced so fast, she could hardly draw a breath. "But . . . but . . ."

"I tried to tell you how I feel by takin' you to

162

dinner. An' givin' you those flowers." His familiar face, so close his breath touched her cheek, lit with fervor. "Those're things a beau would do. Didn't you understand?"

How could she have been so blind? Now she recognized his childish tantrums as jealousy, his desire to please her as signs of affection. Her chest ached. "Oh, Sid . . ."

He sank back, resting his backside on his boot-heels. His expression faded from eagerness to apprehension. "What?"

Sadie caught his hand and held it loosely. She didn't want to hurt him, but she had to be honest. "I'm very flattered that you care so much for me. Any girl would be honored to call you her beau. But—"

He yanked his hand free. "But you don't wanna be that girl." His voice sounded flat. Not angry, not even sad. Just emotionless.

Tears stung her eyes. "I'm sorry." He looked to the side, his jaw muscles twitching. Sadie dared to touch his arm. "You know I care about you. You've always been my favorite cousin. But that's the problem—you've been my *cousin*. My playmate and companion. Not a prospective beau."

The beautiful early summer day lost its luster as Sadie watched Sid battle emotion. Frustration, sorrow, disappointment—they paraded across his face in quick succession while she prayed inwardly for him to understand. Finally he blew out a noisy breath and stretched to his feet. He stood, staring down at her, his eyes empty. And then determination bloomed across his features.

"Sadie . . ." He swallowed. "I'm not willin' to just be your cousin anymore." His shoulders squared. "Whatever it takes to win your affection, I'll do it. I'm gonna woo you like no man's ever wooed a woman before. An' I'm gonna win your love. You wait an' see." He spun and stomped away, his arms swinging.

Sadie sank against the rough bark of the tree, no longer content. If Sid followed through on his promise to woo her, things in Goldtree could become very uncomfortable.

15

Early Monday morning, Asa poured himself a cup of stout coffee and peered out the square window —set low to accommodate his height— into his backyard. Dawn was breaking, sending a rosy glow across the landscape. More than enough light for a man to see where he was going. So where was that Scotty?

He reached into his pocket and retrieved the brief telegram that had arrived Saturday.

DELIVERY MONDAY SUNRISE STOP FIVE SAMPLES STOP CASH TO SUPPLY STOP. Asa scratched his head, yawned, and shoved the telegram back into his pocket. He hoped Scotty was as good as his word, or this too-early awakening would be for naught. Predawn rising was for chickens and dirt farmers.

Memory carried him backward in time to Ohio, his family's farmstead. Cornstalks rustling in the breeze, cows mooing in the pasture, Pa hollering, "Hurry up, Asa, an' bring in that milk!" Never enough money. Or food. Or anything else that mattered. Asa slurped his coffee, swallowing the memories along with the steaming brew. Those days were far behind him. He was a businessman now, with a fine house, half a dozen tailor-made suits, a full pantry, and money in his cash box with plans to get a heap more. He'd never go back to cow-milking or scrabbling in the dirt for a measly living.

But first he needed bottles. He squinted out the window again, willing Scotty to appear. As if the power of thought could make things happen, the squeak of wagon wheels reached Asa's ears. He pressed his face to the windowpane and spotted a wagon pulling up beside the barn, just as Asa had instructed. With a gleeful chortle, he clacked the coffee cup into the tin sink basin and charged out the back door as fast as his short legs would carry him.

He reached the wagon as Scotty swung down from the seat. "You get 'em?" he asked. No need for friendly greetings between superiors and underlings.

Scotty nodded and headed for the rear of the wagon. "Right here." He lifted out a slatted crate with bits of straw poking out from between the narrow bands of wood. He bent over to place the crate on the ground, but Asa waved his hands.

"Somebody might see. Take it in the house."

Scotty sent a glance around the yard, his eyebrows high. "Who's gonna see?"

The snide question set Asa's teeth on edge. So his house was a mile from his closest neighbor. So he didn't expect Sid to fetch the wagon until after eight o'clock. So there wasn't much chance of being seen. He still wanted privacy, and since he was the one paying, *he* would decide where he viewed the merchandise.

With a grunt, he spun toward the house. "Just c'mon." Asa led Scotty to the house and pointed to the table. "Put it there."

Scotty plopped the crate on the checked table-cloth while Asa closed and locked the door and then whisked the curtains together to prevent anyone from peeking inside. Asa caught Scotty's derisive smirk. He decided to ignore it, but he'd give the man a stern warning about maintaining privacy before he left. Last thing he wanted was for somebody—especially that new sheriff who spent his days roaming the whole town—to start putting two and two together.

"Let me see what'cha got." Asa rested his fingertips on the edge of the crate, licking his lips in eagerness.

Scotty dug through the straw and pulled out a short, roundish, yellow-colored bottle. "This here is called an onion bottle. It's imported all the way from Belgium. You can get it in this color or green or clear." He pulled out a second one, similar in height but with a less-rounded shape and a longer neck. "This one, called acorn, is made in the east, so it don't cost as much. Can probably get two acorns for the price of one onion." He set them down side by side beside the crate.

Asa discounted the bottles. Short and squatty, they reminded him too much of his own reflection in the mirror.

Scotty pulled out two more bottles, both slender with smooth lines of deep red glass— one about eight inches in height and the other closer to a foot. "These're hand-blown, so they ain't cheap, but they're the most common. Easy to hold. A fellow can drink straight from the spout." He demonstrated, raising the shorter one to his lips.

Although the ease of handling appealed to him—even his short fingers could maintain a sure grip on either bottle—the long, lean look put pictures of his long, lean sisters in his mind. Asa made a face. "I dunno . . ."

"Well, then, there's always the bordeaux . . ." Scotty held a fifth bottle aloft. Light green in color, the bottle featured a tall body that tapered from shoulder to heel. The neck was short, less than a third the length of the body, but distinct. "Since these're made in a turn-mold instead of hand-blown, you can get 'em for a cheaper price."

Asa took the last bottle and examined it closely. A nearly invisible ridge ran from the spout to the base, the seam created by the mold. But how many men would care about the look of the bottle? What mattered most was what they found inside. He tapped the glass, smiling at the slight ping. "Can I get these in clear?"

Scotty shook his head. "Pale green, like I got there, or aqua."

Asa frowned. Was aqua red? If he had to get a color, he'd like red. It'd match the color of his wine. "Wish you'd brought one of the aqua. Woulda liked to seen the different color."

Scotty just shrugged. He didn't give a description of aqua, and Asa refused to ask.

Asa tapped his fingertip on the bordeaux bottle, his lips sucked in while he thought. He liked the shape, but he didn't want a green bottle. Too much like the cornstalks in his pa's fields. Finally he clasped the bottle by its neck and held it out. "I'll take six gross of these in aqua."

Scotty picked up the taller of the two long, slender bottles. "Sure you don't want these instead? Skinnier—can pack more of 'em in a crate."

An image of Melva and Shelva flashed through Asa's mind. He frowned. "I like this one."

"All right, then." Scotty returned all but the one Asa had chosen to the crate, wriggling them deep into the straw.

"What about corks?" Asa asked, running his finger around the narrow spout.

"Fitted corks come with 'em."

"Good." Asa carried the bottle to his cupboard and shoved it behind the stack of tin plates. "When will I get the shipment?"

"If they come on the train, I'd say four weeks. If you want 'em by wagon—less likely for some-one to peek in an' see what they are—then they'll hafta come in two or three separate shipments. First one'll be here in about six weeks."

Asa sighed. Six weeks . . . seemed like a long time. But by then he'd have at least a dozen barrels of fine wine ready to bottle. "Let's go with the wagon. An' tell them people to use lots of straw. I won't pay for no broken bottles."

Scotty scowled. "You gotta pay up front. Cash to supply, that's what I told you in the telegram."

Asa scowled back, straightening to his full height, which still fell a good six inches shorter than the other man. But what he lacked in stature, he made up for in snarl. "I'll pay half up front an' half on delivery. You do a good job, an' you'll have a steady payin' customer. I ain't one to fly by night."

Scotty chewed his lip, frowning.

Asa marched to the corner of the kitchen and opened a short, low cupboard. He withdrew his cash box and carried it to the table. Using the tiny key he always carried in his pocket, he unlocked the box and pulled out a stack of bills. He began peeling them off, one by one, while Scotty's eyes grew wider with each swish of paper.

"Workin' with me means makin' money. Take it or leave it." Asa ran his thumb over the edge of the bills, creating a steady *thrrrp, thrrrp*. He hid a smile as Scotty nearly drooled, gazing with longing at the stack of greenbacks.

Scotty stuck out his hand. "All right. Half now, half on delivery."

Asa smacked the money into Scotty's palm. "But don't deliver 'em here. I got a little place three miles south. Sits well off the road an' looks like a shack stuck in the side of a hill. There's a 'No Trespassing' sign nailed to a tree at the turnoff, so you can't miss it. I'll want the bottles delivered there. Send me a telegram with one word—'delivery'—in the message the day before they oughtta arrive, an' I'll be sure an' meet'cha there. I'll examine the bottles, an' if I'm satisfied with their appearance, you'll get the rest of your money an' we'll be square."

"If you ain't waitin' there, money in hand, the crates won't get left."

Asa narrowed his gaze. "I told you, I'll be there." He had too much riding on this delivery to risk losing those bottles.

"All right." Scotty picked up the crate and headed for the door. Asa followed, his gaze jumping around the yard, on the lookout for any watchful eyes. Scotty put the crate into the wagon bed and then turned to face Asa. "I hear tell you got a new lawman in town. How you gonna manage to keep him from knowin' what you're sellin'?"

"Sheriff McKane?" Asa snorted. "He ain't a real lawman—just a man our mayor decided to pin a badge on. An' I've figured out his routine. I know where he's gonna be an' when—the man's as predictable as a wound watch. All I gotta do is arrange my shipments while he's otherwise occupied." Asa puffed his chest, proud of how he had everything figured. "'Sides that, he knows I got a shippin' business. Why would he be suspicious of one of my wagons comin' or goin'?"

Scotty didn't look convinced. "Bet he ain't seen you transportin' crates with clankin' bottles before."

"Who says he'll see crates with clankin' bottles?" Asa didn't intend to share his whole plan with Scotty. The fewer people who knew, the better. He aimed a finger in the other man's direction, setting his face into a fierce scowl. "An' you take heed. That money box you saw inside? It won't be in that spot by the end of the day, so don't be thinkin' you can send somebody over to rob me. You keep our dealin's under your hat. You talk to anybody about what I been buyin'—*anybody*—an' I'll contact every lawman from one border of Kansas to the other to be on the lookout for you an' arrest you as a bootlegger. I got a good reputation as a businessman in this state. You? You're nobody—they'll believe me an' you'll rot in jail."

Scotty tightened his fists, but Asa stared him down. The man finally pulled himself onto the wagon seat. "Don't worry, Baxter. Your secret's safe with me. We both stand to profit, now, don't we?"

Asa watched the wagon roll away, a satisfied smile on his face. Yes, sir, they both stood to profit. In no time at all, he'd be the richest man in Clay County. Maybe even in all of Kansas. And then nobody'd look down his nose at Butterball Baxter ever again.

Sadie skipped down the stairs and rounded the corner to enter the mercantile. She plucked a crisp white apron from the pegs just inside the door and tied it over her blue-flowered dress as she hustled for the front door. The Baxter twins wanted the mercantile opened at precisely eight o'clock, not a minute before or after, and Sadie did her best to please her punctilious employers. She turned the lock and pulled the heavy wooden door inward, then placed a brick in front of it to hold it open. The morning breeze whisked through the screen door, and Sadie took a long, slow draft of the sweetly scented air. She loved mornings.

She started to turn back toward the counter, but a fluttering sheet of paper held down by a small hinged box on the porch floor outside the door caught her eye. Puzzled, she creaked the screen door open and stood, half in and half out, with the door propped against her hip. She flicked a glance up and down the street, but no one seemed to be paying her any mind. Bending over, she picked up both items. On the paper, a simple message, scrawled in a familiar hand, caused her pulse to trip.

Dearest Sadie, just a little something so you know I'm thinking of you. All my love, Sid.

Her hands trembling, Sadie folded back the box's lid to reveal a pale blue orb—half of a robin's egg, she realized—nestled on a puff of cotton. She grazed the fragile shell with her fingertip, smiling as a long-ago memory rose from the recesses of her mind.

"Lookit there, Sadie—a nest! Gonna climb up an' take a gander at the eggs. I bet there's three. How many do you think there'll be?"

Sadie grabbed the X of Sid's suspenders, holding him in place as he attempted to climb the tree. "Leave the nest alone! If the mama bird knows you've been there, she won't come back and sit on the eggs again."

Sid wriggled. "Lemme go, Sadie. Who cares if the dumb ol' bird doesn't come back? I wanna see how many eggs there are."

Sadie held tight. "Sid Wagner! Leave 'em be!"

He spun to face her, hands on hips and confusion marring his young face. "What you gettin' so mad about? They're just eggs."

Sadie took a deep breath, battling tears. "It's a robin's nest. It'll have eggs all pretty an' blue like the sky, an' when the babies are big enough, they'll wake me up in the mornin' by singin'. If you pester that nest, you'll take away the song."

Sid stood looking at her for a long time, and then finally he sighed. "All right. I won't pester the nest." A smile broke across his freckled face. "Wanna go catch crawdads?"

Sadie had chased after him that day, relieved because he'd left the nest undisturbed, but also pleased. He'd listened to her. Honored her request. Made her feel as though what she felt mattered to him—unlike neighborhood boys who used their slingshots to terrorize Sadie's feathered friends.

Tears stung as she realized just how important

Sid had always been to her. She loved him. But not the way he claimed to love her.

"Hey there, Sadie. Pretty morning, isn't it?"

Thad McKane's jovial greeting intruded upon Sadie's thoughts. His green eyes twinkled from beneath the brim of his always-present hat. By noon, his cheeks would wear a shadow, but at this early hour they were smooth from a recent shave and still ruddy from his wash at the pump. He stood before her, weight on one hip, with his thumb caught in his trouser pocket. The man always seemed at ease, and being in his presence sent a shaft of warmth through the center of her chest.

She blinked rapidly and offered the sheriff a smile. "It certainly is. Look at that clear sky." The same color as the little eggshell Sid had given her. Her fingers automatically contracted on the box, clutching it tight against her hip.

Thad's gaze dropped to her hand. "What'cha got? A present?"

Sadie nodded.

One dark brow lifted, a look of *uh-oh* blooming across his face. "Is today your birthday?"

Sadie laughed softly. "No."

He blew out a breath. "Whew. Thought maybe I'd missed something important."

Her pulse hiccupped. He thought her birthday was an important day? "My birthday's not 'til September." This would be her first birthday far from home and family. Except for Sid. She bit down on her lower lip and held the little box more tightly.

"So what'cha got there?" Thad asked, bobbing his head toward her clenched hand.

She lifted the box, pressing it to her apron bodice. "A . . . a memory."

"That so?" Thad's lips quirked, raising his mustache a notch. He chuckled, the sound indulgent rather than teasing. "Didn't know you could carry a memory around in a box."

Tears again pricked. Sadie ducked her head. "I suppose a person can carry a memory just about anywhere."

Thad took an awkward step backward. She looked up, surprised by the frown pinching his forehead. He stroked the left half of his mustache with two fingers and then moved another step away from her. "Reckon you're right. Well . . ." He tipped his hat. "You have a good day now, hear?" He strode toward the café, his bootheels thudding against the wide planks.

Sadie watched after him, cradling the box against her heart. His rapid escape stung. Sniffing hard, she stepped back inside the mercantile and allowed the screen door to slam behind her.

"Sadie?" Miss Melva screeched from across the room. "Somebody's been foolin' in these thread drawers an' got things all befuddled. Need the spools sorted an' put back to right."

"Yes, ma'am." Sadie pushed the note and box

into her apron pocket and hurried to the sewing goods area of the mercantile. But even as her hands performed the assigned task, the lump in her pocket turned her thoughts inward. The unexpected gift had touched her, but did that mean she could begin to look at Sid as a potential suitor?

16

Thad removed his hat and slid into the tall booth at the front corner of the café, next to the plate-glass window. Over his weeks in Goldtree, he'd claimed the booth as his own—it was the perfect spot to sit and watch folks head to their places of business. The location let him eat and still be on duty.

He had no more than placed his hat on the table when Cora bustled over, her round, friendly face flushed from the heat of her cookstove. She flashed a bright smile. "Your usual, Sheriff?"

Thad smiled in return. "That'll be fine, Cora."

"Comin' right up." She plopped a thick mug in front of him, splashed coffee into it from a blue-speckled pot, and then rushed off to prepare his two eggs over-easy, ham, and biscuits with butter and honey. The same breakfast he'd enjoyed every morning since arriving in Goldtree.

A few other customers dotted the dining room, visiting softly. They left him alone, though. Some days he wished someone would join him, but his badge set him apart. Folks were willing to give him smiles and hellos, but they seemed uncertain about striking up a real friendship. Except for Miss Sadie Wagner.

He closed his eyes, grimacing. Her comment about carrying memories burned like salt in a wound. Unconsciously, he touched the spot beneath his mustache where a split lip had left a permanent scar. He remembered the day like it was yesterday, although more than twenty years had passed. Yes, a person could carry a memory anywhere, including on his face. He'd grown the mustache so he wouldn't have to look at the thin white line that reminded him of his father's drunken rage. But how could he erase the memories from his heart?

All through his growing-up years, he'd borne the stigma of being "McKane's boy." If he was ornery in school, the teacher would shake her head and say, "I suppose I shouldn't expect more. You're McKane's boy." Folks in town watched him with suspicion, anticipating his doing something inappropriate because, after all, he was McKane's boy. The word McKane became representative of failure, deceit, and immorality.

How many times had Thad ducked his head and avoided eye contact with people so he wouldn't see the derision or distrust in their eyes? He hated carrying the stench of his father's reputation. It would only leave him when he'd finally found a way to make his name mean something more. Something good. Something *pure*.

"Here ya go, Sheriff."

Thad nearly sagged in relief when Cora's cheery voice sent the memories scuttling for cover.

She slid a plate onto the table, then pulled silverware from her apron pocket and clanked the fork and knife next to the plate. "Extra butter on them biscuits, the way you like 'em."

"Thank you, Cora. It looks good, like always." Thad waited until she refilled his coffee mug, then he bowed over the steaming plate to pray. But instead of expressing gratitude for the food, his prayer turned elsewhere. *God, give me the chance to preach—to change lives. Give me the chance to be the man my father never was. Let me find Your approval, an' give me blessed peace.*

Although his hunger had departed, he ate every bit of his breakfast. There'd been too many times in his younger years when he'd gone to bed with an aching, empty stomach. He wouldn't waste food now. When he finished, he thanked Cora again for a good meal, plopped his hat on his head, and stepped out onto the sunny boardwalk. He nearly ran smack into Roscoe Hanaman, who reared back in surprise, then broke into a smile.

"Morning, Sheriff McKane!" He tugged at his snug collar. "Gonna be a hot one today, I reckon. I decided I could do with a cup of cold buttermilk before going to the bank."

Thad had never understood the appeal of buttermilk. To his way of thinking, it tasted too much like milk on the verge of spoiling. But he nodded. "Hope it cools you down." He started to step past the mayor, but the man put out his hand and stopped Thad.

"Sheriff, what did you think of that performance the new little clerk gave in Asa's opera room last week?" The mayor's eyes fairly glittered.

Thad understood the mayor's excitement. Sadie truly had a gift. Why did she choose to use that gift in the cellar of the Goldtree mercantile, though? With a talent like hers, she could sing anywhere. "I thought Miss Sadie did real good. An' folks seemed to enjoy listening to her."

"Whole town's abuzz about that new opera house. I think it'll be the perfect means of drawing newcomers to Goldtree." Hanaman clapped Thad on the shoulder and winked. "Between her amazing voice and her pleasing appearance, there isn't much not to like about her performance."

Thad didn't think the mayor's comments were appropriate coming from a married man. But he wouldn't say so and offend the one who employed him. He replied carefully. "Miss Sadie is a very attractive young woman with a God-given talent. I'm glad folks recognize and appreciate her ability."

"I told Asa I'd get someone from the newspaper in Concordia to write up an article about Miss Sadie's singing. I'm guessing it'll bring in folks from the neighboring communities. More revenue for Goldtree." Hanaman folded his arms across his ample belly and squinted at Thad. "And even more reason to make sure the town's reputation isn't marred by bootleggers." He lowered his voice. "You have any leads yet?"

Thad had covered every square inch of the town, listening close to conversations, observing folks' actions. Although he'd encountered two strangers, drunk and carrying on their own yodeling contest one Saturday night outside of town, he'd yet to see any indication that someone in Goldtree was involved in illegal activities. *Help me root 'em out, God, so I can take off this badge an' pick up my Bible for You.* He shook his head. "Not yet."

Hanaman frowned, but then he gave his head a shake that cleared the expression. "Well, I'm going to take that as a good sign, then. Maybe it was just a rumor after all. That'd be a blessing, now, wouldn't it?"

Thad offered an idle nod, his thoughts elsewhere.

"Yes, sir, things are looking mighty rosy for our little town, between losing the worry of bootleggers and getting that opera house established." Hanaman nudged Thad with his elbow, chuckling. "Of course, bringing in outside folks means fewer seats for those of us who live here. We might want to talk Asa into selling a few of us box seats. Maybe the front row. Or"—the man's face lit, and he waved his fist in the air—"we could have him build in a row of special seats just for box-seat holders along the wall where you were standing Friday night. I assume you could hear Miss Sadie well from that location?"

Thad let his gaze rove up and down the street, his subtle way of telling the mayor he needed to get on his rounds. "Heard just fine from there." Her melodious voice had wrapped itself around his heart, making him hunger for more.

"Well, then, I'll speak to Asa. If we had our own seats on that far wall, it wouldn't take seats away from paying customers." Suddenly, Hanaman paused, his brow beetling. "It occurs to me I'm making an assumption here. You do want to go to all of Miss Sadie's performances, don't you? I noticed you were there both Friday and Saturday nights last week. . . ."

Thad popped off his hat, ran his fingers along the brim as if brushing away dust, then tapped it against his leg. "Can't say I wouldn't enjoy the opportunity. But wouldn't it be best if I stayed on duty if you're hoping a heap of newcomers come into town for the performances? Some of those people just might be ornery—want to stir up trouble."

Hanaman blasted a laugh. "Trouble? In an opera house?" He shook his head, still chuckling.

A movement behind the portly mayor caught Thad's attention. He angled his head slightly and spotted Sadie, broom in hand, stepping out onto the porch. He inched around Hanaman. "You go get that buttermilk, Roscoe, an' I'll get to work." He tapped the tin star pinned to his vest. "Got to earn my pay, you know."

Hanaman laughed heartily and gave Thad's shoulder another solid smack. "You do that, Sheriff. But when I talk to Asa, I'll be sure and have him set one of those seats aside for you. I have the feeling you aren't going to want to miss any of that pretty young lady's singing."

Thad slipped his hat into place as the mayor stepped into the café. He paused for a moment, watching the swish of Sadie's skirts as she put the broom to work on the boardwalk. A slight smile graced her face, and even from this distance he heard her soft hum—"Onward, Christian Soldiers" if he didn't miss his guess. As Roscoe Hanaman had indicated, she was pleasant to look upon. But there was more than looks to Sadie. She had a kind heart and a demeanor that put him at ease. He enjoyed her company. And he wished for more than sporadic stolen minutes of time with her.

Thumping his bootheels to alert her to his presence, he stepped onto the boardwalk. The broom bristles slowed, and she angled her chin over her shoulder. Apprehension showed in her blue eyes as he approached, and Thad kicked himself for giving her reason to be wary. But what should he expect after he ran away from her earlier? Somehow he needed to find a way to bury the ghosts of his past for good.

He stepped right up close to her and dove into his apology. "Sadie, I'm sorry."

She stood silently with her hands curled around the broom's handle, her big blue eyes pinned on his face.

"I shouldn't've took off so quick like I did this morning. You probably thought you did something wrong."

Very slowly, her chin bobbed in a nod.

"It wasn't you. It was the talk about carrying memories." Without conscious thought, his hand lifted to touch that spot where the scar hid beneath carefully combed whiskers. "I reckon just about everybody holds on to things he'd rather forget. An' you talking about memories, it . . . well . . . brought one to mind. I was trying to get away from the memory, not from you."

A sweet, sympathetic smile tipped the corners of her lips. "Then I'm sorry, too." She lowered the broom slightly. "Thank you for telling me, Thad. I didn't want to think I'd offended you."

"You, offend me?" He let a soft chuckle roll. "Not likely." Then he forced an apologetic grimace. "But I figure my taking off offended you. So would you let me make it up to you? I'd like to take you to supper tonight."

She looked surprised. And a little nervous. Maybe he was moving too fast.

"Or tomorrow," he said, "if that suits you better."

"N-no. Tonight . . . would be fine."

Even though enthusiasm didn't color her tone, Thad's heart set up a double beat at her acceptance. "Well, good." He jammed his thumb at the mercantile. "You're done here when?"

"I'm usually finished cleaning up by six-thirty. Then I'll need to change clothes and—"

"No need for changing." He whisked a glance across her full blue-flowered skirt protected by a white bibbed apron. "You look just fine. I'll fetch you at twenty 'til seven, an' I'll ask Cora to set aside a couple pieces of peach pie for our dessert."

Pink stained her cheeks, but she smiled. "That sounds wonderful."

Thad tipped his hat. "I'll see you tonight, then. Have a good day, Sadie." He strode off before temptation to plant a kiss on her sweetly upturned lips got the best of him. And he prayed he'd be able to focus on his job with the promise of time alone with Sadie waiting at the end of the day.

17

Sadie smoothed the stray wisps of her hair into place with a dampened comb and glanced at the little wind-up clock on her bedside stand. Her pulse immediately sped. In only a few more minutes, Thad would arrive. She zipped her gaze back to the mirror to check her reflection once more. Flushed cheeks and bright eyes stared back at her. She pressed her palms to her bodice, willing her silly heart to settle into a normal pattern. Never had she reacted so strongly to the anticipation of someone's presence.

Drawing in a calming breath, she ran her hands over her skirt—the same one she'd worn all day, because Thad had said she looked fine—in an attempt to minimize some of the wrinkles. She snorted in self-deprecation. She'd need an hour with an iron to make the dress look crisp once more. Hopefully, Thad would keep his eyes on her face and not notice her dress. The thought of him gazing into her eyes with the same attentiveness he'd exercised on the porch that morning brought a new bloom of pink to her cheeks.

"Settle down!" she scolded her reflection. "It's just a simple supper at Cora's with the sheriff. It isn't as if you haven't eaten with him before." But her traitorous heart continued its humming-bird's thrum of eagerness.

Bzzzzzzt! The familiar buzz sounded, and Sadie gasped. From elsewhere in the mercantile, one of the Baxter twins bellowed, "Miss Sadie! Get the door!"

Snatching up her skirts, Sadie pattered down the stairs. A shadowed, bareheaded form stood on the other side of the lace-draped window. A smile automatically grew on her face—he'd removed his hat. A sign of a gentleman, Mama would say. She twisted the doorknob and yanked the door open to find Sid on the stoop. Her smile faltered. "S-Sid . . ."

He offered a shy grin. "Hey, Sadie. You off duty now?"

She flicked a glance beyond him, searching for Thad, then returned her attention to Sid. "Yes. I—"

"Good." His grin turned sheepish. "Did . . . did'ja find a box an' . . . an' note this mornin'?"

Sadie's hands flew to her chest. She stared at Sid, aghast at having neglected to thank him the moment she opened the door. Mama would be appalled. "I did. Thank you, Sid." She reached out and grazed his sleeve with her fingertips. "It was so sweet of you." Recalling his claim of devotion on the note, heat rose in her face. She needed to remind him her feelings didn't run as

187

deeply as his. Scrambling for gentle yet truthful words, she licked her dry lips. "Sid, I—"

"Well, good evening, Sid." Thad's voice boomed from her right.

Sadie turned in his direction, then sucked in a sharp breath of delight when she noted he'd traded his plaid work shirt, brown suede vest, and badge for a white cambric shirt and black ribbon tie. He'd apparently shaved again, too, because his cheeks held no shadow of day-old growth. His handsome appearance made her knees go weak. This was no simple supper. In his mind, this was—

She didn't dare allow herself to complete the thought.

"McKane."

At Sid's resentful single-word greeting, Sadie faced her cousin once more. She tangled her hands in her skirt and stammered out, "S-Sid, the sh-sheriff is taking me to supper at Cora's. Can . . . can we talk . . . later?"

Sid's scowl, such a change from his earlier demeanor, made Sadie's chest ache. But then his expression cleared and he took a backward step, waving one hand toward the sheriff. "By all means. Don't let me hold'ja up." Something glittered in his eyes. But not fury. A steely determination. "Since Cora quits servin' at eight, I'll just come fetch you then." He whirled and clomped around the building before Sadie could form a protest.

Thad watched Sid go, then chuckled softly. "Seeing as how we've only got 'til eight, we better get moving, huh?"

His teasing response pleased Sadie more than a show of indignation would have. She stepped forward and took his elbow. "I suppose so."

He gestured for her to precede him through the gap between the buildings, but the moment they reached the boardwalk he offered his elbow again. Considering Cora's sat right next door to the mercantile, she hardly needed escorting, but she took his elbow nonetheless. Inside the café, Thad led her to an empty table on the far side of the dining area and pulled out the stamped-back chair. She offered a smile of thanks as she slid into the seat, then watched him round the table in two long strides before sitting directly across from her.

He'd seated her with her back to the café and its other patrons, providing her with an unobstructed view of himself. Had he done it deliberately so she would focus solely on him? Although it seemed vain to consider it, she hoped he'd placed her in the chair by design rather than chance.

Thad raised his hand and waved at someone, and Sadie glanced over her shoulder in time to see Cora give a nod before scurrying through the kitchen doorway. She looked at Thad again, puzzled. "Isn't she coming to take our order?"

A bashful smile curved Thad's lips. "Well . . . I already told her what we'd want."

She recalled his comment about asking Cora to save two pieces of peach pie. As much as she loved peach pie, she hoped their supper would consist of more than dessert. Lunch—a bowl of ham-and-cabbage soup and two biscuits—was long past, and her stomach rumbled in hunger. But she said, "That's fine."

To her great relief, Cora bustled toward them balancing two plates overflowing with succulent slices of beef, mounds of creamy potatoes swimming in gravy, and round green peas dotted with translucent onions. She placed the plates in front of them and whirled, calling over her shoulder, "I've got a fresh pot of coffee brewin'— I'll bring you cups as quick as I can."

Thad held out his hand, palm up. "Let's go ahead an' pray so we can eat while this food's still hot."

Bowing her head, Sadie took his hand. She thrilled at the feel of his firm, callused fingers closing around hers. Strength emanated from his grip, and then he began to pray, giving her a glimpse of the Source of his inner strength. He offered a simple, straightforward prayer of gratitude for the food and a blessing on the woman who'd prepared it. Then he added, "An' please bless our time together, Lord. May our conversation be pleasing to Your ears. Amen."

His hand slipped away, and he shot her a grin as he held his fork aloft. "Don't know how many times you've eaten here at Cora's, but I can tell you that meat'll be tender. You won't need your knife."

Sadie discovered the truth of his words as she pressed the tines of her fork through the beef and lifted a bite. The well-seasoned meat nearly melted on her tongue, and she released a sigh of satisfaction. The Baxters were good cooks, but nothing she'd eaten at their table compared to the meal set before her by Cora. "Oh . . . this is wonderful."

Thad nodded, forking up a bite of meat dipped in potatoes and gravy. "I have yet to come away from Cora's left wanting."

Diners behind Sadie engaged in conversation, their voices a hum that rose and fell in accompaniment to chair legs scraping on the floor and silverware clanking on plates, but she and Thad ate in silence. She didn't mind not speaking. Somehow just sitting across the table from him, observing his enjoyment of the meal, exchanging smiles and the occasional murmur of appreciation was enough.

Sadie ate every bit of food on her plate, finishing at the same time as Thad. Cora rushed over to whisk away their empty plates, and moments later returned with two huge slices of pie. Plump peaches oozed between layers of flaky crust well dusted with sugar crystals. Sadie groaned, holding her stomach. "Oh my, Cora . . . That is the most beautiful pie I've ever seen, but I don't think I have room for a single bite."

The woman laughed, her eyes crinkling. "You just sit for a bit, let your supper settle. I reckon you'll find room for that pie." She refilled their cups with fresh coffee and hurried off to take care of other customers.

Sadie turned to Thad. "Cora has more energy than two women half her age."

Thad dug into his pie. "Reckon she doesn't have a choice, seeing as how she runs this café on her own. She aims to please her customers with prompt, cheerful service."

She watched Cora buzz from table to table, refilling coffee mugs, swishing a cloth to remove crumbs, carrying empty plates to the kitchen. Her feet never slowed, and her smile never dimmed. "It must be hard for her sometimes, though, keeping up with everything all by herself." Sadie frowned, puzzled. "I wonder why she doesn't hire someone to help her."

Thad swallowed and swiped his mouth with his napkin. "I asked her that myself. Seems as though she could use a second pair of hands in here. But she said she doesn't make enough to pay someone a fair wage an' still earn a decent income. So she does it all on her own." He paused, a fond smile playing on his lips as he watched Cora for a few moments. Then he leaned toward Sadie, lowering his voice. "I'll let you in on a little secret, if you promise not to tell."

Although his tone was light rather than menacing, the comment reminded her of Mr. Baxter's warning to keep the door behind the curtains a secret. A little chill crept up her spine as she gave a jerky nod.

"I hired a couple of local young'uns to keep an eye on her woodpile in the back. When it starts looking low, they're to restock it an' bring me the bill."

Warmth flooded Sadie. "That's a very kind thing to do."

He shrugged, scooping up another bite of pie. "Least I can do for the woman who bakes the best peach pie this side of the Mississippi."

Sadie laughed. The desire to know everything about this kindhearted man washed over her. Resting her chin on her linked hands, she asked, "What's your favorite part of being a sheriff?"

He paused mid-bite. "Hmm. I don't guess I've thought too much about that." He lowered his fork, his expression pensive. "But if I had to say, it'd be helping folks. Whether it's figuring out what happened to the milk bucket that disappeared from their back porch or offering a hand in fixing a loose window. Just . . . helping out." He poked the bite of pie into his mouth.

Sadie smiled. She liked his answer. "I always

thought a lawman's only task was to arrest people who did wrong. But I suppose being a sheriff gives you lots of chances to help folks."

"Sure does." He forked up another bite, then added, "Leastways, for now."

She puzzled at the strange comment. "For now?"

He put his fork on the edge of the pie plate and fixed Sadie with a serious look. "I don't intend to be a sheriff forever, Sadie. I've got a . . . a job to do here, which I plan to do as best I can, but when it's done? I'm going to be a preacher."

"You are?" Sadie hunched her shoulders, envisioning him in a black suit with a Bible draped over his hand. As attractive a picture as her imagination painted, it couldn't compare to his rugged handsomeness in the leather vest, tan cowboy hat, and faded trousers.

"Yep." Sadness crept across Thad's features. "Back where I grew up—in Fairmount, a town not far from Kansas City—folks didn't look kindly on me. My pa . . . he didn't have a good reputation." He stroked the corner of his mustache with one finger, pain flashing in his green-flecked eyes. "I figure if I'm a preacher, then the people in Fairmount'll change how they think about the name McKane. It'll mean something honorable instead of shameful. I'll be able to make amends for my pa's sins, so to speak."

Sadie listened carefully, intrigued by his story. The description of his father hurt her heart.

Thad's pa and her own dear papa were nothing alike. But something he'd said bothered her. Tipping her head, she tried to erase Thad's haunted expression with a soft smile. "I think it's a fine thing to want to preach, but can you make amends for someone else's sins? Isn't each person accountable for himself?"

Thad looked at her, his brow furrowed slightly. Then he released a light chuckle. "I think that's a question I'll be better suited to answer when I'm behind a pulpit. Right now"—he picked up his fork again—"I'm just a small-town lawman enjoying supper with the prettiest girl in town."

Heat flooded Sadie's face.

Thad laughed and pointed at her fork. "Eat up. Don't want to waste that pie, now."

With a giggle, Sadie picked up her fork and dug in. The mingled flavors of peaches, cinnamon, and nutmeg exploded on her tongue. Even though her stomach already ached from the hearty supper, she consumed every bite of the pie and even tamped up the leftover pastry crumbs with the back of the fork's tines. Licking the fork clean, she glanced at Thad and caught his amused grin.

Mortified, she lowered the fork and ducked her head. Hadn't Mama taught her better manners? What must Thad think, witnessing her childish display? He reached across the table and cupped her hand. Her face flaming, she peeked at him through her lashes.

"Don't hide from me, Sadie Wagner." His deep voice, kind yet resolute, sent her heart to thudding against her rib cage. His hand tightened on hers. "Look at me."

Slowly, she raised her head, but her cheeks blazed so hot it took all of her effort to meet his gaze rather than looking past his shoulder to the flowered wallpaper behind him.

His eyes smiled even while he maintained a serious expression. "You never have to be ashamed around me. You enjoyed the pie—what's wrong with that?" He gave her hand a little tug, his brows briefly coming together. "Too many people hunker behind a shield of indifference instead of letting folks know what they really think. I call that putting on airs, and it isn't honest." His face relaxed, his smile enfolding her in a blanketing contentment unlike anything she'd experienced before in a man's company. "So you just be yourself. Always be honest with me, Sadie, no matter what. All right?"

She nodded, but her conscience pricked. Could she really find the courage to be honest with him about everything . . . including her growing affection for him? How would he react if she blurted out he might be a lawman rather than a burglar, but he was stealing her heart? She gulped. "Thad, I—"

"Well, Sheriff an' Miss Sadie . . ." Cora stopped at their table, hands on hips and face wreathed in cheerfulness, even though her shoulders sagged with weariness. "I hate to chase you off, but I'm needin' to clean up in here."

Sadie glanced around, surprised by the empty tables. Why hadn't she realized how quiet it had become in the café? She bounced up, her chair legs screeching against the floor. "I'm so sorry."

Cora chuckled. "No need for bein' sorry." Her words closely echoed Thad's earlier statement. "Kinda nice to see folks enjoyin' themselves. Like I said, I hate to make you leave, but . . ." She swished a dripping cloth at her side, obviously eager to clean their table. "I already put your dinner on your account, Sheriff."

"Not this time, Cora," Thad said. "This one's on me." He dug in his pocket and withdrew several silver coins. He placed two large and three smaller ones in Cora's palm. "Thanks for making that pie up special." Then he tipped forward and deposited a kiss on the woman's round cheek.

Cora blushed crimson and waved her hand at the pair of them. "Out with you now, but you come back anytime. I'll keep a peach pie coolin' on the windowsill for you."

Thad touched Sadie's spine, aiming her for the door. They stepped out on the boardwalk, and Sadie immediately headed for the gap between the café and the mercantile. But Thad caught her elbow, drawing her to a halt. He smiled down at her, his face sweetly attentive in the pinkish glow of dusk. "You were starting to say something before Cora shooed us out."

Sadie swallowed, her mouth suddenly dry. "Y-yes. I was going to—I meant to say—" She licked her lips and started again. "You said be honest, so—"

Like an apparition stepping from shadows, Sid appeared at Sadie's side. "You all done with supper? Can we talk now?"

Sadie nearly wilted. She wanted to resent Sid's intrusion, but a part of her welcomed the rescue. Mama would surely swoon if she knew how close Sadie had come to proclaiming she was falling in love with Goldtree's lawman.

18

Sid, watching out of the corner of his eye as the sheriff leaned in to bid Sadie farewell, ground his teeth. Did the man need to touch her arm to say good night? He bit down on the end of his tongue to keep from protesting when Sadie smiled sweetly into McKane's face and whispered, "Thank you for supper. I had a pleasant time."

The sheriff responded, "The pleasure was all mine, Sadie."

And Sadie nearly simpered in reply.

The moment Thad McKane strode up the boardwalk toward his office, Sid pointed to the bench that sat in front of one of the mercantile's windows. "Let's get comfortable; then we can talk."

But Sadie didn't budge. "Sid, I'm sorry, but our talk is going to have to wait. I haven't practiced yet today. Mr. Baxter gave me three new songs to learn by Friday. I really must work on them."

Irritation tried to rise from Sid's middle. She'd had plenty of time for the sheriff, but now she had none for him? He resolutely pushed the aggravation aside. He would *not* speak harshly to Sadie. "Would'ja mind if I came down an' listened in?" He gave her his best smile. "Then we could talk . . . after."

She nibbled her lower lip, clearly uncertain. Finally, she nodded. "All right."

"Good!" He tried not to sound too eager, but when the word blasted out, he knew he'd failed. Placing his palm on the small of her back, he hurried her through the gap and to the back door of the mercantile. A wall lantern glowed inside the door, illuminating their way down the hallway. They entered the main part of the store where the light didn't reach. Shadows loomed, making the room appear menacing.

Their feet echoed on the floorboards as they inched forward, feeling their way, and Sadie shivered. "It's always so creepy in here at night."

Sid squinted through the shadows and located a darker gray square ahead—the doorway to the storeroom. "Stay here. I'll fetch the lantern an' come back for you." He let his hand slide from her waist. "No need to be scared—I'm here."

Scuffing his way to the storeroom, he wondered if she remembered how many times he'd played protector for her in childhood. He'd fought school-yard bullies who dared pull her pigtails, and he'd escorted her home on moonlit nights when she'd stayed too late studying with the piano teacher in Dalton. If she'd let him, he'd spend the rest of his life protecting her.

He fumbled on the shelf for the lantern and matches. A flick of a match on the underside of the shelf brought a welcoming glow. He quickly lit the lamp and hurried back to the doorway. "All right, Sadie—here you go."

She joined him, and together they moved down the back stairway to the cellar and on into the singing room. Sadie headed immediately to the piano on the stage, and Sid followed with the lamp held high. He set the lamp in one of the brass holders attached to the piano's smooth face. Then, stepping behind the piano, he rested both arms on its top and watched Sadie pull out the stool and lay out several loose sheets of music. The pages, all marked with lines and dots, meant nothing to him. But somehow Sadie found a melody hiding in the strange scratchings.

He remained very quiet while she practiced, hiding a smile when she huffed at misplayed notes or closed her eyes to repeat a certain phrase until it pleased her. He watched her face change as she sang, mesmerized by the transformation. Some-how singing made Sadie glow from within, magnifying her natural beauty. *I love you, Sadie. I want you to be mine.* The words quivered on the tip of his tongue, and it took every ounce of self-control he possessed to hold them inside.

Time slipped by, and Sid's feet began to complain about standing still, but he didn't budge. He wouldn't disturb her. At last she closed the cover over the keys, restacked the pages, and lifted her face to him. "I'm done. For now." She yawned, holding her dainty hand over her mouth, and then she stretched both arms over her head. "Oh my, I'm tired."

Was she hinting she wanted to turn in? But they hadn't talked yet. In the lantern's glow, her yellow hair shone like morning sunlight. He wished he had the courage to coil one of the loose strands dangling from her temple around his finger. "You coulda been done a lot sooner if you hadn't gone to the café with McKane." He hadn't intended to sound accusatory, but it came out that way anyway.

She shot him a frown. "Sid . . ."

He held up both hands in surrender. Then he rounded the piano and braced one hand on his knee, leaning close to her. "But I'm hopin', in the future, you'll be goin' out to supper with me instead o' him."

Her gaze zinged away, and she pulled her lower lip between her teeth.

Gathering all his courage, Sid caught her chin in his hand and lifted her face to him. He wished his fingers would stop trembling, but the glory of her soft skin nearly undid him. "Did'ja like the little present I left for you today?" With her face caught in his fingers, she couldn't nod. But he saw a soft look creep into her eyes. She liked it. He smiled. "Y'know, Sadie, I loved you even back then. You've always been important to me."

She swallowed, the sound loud in the silent room. She leaned back slightly, removing herself from his quivering grasp. "I . . . I know, Sid. And you've been important to me, too. Always my favorite—"

He covered her lips with his fingers. "Don't say 'cousin.' 'Cause we aren't."

She shook her head, giving him a pleading look. "But, Sid, I've always thought of you as my cousin. How can I just set that aside after all these years?"

"By rememberin' we aren't really related."

Hurt flickered in her eyes. "But then I have to remember Papa isn't really my father. And I want to think of him as mine."

Sid sighed. Why'd she have to be so stubborn?

He reached for her again, but she leaned away. Sid bolted upright, jealousy straightening his spine. "I didn't notice you actin' all shy when McKane cozied up to you."

Red flags of temper flashed on her face, and Sid knew he'd made a mistake. But he couldn't take the words back. And he didn't want to. He intended to court Sadie. She might as well know how he felt about her spending time with Thad McKane.

"I consider the sheriff a friend, Sid, and—"

Sid snorted. "Sheriff . . . Don't let that tin badge fool you. He's no lawman."

Sadie blinked at Sid, her lips parting slightly in surprise. "W-what do you mean?"

Sid balled one fist on his hip. "Asa Baxter told me—Mayor Hanaman brought McKane to town to play lawman, make the town look like a safe place so new families'd move in. But he isn't a *real* sheriff." Leaning in again, Sid dropped his voice to a near whisper. "You think you know him, Sadie. But you don't. He's a stranger. But me? We go way back."

Sadie sat in silence, staring into his face. She didn't smile, but she didn't try to retreat, either.

He went on softly, sweetly, adopting the tender tone he'd use to placate a frightened horse. "You *know* me, Sadie. Haven't I always been there for you? An' now you're here, in the same town as me, finally singin' your songs on a stage for folks' pleasure." Lifting his hand, he eased his fingertips along the line of her jaw. Soft . . . so soft. His heart lurched. "I arranged all that 'cause I love you, Sadie."

Without warning, she shot to her feet, nearly tipping the piano seat. Her expression turned frantic. "Sid, I—" But instead of finishing the sentence, she turned and ran up the middle aisle.

Sid snatched up the lantern and stumbled after her. "Sadie, wait!" But she clattered through the open doors at the hallway, her footsteps pounding on the stairs. He trotted after her, pausing to latch the doors before making his way upstairs. By the time he reached the main room of the mercantile, she was long gone—probably closed in her room. He wouldn't pursue her there.

He returned to the storage room, blew out the lantern, and slid it onto the waiting shelf. Then, standing in the dark room, he made a silent vow. He wouldn't say the words "I love you" to Sadie again. They obviously scared her. But he'd *show* her how he felt.

Squaring his shoulders with determination, Sid made his way out of the quiet store. He'd win her over. It was just a matter of time.

There were times over the following weeks Sadie thought she might pull out her hair in confusion. Each day, she discovered a little something on the front porch, just outside the door. Even though no notes accompanied the items, she knew Sid left them. The gifts, although never elaborate, were sweet and thoughtful. Clusters of wild flowers, a bag of black gumdrops —her favorite—hair ribbons, a book of poetry . . . But instead of making her feel cherished, they left her feeling smothered. And manipulated. She hated herself for being unappreciative, yet she couldn't shake the honest reaction to his persistent bid for her affection.

She also grappled with Sid's statement about Thad not being a legitimate lawman. Thad had asked her to be honest with him at all times, yet if Sid had spoken the truth, Thad hadn't been completely honest with her. She wanted to ask him to verify or deny Sid's claim. She had ample opportunities to broach the subject—Thad stopped by the mercantile daily to purchase supplies or a bag of candy sticks to share with Goldtree's youngsters or to simply chat with either Sadie or the proprietresses. Yet she held the question inside. A part of her feared his response.

So she poured her confusion into a letter to her parents and sent it off, praying for a speedy reply. She trusted Mama and Papa to wisely counsel her. Until she heard back from them, she vowed to hold both Sid and Thad at bay. But she found it more difficult than she cared to admit. She missed the carefree relationship she'd once shared with Sid and wished to resume it, and she longed to explore the flickers of love stirring to life within her heart for Thad.

Several times either Miss Melva or Miss Shelva snapped their bony fingers in her face to draw her from inner reflection to reality. Most times the ladies laughed and teased Sadie about drifting away into dreamland, but other times she witnessed impatience in her employers' eyes. She needed to find a means of dealing with her jumbled emotions before she jeopardized her job.

The only time she managed to forget Sid's unwelcome pursuit or Thad's possible duplicity was when she was singing. The stage became her refuge, and she found herself wishing away the hours to Friday and Saturday nights, when she could pour all of her passion into song and allow the exuberant applause of the audience to carry her away from her troubles.

The second Friday in July, as Sadie prepared to refill one of the glass-front storage drawers with dried navy beans, Miss Melva swooped in and snatched the wooden scoop from her hand. "Just saw the mail stage pull out. Sister'n me's expectin' a package from Boston. A newfangled medicine for"—she dropped her normally strident tone to a hissing whisper—"female troubles." Her voice rose again. "Go on over an' see what come in today." She gave Sadie a little push toward the door.

Sadie brushed away the fine dust raised by the

beans from her apron skirt as she headed out the door. A hot gust of wind greeted her, hurrying her across the street. The screen door slapped into its frame behind her as she entered the post office and stepped to the counter. Mr. Rahn turned, the mail pouch dangling from his wrist and a cluster of letters fanned like a hand of cards between his fingers. He sent a weary smile in Sadie's direction.

"Don't tell me—you're here to fetch the medicinal concoction the Baxter sisters ordered."

Sadie raised her eyebrows in surprise. "How did you know?"

The man snorted. "Because they've pret' near pestered me to death, wantin' to know when those bottles of Dr. Kilmer's miracle cure'd get here. I finally told 'em not to come ask again— I'd deliver 'em myself when they arrived."

Sadie giggled. How sneaky of Miss Melva to send Sadie in their stead rather than facing Mr. Rahn's ire. "Well, I'll leave you alone, then." She turned to leave.

"Wait up there, Miss Sadie." The man flopped the pouch onto the sorting table and crossed to the counter. He held out two envelopes. "These come for you—both from Dalton, Indiana."

Sadie couldn't stifle her exclamation of joy. She reached eagerly for the letters and examined them. One from Mama and one from Papa. She crinkled her brow. Why had they written separately? Then she noticed the date inked over the postage stamp—Papa's had been sent three days prior to Mama's. Yet they'd arrived at the same time. Apparently a holdup along the line delayed the arrival of Papa's letter. She smiled. How exciting to receive both letters in one day. And how exciting to find a letter solely from Papa. He usually just jotted a few lines at the end of Mama's lengthy discourses. An entire letter from him was an unexpected treat.

Mr. Rahn grinned. "Busy day for folks in Dalton sendin' letters. Got one over there for Sid, too." He stretched his hand toward the letters scattered on the table. "You wanna take it to him? Seein' as how you're family an' all, I don't reckon the United States Postmaster General would have cause to complain."

She wasn't ready to seek out Sid. She took two backward steps toward the door. "No, thank you, Mr. Rahn."

The man looked at her as if she'd suddenly broken out in green warts. "Well, then . . ." He scratched his chin. "Sid don't come in every day, the way you folks at the mercantile do. When you see him next, would you tell him he's got a letter over here waitin'?"

Sadie assumed Sid would come to the opera house that evening—he hadn't missed a performance yet and he always arrived early. They wouldn't be able to engage in a lengthy conversation if she was preparing to sing, but she could mention the letter. "Yes, sir. I'll tell him." She scurried out the door and stepped into the street, eager to return to the mercantile where she could find a quiet corner and read her letters.

"Runaway wagon!"

The cry took Sadie by surprise. She came to a startled halt and looked up to see a fully loaded wagon, pulled by two enormous, galloping horses, bearing down on her. With a shriek of terror, she reached to lift her skirts and run. The letters fell from her hand, and the wind immediately whisked them down the street.

Sadie cried out in alarm and spun toward the escaping squares of white. But before she could take a step, someone's arms coiled around her waist and flung her to the ground. The wagon rattled past, inches from Sadie. Two men on horseback and three on foot chased after the escaping wagon. Dust billowed in her face, and she squeezed her eyes closed against the onslaught. Coughing, she tried to scramble to her feet and retrieve her letters. But strong arms held her fast. Then an angry, masculine voice thundered in her ears.

"What in tarnation did you think you were doing? You could've been killed!"

She angled her head to peer over her shoulder. Thad lay beside her, his arm draped across her waist. Fury blazed in his eyes.

19

Thad rose and reached for Sadie. His hands shook worse than tree leaves in the stout Kansas wind. Fool woman! She'd scared him out of ten years of life at least. He caught her wrists and pulled her upright. She found her footing quickly, but he didn't let go.

"Didn't your mama teach you to look into a street before trying to cross it? You came within a hairsbreadth of being run down!" An ugly picture formed in his head, and he gritted his teeth, willing it to depart. His hands involuntarily tightened. "You gotta be careful, Sadie!"

She wrenched free of his grasp, then rubbed her wrists, glaring up at him. "I didn't step in front of the wagon deliberately. I was—"

"Being a plumb fool!"

A small crowd gathered on the boardwalk, their excited mutterings competing with the pounding rush of blood in his ears. He waved his hand at the throng. "Go on about your business, folks." He waited long enough to make sure they'd follow his direction. Then he whirled on Sadie, who'd lifted her skirts as if ready to take off. "Not you! You stay put."

She clutched her skirts in her fists, her poised body emanating impatience.

He aimed his finger at her face. "I ought to haul you in for being a public menace."

Her jaw dropped, and her eyes widened.

He ignored her aghast expression and grabbed her arm. "Since it isn't safe to leave you unattended, I'll take you across the street." She wriggled, but he held tight while looking up and down Main Street. "Then we'll establish a new rule for you—no crossing without a chaperone." The street was clear, so he took one forward stride.

She dug in her heels and fought against his restraining hand. "Thad! Let me go right now!"

"No, ma'am." He pulled, drawing her along beside him. "As sheriff, my job's to protect folks. An' you obviously need protecting."

Her tumble in the dirt had jarred loose the coil of hair she always wore on the back of her head. Tangled strands of yellow hair waved over her shoulders and in her face. She slapped at the tresses, demanding her release in the most abrasive tone he'd ever heard, but he continued to pull her across the street. They neared the mercantile boardwalk, and Miss Melva and Miss Shelva came flying out of the building, hands outstretched. They met Thad and Sadie at the edge of the road.

Thad was forced to relinquish his hold when the twins wrapped their long arms around Sadie, sandwiching her between them. Their crooning and exclamations of concern rose above the wailing wind. Thad plunked his hands on his hips and waited for their hubbub to calm so he could talk to Sadie once more. The girl had been moony and distracted for weeks, and he would get to the bottom of her preoccupation before she ended up hurting herself.

From the circle of the Baxter sisters' arms, Sadie cried, "Please, Miss Melva and Miss Shelva! You must let me go!" She broke free and stumbled south, her gaze bouncing everywhere.

Thad thudded along behind her, flicking a glance over his shoulder at Miss Melva and Miss Shelva, who stood in the road with arms akimbo, glaring after them. He offered the pair a sympathetic grimace before double-stepping to reach Sadie's side.

"What do you think you're doing now?"

Sadie pounded onward, arms pumping with determination. She sent him a brief, furious look. "I'm retrieving my letters! They fell out of my hand when the wagon frightened me, and then you tackled me. I couldn't get them before the wind carried them away."

Letters. So that's what she'd been thinking about instead of looking where she was going. Thad tried, but he couldn't conjure up much sympathy for her. Not after she'd nearly killed herself. But he scanned the roadway, too, staying close at her side. "The way the wind's blowing today, they're probably in Ottawa County by now."

She spun to face him, balling her hands into fists. Tears glittered in her eyes. "Then why wouldn't you let me go after them once the wagon had passed? If you'd only allowed me to go after them, I might not have lost them for good!"

He gawked at her. Was she blaming *him* for the loss of the letters? "Now listen here—"

"No, *you* listen, Sheriff—if you really *are* a sheriff." Her blue eyes blazed, her sweet face set in a scowl of pure venom. "I've been waiting for word from my parents—waiting and hoping—and finally letters arrive. But before I even have a chance to open them and find out what Mama and Papa think is best for me to do about my feelings for you, you come along and—"

Thad had heard enough. She obviously had no inkling how frightened he'd been. He might have lost her. And he hadn't yet told her how much he cared for her. Well, he wouldn't wait another second. But she wasn't in a state to listen to words. He'd have to show her.

With a growl, Thad gathered Sadie in his arms. She let out a little squawk of surprise, but he cut it short with a firm, heartfelt, possessive kiss.

Sadie pulled back and stared into Thad's face. She nearly went cross-eyed, he was so close, but she glimpsed her own startled reflection in his pupils. He'd kissed her. Her knees quivered, her spine turned to jelly, and she stood completely power-less within the circle of his arms.

"Sadie," Thad said, his gaze boring into her. He kept his voice low, almost a growl. "Don't ever scare me like that again. If anything had happened to you, I—" With a groan, he pulled her close again.

Her cheek pressed to his chest, the points of the tin badge pricking her flesh. His heartbeat pounded fast and sure beneath her ear. She remained snug in his embrace for long seconds, absorbing the wonder of the moment. Her lips still tingled pleasantly from the pressure of his. She tasted the essence of coffee and salty ham. And she'd eaten oatmeal for breakfast.

Won't Mama be shocked when I write and tell her Thad—

Her letters! Sadie pushed hard against Thad's chest, freeing herself. "Please, please, Thad. Help me find my letters. They were from Mama and Papa, and I have to know what they said." Her vision blurred with the spurt of tears.

Thad caught both her hands, but the grip was tender rather than punishing. He rubbed his thumbs over her knuckles, and even though she wanted to go seek her letters, she didn't try to remove herself from the simple caress. "Sadie, I'm sorry, but those letters're surely gone. The wind . . ."

He lifted his face to the gusting wind, and Sadie did the same. The hot blast dried the tears as soon as they snaked down her cheeks. Her hair waved across her face in tangled ribbons, and her dust-streaked apron billowed. Thad was right. She'd never find those letters. She hung her head, biting on her lower lip to hold back sobs of disappointment.

He curled his arm around her shoulders. "Let's get you back to the mercantile. Maybe Miss Melva an' Miss Shelva'll let you go lie down for a while. Give you time to recover from your scare."

Sadie didn't need to recover from her scare. Thad's kiss had completely chased away the panic of that moment. But she needed to explore all of the emotions his kiss had stirred. And she needed Mama and Papa's advice more than ever.

Thad delivered her to Miss Melva and Miss Shelva, who clucked over her and patted her and made her feel positively cosseted. If she'd questioned their affection for her previously, all uncertainties were laid to rest as Miss Shelva escorted Sadie up to her room, knelt on the floor to remove her shoes, and then tucked her into bed as tenderly as a mother caring for her newborn. The woman tiptoed to the door and whispered, "You sleep now, Sadie. Me an' Sister'll be just fine the rest o' the day." She closed the door behind her with a soft click.

Sadie rolled onto her side and stared at the framed portrait of her family. Stretching out one hand, she grazed first Mama's and then Papa's face with one fingertip. She sighed. "What did you advise me? How I wish you were here right now to help me sort through my feelings. . . ." She closed her eyes against the image of their dear faces, and within minutes she slipped into sleep.

A discordant, prolonged creak awakened her. She fluttered her eyes open, squinting into her room. A pale path of waning sunlight angled from the window to the foot of the bed, exposing a flurry of shimmering dust motes. What time was it? Sadie rubbed her eyes and squinted at the little clock beside her bed. Then she gasped and leaped out of bed.

The moment her feet hit the floor, both of the Baxter twins burst into Sadie's room. Miss Melva clasped her hands beneath her pointy chin. "Did we scare ya?"

Miss Shelva hovered behind Miss Melva, her pale eyes wide with concern. "We tried to be quiet, but them hinges made a racket."

Miss Melva swung on her sister. "Wasn't Asa s'posed to oil them things?"

Miss Shelva scowled. "Sure was. Gonna hafta get on him."

While they fussed about the creaky hinges, Sadie flew to her wardrobe and pulled her cinnamon-colored singing dress from its hook. She scrambled out of her work clothes, unmindful of the watching eyes in the room. She'd be late for the stage if she waited for the sisters to clear out.

"Miss Sadie, what're you doin'?" Miss Melva scuttled to Sadie's side.

"I've got to get dressed." Sadie sent a panicked look toward the little clock. "Folks'll be here soon."

Miss Melva's jaw dropped. Miss Shelva stepped up beside her sister, her face a perfect replica of dismay. "You're singin'?" they chorused.

Sadie swallowed an hysterical giggle. "Of course I'm singing. Those horses"—and Thad's unexpected kiss—"didn't knock my voice loose." She finished buttoning her dress and then dashed to the bureau for her hairbrush. She winced as the bristles snagged on tangles. "Will you go down and let Mr. Baxter know I'm on my way?"

The pair exchanged an uncertain look. "But you ain't even et supper yet," Miss Melva protested.

Sadie jerked the hairbrush through a particularly snarled area of hair. Her scalp stung, and she feared she'd strip herself bald if she didn't take more heed, but there wasn't time for caution. By now, people were surely settling into seats in the opera room. "I'm not hungry. Truly. Now please, go let your brother know I'm coming."

The sisters snorted their disapproval, but they

departed, stomping in unison on the hardwood floor. Left in peace, Sadie finished brushing her hair, then sat on the edge of the bed to don her shoes. Her clumsy fingers resisted pulling the laces tight. Tying a neat bow—something she'd been doing since she was six years old—proved challenging. But finally both shoes were tied and she was ready to go.

She careened out of the room and ran smack into a large, solid form. The wind left her lungs, and she grabbed the wall to keep from falling. For a moment, her vision went fuzzy, and she blinked several times to clear it. She focused on Mr. Baxter, who stood glaring at her.

"You're late," he barked.

"I . . . I know." Sadie forced herself to stand upright. Her right cheekbone throbbed. She'd apparently banged it against his forehead, because a round red spot showed above his left eyebrow. "I fell asleep, and—"

"So my sisters told me. But just like I told them, it's no excuse." He grabbed her arm and gave her a little push, sending her skittering toward the stairway. Dizziness struck—would she tumble down the stairs? He grabbed her arm again, holding her upright. "Since I had to put Melva an' Shelva in charge of takin' the last tickets, I lost count of how many people came through the door. But it promises to be a full house tonight. If I have to refund tickets, it'll come out of your pay. So get on down there an' sing like your life depends on it, girlie." He released her, giving her arm a rough shake. "If you don't measure up, there'll be others willin' to fill your spot."

"Yes, sir!" Sadie scurried for the stairway. She passed Miss Melva and Miss Shelva as she rounded the corner for the cellar staircase, but she ignored their hangdog looks. She didn't dare pause to reassure them—not with Mr. Baxter clomping behind her, red-faced and angry. Although her heart pounded faster than the hooves of the horses pulling that runaway wagon, she managed to square her shoulders and enter the opera house with her head held high. At her entrance, a smattering of applause spread across the room. The warm welcome calmed the fringes of Sadie's tattered nerves, and she stepped onto the stage between the polished pillars and cast a smile across the sea of expectant faces.

Although she usually began with a hymn, she whispered to the pianist to play a simple ballad as her opening piece. The slow pace and story-telling quality of the song gave her an opportunity to overcome her breathless state. Her boss stood at the back of the seating area, arms folded over his brocade vest and a stern frown on his face. Sadie aimed her focus to the wall beyond him and allowed the music, once again, to carry her away.

As she sang, she gained strength, moving from piece to piece with an ease as natural as breathing. She took her gaze away from the wall and allowed it to drift across the faces of her listeners. Rapt expressions fueled her desire to do her very best, and her voice rose in response to the audiences' obvious pleasure. She shifted her body slightly, turning her face toward the south wall, where Mr. Baxter had built a narrow platform and secured a single row of seats—what he'd termed "box seats." Her gaze encountered Thad's. Her heart skipped a beat, and her voice tripped in response. She looked quickly past him and encountered Sid on Thad's right. His ardent expression made her mouth go dry.

Jerking forward once more, she pinned her gaze to the back wall and managed to complete the recital without mishap by staring at a small crack zigzagging like a bolt of lightning from the ceiling to the top of the doorframe. At the close of her final number, the audience rose as one and offered a standing ovation. Sadie dropped into a prolonged curtsy, her head low, her heart thrilling at their exuberant praise.

As had become her custom, she exited down the center aisle while the attendees remained in their rows, nodding and smiling in thanks. When she reached the end of the aisle, she headed for the doorway. Before she could pass through the opening, though, a hand snaked out and grabbed her elbow. Sadie froze.

Mr. Baxter leaned close, his breath warm on her

cheek. "Go on up to your room 'til everybody clears out, but then come back down. I wanna talk to you."

Sadie offered a quick nod, and he released her arm. She scurried up the stairs, her heart pounding in trepidation. *Oh, Lord, please don't let him discharge me!*

20

Asa paced along the edge of the stage. He'd extinguished most of the lights but left one wall of sconces—those above the row of box seats—burning. The domed sconces couldn't penetrate the darkness of the entire room, leaving the stage area cloaked in gray. The shadows gave the room an element of secrecy that appealed to him.

The *pat-pat* of footsteps alerted him to Miss Wagner's approach. He turned toward the double doorway as she stepped through. The apprehension on her face boosted Asa's feeling of power. He plunked his fists on his hips and pasted a stern scowl on his face as she made her way up the aisle to meet him.

"M-Mr. Baxter?" She bit down on her lower lip and clasped her hands at her waist.

He allowed a few seconds to tick by, giving

her an opportunity to squirm, before he released a little grunt that made her jump. "You sang good tonight. Folks were pleased."

She looked so confused he almost laughed. He'd complimented her—done it deliberately—but in such a disapproving tone, he'd befuddled her good. Swallowing his humor, he went on.

"Now that I know what kind of audience I can get in here for your *hymns* an' such"—he didn't bother to hide his derision for her choice of songs—"it's time to expand an' try some new things, too."

Miss Wagner's brow pinched. "N-new things?"

Asa stalked to the corner of the stage and snatched up the stack of music he'd been collecting. He marched back to where she waited, looking as timid as a church mouse, and thrust it at her. "Startin' at the end of July, gonna open up the opera room on Tuesday nights. For special performances."

She flicked through the music, her gaze scanning the titles. "These are . . . these are very different from my usual numbers."

He snorted. "S'posed to be. That other stuff you do—it suits a mixed audience. But these Tuesday shows? They'll be for men only."

Her fingers tightened, creasing the music sheets. "B-but—"

Asa plowed over the top of her protest. "Eight to eleven. Since it's a longer show, you'll earn more. Five dollars a night."

Her eyes flew wide. "Five dollars!"

His sisters paid the girl five dollars for a full six-day week in the mercantile. He'd known the sum would astound her. Asa grinned. "That's right. Since this show'll go later, I'll talk to Melva an' Shelva about lettin' you off on Wednesday mornin' from now on. Maybe even see about them givin' you either Friday or Saturday afternoon free, too, to give you more time to relax before performances. They might cut your pay some, but you'll be makin' it up with your singin', so it shouldn't hurt ya none. You'll still have plenty to send home to your ma an' pa."

He spoke briskly, confidently. Little mouse like her wouldn't dare to argue with the tomcat. "I already put out the word about these special nights of entertainment for menfolk, due to start the twenty-third of July. That gives you a little over a week to learn these songs. Girl smart as you oughtn't have any trouble pickin' 'em up."

Miss Wagner was examining the sheet music again, her brows low. Her lips quirked off to the side, as if she chewed the inside of her mouth. It tickled Asa to see her so deep in thought. While she was busy thinking, he bustled to the far corner of the room and pulled back the curtain. The ruby-colored dress he'd special-ordered from Chicago hung on a hook. He'd ordered a hat, too—a befeathered black velvet with seed pearls, bold red glass stones, and a rolled brim that'd sit low over Miss Wagner's eyes. He'd seen a saloon girl wear a similar hat, and the picture had never left his mind. He couldn't wait to see Miss Wagner's pale blond hair set against the rich black velvet.

He pulled the dress from its peg, scuttled back to the stage area, and held the frock out to her. "Got a dress for you to wear for them Tuesday shows, too—somethin' that'll please the men for sure."

She lifted her gaze from the music and looked at the dress. Her eyes widened into saucers of surprise, and her face drained of color. "Th-that's a . . . a bawdy dress, Mr. Baxter! I could never wear anything so scandalous!"

Asa scowled fiercely. He wadded the dress in his fists. "Not askin' you to wear it to work or to Sunday service. Just for these performances." He jammed it toward her, and she recoiled. He grunted in frustration. "I paid a goodly amount to have this dress made for you, Miss Wagner, an' you're gonna wear it."

She stumbled backward, shaking her head. "I'm sorry, Mr. Baxter. But I . . . I can't wear that dress. And I can't sing these songs." She extended her arm, offering him the rumpled sheets of music. "I'm more than happy to continue performing Friday and Saturday nights, but you'll need to find another singer for your Tuesday evening programs."

Asa crunched his brow so tight his head hurt.

"If I find someone else for Tuesdays, I'll ask that same person to sing on Fridays an' Saturdays, too. That'll put you off the stage, Miss Wagner. That what you want?"

He watched a war play across her pale face. She'd come around. She had to—she needed the money. Besides that, he'd seen her sing. She came to life on that stage. Singing for an audience delighted her as much as making money pleased him. Maybe even more. And making money thrilled him deeper than anything else in the world.

She cleared her throat. "Mr. Baxter, I thank you for giving me the chance to sing for the folks of Goldtree." Tears glittered in her eyes. "But what you're asking me to do now . . . I'm sorry. Find another singer." She bounced the music at him. When he wouldn't take it, she dropped the handful and ran from the room.

Asa stared after her, too stunned to give chase. He stood for several minutes holding the red dress. Then he cursed and threw the dress on top of the scattered sheets of music at his feet. Find another singer? How would he find another singer willing to come to this podunk town? And even if he found one, how would she learn the music in time for the opening of his most promising money-making venture yet?

Raising his curled fists, he growled at the ceiling. His carefully laid plans were coming undone at the seams. She'd crossed him. And *nobody* crossed Asa Baxter. Scooping up the dress and the music, he made a silent vow. He'd change Sadie Wagner's mind. His hands paused, a sly grin finding its way to his face. And he knew who to use to do it.

Sadie weighed the paper cone of sugar, rolled the top closed, and handed it across the counter to Mrs. Hanaman. "That's five cents."

The woman dug in her little beaded reticule and withdrew a round silver coin. "Here you are, Miss Wagner." As she took the paper cone from Sadie, she added, "Roscoe and I so enjoyed your performance last night. I'm delighted he purchased season tickets—the first offered by Mr. Baxter—so we won't miss a single performance. Will tonight's repertoire be the same as last evening's?"

Sadie was too heartsick to try to make changes for what would be her final time to sing on the Goldtree Opera House stage. She nodded.

Mrs. Hanaman beamed. "Oh, such a delight. There are several numbers I wish to hear again."

Sadie's lips quivered with her attempt to offer a genuine smile. She swallowed the tears gathering in her throat. "Thank you, Mrs. Hanaman. I . . . I do enjoy singing."

Mrs. Hanaman cupped Sadie's hand. "And you have a gift for it. I've attended vocal recitals in several eastern cities. Your performance equals and even exceeds many of those. Any number of people possess the ability to sing the notes, but you, my dear, sing the *music*." Her words of praise increased the fierce ache in the center of Sadie's breast. "Such an asset to Goldtree you are, Miss Wagner."

Sadie ducked her head, embarrassed yet pleased by the woman's commendation. "Thank you, ma'am."

"You're very welcome." She tucked the small bag of sugar into the bend of her elbow, bestowing another smile. "I shall see you this evening." She strode out, the ostrich plume of her hat gently bobbing in time with the swirl of her emerald skirts.

Miss Melva peered over the top of a shelf, watching Mrs. Hanaman's exit. After the screen door closed behind the woman, Miss Melva scurried to the counter. "Somethin' about that lady puts my teeth on edge."

Miss Shelva poked her head from the storage room and blared, "Now, Sister, don't be bitin' the hand that feeds you. The Hanamans do a heap o' purchasin' in here. We need their business."

Miss Melva scowled at her sister. "I ain't sayin' it *to* her, just *about* her. An' Sadie here ain't likely to repeat it." Turning back to Sadie, she lowered her voice somewhat. "She's lived most o' her adult life right here in Goldtree, but when she was still a girl, her ma sent her back east for a

year or two with an aunt who planted all sorts o'
highfalutin' ways in her. She's just so hoity-toity a
body can't hardly have a conversation with her."
She sniffed, lifting her pointy chin. "Don't see
how she's better'n anybody else. Just 'cause her
husband owns the bank, an' she wears them
fancy dresses an' pea-sized diamond stones in her
ears." Miss Melva pinched her own naked ear-
lobe and then slicked her hands down the front
of the bleached muslin apron covering her simple
calico dress.

Sadie searched for words to reassure Miss
Melva of her worth—obviously she found herself
lacking. Stretching her hand across the counter,
she captured her employer's bony wrist and gave
it a gentle squeeze. "I think it's better to have a
heart of gold than an overflowing money box.
You and Miss Shelva possess two of the purest
hearts I've ever known."

Miss Melva charged around the counter as Miss
Shelva charged out of the storeroom. They
encircled Sadie in a combined hug that nearly
stole her breath.

Miss Melva bawled, "That's the nicest thing
anybody ever said to us."

"You plumb turned our heart inside out,
Sadie," Miss Shelva added.

Sadie noted Miss Shelva's use of "heart" rather
than "hearts." Sometimes she believed the
women viewed themselves as two halves of one

person. She wriggled her arms free and wrapped one around Miss Shelva and the other around Miss Melva. Tears stung the back of her nose. If Asa made things difficult for her now that she'd turned down his demand for her to sing bawdy songs and dress like a saloon girl, she might have to leave Goldtree. It would be very difficult to say good-bye to the spinster sisters, who railed at each other yet embraced Sadie as if she were their child.

The little bell above the screen door jangled, alerting them to the arrival of another customer. Sniffling, the twins released Sadie and dabbed their eyes with their aprons, their movements perfectly in tune with one another. Miss Shelva bustled back toward the storeroom, calling, "I gotta finish unloading them crates o' shoes."

Miss Melva headed for the stairs. "I'm gonna put our lunch on. Sadie, you mind the store!"

Sadie quickly swished her apron across her eyes, then turned to greet the customer. She jolted in surprise when she found Thad standing on the opposite side of the counter. Her pulse skipped, and her breath followed its lead, refusing to flow smoothly but instead releasing in stuttering gasps. Remembering their last encounter—his anger followed by a possessive kiss—she found herself torn between throwing herself into his embrace or running upstairs, where she could hide from the tumultuous emotions he created within her heart.

She pressed her sweat-damp palms to the scarred top of the counter and pasted on the semblance of a smile. "G-good day, Thad. What can I do for you?"

He rested one elbow on the counter and leaned in, his green eyes shimmering. "You can forgive me."

She blinked twice, too surprised to speak.

"I wanted to ask you last night after you were done singing, but Asa said you were turning in early, so I didn't stay around." He sighed, his breath stirring the little wisps of hair that always escaped her bun. "I was pretty hard on you yesterday."

Your lips weren't hard at all. She stared at his lips, the upper one shielded by the coal-black mustache. His whiskers were so soft, she hadn't even noticed their intrusion when he'd kissed her.

"It's just that I was so scared," Thad continued. "You could've been run down. Hurt. Even killed." His face contorted. "The scare turned to anger real quick, but I shouldn't have been so rough with you. I'm truly sorry, Sadie. Will you forgive me?"

Sadie ducked her head. She'd spoken harshly to him, too—accused him of losing her letters and of masquerading as a sheriff. She'd never know what Mama would have advised concerning Thad, but somehow in that moment Mama's opinion didn't seem to matter. She only cared about her own feelings. Peeking at Thad through her eyelashes, she whispered, "I forgive you. And will you forgive me for attacking you with accusations? I . . . I was wrong, too."

A tender smile lifted the corners of his mustache and brought out tiny starbursts at the corners of his eyes. He plucked off his hat and set it aside before placing his hand over hers.

"All is forgiven." He squeezed her hand. "We're friends again?"

Sadie raised her face to meet his gaze. She laughed softly. "We never stopped being friends." How strange to fully trust this man with whom she'd only so recently become acquainted, yet the weeks of wonder and worry melted away beneath the warmth of his smile. Regret smote her. She'd wasted precious time—days she could never recapture—wondering if he'd misled her.

"There's something else I want to ask you, too." His hand still holding tight to hers, he glanced around the empty mercantile. Then he leaned across the counter, his face so close to hers his breath kissed her cheeks. "This isn't hardly the time or place, but I don't want to waste another minute. Sadie, would you do me the honor of allowing me to court you?"

Sadie gasped. Her free hand flew up to clamp over her open mouth. She stared at him.

"I know we haven't known each other for very long, but I know enough to see you're perfect for me. You love God, you want a big family some-day, you're hardworking. And I can see us serving a congregation together—me preaching, you singing . . ." He smiled, his fingers tighten-ing on hers. "We were made for each other, don't you see?"

Yes, Sadie did see. With a shaky laugh, she forced her hand away from her face and placed it over the top of Thad's, sandwiching his hand between hers.

"So may I court you, Sadie?" He seemed to hold his breath, waiting for her answer.

Her chest heaved in several little bursts of air and then she exclaimed, "Yes!"

Thad pulled loose to plant his palms on the counter and then leap over the wooden barricade separating them. He wrapped her in a hug that lifted her feet from the floor. Sadie squealed, flinging her arms around his neck and holding tight. He laughed, the sound joyous, and Sadie responded with an echoing trickle of laughter.

"What'n tarnation are you two doin'?"

Sadie peeked over Thad's shoulder at Miss Shelva, who glowered at them from the storeroom doorway.

The older woman pointed her bony finger at Thad. "Thad McKane, I don't care if you are the town's sheriff, you got no business comin' in here an' accostin' our clerk!" She marched forward, her heels echoing noisily against the floorboards, and caught Sadie's arm. With a mighty tug, she freed Sadie from Thad's grip and shook her finger again. "Now you'd just better explain yourself, young man."

Thad's lips twitched with his grin. "Can't a man give his intended a hug?"

Miss Shelva jolted. "Intended?" She captured Sadie's shoulders and stared into her face. "That so, Sadie? He's your beau?"

Beau—such a wonderful word! Sadie giggled. "Yes, ma'am."

Miss Shelva scowled. "Since when?"

Sadie sighed. "Since *now*."

Miss Shelva pursed her lips so tightly they disappeared. She looked from Sadie to Thad to Sadie again. Then she spun on Thad. "All right, then. But you can't be comin' in here, snatchin' Sadie off the floor anytime you please. There's rules for courtin', you know, an' just 'cause Sadie don't got folks here in town to keep an eye on her don't mean nobody'll be watchin'. Me an' Sister'll be keepin' watch on you, an' you just best behave yourself, Thad McKane!" Tears winked in the older woman's eyes. Her chin quivered. "We happen to be more'n just a mite fond o' Miss Sadie."

Thad reached out and embraced Miss Shelva. "I'm a mite fond of her myself, an' I promise not to do anything untoward. You've got my word on it."

Miss Shelva patted Thad's back, sniffed, and jerked loose. She gave him a fierce scowl. "See that you keep it." Then she spun and charged for the stairway, bellowing, "Sister! Our Sadie's gone an' got herself a beau!" She disappeared around the corner.

Thad chuckled, shaking his head indulgently. "Those twins . . . they're something."

Sadie caught his hand. "You're something for being so kind to them."

His tender gaze bore into hers, and his thumb slipped up and down, caressing her wrist. Tremors of pleasure climbed her spine. What had she done to deserve the affection of a man like Thad McKane? She released a self-conscious giggle. "Now that no one's looking, could you hug me again?"

With a wink, he teased, "Sounds as if Miss Melva an' Miss Shelva are planning to keep watch over the wrong half of this courtship."

Fire seared her cheeks.

He threw back his head and laughed. "I think I've got something you'd like even better than a hug."

Sadie's heart set up a double beat. Would he kiss her again? But he pulled his hand from hers and slipped it beneath his vest. He held out a rumpled, dust-smeared envelope. Papa's wobbly hand-writing covered its front. Sadie squealed and yanked it from his hand. "My letter!"

"Only one. Couldn't find the other." Thad's voice held regret. "But this one was caught in some brambles on the edge of town."

Sadie stared at him in amazement. "You went looking for them?" She'd thought finding them an impossible feat. He'd even said so—that they were probably in the next county. Yet he'd hunted them anyway.

He grinned boyishly. "Had to at least try. I know how precious words from home are." Pain laced his brow, but he swiped his hand over his face and cleared the glimpse of anguish. He grabbed his hat, holding it against his thigh, and took a giant step toward the door. "I'll take my leave so you can get back to work." Glancing around at the still-empty store—an uncommon happening for a Saturday noon—he added, "Or maybe sneak away somewheres an' read your letter."

She hugged the filthy envelope to her heart, envisioning the dear man who'd penned the words inside. "I am eager to read it."

"Then you do that." He slipped his hat over his hair, settling the brim low. Although the brim cast his eyes in shadow, Sadie glimpsed the sparkle of his smile. "I'll see you this evening, Sadie, in the singing room." He turned on his heel and opened the door. The bell jangled a merry farewell.

Sadie sank onto the little stepstool behind the counter and started to peel back the flap. But before she managed to remove the pages of the letter, a sudden thought stilled her hands. She'd told Mr. Baxter she wouldn't wear the red dress or sing the songs he'd chosen. If she didn't sing, she wouldn't be earning the extra money Mama and Papa needed. If she weren't able to earn enough to support her family, it didn't make sense to remain in Goldtree.

At the time she'd told Mr. Baxter to find someone else, she'd believed she was doing the right thing. But now she considered the loss of so many precious things—time with Miss Melva and Miss Shelva, earning enough money to meet the needs of her family, and the pleasure of a courtship with Thad.

Closing her eyes tight, she pondered whether doing something questionable might be right if it carved the pathway to so many good things.

21

Sid paused at the corner of the mercantile, moving out of the path of others filing through the alleyway. He'd thought Asa Baxter a little foolish, putting the entryway to the singing room at the rear of the big building, but it sure didn't seem to hinder folks. They came in a steady stream. Good thing he'd reserved one of the special box seats.

Cost him more to sit in one of the seats on the raised platform, but it meant he didn't need to rush right down—he had a spot waiting.

He felt his tie to be sure the knot was still tight, then brushed his hands over the lapels of his best jacket. He didn't want a speck of dust to spoil his appearance. He'd continued to leave little surprises for Sadie on the mercantile's porch but otherwise kept his distance, not pushing Sadie too much. But tonight he intended to stick around after the show, steal a few moments with her, maybe even steal a kiss so she'd know for sure how much he cared for her. His mouth went dry at the thought of pressing his lips to hers. He'd waited so long to claim Sadie as his own.

"Hey there, Sid."

Sid looked up at the cheerful greeting and found the town's postman and his wife smiling at him.

"You heading to the program?" Mrs. Rahn asked.

"That's right." Sid tugged the bottom of his jacket, putting the buttons into alignment. "I haven't missed one of Sadie's shows yet."

"She's got a beautiful voice," Mrs. Rahn said.

Mr. Rahn held up three fingers. "This is our third time to hear her. The wife an' me have enjoyed it every time."

Pride squared Sid's shoulders. "We always said Sadie'd be makin' audiences happy."

The couple chuckled, and Mrs. Rahn said, "I reckon you were right." She gave her husband's arm a little tug, turning toward the porch.

But Mr. Rahn stayed planted. "Don't know if Miss Sadie's mentioned it, but you've got a letter waitin' at the post office—somethin' from Indiana."

"I haven't seen Sadie lately. Work's kept me pretty busy," Sid replied. That work would allow him to save enough money to buy Sadie a fine home. It'd all be worth it in the end.

Mr. Rahn said, "Might wanna stop by on Monday an' pick it up."

Sid's folks had only written to him once before, begging him to return. He wasn't eager to read another guilt-invoking plea, but he nodded. "I'll come by Monday for sure."

"Good. Good." Mr. Rahn gave in to his wife's prompting, and Sid followed the couple. He stepped onto the porch and nodded at Asa, who stood beside the door collecting tickets.

Asa stopped Sid with a hand on his arm. "Hold up. I need to talk to you."

Sid swallowed a protest. He wasn't on duty right now, but he shouldn't argue with his boss. He stepped off the porch and waited in the sparse grass nearby, fidgeting, until the last person had entered the back door.

Finally Asa turned to face him. "We got a problem."

Sid frowned. "What's that?"

"Your cousin." Asa folded his arms over his

chest and peered down at Sid from his perch on the porch floor. "She's refusin' to add another night of singin' to her duties."

Protectiveness welled. Sid jammed his hands into his jacket pockets to keep Asa from seeing how they balled into fists. "She's already singin' two nights. That's a lot of performin'. Takes its toll on her."

Asa tipped toward Sid, his eyes narrowing into slits. "Ain't askin' her to sing every night of the week. Just one more night. But she refuses." A smug look crossed the man's jowled face. "I told her if she didn't want to follow my schedule, I'd just find somebody else. So that's what I'm fixin' to do."

Sid's thoughts raced. If Sadie couldn't sing, her income would drop considerably. If she couldn't make enough money in Kansas to provide for her family's needs back home, she might pack up and return to Indiana.

Asa went on. "Seems to me you got me into this mess—convincin' me to give her a try. An' now she's runnin' out on me. I ain't too happy about it, Sid, I don't mind tellin' ya."

Sid swallowed.

"Now, it ain't that I dislike you. You've been a real good worker for me. Truth is, I was hopin' to advance you in my freightin' company—more responsibility, better wage. But now . . ."

Sid curled his hands over the railing. "What

can I do to make it up to you?" If he lost his job with Asa, he'd end up back in Indiana, too. Back in the mines, just like his pa and uncle, breathing in black dust, worrying about cave-ins, never getting ahead. Advancing in Asa's company was better than anything waiting at home, even if it meant Sadie was there, too. Somehow he'd fix this so both he and Sadie could stay here in Kansas instead of throwing away their dreams.

Asa leaned forward, nearly nose to nose with Sid. "Convince her to sing all three nights. It's that simple. She keeps her job, you keep your job. I'm happy, you're happy. Seems like it'd be best for everybody, now, doesn't it?"

Sid looked into Asa's smirking face. The man had him trapped, and he knew it. Sid sighed, lowering his head. "All right. I'll talk to her."

Asa clapped him on the shoulder. "Good boy. I knew I could count on you. Oh—one more thing . . ." He glanced around the yard, then put his face close to Sid's ear. "This extra night of singin'? It's by invitation only—real special. So don't be talkin' it up around town. Some folks might be offended, knowin' they ain't been asked to come."

Sid frowned. Something sounded fishy about the setup. Before he could question it, Asa pulled open the door. A sweet melody drifted from the cellar.

"Show's started. Better head down." Asa

chuckled, the sound more menacing than merry. "Sure would be a shame to silence a voice like Miss Sadie's. Yes sir, sure would be a shame . . ."

Sid shot past Asa. Sadie would keep singing. Whatever it took, she'd keep singing. He'd see to it.

Thad stepped out of the sheriff's office in time to tip his hat to Miss Melva and Miss Shelva, who bustled by in their Sunday best on their way to the Episcopal church. The pair nodded in unison, their feet stepping in perfect tempo on the boardwalk. "Have a blessed Lord's day, Sheriff," they chorused in voices that reminded Thad of honking geese.

"Thank you, ladies. You too."

Over his weeks in Goldtree, Thad had determined every resident's place of worship. He wished he could settle in with one congregation, but he didn't want to play favorites—didn't figure it would look right. So he continued rotating from church to church. Today he'd attend the Congregationalist church.

He turned in the opposite direction the Baxter twins had gone and caught sight of Sadie at the other end of the block, preparing to cross the street. Although he knew it wasn't polite to shout at a lady, he cupped his hands beside his mouth and hollered, "Sadie, wait!"

Thad broke into a trot, his boots thundering on

the planked boards. She waited, the toe of one boot peeping from beneath the full skirt of the brownish-red dress she wore to church each Sunday and for her performances. The dark color provided a perfect backdrop for her shimmering locks of gold. She looked so lovely there in the sunlight, a Bible cradled in her arms and a little hat perched slightly askew on her carefully combed hair, that he couldn't stop a smile from growing.

"I'll walk with you. It's my Sunday for Reverend Wise's teaching."

Wordlessly, she slipped her gloved hand into the curve of his elbow. Together they crossed the street. He puzzled at her odd silence. She'd been standoffish and skittish in the weeks prior to him tackling her in the street, but he thought their talk yesterday afternoon had chased away her reserve. He stifled a chuckle, remembering how she'd asked for another hug after agreeing to allow his courtship.

Then his humor faded as he recalled how she'd skirted past him after her performance last night, murmuring the excuse that she was tired and wanted to turn in. He'd been understanding, but later when he'd made his nightly rounds, he'd spotted her sitting on the back porch stairs with her cousin, Sid. He'd kept his distance, not wanting to intrude on a private conversation, but now he wondered what they'd discussed.

His warmly affectionate Sadie had faded into a cool, distant woman again.

They entered the clapboard building without her uttering a single word. The two long benches behind the minister's lectern which served as a choir loft were already filled. He gave a nod toward the front. "You better skedaddle. Choir's in place."

"I'm not singing today." She spoke so softly, he almost missed her words.

"You feeling sickly?" If she were ill, it would explain her strange behavior.

She shook her head.

"Well, then, why not go sing?"

Turning her face away, she set her lips in a firm line and didn't answer.

What had gotten into her? He wouldn't have guessed she'd be prone to fits of moodiness. Swallowing his irritation, he pointed to an empty bench midway between the front and the back. "Let's sit there."

She pulled her hand free of his elbow and gave him a sad look while shaking her head. "I'll sit with Cora."

Thad glanced around the half-filled sanctuary and spotted Cora on a crowded bench near the front. There wasn't room for both of them up there. "You don't want to sit with me?"

Again, that sad shake of her head. She made her way up the center aisle and slid in next to the café owner, who welcomed her with a soft smile Sadie didn't return. Thad crunched his brow. At least her uncharacteristic detachment extended beyond him to others. It was small consolation, but consolation all the same.

He plopped down on the end of the bench he'd chosen and tried to pay attention as the choir rose and opened the service with a hymn. But he sent furtive glances in Sadie's direction throughout the service. As much as he wanted to listen to the minister's lesson, her odd demeanor troubled him even more than the rumor that had reached his ears about a shipment of bottles and corks delivered to an abandoned dugout east of town. One of the local farmers had glimpsed the crates being unloaded and stored in the dugout. But when Thad went out to investigate, the place was empty. He'd seen lots of wheel tracks, and the dust had been stirred up inside the little shelter, giving evidence of recent activity, but nothing remained that would provide a hint as to who'd been there and why.

He'd hoped the tale about the bottles would finally lead him down the trail to the unknown liquor maker. But without so much as a cork to prove the bottles existed, he was as clueless now as he'd been when he first moved to town. Hanaman was getting impatient with him, pressing him to make an arrest. But who should he arrest?

To his surprise, he glanced up to see that everyone else was standing. He leaped up, mortified by the titters of a trio of children seated behind him. Some minister he'd be if he couldn't even pay attention to someone else's sermon. He joined the congregation in singing the closing hymn; then he watched for Sadie to pass by so he could walk out with her and get to the bottom of her aloof behavior. But Doyle Kirkhart, the town barber, stopped to talk with him, and by the time they'd finished their conversation Sadie had disappeared.

With a groan of frustration, Thad charged across the grassy yard to the corner. He scanned the street, but he didn't see her anywhere. He rubbed his chin, trying to decide what to do. He had the fixings for a simple lunch, so he could walk to the mercantile, ring the buzzer, and ask her to join him for another picnic. Maybe he could pry loose what was troubling her. But what if she wouldn't tell him?

He slapped his hat on his head. Females! One minute smiling and forgiving, the next taciturn. He set his feet in motion, stirring dust with every pounding footstep. He wouldn't spoil his Sunday playing twenty questions with Sadie. As he closed himself in his little living area at the back of his office and reached for his supply of bread and cheese, his righteous indignation fizzled and died.

Who was he fooling? Sadie's sorrow was his

sorrow. He felt it in the depth of his soul. She wanted some privacy or she wouldn't have sneaked off without speaking to him. So he'd give her privacy. For now. But come tomorrow, he'd stop by the mercantile and ask if she'd changed her mind about allowing him to court her. And he prayed she wouldn't say yes.

22

Sadie hid a yawn with one hand while unlocking the mercantile door with the other. She'd gotten very little sleep last night, and even less the night before. Bits and pieces of her conversation with Sid from Saturday evening—"He'll fire us both if you don't sing at those special invite-only shows, Sadie"—collided with advice from Papa's letter—"I know it's hard for you to be far away, Sadie-girl, but the Lord is always with you. Follow His ways, and you'll land on your feet every time." Sadie felt certain doing what Mr. Baxter asked wouldn't be pleasing to God. But not doing it would create so much conflict. For her, for Sid, for her family. So what was best?

She crunched her eyes tight and whispered the same prayer she'd offered a dozen times in the past two days. "Lord, show me what to do." But when she opened her eyes, only the familiar street scene of Goldtree greeted her. How she wished God would pen His reply across the awakening sky so she'd have clear direction.

As if sent on a lightning bolt, another bit of wisdom from Papa's letter winged through Sadie's memory: *"Keep reading your Bible every day and talking to God."* Guilt pricked. In the past weeks, she'd failed dismally in following her parents' example. At home, Papa read nightly to the family. But here in Goldtree, between working at the mercantile and preparing for her perfor-mances, it seemed she never had a minute to spare. Exhaustion at the end of the day encouraged her to drop into bed at night for sleep rather than taking the time for Bible reading or prayer. How disappointed Mama and Papa would be if they knew.

Shame lowered her head, and out of the corners of her eyes she caught sight of a little wax-paper-wrapped bundle waiting on the porch. She sighed. She'd told Sid on Saturday night to stop leaving her the gifts, but apparently he'd chosen to disregard her request. She appreciated his kind consideration, even while she rued his bold persistence. Yet no matter how many thoughtful deeds Sid performed, she still viewed him as her childhood playmate and cousin. Never a beau. If only her heart would rise and take wing within her chest when Sid approached—the way it responded to Thad's presence—how much simpler things would be.

Sadie lifted the package and peeled back the paper, revealing a sweet roll from Cora's. Still warm. He must have been there only moments ago. The scent of cinnamon wafted upward, tickling her nose. Sadie had always loved the scent and flavor of cinnamon—it reminded her of Mama's apple pastries—but today her stomach roiled. Sighing, she scuffed her way to the storeroom and tossed the sweet roll in the rubbish bin. She stood, staring down at the treat, tears threatening. Until she was able to put her worries to rest, she wouldn't be able to eat or sleep. Or allow herself a moment of time with Thad.

One tear rolled down her cheek, and she whisked it away with the back of her hand. It had nearly broken her heart to hold herself aloof from him yesterday after he'd been so kind, retrieving her letter and asking to court her. But if she were going to leave Goldtree, she must protect her heart. And his.

"Sadie?" one of the twins bawled from the main room. "Where are you?"

Sadie bustled out of the storeroom. "I'm right here. What do you need?"

Miss Shelva rattled off a list of duties she expected Sadie to accomplish during the morning. Sadie sprang into action, and the hours slipped quickly by. At noon, Miss Shelva hung the little hand-scrawled "LUNCH—BACK AT 12:30" sign on the door and ushered Sadie upstairs, where Miss Melva had their simple meal waiting on the kitchen table.

Although the soup and rolls looked inviting, Sadie couldn't carry a single bite to her mouth. Each time she tried, her throat constricted and she knew she wouldn't be able to swallow. She lowered her spoon to the table and sat back in her chair. "May I be excused?"

"But you ain't even ate a bite yet!" Miss Shelva scolded.

"You didn't eat breakfast, neither," Miss Melva said, waving her spoon at Sadie. "Gonna waste away to nothin' if you don't eat."

Miss Shelva put in, "How you expect to keep up your strength with no food in your belly?"

Miss Melva chuckled and poked her sister on the arm. "Maybe we oughtta fetch the sheriff—reckon he could convince 'er to eat."

Sadie's face flamed. Miss Shelva opened her mouth to add her comments, but before she could speak, Sadie pushed away from the table. "Excuse me," she said, and fled. She zipped past her bedroom door. If she went in, one or both of the sisters would surely follow. So she clattered downstairs instead. Both twins called after her in strident tones to come back, but she ignored their insistent appeals. It was her lunch break—she'd use it as she pleased. And right now she needed time alone more than she needed food. She had to *think*.

When she reached the bottom of the staircase, she pushed open the back door and ran across the small yard. A huge cottonwood grew at the far edge of the property, casting dappled shade across the sparse, wilted grass. She sank down beneath the tree, using a few gnarly roots as a lumpy seat, and leaned against the rough bark. Closing her eyes, she began an earnest, lengthy prayer for guidance. For wisdom. For peace.

"Give me an answer now, Lord," she begged, "so I know what I'm to do."

"Sadie."

She gasped. Her hands flew upward to prevent her wildly thudding heart from leaving her chest. *God?* Then she spotted Sid a few feet away, his face somber. "Oh my . . . I thought—" Had she really thought the Lord would speak aloud to her? She shook her head in self-deprecation. "You frightened me. What are you doing here?" Couldn't people leave her alone for even a few minutes?

"The Misses Baxter told me you'd taken off. Glad you didn't go far. I . . . I gotta tell you something." Sid bent on his haunches before her. He pressed a crumpled sheet of stationery against his knee, smoothing the page. "Sadie, I got a letter from home. An' . . . it's bad news."

His sober expression, coupled with the catch in his voice, sent a chill through Sadie's limbs.

She braced her palms against the cool ground. "W-what?"

With his eyes on the paper, Sid drew in a deep breath and released it slowly. "Pa wrote to let me know about Uncle Len." His eyes flicked to meet hers, then dropped again.

Papa? Sadie's pulse beat so hard in her temples she could hear the blood rushing through her veins. Fear took a stranglehold, holding her voice captive.

"The infection in his leg . . ." Sid gulped, his head low. "He died, Sadie. Over a week ago."

Sadie shook her head wildly, tendrils of hair slapping against her cheeks. "No!" She dug her fingers into the moist dirt beneath the tree. "No, he can't be dead. He just sent me a letter. And Mama would have told me if he was gone." But even in her panicked state she recalled the date the letter from Papa had been mailed. Three days earlier than the one from Mama, which had blown away. Surely the lost letter contained the heart-breaking report.

With a start, Sadie realized Papa must have penned the letter only a day or two before succumbing. During his final hours, she was on his mind. How much he loved her, even though she wasn't truly his.

Papa . . . oh, Papa, no . . . Her mind screamed the words, but somehow her tongue refused to work. Sid's image swam as tears flooded her eyes. She pressed a fist to her mouth to hold back wails of agony. She tasted earth on her fingers—a familiar flavor from years of gardening with Mama, of digging fishing worms with Papa, of making muddly-mud pies for Effie. *Oh, I want to go home!*

She jolted to her feet and stumbled toward the mercantile.

Sid pounded after her. "Sadie, wait."

He caught her arm and spun her around. The sun hit her full in the face. She squinted at him, wriggling to free herself. "Let go. I have to pack. I have to arrange for a stage. I have to—"

"Go home?" He barked the question. "Going home won't bring him back." Sid's harsh voice stung like a lash. "Going home won't change nothin'."

"B-but, Sid, I . . ." A sob choked off her protest. She placed her hands against his chest, which heaved with the force of his rapid breaths.

Sid gave her a little shake. "He's gone, Sadie. An' that means he won't ever be able to care for your family again. Don't you see what you gotta do? You gotta stay here. Work. Keep earnin' that pay. At least until Effie or the boys're bigger an' can help out some, too."

Sadie threw her arms outward, dislodging Sid's hold. She turned her back on him, hugging herself. Silent sobs shook her body. She wanted Mama. She wanted her mother's comfort. But Sid was right—going home meant giving up the source of income that would feed, house, and clothe her mother, sister, and brothers.

"Your ma needs you, Sadie, but not there. She needs you here. She's gonna be countin' on you more than ever now." His words filtered through the numbing shock, making her wonder if he'd read her secret thoughts. Warm hands curled over her shoulders. "You can't go back. There's nothin' waitin' for you there."

She nodded jerkily, finally recognizing the truth of his statement.

"But here . . ." Sid went on, his voice soft and convincing. "Here you got the means to take care of your family."

Sid was right. It would be selfish to go home. She'd come to Kansas to gain employment—the type of employment unavailable in Dalton. She had to stay. Mama and the children depended on her. Hadn't Papa even said so in his letter? In her mind's eye, she saw the line written in Papa's oversized, messy script: *"You're a good girl to put your family first, Sadie-girl. I'm proud of you."* She'd continue making him proud. She'd care for her family the only way she knew how.

But would the twenty dollars a month from her mercantile job be enough? No, she needed the singing money, too. Her mouth went dry. Mr. Baxter would find another singer if she didn't agree to perform all three nights. She bolted toward the mercantile.

Sid trotted alongside her. "What're you doin'?"

"I've got to ask Miss Melva and Miss Shelva for permission to go find Mr. Baxter. I have to talk to him—to tell him I'll keep singing."

Sid grabbed her arm, his eyes wide. "You're gonna do it? The private shows, too?"

Sadie swished her hands over her eyes, removing the remaining vestiges of tears. She heaved a shuddering sigh. "I have no choice. He told me it's all or nothing." *I'll do it, Papa, so Mama and the children won't go hungry.*

Sid blew out a breath, his face breaking into an expression of both joy and relief. "Go ask, then. If they say yes, I'll take you out to his place myself—I gotta exchange wagons anyway. You better talk to him before he finds another singer." Sid gave her a gentle push toward the door. "Hurry, Sadie."

Sadie stepped up on the stoop, but she didn't hurry. She couldn't. Her feet felt as though they'd turned to lead.

23

Asa squeaked the cork into place with his thumb and then held up the slender bottle by its throat to the shaft of sunlight streaming through the barn window. The red wine filling the bottle turned the aqua glass a muddy shade of purple. He'd been disgusted when he'd discovered aqua meant greenish-blue, but now he chortled, delighted by the sight. No one would guess the bottle's true contents—especially with his cleverly designed labels intact.

He set the bottle on the worktable and reached for the glue and a paper label:

Baxter's
⌒ FANCY ⌒
RED WINE
Vinegar

Very carefully, he applied glue to the upper third of the label. When the shipment reached its destination, the receiver could score the label with a razor blade and tear away the word "vinegar," leaving the "Baxter's Fancy Red Wine" intact. Took a steady hand and careful thought to brush on the right amount of glue and then center the scrolled label between the bottle's barely visible seams. But Asa had perfected the task over the past few days, readying his first shipment.

With another raspy chortle, he placed the bottle in the crate at his feet. He balled his hands on his hips and surveyed the fruits of his labor. Nine more crates sat on the barn floor, each containing an even two dozen bottles, ready for Sid to load in the wagon and transport to Abilene. The saloon owners who'd been shut down by Kansas's prohibition laws would be thrilled to buy his illicit liquor.

But he wouldn't sell all of it to former saloon owners. He'd need a supply for his Tuesday nights of poker, roulette, and blackjack. He didn't figure the Tuesday crowd would be as fond of his wine as they would the homemade beer waiting in kegs in the hidden room under the mercantile, but he'd have some on hand anyway. Asa rubbed his palms together, imagining the piles of money he'd soon amass. The thought made him giddy.

Yes, sir, ply them with enough drink, and the men would gamble all night. But he'd have to limit their imbibing and then shut things down at a reasonable hour. After all, the fellas had to return to work the morning after, and a bunch of red-eyed, dragging workers would certainly signal something was awry. He couldn't risk attracting that snoopy sheriff's attention. What had Hanaman been thinking, bringing a lawman to Goldtree?

But Asa wouldn't make it easy for the sheriff. Nobody'd hear the activity in the mercantile cellar—sturdy concrete walls absent of windows would hold the sound inside. And nobody'd see men coming and going from the mercantile, because they'd use the tunnel leading from his barn to the cellar. A half mile in length and reinforced with sturdy timbers, it had taken Asa almost four months to finish the secret passage-way. But now it was done, and he could open his gambling room to men eager for some fun.

The rattle of wagon wheels drifted from outside. Asa smiled—Sid, arriving to load the "vinegar." Rolling down his sleeves and fastening the cuffs around his thick wrists, he sauntered to meet the boy. To his surprise, Sid wasn't alone.

Asa scowled, jamming a stubby finger in Miss Wagner's direction. "What's she doin' here?"

The moment Sid set the brake, Miss Wagner scrambled down from the high seat and faced Asa, her expression pleading. "Have you located a singer to replace me?"

Asa crunched his lips to the side and folded his arms over his chest. What with needing to get that wine into bottles, he hadn't had a chance to send out a single inquiry. But Miss Wagner didn't need to know that. "Why?"

"B-because I . . ." Tears pooled in the girl's eyes. "I need the job. I need the money to . . . to send home to my mother. My father . . ." A tear trailed down her pale cheek. She didn't even bother to wipe it away. "He died. So . . ."

Asa rubbed his prickly jaw. Not that he gloried in the girl's loss, but the timing couldn't have been better from his standpoint. A desperate employee was a reliable employee. She'd do what he asked without question. And her voice—as well as her more-than-pleasing appearance—would continue to draw customers. Asa wanted to jump up and down with glee at this turn of events, but he kept his feet firmly planted and maintained a stern tone.

Squinting, he pinned her with a firm look. "If I say you can stay on, you gonna change your mind on me? 'Cause if I commit to keepin' you, I don't wanna get left standin' high an' dry"—he almost choked on his own unintentional pun—"if you decide it's too much work or you don't like the songs I pick."

She swallowed, but she didn't shrink away as she had the last time they'd talked. "I won't change my mind. I-I'll sing whatever songs you choose, and I'll work three nights a week." She paused, her expression apprehensive. "The pay . . . the pay is still the same?"

Oh, it would gratify Asa to lower the amount and watch her squirm. But that'd be just plain cruel, considering she was mourning the loss of her pa. Asa didn't understand that kind of mourning—he couldn't honestly say he'd been sad standing beside his pa's grave—but it was clear the girl was torn up. He wouldn't rub salt in her wounds. "Pay's the same."

Her shoulders wilted. "Thank you, Mr. Baxter."

He flipped his hand in reply, then scowled at her. "One more thing. These Tuesday shows? They ain't for everybody."

Her brows came together. "Yes, you told me. They're for m-men only."

"That's right. But not for *all* men." Asa arched one eyebrow, squinting with the opposite eye. "These're special shows for certain fellas. A kind of . . . private society, you might say." In the big cities, highfalutin' men gathered together in by-invitation-only dens to smoke cigars and complain about the country's leaders. Who would've thought Butterball Baxter would grow up to play host to such exclusivity?

"Only men comin'," Asa went on, "will be those I choose to invite. So you don't be talkin' up the Tuesday show. Let me do the advertisin'. An' you make sure you don't let nobody see you a-creepin' downstairs on Tuesday nights. Don't wanna rouse questions. You got it?" He waited until she nodded in agreement, then he looked at Sid, who hadn't budged from the wagon seat. "S'pose you gotta take her back to town now afore you can get that load ready for transport." He injected as much disgust into his tone as possible even though an hour delay wouldn't affect the deal.

Sid shrugged. "I've already got my gear packed an' ready to go. So if you'd rather, I can load the crates real quick an' drop Sadie off at the mercantile on my way out of town."

The last thing Asa wanted was Sid carting his wine down the middle of Goldtree's Main Street.

He coughed and waved both hands in the air. "Take 'er to town first. Then hightail it out here an' get to loadin'."

"Will do."

Asa took Miss Wagner's arm and urged her to climb aboard. After she settled herself on the seat, tucking her skirts beneath her just so—she sure was a graceful thing—she peered down at Asa. Gratitude shone in her blue eyes. "Thank you again, Mr. Baxter." Her chin quivered. "My family will appreciate the money I can send."

Asa slipped his thumbs into the pockets of his vest and offered a solemn nod. He watched the wagon roll off his yard, holding his delight inside until he was certain the young folks were out of range of sight and hearing. Then he did a little jig right there in the sunshine and let out a whoop of jubilee.

When Sid drew the wagon to a stop in front of the mercantile, Sadie placed her hand over his arm. "Thank you, Sid, for taking me to see Mr. Baxter. I feel better now, knowing I'll have the means to see to Mama's and the children's needs." Yet her assurances didn't remove the stone of dread from her stomach.

Sid patted Sadie's hand, offering a sympathetic look that brought a fresh rush of tears to her eyes. "I'm sorry you can't go back to Dalton, Sadie—I know how much you wanna see your ma."

"And attend Papa's service." Sadie bit her lower lip, controlling the desire to weep. Papa was no doubt already in the ground. She'd always hated viewing the headstone that marked her real father's resting place. Perhaps it was a blessing to be far away. She wouldn't have to carry a picture in her head of Papa lying in a pine box or of shovelfuls of dirt being emptied into his grave. Drawing in a breath to clear her tears, she grasped the edge of the wagon and climbed down.

Sid leaned sideways, reaching one hand to her. She clung to him, grateful for the comforting touch. He said, "I'll be gone most of the week. This load I'm takin' for Asa is goin' all the way to Abilene." His chest puffed with pride. "Asa's promoted me to chief freightsman. Better wages."

Her apron flew up, tossed by the wind, and she pulled free of Sid's grasp to push it back down and hold it there. "Th-that's wonderful, Sid. Congratulations."

"Thanks. But it's also longer hours." He grimaced. "Wish I didn't have to leave you now, especially after gettin' such bad news."

Bowing her head, Sadie silently petitioned God for strength. "I'll be fine, Sid." She released a mirthless chuckle. "If I have to learn a whole new repertoire of songs, I'll be too busy to think much. That will help."

"Well . . ." He gazed down at her, clearly reluctant to leave.

She bobbed her head, forcing her lips into a smile. "You better go. Mr. Baxter's waiting."

"Yep, I know." His shoulders heaved with a mighty sigh. He released the brake. "I'll come see you soon as I get back to town. Bye now, Sadie." He slapped down the reins, and the wagon jolted forward, leaving Sadie standing in a puff of dust.

With Sid's departure, Sadie needed to return to work. But her feet remained planted in the dirt road, unwilling to carry her forward. She had no desire to enter the mercantile. She preferred to find a quiet place and give vent to the grief that squeezed like a band around her chest. When she was little and wanted to mope, Papa had teased her doldrums away or put her to work. *"Busy hands'll keep the ache away,"* he'd said. She clamped her hand over her mouth. He'd been the dearest, most loving papa any girl had ever had.

"Sadie? What're you doing out there in the street?" Thad's voice—curious, carrying a teasing note—reached her ears.

She spun to face him. His image swam behind the spurt of tears.

The impish glint in his eyes melted quickly to concern. In two broad strides, he reached her and curled his arm around her waist. He guided her onto the boardwalk beneath the shade of the mercantile's porch roof and then took hold of her shoulders. "What's wrong?"

Sadie stared into his compassionate face. One

joyous thought penetrated her cloak of sorrow: If she remained in Goldtree, she could continue to see Thad. Tears spilled down her cheeks in warm rivulets. She grasped his wrists and clung, taking deep, shuddering breaths. His hands tightened on her shoulders, their pressure reassuring. He was here. He cared.

"Sadie?" His voice turned husky, evidence of his concern. "Something was wrong yesterday. What is it? How can I help?"

Yesterday's concern had been erased, but today's heartache needed release. She choked out, "My papa died."

Without a moment's hesitation he pulled her against his chest. One palm cupped the back of her head, the other pressed firmly to her back, holding her snug within the comfort of his embrace. She sobbed, her hands clutching handfuls of his shirt. His leather vest, redolent of his masculine scent and warm from the sun, provided a pillow for her cheek. With her eyes squeezed shut, she clung, absorbing his strength, his sympathy. No hug ever had been as needed or treasured as the one Thad now offered.

She was dimly aware of his feet shuffling, drawing her along with him while maintaining his hold. She opened her eyes and realized he'd moved between the mercantile and the café, out of sight of anyone else on the boardwalk. The narrow alleyway, shrouded in shadow, became a place of beauty as Thad held her, rocked her, murmured soothing words. Sadie didn't know how long she stood, her face buried against his sturdy chest, until the wracking sobs finally calmed. But she sensed he would have remained in that slice of shade, offering the strength of his presence, until the sun went down if she'd asked it of him.

"Busy hands'll keep the ache away." Papa's long-ago words reminded Sadie she needed to return to work before the Baxter twins sent out a posse in search of their missing clerk. She reluctantly backed away from Thad's arms and wiped her face with her apron skirt. Then she sucked in a steadying breath that squared her shoulders. "I . . . I need to go inside."

His warm hands held to her upper arms. A gentle hold, matching the gentle empathy shining in his eyes. "If you need a ride to the stage station in Macyville, I can take you."

Sadie shook her head. "I'm not going home." Her voice sounded funny—tinny and hollow. She sniffed hard. "Mama will need the money I make more than anything else. Now that Papa will n-never get well—" How tenaciously they'd all clung to hope for Papa's recovery. A twinge of anger pinched her chest. "Someone has to provide for the family. They're all depending on me."

Thad shook his head. "I admire you, Sadie. You've taken on a big responsibility." He drew

264

her close again, planting a kiss on the top of her head and then another near her temple. She turned her face slightly, hoping his lips might find hers and provide a welcome distraction from the ache that filled her chest. But instead he slipped his arm around her waist again and aimed her toward the boardwalk.

Disinclination to leave the welcoming comfort of his embrace slowed her pace, and he matched her stride by tempering his. His actions bespoke of a desire to hold her near. In spite of her deep sadness, appreciation welled. She tipped her head, grazing his shoulder with her temple. "Thank you, Thad."

He smiled sadly, his eyes crinkling. "If you need me, just come on down to the office." His gaze whisked up and down the street, then met hers again. Regret now tinged his features. "Wish I could do more than offer sympathy, but—"

She boldly placed her trembling hand on his forearm. "It's exactly what I need."

He nodded, his gaze boring into hers so intensely she wondered if he could read the errant thought that tripped through her brain: *I've lost my precious papa, but at least I don't have to face losing you.*

24

Thad sat astride the horse loaned to him by the town's blacksmith, holding the roan to a sedate clip-clop even though he wanted to give the big beast free rein and let it gallop. He received a reckless thrill from racing along a dusty road lined by pastures and wheat fields, the wind tugging at his hair and the thunder of hooves filling his ears. But he had several miles to cover, and it would be irresponsible to tire the horse.

Since his daily treks around town hadn't turned up any clues to the suspected illegal dealings, he'd decided to expand his territory. For the past few days, each afternoon he'd borrowed a horse and set off in a different direction to explore the surrounding farmsteads. He'd inspected the farms north, east, and west of town without uncovering anything suspicious. But he hadn't wasted his time—the visits had given him a chance to get acquainted with the area farmers.

Some were too busy to chat, but one woman had given him a glass of cold milk and a slice of gingerbread, and two others had begged favors—helping hack out a tree stump from the center of a garden plot and rounding up a runaway pet goat.

Dislodging the ungainly stump had been a heap sight easier than capturing that stubborn billy goat. But—Thad chuckled, remembering—the smile on the children's faces when he'd dragged the pet home had eased his aggravation.

Nope, he didn't mind offering a helping hand—he'd probably perform similar deeds when he served as minister someday. People always turned to their preachers when they needed to unburden themselves or to pray with a trusted friend. Or when they needed some comforting. Like he'd given Sadie on Monday.

His heart gave a double thump in response to her name. When he'd held her as she'd cried, he'd experienced a strong urge to sweep her into his arms and carry her someplace where sadness and sorrow could never touch her again. He'd held her once before—the day she'd stepped into the path of the runaway wagon—but it was different Monday. His first embrace had been one of desperation. The second expressed devotion. And it had left him wanting more.

He pulled the reins, guiding the horse on a gentle bend in the road. Too bad he couldn't redirect his feelings with a simple tug. As he'd cradled Sadie close, listening to her cry while her tears soaked his shirt, he'd yearned to kiss her. As a means of comforting her, yes, but even more to communicate how he felt about her. She'd agreed to his courtship, but responsibilities kept them apart.

You think you're busy now as a sheriff, just wait. You won't be any less busy once you're a preacher. The errant thought took him by surprise. But he pushed it aside. Being busy doing God's work shouldn't be a burden. He must be extra tired, letting gloomy ideas come into his head. The sun beat down, heating his head through his hat and raising perspiration on his face and back, but a chill of pleasure tiptoed up his spine as he returned his thoughts to Sadie.

Listening to her sing, seeing the passion light her heart-shaped face, stirred something deep inside of him. When she smiled, it warmed him. When she giggled, it lightened his heart. She was fine to look upon—no man could deny her beauty —but her loveliness went beneath the surface to her character. Her determination to bear responsibility for her mother and siblings' care touched him.

He wished he could help her so she wouldn't have to work so hard. And, selfishly, he wanted more time with her. She worked all day in the mercantile and then spent the evenings preparing for the opera house performances, leaving her little time for relaxation. However, when he'd stopped by the mercantile this morning to check on her, she'd agreed to have lunch with him Sunday—another picnic in the park. "Under our tree," she'd said and then colored prettily.

The horse suddenly nickered, shaking its head,

and it seemed to give a skip, as if it wanted to turn itself around. Thad pulled back on the reins, bringing the animal under control. "Whoa there, big fella. What's the problem?" Then an odor reached his nose—the essence of something rotten. The horse danced in place, snorting in protest. Thad couldn't blame the horse. The odor nearly singed his nose hairs.

He looked around, his face puckered in distaste. What was that? A dead animal? He'd smelled the rotting flesh of buffalo when he was a boy, and he'd never forgotten it. This smell had a putrid edge to it, but it also reminded him of rising bread dough. Suddenly, without warning, another memory rose from the recesses of Thad's mind. His body jolted in response, his hands tightening on the reins. *We've found it, haven't we, Lord?*

The horse snorted again, eager to leave the area. "All right, boy," Thad said, "we'll move. But you aren't gonna like it much." Wrinkling his face in distaste, he tapped his heels on the animal's sides. The horse bounced its head in protest, but Thad ignored the animal's complaint and rode toward the scent rather than away from it.

"A cave?" Roscoe Hanaman stared at Thad, his jowls sagging with the weight of his slack jaw. "Why, I never heard tell of any caves around Goldtree."

Thad leaned back in the chair across from the

banker's desk and nodded. "I wouldn't have believed it if I hadn't seen it myself. It was well hidden. If it hadn't been for the wind carrying that distinct scent"—how many times had he been forced to bear the offensive odor on his father's breath?—"I wouldn't have found it."

Hanaman shook his head. "But why haven't we picked up on the . . . er . . . aroma before now?"

Thad shrugged. "It being south of town, the north wind's going to carry the scent away from most folks. Besides, it's a good distance from town, so if anybody did notice it, they'd just reckon it's a dead animal. Not until you get close can you pick up the yeasty smell." Somebody'd chosen their spot well, off the road and surrounded by saplings with low-growing branches. The bootlegger had even added piles of brush around the cave's opening and across the wide pathway weaving out of the trees to the road to further conceal the location.

"I'm gonna go back tomorrow with a lantern and do some more exploring," Thad said. "It was black as pitch in there. Could hardly see a thing, but I didn't need my eyes to smell. . . ." He tapped his nose, cringing. "I knew I'd found the bootleg camp."

Hanaman leaned toward Thad, nearly licking his chops in anticipation. "So you'll be able to make an arrest soon? Take this lawbreaker out of operation?"

The man's impatience stirred Thad's ire. Maybe he shouldn't have shared his finding with the mayor. He'd probably opened himself up to even more pressure. "I'm just here to give you a report, Roscoe. I still don't know who's behind this." So far he'd explored an old shack with signs of recent activity and a cave with a beer-brewing setup. But the two places were miles apart. What was the connection between them? "I don't even know who owns the property."

Hanaman pointed one finger in the air. "Ask Rahn at the post office. Since he serves as the clerk of Five Creeks Township, he's got information on every land deed."

"It's possible," Thad continued, filing away Hanaman's suggestion for later use, "that the person making the liquor is trespassing. Only a fool would put the operation on his own land. So I've got work to do yet."

Hanaman scowled. "How much longer, Sheriff? We need to bring this man down quickly."

Thad couldn't give a certain answer, so he lifted his hat from his knee and rose. Sliding the hat into place, he said, "The minute I'm ready to make an arrest, you'll be the first to know."

Hanaman came around the desk, scowling. "Well, see that it's soon." He opened his door and ushered Thad into the main lobby of the bank. Several folks stood in line at the teller's window, and Hanaman cast a beaming smile across them.

The man could change expressions quicker than a lizard changed its colors. "Good day, folks, good day. Might I be able to assist any of you?"

Two of the customers left the line to approach Hanaman, and Thad made his exit while the banker was otherwise occupied. He returned the horse to the blacksmith's shop and requested its use for the next day from the owner, Bill Kimbrough.

"Sure thing, Sheriff," the affable man replied. He released the horse into the attached corral. "Tell you what, I'll just leave the saddle an' such in the first stall there where you can get to it. Anytime you need to use ol' Thunder, just help yourself. I won't lend him out to nobody else. If he turns up missin', I'll just assume you've got him. That work for you?"

"That's very generous of you, Bill," Thad said, clapping the other man on his broad back.

"Least I can do for the man who keeps law an' order in Goldtree." Bill laughed, the sound deep and rumbling.

Thad grinned in reply and headed for his office. But his feet took him past his door and on to the mercantile. The business would close in another half hour—maybe the Baxter sisters would release Sadie early and he could take her to Cora's for supper before she went down to the singing room to practice. The thought of a few minutes of time with Sadie sped his footsteps.

The little bell above the screen door sent out a tinny jangle as he crossed the threshold. Miss Melva drowned out the bell's clatter with a screech of welcome. "Howdy again, Sheriff. Wasn't you just in here this mornin'?"

Miss Shelva, arranging cans of peas in the front window, tittered. "Mornin' was a long time ago, Sister. 'Sides, he might've forgot somethin' . . . like how purty Miss Sadie looks in that yellow dress she's wearin' today."

"How could any feller worth his salt forget somethin' like that?" Miss Melva bantered back. "Ain't likely, to my way o' thinkin'."

Thad pursed his lips. The women were enjoying his new position as Sadie's beau even more than he was. He glanced around, his brow pinching. "Where's Sadie?"

Miss Melva squinted one eye at Thad. "So you sayin' the reason you come in was to talk at her?"

Thad nodded, bracing himself for a scolding for taking Sadie's attention away from work.

Both women left their tasks and flew at Thad, hands wringing, faces wearing matching frowns of concern. Miss Shelva spoke first. "We're worried as worried can be about Sadie."

"She's just so sad-lookin' all the time," Miss Melva said. "Can't hardly raise a smile out of her. An' she don't eat."

The pair exchanged an appalled look, both *tsk*ing. Miss Shelva said, "I keep tellin' her she's gonna make herself sick if she don't eat, but she just pecks at her food."

"Sister even cooked up a mess o' peach tarts, since we all know how much Sadie likes peaches." Miss Melva threw her arms wide. "She didn't eat nary a one! Two bites—that was it."

Twin tears shimmered in Miss Shelva's eyes. "We're wonderin' if maybe we hadn't oughtta send her back to Indiana afore she fades clean away from homesickness."

Thad pinched his chin. The sisters tended to overdramatize, but even in the brief snatches of time he'd been able to carve out for her, he'd noted Sadie's lack of sparkle since her stepfather passed away. He understood mourning—she'd obviously adored the man—but he hadn't realized she'd resorted to not eating. Yet she'd agreed to meet him for a picnic on Sunday, so surely she just needed the right kind of prompting to eat. Imagining how the Baxter twins probably encouraged—shrieking in her face—he decided the best way to boost Sadie's appetite was to give her a break from the well-meaning but forceful mercantile owners.

He repeated his earlier question. "Where's Sadie?"

Miss Melva waved her hand toward the rear of the store. "Sent her out back to burn trash."

Miss Shelva's bushy gray eyebrows rose. "You gonna talk to her?"

Thad nodded. "With your permission, I'm going to invite her to Cora's for supper."

The pair broke into bright smiles and identical chortles. Miss Melva flicked her fingertips on Thad's arm. "You got our permission, Sheriff, to take Sadie to supper. Take her right now, if you've a mind to. That barrel'll burn itself out without watchin'."

"An' you give her a good talkin'-to about maybe goin' home," Miss Shelva said. Her smile faded. "I'd miss her somethin' fierce. What a sweet girl she is. . . ."

"She wouldn't hafta be gone forever, Sister." Miss Melva patted her sister's back then swung a pleading look on Thad. "Goin' home for a while, though—to see how her ma an' all them little brothers an' her sister're makin' out now that her pa's gone—would do her a world of good."

Thad gave each woman's arm a squeeze, earning matching blushes and titters, then headed for the back door. With each step, his resolve to cheer Sadie grew. When he was a preacher, he'd need to be able to offer comfort as well as sound advice. Ministering to Sadie would be good experience. More than that, he yearned to see her unburdened and happy again. *Please, Lord, ease her pain.*

He pushed open the door and spotted Sadie at the far corner of the yard, poking a stick into a barrel from which smoke rose like a writhing snake. Her yellow hair gleamed in the sunshine, curling strands dancing in the stout breeze that plastered her dress and apron to her slender form. His heart caught in his throat. He didn't want to suggest she leave Goldtree. But he shouldn't be selfish. A preacher wouldn't be selfish.

Squaring his shoulders, he took off across the yard. *Give me strength, Lord, to do what's best for Sadie.*

25

"I am not going back to Indiana, Thad, and I don't wish to discuss it any further."

Thad ground his teeth, stifling a growl. In the half hour since he'd slid across from Sadie into his familiar booth at Cora's café, she'd stubbornly refused every one of his suggestions—including the one to dig into the delicious stew Cora had delivered to their table. His bowl was empty, but hers held congealed broth dotted with chunks of beef and vegetables. Unappetizing. He doubted she'd eat it now. But he pointed at her bowl anyway.

"An' what would your mama say if she saw how you're letting food go to waste?" He supposed he sounded like a nag, but concern for

Sadie sharpened his tone. "You can't go on like this—not eating, working all day an' then singing at night. You're gonna wear yourself out an' be of no use to anybody."

She set her lips in an obstinate line.

Thad sighed, reining in his frustration. Being quarrelsome hadn't gotten him anywhere. Maybe he should try a gentler approach. "I'm not trying to rile you. I'm worried about you. So are Miss Melva an' Miss Shelva."

Tears shimmered, but she blinked and chased them away.

He pushed his bowl aside and rested his arms on the table, leaning in. "We're not trying to send you off for good, Sadie. All of us, especially me"—a blush stole across her pale cheeks, pleasing him—"want you to come back. But don't you think it'd be easier to set your mourning aside if you had the chance to go home, see your family, an' say a proper good-bye to the man who raised you?"

Her stiff shoulders wilted. She poked at a dried biscuit on the little plate beside her bowl. "It isn't that I don't want to see my family. I . . . I worry about Mama . . . how she's doing. She's buried two husbands now." Sadie's chin crumpled as tears threatened. But she shook her head hard, determination squaring her jaw. "But I can't leave. It would take a week to get there, another to get back. That's too many days of no work. I have to work to get paid. So . . ." Her voice faded to silence.

Thad cupped his hand over hers. "You've made good money with your singing." He'd been shocked when she'd shared what Asa Baxter paid her. If he was interested in accumulating wealth, he'd take up singing lessons. "Haven't you set extra aside—enough to get by for a month or so?"

Sadie pulled her hand free and lifted her cloth napkin, dabbing her mouth. Thad thought it a silly thing to do—a person couldn't get messy when she didn't eat. She lowered the napkin to her lap and stared down at it. "I send almost everything to Mama. And I'm sure she's had the sense to set some of it aside. But if I leave, Mr. Baxter will have to close the opera house for a few weeks. Or he'll find another singer to take my place."

Thad detected a note of fear in her voice. "He might have to find somebody else for a few performances, but then you'd be back to singing again."

Her head bounced up. "No. He's already warned me. If he brings in someone else, it will be for good. And now that he's starting—" She turned sharply away, biting down on her lower lip.

"He's starting what?" Thad prompted.

She angled her face slightly to peek at him. "It isn't important. But my singing *is* important. Making money is important. Papa worried about his sons growing up to work in the mines. He always talked about wanting his boys to go to college someday—to be more than common laborers. That can't happen unless Mama has money to pay for their education. So I can't take time away to go home, even for a visit. I have to work."

She slid from the booth, tossing her napkin over the bowl of stew. "Thank you for the supper, Thad, but I must practice now. I have new songs to learn for . . . for next week." She dashed out of the café before Thad could form a protest.

He sat, fingers pinching his chin and brow pulled low, replaying their conversation. Something had Sadie rattled. Had Asa Baxter threatened her, or were her own desires to earn as much money as possible holding her captive? Either way, she was bound to make herself sick if she didn't let loose of fretting. He dropped some money on the table to pay for their meal and then pushed out of the booth. Sadie might view him as a pest, but he intended to go down to the singing room and try once more to talk sense into her.

When he stepped out onto the boardwalk, he spotted one of Asa Baxter's freight wagons pulling into town. Sid Wagner sat on the high seat. He'd left on Monday—for Abilene, someone had mentioned. Thad had thought it too bad he'd been gone the same week Sadie got the news on her stepfather. Having her cousin close by would've been a comfort to her. But now that Sid was back, maybe he could help convince Sadie to take a break.

Thad stepped into the street and waved his hands. "Hey there, Sid! Hold up for a minute!"

Sid pulled back on the reins, drawing the wagon to a stop. He peered down at Thad, his face both tired and wary. "What is it, Sheriff?"

Thad noticed Sid adopted an insolent edge when addressing him, but he decided to ignore it. He propped one boot on the wheel hub and hooked his elbow on the edge of the seat. "Need to talk to you about Sadie."

Sid lost his belligerent look in an instant. He set the brake and came half out of the seat, wrapping the reins around the handle with clumsy motions. "Is she all right? Is she hurt?"

Thad hadn't intended to panic the man. He held up one hand. "Whoa there, slow down. She's fine. Leastways, she isn't sick. Except at heart."

Sid plopped back on the seat and scowled. "What're you tryin' to say?"

Another wagon rolled up behind Sid's. Thad needed to let Sid get out of the street. "Park this thing an' then come to my office. We'll talk there."

The man didn't look happy, but he nodded. Thad headed to his office and waited in the doorway while Sid angled the wagon close to the board-walk, set the brake, and hopped down. His feet scuffed. The days of travel had left him dirty, tired, and—if Thad guessed right—grumpy.

But this was important. It couldn't be put off.

Thad gestured Sid inside, then closed the door. Only two chairs occupied the office, one by the table that served as his desk and the other in the corner. Thad dragged them to the center of the floor, aimed them face-to-face, then said, "Sit."

Sid folded his arms over his chest. "I've been sittin' on that wagon seat for longer'n I care to admit. I'd ruther stand. Now . . . what's wrong with Sadie?"

If Sid was going to stand, Thad would, too. He hooked his thumbs in his back pockets, pretending a nonchalance he didn't feel. "She's worn out, Sid. Working all day, every day but Sunday in the mercantile, practicing in her room in the evenings, then singing every Friday and Saturday night. She hardly gets a chance to rest. And this past week, mourning over her stepfather, she hasn't eaten enough to keep a bird alive. Miss Melva, Miss Shelva, an' me all think she needs a break. But we can't talk her into going back to Indiana for a visit. So I was hoping maybe you would—"

"You want me to talk her into going home?"

"That's exactly right."

"I . . . I can't do that."

Thad frowned. "Why not?"

Sid fidgeted with his shirt button, his gaze bouncing around the office. "Just can't, that's all."

Thad grunted. "But don't you think it'd be good for her?"

Sid set his feet wide and imitated Thad's stance—thumbs in pockets, chin angled high. Thad got the feeling he was about to be challenged to a duel. "Maybe. But it ain't for me to say. It's gotta be Sadie's choice, an' it seems to me she's already made it if she's told you she's stayin'." His eyes flicked to the side, avoiding Thad's gaze.

"But she'd listen to you, you being her cousin. Somebody she knows an' trusts. So why don't you—"

The muscles in Sid's jaw clenched. "She's gotta sing."

Something in Sid's words made the fine hairs on the back of Thad's neck prickle. "She's *got* to sing?"

Sid spun and clomped toward the door. He grabbed the door handle and sent a murderous glare over his shoulder. "McKane, let Sadie be. If she wants to go home, she'll go. If she wants to stay, she'll stay. But don't be pesterin' her, 'cause—" He clamped his lips closed. Then he blew out a mighty breath. "Just leave her be." He stormed out of the office.

Thad sank into the closest chair, his mind whirling. He might only be a temporary lawman, but he knew suspicious behavior when he saw it. Sid and Sadie were hiding something.

His chest tightened. Did he really suspect Sadie of deceit? The stew soured in his stomach.

Sid had told him to leave Sadie alone, but he couldn't do it. Every instinct told him Sadie's lack of appetite had less to do with sorrow and more to do with a pressure to appear on that opera house stage. He had two mysteries to uncover now. But he was more concerned about the one affecting Sadie.

He shot out of the chair, out of the office, and down the boardwalk. Sadie had said she needed to practice, so he knew where to find her.

Sadie's fingers tripped lightly on the ivory keys, the notes providing accompaniment to the song rasping from her throat. She needed to sing with greater feeling, but her vocal cords refused to cooperate. The title of the song, "Hold Me Tighter in Your Arms," brought sweet memories of the day Thad had whisked her into the alleyway and held her while she'd cried, but the lyrics stole the innocence of her memories.

Mama would call the words indecent. Seductive, even. Sadie found it difficult to form the lyrics, let alone sing them with the feeling Mr. Baxter would expect. Hence, her throat closed, creating a husky tone that didn't sound like her at all. Which was fitting, because she didn't feel like herself, singing rollicking tunes called "Little Brown Jug" and "Ben Bolt."

But at least, she consoled herself as she finished the song and reached for another piece of music, she would still be able to sing her familiar hymns and sweet ballads on Friday and Saturday nights. She needn't limit her repertoire to these questionable offerings. She only wished the realization would eliminate the guilt that continued to prick at the back of her heart.

As she laid the next sheets of music across the piano's music ledge, a faint creaking sound reached her ears. She paused, looking toward the carved double doors at the back of the room. She'd left them slightly ajar. For some reason, being closed in the windowless room—regardless of its ostentatious appearance and even with all the lights glaring—left her unnerved. But she couldn't leave the doors wide open without the music drifting along the hallway and up the stairs, so she compromised by leaving only a gap that offered a glimpse of the hallway beyond.

Looking at the doors now, she frowned. She'd left only a six-inch opening, but the gap was wider than that—at least a foot's clearance. A slight draft might have moved one door, but both of them? Someone must have given them a slight push, making the hinges squeak. Yet no one stood in the opening.

A chill wiggled down her spine, and her pulse sped. She called, "Is someone there?" She tipped her head, listening closely, but no one answered.

She took several calming breaths. Obviously she'd left the doors open wider than she'd thought. She needn't sit here like a child waiting for a bogeyman to jump out of the shadows. But she shouldn't leave the doors so wide, either.

On shaky legs, she skittered up the aisle and caught the door handles. She pushed the doors inward until a scant four-inch gap remained. Her heart pounded. Oh, how she hated feeling all hemmed in. But better to keep the sound muffled. Mr. Baxter would not be pleased if the sound carried beyond the cellar.

With a sigh, she turned to go back to the stage, but another sound—the click of a door latch—froze her in place for ten fearful seconds. Then she spun toward the gap, peeking at the shadowed hallway beyond. *Someone* had just closed the door at the top of the cellar stairs. So she hadn't imagined her visitor. But the person was gone now.

"You're safe, Sadie," she whispered, her voice too low to create an answering echo. "It was probably Mr. Baxter. He came down, realized I was practicing, and decided not to bother me. Yes, surely that was it." But her pulse continued to race. She gave herself a little shake and spoke more firmly. "Don't be a ninny. Just go sing." Hugging herself, she hurried back to the piano. The sooner she finished practicing, the sooner she could go upstairs again.

She sat on the little piano stool and placed her fingers on the keys. She began the introduction to "Lily Dale." While she played and sang, she repeatedly raised her head to peek over the piano's sleek top for evidence of an intruder. By the end of the song, she'd convinced herself she had no reason for concern. At the first opportunity, she'd ask Mr. Baxter if he'd come down to the opera room. If he denied having visited, *then* she would worry.

26

Thad settled into his reserved box seat in the opera house. Mr. Baxter had cheerfully assigned him the first seat in the recently added row beneath the gas sconces, a location that provided a straight view to Sadie's profile as she sang. The position of one pillar shielded her partially if she shifted too far forward on the stage rather than remaining directly beneath the overhead chandelier, but all in all, it was a good seat and he was glad to claim it as his own.

The past week had been one of the hardest he'd ever remembered. As much as he wanted to spend time with Sadie, he'd avoided her. He blamed it on needing to haunt the cave opening, waiting for the unknown bootlegger to make an appearance, but the truth was he didn't know what to say to her.

Although he'd fully intended to speak to her when he'd entered the underground singing room over a week ago, the song—delivered in a husky, almost suggestive tone—had stopped him in his tracks. Why had Sadie chosen such a coarse number? He felt a blush building, thinking about the lyrics that had slipped from her sweet lips. Glancing around at the audience, which waited in hushed expectation for the performance to begin, he wondered how they'd react when she opened her mouth and began singing about the pleasant pressure of a man's hand on her spine.

Roscoe and Miriam Hanaman wriggled into their seats next to Thad's, Roscoe's natural bulk and Miriam's voluminous dress of plum velvet making it a tight fit. The mayor's wife beamed at Thad. "Good evening, Sheriff. Are you eager for another of Miss Sadie's impressive performances?"

Thad nodded, even though his stomach churned. "Yes, ma'am. Wouldn't miss it."

Roscoe Hanaman chuckled. "Miriam won't allow me to miss a single performance. These shows are the best part of her week, she says." He bumped Thad's arm with his elbow, winking. "Almost makes me want to take up singing, so I can be the best part of her week."

"Oh, Roscoe, you silly goose!" Mrs. Hanaman slapped playfully at her husband's wrist. The two of them laughed merrily.

Miriam shifted to visit with the person on her left, and Roscoe leaned closer to Thad. He whispered, "What more have you turned up since we spoke last?"

Thad grimaced. He had little new to report in revealing the instigator, but he shared what he'd discovered. "Somebody's got quite an operation out there. The cave went a lot deeper than I expected. Three different chambers, each containing a good-sized still. I found at least thirty jugs, already full, in the middle chamber, an' nearly a dozen empty barrels. I reckon whoever set it all up is getting quite an output." He shook his head, frustration rising to pinch his chest. "But I couldn't find a thing to help me identify our bootlegger."

Roscoe frowned. "But the man's got to go out and check his stills every day, doesn't he? Why haven't you spotted him?"

Thad gritted his teeth, holding back a defensive retort. How could he sit beside that cave entrance all day and still be on duty in town? He forced an affable tone. "I'm out there as much as I can be without making the townsfolk wonder why I'm not on duty."

"Hmm." Roscoe pooched his lips, making his mustache twitch. "Maybe we should hire someone to camp near the cave and watch the area."

Thad quirked one eyebrow. "You want me to post somebody out there? I'd have to tell them why they were watching . . . and I thought you wanted this to be our little secret."

Hanaman sighed. "You're right. I guess you'll just have to go out more often."

Before Thad could reply, a flurry of movement caught his eye—Sadie coming up the middle aisle in her familiar dress, her hair cascading over her shoulders in a shimmering curtain. As one, the audience rose and broke into applause. Thad stood, but his shaking hands refused to connect with each other. How quickly she'd won their admiration. But they hadn't heard her new repertoire yet.

When Sadie stepped onto the stage, folks settled back into their seats to a chorus of creaking metal joints and excited whispers. They aimed their faces straight ahead, and their voices fell silent. Sadie nodded to the pianist—her signal to begin. She opened the program with a hymn, then moved into a ballad. Three more hymns, another ballad. Thad sat tense, hardly daring to breathe or blink, waiting for the song he'd overheard to find its way into the program. But after an hour, she sang what had become her traditional closing number—"Eternal Father, Strong to Save"—and by the time she'd finished to rousing applause, Thad wondered if he'd imagined her practicing an unseemly selection.

Sadie made her way up the center aisle, smiling, shaking hands, bobbing her head in silent appreciation, then disappeared behind the double doors. Thad started after her, but Roscoe caught his arm and drew him to the corner to discuss the cave and the stills. By the time he and the mayor finished talking, it was too late to seek out Sadie. So he decided to come back Saturday night and listen. Maybe she'd insert the new songs into Saturday's performance.

Saturday dragged longer than any day in Thad's memory. He spent a significant portion of it watching the break in the trees that led to the cave. But to no avail. The bootlegger kept himself hidden. When the evening finally arrived, Thad took his seat, once again so tense his leg muscles quivered in apprehension. As she had on Friday, Sadie sang hymns and ballads—a different collection than the night before, but nothing of a questionable nature. By the close of Saturday night's show, his confusion had reached unreasonable heights.

He scuffed his way to his office, his thoughts reeling. When he'd taken her to supper, Sadie had told him she needed to practice for "next week's performance." He'd clearly heard her singing a song one might hear in a saloon or from the lobby of a house of ill repute. If the song wasn't a part of her opera house repertoire, then why did she need to learn it?

"Ack! Help! Help!"

The hysterical screech roused Sadie from a

sound sleep before dawn on Sunday morning. She leaped out of bed and raced into the shadowy hallway, her nightgown tangling around her ankles. Miss Melva stumbled out of her bedroom and joined Sadie.

"Help!" The cry came again.

"That's Sister!" Miss Melva hollered, her face white. She looped elbows with Sadie and together they thundered down the stairs and around the corner into the mercantile, nearly colliding with Miss Shelva, who stood just inside the door leading into the merchandise area.

Only muted light filtered through the plate-glass windows, but even with the room cast in gray shadows, Sadie spotted the source of Miss Shelva's distress. The place was a shambles! The twins clung to each other, blubbering.

Sadie pushed past the sisters and ran barefooted out the front door, which stood ajar, and up the boardwalk to the sheriff's office. The door was locked, so she pounded her fist on the solid wood while peering through the glass. Moments later, Thad careened from the back half of the office, his shirttails flapping.

He threw open the door. "What're you doing out here in your nightclothes?"

Only then did Sadie remember her state of undress. Heat seared her face, but she couldn't allow embarrassment to keep her from her task. Clutching fistfuls of fabric at her throat with one hand, she caught Thad's sleeve with the other and gasped, "The mercantile's been robbed!"

Thad's eyebrows flew high. Without another word, he pounded behind her, his bootheels an echoing intrusion in the morning's calm. Sadie left Thad listening to Miss Melva and Miss Shelva and darted upstairs to put on a dress and twist her hair into a simple braid before going back to the mercantile. By then, the sun had crept high enough to illuminate the scene, and Sadie couldn't hold back a gasp when she saw the damage in full light.

The twins and Thad stood at the counter, surveying the mess, and Sadie crossed directly to her employers. She hugged first Miss Melva, then Miss Shelva. "I'm so sorry this happened."

Thad sent a stern look in her direction. "Miss Melva an' Miss Shelva say they didn't hear a thing last night. But something like this"—he swept his hand, indicating the tumble of cans, strewn cloth bolts, and overturned crates—"had to have made a heap of noise. Did you hear anybody down here last night?"

Sadie bit down on her lower lip and shook her head. Guilt assailed her. She'd gone to bed late, having stayed up to pen a lengthy letter to Mama and the children, then had put her pillow over her ears to muffle the loud snore emanating from one of the twins' bedrooms. The pillow must have blocked the sounds made by the thieves. "I'm sorry. But no, I didn't hear anything, either."

"Why would somebody wanna rob us?" Miss Melva's gray hair stood out around her head like a lion's mane. Her faded eyes flooded with tears. "We give credit to anybody who asks. No need to steal from us."

"No need at all," Miss Melva added.

Miss Shelva drew in a shuddering breath. "Well, Sister, reckon we won't be attendin' Sunday services this mornin'. We gotta get this place in order by tomorrow. Else customers won't be able to find a thing." With sniffles and disheartened sighs, the pair shuffled into the mess and began picking up.

Sadie looked into Thad's grim face. "Could you ride out and let Mr. Baxter know what's happened? I think Miss Melva and Miss Shelva would appreciate his support."

Thad muttered, "Can't imagine him being much help, but yes, I'll go get him." He high-stepped over several discarded cans and gave each of the Baxter twins a hug, promising to return soon. Then he strode toward the door. Just before leaving, he paused and looked back at Sadie. Her heart caught, hoping for a word of comfort or a sweet wink—anything. But he merely stared at her with an odd expression on his face for the space of several seconds, then clomped out without a word.

• • •

Sid latched the gate on the freight wagon Monday morning and turned to face Sadie. "Well, that's that. Guess I'm ready." He tried not to frown when he looked at her. She appeared even thinner than she had a week ago. And sadder. He wished he had time to stay and talk, the way she'd asked. She said she had something important to talk to him about, but it would have to wait until he returned from his trip. Asa had promised him a daylong break in between deliveries when he got back. A full day of no work would be nice. And it'd give him time to take Sadie to supper, for her to share whatever secret she carried.

She linked her hands behind her back, peering at him with dark-rimmed eyes while the wind billowed her skirt and tossed one loose strand of hair across her cheek. "I wish you didn't have to go. It's kind of frightening right now, knowing somebody broke into the mercantile and caused such destruction."

Sid had heard about the break-in as soon as he'd returned to town yesterday evening, but he could make little sense of the situation. When somebody broke into a place, they usually stole something. But the Baxters insisted nothing was missing, so someone had merely ransacked the mercantile. He gave Sadie's shoulder a squeeze. "Now, you heard what the sheriff said. Probably some kids playing a mean prank. No need to be afraid."

"I suppose." She heaved a sigh, then looked at him again, a weak smile curving her lips. "So . . . are you heading to Abilene again?"

"Beloit this time, but it'll be just as many days as last week."

How he hated being gone more days than not. But Asa had doubled his salary. He was already looking at moving into a nicer house— one with a real front porch and maybe a carriage shed out back so he could buy a buggy and a horse. Thinking of the things he'd be able to provide for Sadie made the separation bearable.

She sighed. "I'll miss you."

The simple statement made him smile. If they weren't out in the open where anyone passing on the boardwalk would see, he'd snatch her close in a hug. Maybe even give her a kiss. But he couldn't do something so brazen in the middle of the street. So he teased, "Aw, you'll just miss the little goodies I leave for you on the porch."

She ducked her head, showing him the neat part in her hair.

"But don't worry. When I get back, I'll have somethin' special for you to make up for it." He'd heard Beloit had a store that sold jewelry and pretty gewgaws. He might not have the courage to buy Sadie an engagement ring or brooch just yet, but surely she'd appreciate a pretty china figurine or painted hair receiver—something more lasting than the little things he'd picked up for her thus far.

She shook her head, one loose strand of hair bouncing along her cheek. "You don't have to buy me anything, Sid. Just be safe and . . . and hurry back, all right?"

His heart caught. It was the kind of thing a wife would say when her husband took off on a trip. His arms itched. Watchful eyes or not, he should pull her close. But she was already stepping up on the boardwalk, out of reach. "Will do," he said, his throat tight. He climbed into the seat and took up the reins. "Bye, Sadie."

She waved, and he gave the reins a flick. The horses strained against the rigging, and the wagon rolled down Main Street. One wheel jounced over a rock, and Sid heard a clink. He glanced into the bed, frowning. The crates were all stamped "Navy Beans," but beans didn't clink. Should he stop and pry open the crates to find out what made the noise?

"Don't be foolish," he berated himself. The rock probably bounced up under the wagon and hit a piece of metal. He faced forward and clicked his teeth on his tongue. "Get up there, now," he commanded Rudy and Hec. The horses obediently broke into a gentle trot.

He ought to reach Brittsville by noon or shortly after. The town didn't have a café, but the stationmaster's daughter was a good cook. If a stage was due in at some point during the day, she'd have something simmering on the stove, and he'd buy lunch from her. The last time he'd been in Brittsville, he'd only had to pay twenty-five cents for a big bowl of beans with chunks of bacon, biscuits, and so much coffee he sloshed when he left. A bargain. And he'd thoroughly enjoyed chatting with the comely young woman. If he hadn't already given his heart to Sadie, he might even consider taking up with her.

Even Sadie had expressed dismay when she'd packed his basket of supplies for this trip. "A man needs more than dried beef, cheese, and crackers, Sid," she'd said, shaking her head. "Why not ask Cora to make some decent sandwiches for you? Or maybe you could take one of her fruit pies." Then she'd sighed and added, "If I had a house with a kitchen, I'd bake a batch of corn bread or cook up a pot of stew you could take and reheat on the trail."

In the end, he'd allowed her to tuck several strings of licorice and a bag of gumdrops into the basket so he'd have a sweet treat. His heart had thrilled at her desire to fix something special for him. Surely that meant she was starting to look at him differently. And as soon as he had a nice house—including a kitchen with a real built-in cupboard and the best stove he could buy—he'd come right out and ask her to be his wife.

Caught up in his thoughts of his future with Sadie, he gave a start when the horses both lifted their noses and snorted. He squinted ahead against the bright morning sun and spotted a horse and rider, the horse's rump hidden by thick brush. As Sid approached, the rider urged the horse onto the road, holding up his hand. With the sun in his eyes, Sid didn't recognize the man at first, but when he called out, Sid knew the voice. He grunted in aggravation. Couldn't he get away from Goldtree's sheriff?

Sid set the brake but kept his hand on the wooden shaft. "What're you doin' out here, McKane?"

"Makin' my rounds," the man replied in a friendly manner.

Sid looked around. Not a farmhouse in sight. Why did the sheriff need to make rounds out here where nobody lived? He started to ask, but he caught the man peering into the back of the wagon.

McKane leaned over and patted the wooden top on one crate. "You headin' out on another delivery?"

Sid nodded.

"Baxter's been keeping you busy lately. Where to this time?"

Sid didn't see how his job as drayman was any of the sheriff's business, but he answered anyway. "Beloit."

McKane grabbed the brim of his hat and shifted it around a bit, as if he was scratching his head. "Isn't that east of here?"

"Yep. But the best roads are from Goldtree to Brittsville, then Brittsville to Beloit. A little longer, but easier on the horses." Sid had no idea why he bothered with such a lengthy explanation, but for reasons he couldn't explain he suddenly felt uneasy in the lawman's presence. "Takin' a load of beans to the liveryman over in Beloit."

McKane's eyebrows shot up. "Beans? To a liveryman?" He laughed, and his horse shied at the sound. Giving the big animal a pat on the neck, he added, "Seems like an odd thing for a liveryman to request."

Sid hadn't thought much about it when Asa told him where to take the crates, but now that he'd said it out loud, it did sound strange. He shrugged. "I just do what I'm told."

For long seconds, McKane stared into Sid's face, as if searching for something under Sid's skin. Sid got twitchy beneath the man's intense scrutiny. He wanted to get going.

Finally, McKane smiled. "Well, reckon I better send you on. Beloit's a good distance. Have a safe trip, Sid." He backed the horse away from the wagon and touched the brim of his hat before trotting his horse into the bushes again.

Sid released the brake and chirped to the horses. As the wagon rolled onward, he glanced over his shoulder and caught the sheriff watching after him. He experienced a little chill of unrest. The sheriff was up to something. But what?

27

Thad watched the freight wagon roll over a gentle rise, discounting Sid Wagner as a suspect. When he'd seen the neatly stacked crates in the back of the wagon, he'd wondered if Sid might be coming to the cave to fill those crates with jugs of beer. But no hollow thud sounded when he'd patted the crate—it was already full. Of beans. For the liveryman in Beloit.

Thad chuckled. It seemed a little strange, but who knew why a man who rented out wagons for a living wanted a couple dozen crates of beans. Maybe he ran a boardinghouse, too, and needed to feed his boarders. Maybe he just liked beans. Either way, Sid hadn't appeared to be interested in slowing that wagon until Thad stopped him, so he probably wasn't heading to the cave.

Sweat trickled down Thad's temple, and he reached for the water canteen on the back of the saddle. He guzzled a drink, grateful for the cool water on his parched throat. It promised to be a hot day—typical of late July in Kansas. But he intended to spend time at this post until he'd finally caught somebody heading to that make-shift underground brewery. He'd rather be in town than on this roadside, walking the streets instead of straddling this horse. It was quiet out here—lonely. He missed being able to tip his hat to the ladies, toss an errant ball back to a group of rowdy youngsters, and stop by the mercantile for a handful of jelly beans and bit of conversation with Miss Sadie.

His heart twisted. On Sunday, they'd had to cancel their picnic after the disaster in the mercantile. Hadn't seemed right for her to leave when the Baxters needed her help cleaning up. But it had taken his only chance to talk to her about the song she'd been singing. He felt sneaky, knowing about it without her awareness. The sooner he could talk to her, the better.

A rustle caught his attention. Somebody was coming. But not along the road—through the brush. The horse nickered, and Thad stroked the animal's neck, whispering, "Hush now." Thad's pulse tripped into double beats. He slid from the saddle, catching the horse's reins and wrapping them loosely around the closest sapling. The horse rolled his eyes, tossing his head.

"Shhh, boy," Thad intoned, his senses alert.

The rustle came again, closer this time. Thad inched around the horse, placing his feet carefully to avoid alerting the intruder to his presence. Off to his right, he spotted a movement. Another rustle, followed by the thrashing of brush. Thad crouched, his fingers flexing in anticipation.

Then when the leafy branches moved again, he let out a whoop of warning and leaped directly into the visitor's pathway.

Sadie placed the final bolt of cloth on the fabric table, then raised her apron skirt and wiped her brow. The heat was unbearable today. Not even opening both the front and back doors to allow a cross breeze helped. And the gusts of hot wind carried in dust as well as blew the little paper signs advertising the week's specials from their restraining tacks.

How far might Sid have traveled by now? Had the wind slowed him down? He must be miserable, high on that wagon seat with the sun beating down and grit peppering him. And how much more miserable he'd be when he learned she'd agreed to court Thad. She wished she'd had the chance to talk to him before he'd left. The longer she waited, the more likely it became he'd hear it from someone else. The news would hurt him—something that pained her—but she had to let him know. His comment about finding her something special in Beloit told her he hadn't released his desire to become her beau.

Sadie glanced at the ticking wall clock and sighed. Closing time was still two hours away. How she wished she could go to Republican Creek, which flowed a quarter mile behind town, and dip her feet in the cool water. Perhaps

stretch out along the bank beneath some shelter-
ing cottonwoods and sleep the remainder of the
afternoon. But tasks awaited attention.

Wearily, she turned toward the counter. Just as
she took a step, the screen door flew open, causing
the little bell to clang wildly. Gasping in fear—
had the mischief makers returned?—she spun
toward the door. Thad stepped over the threshold
and stopped in a wide-legged pose, his hat in his
hand and his hair standing in sweat-damp spikes.
A pungent, telltale odor accompanied him.

Sadie pinched her nose and spluttered, her
eyes watering. "Oh, Thad . . . phew!"

Miss Melva bustled from the corner of the store,
waving both hands at him. "Fool man, get outta
here! You're gonna stink up the whole place!"

From the other side of the store, Miss Shelva
began coughing. "Out! Out!"

Thad didn't budge. "I need tomatoes. Lots of
'em. Many as you've got."

Miss Melva planted her hands on his chest,
gave him a push, then skittered away, her face
pinched with distaste. "We'll deliver 'em to your
office. Now get out afore that stink fixes itself to
every piece o' merchandise in the store!"

Thad departed in a stiff-legged gait. The Baxter
twins fluttered around in confusion for a few
minutes, fanning their shelves of goods as if to
chase away the lingering odor. Sadie thought
their actions ludicrous, but she couldn't blame

them for wanting to rid the store of the stench. Nature surely possessed no more unpleasant aroma than the one excreted by skunks.

Miss Melva charged into the storeroom and returned with an empty crate. Flinging her arm toward the back door, she said, "Sadie, go fetch Asa's wheelbarrow an' hike it on in here."

Miss Shelva dove into the aisle where canned goods lined the shelves. "We'll fill it up with every last can o' tomaters in stock, but I don't reckon it'll be near enough."

Miss Melva cringed. "You're right, Sister. The sheriff's a good-sized man. Then there's his clothes, too."

"Probably need to go house to house an' see if any ladies'll be willin' to let loose o' some o' their home-canned tomaters."

"Seein' as how tomaters've been on the vine a good month already, surely folks around town'll have some to spare."

Sadie stood rooted in place, her head bobbing back and forth from sister to sister as she tried to keep up with their fast-paced conversation.

"Sadie, take the wheelbarrow an' bother every neighbor up an' down the street. Gather as many tomaters—canned or fresh from the vine—as you can find," Miss Shelva directed.

Miss Melva pointed at Sadie. "Then take it all to the sheriff's office an' lend him a hand."

Sadie pressed both palms to her bodice. "Me?"

" 'Course you." Miss Melva balled her hands on her scrawny hips. "Only fittin' you do it, seein' as you an' the sheriff have taken up company with one another."

"Neither Sister nor me could do it," Miss Shelva added, her thin face flooding with color. "Why, we're maiden ladies. What would folks think?"

Sadie was a maiden lady, too, even if she were being courted by Thad. She spluttered, "But . . . but . . ."

Miss Shelva gave her a little push. "Just do as we say."

Sadie reluctantly plodded in the direction of the back door.

Miss Melva called after her, " 'Sides, Sheriff's gonna need his clothes cleaned, too. He can just plunk himself an' his clothes in the washtub. Nothin' unseemly 'bout you scrubbin' a fully dressed man."

Despite Miss Shelva's proclamation, Sadie nearly died of embarrassment when she knelt next to the iron washtub where Thad hunkered, his knees under his chin. He'd dragged the tub out to the sparse patch of grass between the office and a storage shed rather than being closed in his tiny living space with the awful smell. But even outside, with the wind blowing, Sadie couldn't escape the stench.

"I wish I had a clothespin," she said as she

emptied a quart jar of Mrs. Rahn's last year's tomatoes over Thad's head. The inside of her nose felt fairly singed.

"You think it's bad now, you ought to have been there when the consarn animal let loose." He hunched his shoulders while Sadie used a bath brush to grind the tomatoes into the fabric of his shirt. "I couldn't even see, my eyes watered so bad. An' the horse took off, leavin' me afoot." He grunted. "Took me a full two hours to walk back to town, all the while breathing in what the skunk sprayed all over me."

Sadie groped blindly for another jar, her nose pressed against the shoulder of her dress. Her fingers located one, and she popped the wire latch. "It's hard to imagine one small animal being capable of creating such a powerful aroma."

"Wasn't just one," Thad groused. "I startled a whole family—mama an' four babies. An' they all let loose."

A picture formed in Sadie's head, and before she could stop herself, a snort of laughter blasted. She covered her mouth, but her entire body shook as mirth overtook her.

Thad glowered at her. "It isn't funny, Sadie. Folks clear over in Ottawa County are probably asking themselves right now, 'Where's that smell comin' from?' "

Sadie laughed harder. Amazing how good it felt to laugh. She couldn't recall the last time she'd laughed so freely. She begrudged the cause of her amusement—poor Thad, suffering so—but she gloried in the ability to give way to uninhibited laughter. Wasn't there a verse in Proverbs that declared laughter was good medicine? Weight seemed to fall from her shoulders with each jostle of uncontrolled humor.

Thad, however, was not amused. "I mean it. Stop laughin'. How'm I gonna be able to surprise anybody with skunk smell all over me? It'll probably never come out of my leather vest or my hat. Dumb animal just ruined my chance of sneak—" He broke off, clamping his jaw tight.

Sadie buried her face in her apron to bring her laughter under control. Her voice muffled, she asked, "Ruined what?"

Thad folded his arms over his chest, hunkering down. "Nothin'. Never mind." He sent a crinkled-nose glare in her direction. "Can't you hurry? My legs are cramping up in here."

She swallowed another chuckle. He reminded her of one of her younger brothers, his lower jaw poked out and brow all crunched in a pout. But she could hardly blame him for being grumpy, considering what he'd been through. Biting down on the end of her tongue to avoid so much as a snicker, she dumped every last can and jar of tomatoes over Thad.

Bits of tomato caught in his hair and on his shoulders. Juice dripped down his face, chest, and back. He resembled a chicken in a stew pot, but she kept the comment to herself and used his bath brush to grind the tomatoes into his clothing, hair, and exposed skin.

An hour later, he dumped the tomato mess into the alley, turned the tub upside down beside the shed, then walked over. Sadie hid a smile at the little trail of tomato bits he left behind. He propped his fists on his hips. "Well? Do I smell any better?"

Truthfully, he still stunk. Of skunk *and* tomato. But at least the pungency of the skunk odor had been mellowed. "It's better," she said. She began stacking the empty jars in the crate to return them to their owners. Thad reached for the empty cans scattered across the yard and tossed them into the wheelbarrow.

Sadie smiled, finding pleasure in working side by side with Thad under the hot sun, the wind tousling their hair. "You'll want to change out of those clothes as quickly as possible," she advised. "Wash them and use a vinegar rinse—I seem to recall Mama using vinegar to battle fierce odors. Then hang them in the shed for a few days to let them air out."

Thad smacked another can into the wheel-barrow with such force it bounced out again. With a little grunt, he scooped it up and put it back. "Wish I could hang myself in the shed." He sniffed his own arm and grimaced. "Enough stink on me yet to offend all of Five Creeks Township."

Placing the last jar in the crate, she squinted up at him. "Where did you encounter the skunk family?"

"It doesn't matter."

She coughed to cover a chortle. How could he be so attractive even in his grumpiness? She started to lift the crate, but he darted to her side and took it from her. He put it on top of the cans in the wheelbarrow, taking care not to rattle the jars. Even in a state of temper, he was a gentleman and exercised restraint. She believed she'd been given a glimpse of Thad's character in the last hour, and she liked what she saw.

But she didn't like how he smelled. She skittered to the other side of the wheelbarrow to be upwind of him. Offering a smile, she said, "Well, I suggest you avoid that area from now on. After you scared her babies, that mama skunk will probably be on the lookout for you." She'd hoped her teasing comment might raise a smile, but he stared into her face, his lips set in a grim line and his forehead furrowed. His solemn-yet-puzzled expression made her stomach churn with apprehension. "Is something wrong?"

He took a step forward. She automatically retreated—not out of fear of him, but to avoid the unpleasant aroma trapped on his skin and tomato-stained clothing. His frown deepened. "Sadie, there's something I need to ask you."

Why did he sound so ominous? She licked her dry lips. "A-all right."

"It's about—"

"Whoo-*ee!*" The exclamation blasted from Sadie's left. She shifted her gaze and spotted Mr. Baxter at the back corner of the sheriff's office. He waved his pudgy hand in front of his face, his mouth puckered up as if he'd just bitten into a sour pickle. "Who got skunk-sprayed?" Then he looked Thad up and down and chuckled. "Reckon I already know." Shaking his head, he strode forward a few feet, keeping a fair distance between himself and Thad. "All them tomater stains give ya away."

Thad glanced down his own length and grimaced. "I need to get changed." He started toward the back door of the office, then paused and looked at Mr. Baxter. "Did you need me for something?"

The other man shook his head, his lank gray hair flopping. Two oiled strands caught in the breeze and stood up like a pair of crooked cockroach antennae. "Nope. Come to fetch Miss Sadie here. Got some business to discuss with her."

Thad sent Sadie a disgruntled look. Sadie nodded in understanding. Duty always seemed to steal their time together. He blew out a breath. "Go ahead, Sadie. I'll come by the mercantile tomorrow after closing. Hopefully, I'll smell fresh enough to be around decent folk by then.

We can go to Cora's for supper. An' talk." The last word carried a hidden meaning.

Sadie flicked a glance at Mr. Baxter. Tomorrow was Tuesday—opening night of his special shows. Apparently Thad wasn't on the invitation list or he'd know she wasn't available. Mr. Baxter had warned her not to speak of the Tuesday night shows, so she didn't know how to respond.

Mr. Baxter coughed out a laugh, aiming his leering grin in Sadie's direction. "Reckon congratulations are in order. My sisters tol' me how you an' the sheriff've decided to keep company. Fine match, fine match." His mouth formed a grin, but his eyes glimmered with something other than approval.

Thad took another step toward the building. "Well, if you'd excuse me, I'm gonna—"

"Sheriff, hate to say it, but Miss Sadie ain't gonna be free for supper tomorrow night." Mr. Baxter's grin turned sly. "Her an' me . . . we got plans."

Sadie cringed. Mr. Baxter made it sound as though the two of them were in cahoots together. Which, she supposed, was true. But his tone seemed intended to garner a jealous response.

Thad slipped his thumb into his trouser pocket and squinted at Mr. Baxter. "That so?"

"Uh-huh. Been set for a couple weeks already, so your supper'll have to wait." Mr. Baxter sputtered out another fake cough. "Prob'ly best anyway. That skunk smell ain't goin' nowhere for a while. Cora'll chase you out of her café with a wooden spoon, you go an' smell up the place."

Sadie looked in confusion from man to man. Why was Mr. Baxter deliberately baiting Thad? The muscles in Thad's jaw clenched and unclenched, then he shook his head, releasing a rueful chuckle.

"I reckon you're right, Asa. Last person I'd want to rile is Cora, seeing as how she feeds me on a daily basis." He shifted his attention to Sadie, but his expression didn't soften. "Since you're busy tomorrow, I'll stop by sometime Wednesday an' we'll figure out an evening for us to maybe go for a ride. Do some talking. That sound good?"

She and Thad, all alone, away from town . . . Did eagerness or foreboding account for her scampering pulse? Sadie nodded. "That's fine, Thad." She reached for the wheelbarrow handles.

Mr. Baxter quickly swaggered over and pushed in front of her. "Here now, little lady, you shouldn't be doin' heavy work such as totin' wheelbarrows. You just step aside an' let me take care of this." He flashed a grin at Thad. "Bye, now, Sheriff. Stay away from skunk dens now, you hear?"

28

Asa scuffed his feet, stirring up dust, as he propelled the wheelbarrow toward the mercantile. Hot wind blasted him, adding to his temper. What'd the little singer gal think she was doing, taking up with the sheriff? Sure as the sun rose in the east, she'd slip and talk about the Tuesday night shows. Wasn't it enough some ornery fellas had torn apart the mercantile, trying to find Asa's stash of beer? He'd managed to persuade the sheriff that the whole thing had been a prank, but the lawman would surely nose around if Miss Wagner yapped. Then all of Asa's carefully laid plans would shatter like a wine bottle elbowed off a table.

He managed to hold his irritation inside until they'd reached the back side of the mercantile. Then he whirled on the girl and hissed, "Whaddaya think you're doin', girlie?"

Miss Wagner's eyes widened. She zipped a quick look back and forth before aiming those big blue eyes on him again. "I . . . I don't understand."

"Agreein' to be courted by the sheriff." Although he held his volume to a near-whisper, he injected venom into his tone. Scowling fiercely, he pointed his finger directly at her face. "You're askin' for trouble. A man bent on courtin' wants every minute he can steal with his intended. How you gonna keep silent 'bout your Tuesday night singin'?"

She worried her lip between her teeth, dropping her gaze to the dry grass at their feet. "I'm not sure. I don't want to lie to him. . . ."

"Well, you sure can't tell him the truth!" Asa's volume raised a notch. He clenched his fists and deliberately lowered his voice. "Listen, girlie, I pay you good to work for me. Part of the reason I pay good is I demand a lot. Most important thing I expect is loyalty. An' I don't see how you can be loyal to me *an'* be spendin' time with the sheriff. So you're gonna have to decide which you'd rather have—a beau or a job."

She stared at him, her hands wringing together. She opened her mouth as if to protest, but then she snapped it shut and nodded. Her head low, she said, "Y-yes, sir."

That was more like it. "All right, then." Asa waved toward the back door. "Best get inside. Mercantile's closin' soon, an' my sisters'll want your help with cleanin' up. But right after supper you get on down to the singin' room an' practice."

She lifted her head so quick he wondered that her neck didn't pop. "Will you listen to the practice, the way you did last week?"

Asa pulled back, crunching his face. "What're you talkin' about?"

Miss Wagner hunched her shoulders. "I meant to ask you earlier, but we've not had time alone." She whisked another glance across the empty yard as if she expected someone to jump out of the bushes at her. "Last week when I was practicing the songs you . . . you gave me, someone came down to the cellar and listened at the door. I thought it was you."

Something began to boil in Asa's middle. "I been too busy to sit in an' listen to your practices." Between sneaking to the cave at night to check his stills and bottling liquor during the day, Asa hardly had time to draw an extra breath. He leaned close, scowling. "You *sure* somebody come down?"

The girl chewed her lower lip and nodded.

Asa huffed out an aggravated breath. Couldn't've been his sisters—they were too scared to go down under the ground. And Sid had been out of town, making deliveries. But he had an idea who might've been sneaking around, checking on the girl. He curled his hands into fists and stifled a growl. "Well, don't you be worryin' none. Nobody'll bother you anymore. You just make sure you're good an' ready for tomorrow night. Wanna open with a rip-roarin' show guaranteed to bring the fellas back again an' again. Now scoot."

The girl skittered inside without a backward

glance. Asa cackled to himself. When he was a kid, he'd noticed only the tall, good-looking boys got the girls to do their bidding. Asa might be short and homely with a balding pate and a paunchy gut, but he had one very pretty girl in the palm of his hand. He swaggered around the building to the hitching post, where Percival drowsed in the late-afternoon sun, the silver bangles on his saddle gleaming like stars.

With tugs on the reins and a few pushes on Percival's hindquarters, he maneuvered the big stallion alongside the porch railing. Grunting with exertion, he climbed from the boardwalk onto the railing and then heaved himself into the saddle. Percival snorted as Asa's weight settled on his back, and Asa bounced his heels on the horse's ribs to show his lordship.

"Giddap now, Percival. Home." Asa jerked the reins, turning Percival toward the road. The horse obediently broke into a trot, and Asa held tight. He kept his gaze aimed ahead, but even so he was aware of folks giving him a look as the horse made his majestic exit from town.

Asa smirked. So he wasn't a handsome man. Looks faded. But money was power. He had money. Lots of money. And lots of power. Wouldn't those school bullies be jealous when Butterball Baxter returned to High Ridge, Ohio, and built his mansion smack-dab in the center of town? He sniggered, imagining their stunned faces. Then he sobered. Before he could see his plans through, he had to eliminate the one barrier to his success.

He gave Percival's glossy sides a kick, hurrying the big horse into a steady lope. "Giddap there. I got work to do."

Sadie held the little flickering lantern in front of her and tiptoed up the stairway, determined not to rouse Miss Melva or Miss Shelva. Holding her breath, she made her way along the short hallway to her room and then closed her door behind her with a gentle click. Once inside her room, she placed the lantern on the top of the dresser, released her lungful of air, and cast all caution aside.

With jerky motions, she yanked the black velvet hat from her head and tossed it on the little chair in the corner. The red dress quickly followed. She skimmed out of her slip and chemise, leaving them in a heap on the floor, and whisked into her nightgown. The buttons proved tricky, her trembling fingers refusing to cooperate, but finally she fastened the gown to her chin. Snatching up her brush, she attacked her hair with vicious strokes, a feeble attempt to remove every remnant of the past three hours from her memory. But after several minutes of frantic brushing, she'd accomplished little more than adding a stinging scalp to an equally aching heart.

Setting the brush aside, she sank onto the bed. Tears pricked. If she filled the washtub and scrubbed herself with a bar of St. Croix soap, would she feel clean again? Surely Thad's skunk smell was preferable to the indecorous essence she now carried. Burying her face in her hands, she leaned over her lap and tried to erase the images from her mind. But they played out before her closed lids, as persistent as the little moth now bouncing against the lantern's globe.

The beginning of the evening had felt like any other performance, except for the all-male audience—an audience that changed frequently, with men coming and going through the doorway Mr. Baxter had exposed by tying back the curtains. With each visit to the other side of the door, the men became rowdier, clumsier, more jovial. And more leering. She shuddered, shrinking into herself as she recalled the sour-smelling man who'd joined her onstage toward the end of her performance. The moment he slung his arm around her shoulders, two others jumped up and yanked him away, starting a scuffle that lasted nearly ten minutes before Mr. Baxter got them settled down again.

Dropping her hands, she sat straight up and sucked in several breaths, trying to clear her senses of the sickly sweet odor that had hung over the opera room by the night's end. The strength of the stench and the boisterousness of the men had increased at the same rate until Sadie wanted to run from the room and hide. Although Papa hadn't been a drinking man, many of the other miners were. She'd witnessed their behavior when they'd sampled what Mama called the devil's brew. So Sadie knew the men were imbibing on the other side of that door. She also knew it was illegal. How had she gotten herself tangled up in providing entertainment for drunkards?

With a groan, she fell sideways onto the bed and pulled up her knees, curling into a ball. The weeks stretched ahead of her, each requiring another performance under similar circumstances. How would she survive? "I can't do it. I can't sing to men who ogle me and sway in their seats and shout out crude comments. I must tell Thad—"

She snapped her jaw shut, sending the thought from her mind. She couldn't tell Thad what was happening in the opera room on Tuesday nights. Mr. Baxter would be arrested, and she'd lose her singing job. She must sing. She must send the money home to Mama.

Rolling to her other side, she peered through the meager lantern glow at the family portrait. Her gaze fell on Papa's dear, handsome, steadfast face. Tears welled in her eyes, distorting his sweet image. "Oh, Papa, this long-held dream to be a singer . . . it's become my nightmare. We thought my coming here was an answer to prayer, but now . . ." An anguished wail left

Sadie's throat. "Why did you have to get hurt and die? I need you. I *need* you . . ."

In the morning, Sadie frowned at her image in the little mirror above the dresser. Red-rimmed, puffy eyes stared back from a pale face. She pinched her cheeks until she raised a rosy hue. Then she dipped a handkerchief in her washbowl, wrung it out, and held it over her aching eyes for several minutes. She peeked again. The ministrations had accomplished little. She sighed. Did she really believe some cool water would hide the effects of a sleepless night?

She twisted her hair into a coil and secured it with pins, her stomach whirling in apprehension. Thad had promised to come by and arrange a time for them to go for a drive. So they could talk. Mr. Baxter had demanded she end her courtship with the town's sheriff, and now that she'd involved herself in illegal dealings, she had no choice. Spending time with Thad, holding the secret inside, would be too difficult. She must break all ties with Thad.

But would she find the strength to do so? Although she'd only known him a short time, she felt drawn to him. She admired him, respected him, and felt safe with him. He didn't shower her with flowery praise or offer little gifts of adoration, yet she knew he cared for her. She saw it in his eyes and in the tenderness of his smile. In his presence, she experienced the contentedness of homecoming. Telling Thad she couldn't accept his courtship would be even harder than continuing to sing on Tuesday nights. But she would do it. For Mama and the children, she would do it.

She left her room but headed straight down the stairs rather than going to the kitchen for breakfast. Miss Melva and Miss Shelva would scold, but she couldn't eat. Dread thoroughly filled her middle. Maybe she'd have room for food after she'd talked to Thad. Surely this awful lump of trepidation would lift once she'd followed Mr. Baxter's orders. She went through her usual routine of unlocking the front door and propping it open. A rain-scented breeze coursed through the screen door.

Sadie stepped to the edge of the boardwalk and peeked at the sky. Gray clouds hung in rippling waves, resembling dozens of sheets suspended by their corners. She shivered, even though the air was warm and moist. A summer storm was brewing. She hoped Sid wouldn't run into foul weather as he traveled back from Beloit. And she hoped the stormy sky wasn't a sign of how Thad would respond when she told him he could no longer court her.

She turned to go back into the store, but her nose caught the faint whiff of skunk. Her mouth went dry, and she turned slowly. Thad stood at the corner of the mercantile. The sight of him—green eyes shaded by the brim of the familiar cowboy hat and six-pointed star shining on his chest—sealed her feet in place. She wanted to smile a greeting, but her face felt frozen. So she stared, unblinking, waiting for him to speak.

He lifted his hand and removed his hat, but he didn't approach. "Sadie . . ."

She gulped. "Thad." Tangling her hands in her apron, she forced her clumsy tongue to form words. "How are you this morning?"

A rueful grin lifted one corner of his lips. "Still stinky. That's why I'm staying over here."

Sadie wished she could giggle at his statement, but she couldn't summon even a smidgen of levity. She flicked a glance skyward. "A storm is brewing. Guess that means we . . . we won't be able to take that ride this evening after all."

He turned his gaze toward the clouds. Bouncing his hat against his thigh, he looked at her again. "No need to be so quick to abandon our plans. I could rent that covered buggy from Bill Kimbrough. It'd keep us fairly dry, I think, if it's still raining by evening."

Sadie had seen the mayor and his wife riding around town in the black leather Phaeton buggy and had wondered what it would be like to sit beneath the fringed canopy on the narrow, tufted seat with Thad. Thanks to Mr. Baxter's demands, she'd never know. "I . . . I don't think so."

His brows beetled, but she sensed that puzzlement rather than anger created the reaction. "How come?"

Guilt took a throttlehold on her heart. She couldn't meet his gaze. So she shifted her face slightly, peering beyond his shoulder. "I . . . I don't have time. I have to w-work." Bits and pieces of last night's performance returned to haunt her.

"Mercantile closes at six. Bedtime's at—what?—nine-thirty or ten?" Thad's gentle voice held a teasing note. "Seems as though we'd be able to fit an hour-long drive in there."

"I know, but . . ."

"Are you like a cat—get all ruffled up if you get wet?"

The first splat of fat raindrops landed on the street. The heavy drops left little dents behind. Sadie felt as though his sweet teasing left bruises on her heart. She wished he'd get frustrated. Demanding. Indignant. Then it would be easier to send him away. "No, I'm not afraid of the rain."

His expression turned serious. "Sadie, I've been needing to talk to you about something. I don't want to put it off any longer. It's important."

She swallowed. "I'm sorry, Thad. I just can't . . . tonight."

"Well, then, how about tomorrow?"

"Not tomorrow either."

He flicked the hat back and forth against his

trouser leg, the soft *whish-whish* competing with the patter of raindrops landing on the porch roof overhead. "Friday an' Saturday nights you have to sing, so how about Sunday afternoon? I'll reserve the buggy." A faint grin creased his smooth-shaven cheek. "By then, I oughtta be fully rid of all the skunk smell, an' this rain will have cleared. We'll have a nice drive."

Agony twisted her chest. "Not Sunday either."

He sighed, the first hint of impatience. "Well, then, you pick the day an' time."

She wove her fingers together and pressed her hands to her trembling stomach. "That's the problem, Thad. I can't choose a day or time. I'm . . . I'm just too busy. And . . ." Sucking in a breath of fortification, she finished in a rush. "It isn't fair of me to always put you off, so . . . so maybe . . ."

Despite his stated intention to maintain distance between them, he strode forward. Dropping his hat onto the porch floor, he took hold of her upper arms. He dipped his knees and looked directly into her face. "Are you saying you'll *never* go driving with me?"

Sadie's chin quivered. Her chest grew so tight it hurt to breathe. *Help me. Help me,* her thoughts begged. Her throat closed, her tongue too thick and clumsy for speech. So she nodded mutely.

"But why?"

His genuine confusion nearly broke Sadie's

heart. But what could she say? At least Thad would never witness her in that red satin dress, singing lusty songs.

Apparently he wearied of waiting for an answer, because he released her and took one backward step. His eyes glinted, his irises darkening to evergreen. "I thought we were building something special, but . . ." He bent over stiffly and retrieved his hat, slapping it onto his head in one smooth motion. "I guess I was wrong. All right, Miss Sadie. I won't bother you anymore."

He turned and strode away, the thud of his bootheels on the planked boardwalk matching the first rumble of thunder.

29

Somehow Sadie made it through Wednesday and Thursday without breaking down. But it took every bit of self-control she possessed. Although Thad didn't set foot in the mercantile, she saw him everywhere. Each time she glimpsed the jar of candy sticks, she envisioned his fingers grasping a sackful of the striped treats to share with the town's youngsters. In a green bolt of calico, she saw the color of his eyes. While organizing a shipment of men's razors in the glass case on the counter, her fingers brushed the soft velvet backing and immediately she thought of the softness of Thad's mustache against her lips.

She'd sent him away, but she couldn't escape him.

Miss Melva and Miss Shelva clucked over her like a pair of overprotective hens, aware that Sadie's heart was breaking. They threatened to march on down to the sheriff's office and give Thad a good tongue-lashing, but Sadie managed to hold them at bay. It warmed her that the spinster twins were willing to stand up for her, but her heartache was her own doing—not Thad's. And she told them so, earning a fresh round of questions she couldn't answer.

Oh, how she wished she could tell them about the activities in the mercantile's cellar on Tuesday nights. Unburdening herself would relieve the weight of responsibility. But telling them would be selfish. They adored their brother. It would kill them to know he took part in illegal activities. Their ignorance saved them from distress and also allowed them to be innocent of any wrong-doing. She couldn't tell anyone. Except Sid.

She counted down the hours to her cousin's return. Thankfully she had no need to hurt him with news of her courtship with Thad. Instead, she would share her concerns about Mr. Baxter's Tuesday night shows. Together they would find a solution to the problem.

On Thursday, about a half hour from closing time, the little bell above the mercantile door jangled. Sadie, busy stacking hosiery in a basket in the back corner of the store, didn't bother to look up until Miss Shelva screeched, "Sadie! Your cousin's here an' wants to see you!"

Sid! Sadie dropped the rolled stockings, which bounced across the floor. Stepping over the fallen items, she flew around the shelves and straight into Sid's surprised embrace. The moment she buried her face in the curve of his shoulder, tears spurted.

His low chuckle vibrated. "Did'ja miss me?"

Miss Shelva answered while Sadie continued to hide in Sid's musty-smelling shirt collar. "She's been moony all week. She's sure as shootin' been missin' *somebody*."

Sadie knew the someone to whom Miss Shelva referred, but Sid obviously thought otherwise. His arms tightened on Sadie, the hug possessive. He whispered, "I missed you, too."

A strong hand curled around Sadie's upper arm and pulled her free of Sid's hold. Miss Melva kept a grip on Sadie while she glowered at Sid. "This girl's in need of a little cossetin'. Take her next door, make her eat some peach pie at Cora's, an' then bring her back with a smile on her face."

Sid beamed. "Yes, ma'am!" He held out his elbow. "You heard the lady. Let's go, Sadie."

"But . . . but I'm still on duty." Sadie looked from Miss Melva to Miss Shelva.

Miss Shelva waved both hands at Sadie. "Go! You're just about useless right now anyway, what with your mind on other things." Although her words were blunt, her tone wasn't unkind.

Miss Melva leaned down and rasped in Sadie's ear, "Best cure for a heartache is time with an attentive fella. So go on now. Find your smiler again." She gave Sadie a little push toward Sid. "Take good care o' our girl now, y'hear?"

"I will." Sid caught Sadie's hand and placed it in the bend of his elbow. He escorted her onto the boardwalk, but instead of leading her to Cora's, he took her around the corner to the alleyway. Then he captured her in another hug. He sighed against her hair. "Ah, Sadie, makes me so happy to have you run to me that way. The whole time I was gone on this trip, I was thinkin' about you. An' I—"

Sadie wriggled loose. "Sid, I have to talk to you."

He grinned at her. "Why, sure. That's what we're doing—talkin'."

"About something *important*."

His eyes sparkled. "I got somethin' important on my mind, too."

Sadie let out a long sigh. "Sid, please . . . can we go somewhere private?" She glanced up and down the alley. Although no one was nearby, she still felt too vulnerable out in the open.

Sid slipped his arm around her waist and urged her back toward the street. "Tell you what, Asa's expectin' me. I need to take the wagon to his place. You can ride out with me."

Apprehension struck so fiercely she jolted. She started to protest, but Sid went on. "We can talk on the road—it'll be just the two of us. Nice an' private. All right?"

Although still hesitant about seeing Mr. Baxter, she offered a jerky nod. Sid helped her into the wagon. He settled beside her, released the brake, and took up the reins. With a broad smile, he chirped to the horses, and the wagon rolled forward.

Sadie waited until they'd left the town behind before shifting sideways on the seat to face her cousin. "Sid, I sang Tuesday night in the opera room."

Sid shot her a quick, interested look. "How'd it go?"

Sadie swallowed the bitter taste that filled her mouth. "Awful." She told him about the open doorway and the odor wafting from the other part of the cellar. She described the change in the men after trips into the other room. His face hardened when she shared some of the remarks the raucous audience members made while she sang. She finished, "I don't know what to do. Mr. Baxter is certainly providing liquor to the Tuesday night customers. I need this job, but I can't participate in something illegal."

Sid clenched his jaw. His eyes turned steely. "No, you can't."

Hope ignited in her chest. "So you'll talk to him? You'll fix things?"

"Don't worry, Sadie." Sid transferred the reins to one hand and placed his free hand over hers, which she clutched together in her lap. "I'll fix things."

Sid drew Hec and Rudy to a halt outside the barn. He wished he'd left Sadie in town, where she'd be safe from any fracas that might erupt between himself and his boss. Anger burned deep within his soul. He'd battled bullies for Sadie in the past, and even if Asa Baxter was his employer, he wouldn't hesitate to punch the man right in the nose if everything Sadie said was true. How could Asa have allowed her to be mistreated? Paying her five dollars for a few hours of work didn't earn him the right to let men abuse her.

He hopped down and held out his hands to Sadie. He assisted her to the ground, then pointed to a low bench tucked in the slanting shade of the tool shed. "Have a seat. I'll find Asa an' we'll get this Tuesday night show figured out."

"Thank you, Sid."

The relief shining in her blue eyes refueled Sid's determination to rescue her. "Don't worry," he said, offering a wobbly smile. "Everything'll be all right." He watched her scurry to the bench and seat herself. Then he lifted his hand in a wave and stalked into the barn. Even though Asa was a man of wealth, he seemed to spend more time in his barn than in his house. More often than not, Sid found him puttering around in the huge wooden structure when he returned the freight wagon after a delivery.

He entered the barn, blinking as his eyes adjusted to the lack of sunlight. Asa had closed all the shutters, shrouding the building in deep shadow. Squinting through the murky gloom, Sid called out, "Asa? You in here?"

A scraping sound reached Sid's ears, and he looked up to the loft. But no wisps of hay flitted down, alerting him to someone's presence. The muffled *scrrrape* came again, and Sid looked around in confusion. "Asa?"

Like a badger emerging from a hole, Asa's head popped up from the hay-strewn floor. "Sid, that you?"

Sid strode forward, his brow furrowed. Up close, he noted steps carved of dirt leading downward. A wooden door folded back against the barn wall. Asa came all the way up, his feet scuffing on the dirt and creating the noise Sid had heard. He pointed to the hole. "You got a cellar in the barn?"

Asa smacked the door into place and kicked hay over the planked wood, effectively hiding it from sight. Then, swishing his hands together, he faced Sid. "You're back early. Everything go all right in Beloit?"

Sid shook his head as if to clear it. Was the man deaf? Or had he just chosen to ignore Sid's question? Well, two could play the change-the-subject game. Planting his fists on his hips, he shot Asa a challenging look. "Sadie told me about the Tuesday night show. Said half the fellas who came were drunk. You the one supplyin' 'em with liquor?"

To Sid's aggravation, Asa released a chortle. He pushed past Sid, crossing to disappear behind a stall wall. "So what if I am?"

Sid followed. He watched Asa wrestle a canvas sheet over a stack of crates. "Liquor's been outlawed in Kansas. You could get yourself in a heap o' trouble sellin' it. An' you're puttin' Sadie in harm's way, stickin' her in a room with a bunch of liquored-up men bent on a good time." When he considered what might have happened, indignation filled him. He marched forward and caught Asa's shoulder, spinning the man around. "You can't be expectin' her to stand on that stage an' entertain men who aren't in full control o' themselves."

Asa's beady eyes narrowed. He brushed his shoulder with pudgy fingers, as if removing Sid's touch from the black broadcloth. "Gettin' a mite pushy there, boy." His voice held a warning note. "You might wanna remember you work for me.

As does your cousin. An' if you wanna get paid, you—an' she—will do as you're told." He started for the center of the barn, but Sid stepped into his pathway.

"Ain't right." Sid forced the words past clenched teeth. "You can't be—"

"Can't?" Asa screeched louder than Sid had ever heard him. "*You* are tellin' *me* I can't run my business the way I see fit?" He threw back his head and laughed—a guttural sound.

"Yes," Sid said, "an' you best pay heed. 'Cause I won't let you do anything that'd hurt Sadie."

Still chuckling, Asa said, "That so? An' just how you think you're gonna stop me?"

Sid ground his teeth, battling the urge to plant his fist in Asa's beefy face. Before he could form a reply, Asa chuckled again.

"Boy, you got nerve, I'll say that for you. But you oughtta take a step back an' do some deep thinkin' before you say another word." Folding his arms over his chest, Asa smirked at Sid. "Way I see it, we're in this business together— you, me, an' your sweet little cousin."

Asa's conniving tone sent chills up Sid's spine. He frowned, his fists twitching. "How so?"

"Well, now, it's true I been makin' liquor. Beer an' wine—quality brew, both of 'em. Folks'd be hard pressed to find anything better. An' I got customers lined up from here to the borders of Nebraska an' Oklahoma, just waitin' to buy." Asa propped his elbow on the top rail of the stall. "Those Tuesday night shows? They're more for the men puttin' their hands to a deck of cards or bettin' on a roulette wheel than actually drinkin'."

Gambling? Sid gaped at Asa, uncertain he'd heard correctly. The man was breaking the law in every direction!

Asa continued calmly. " 'Course, havin' the liquor in their bellies does seem to loosen their purse strings. So plyin' 'em with drinks adds to my coffers quite nicely."

Sid shook his head. "But why involve Sadie?"

Asa snorted. "Pretty little gal like her is as much a draw as the beer, my boy. An' if somebody should come down the mercantile stairs, all they'll see is a bunch of men enjoyin' a special performance. She's my distraction, so to speak."

Sid quivered with the force of his fury. "Well, she ain't gonna be your distraction anymore. She won't be doin' those Tuesday shows."

Asa didn't even blink. "Oh yes, she will." He lowered his arm slowly, his knowing leer fixed on Sid's face. "You know good as me how much she wants to sing. How much she *needs* to sing to provide for her poor widowed mama an' all those fatherless tykes at home." Asa *tsk*ed, shaking his head. "Why, what'll her family do if she stops? Starve, most likely. She don't want that on her head."

Sid reached out and grabbed Asa's coat front,

wadding the fabric in his hands. Nose to nose with Asa, he growled, "She ain't gonna sing on Tuesdays no more. An' I'm gonna tell Sheriff McKane what you're doin' down in that singin' room."

"You watch yourself, boy." Asa planted his hands on Sid's chest and pushed. Sid stumbled backward, and Asa straightened his coat. "She *is* gonna sing, an' that's final." Then he replaced his scowl with a knowing grin, folding his arms over his chest. "As for tattlin' to our fine sheriff . . . you ain't gonna do it. You're in just as deep as I am."

"Me? How so?"

"Makin' an' distributin' liquor's against the law, right? Well, I might be the one makin' it, but you been the one distributin' it."

Sid's heart kaboomed in his chest. "What?"

"Them crates you been takin' to Abilene an' Beloit? Wine. All wine." Asa ambled toward the barn's wide opening. "If you turn me in, I'll just name you as my partner. You'll go down as quick as me. An' your dear little cousin'll come tumblin', too."

Sid pounded after Asa and blocked him from leaving the barn. "The sheriff won't believe I'm involved."

"You don't think so?" Asa stared at Sid as if he'd taken leave of his senses. "Who brought Sadie to town to perform in the opera house? Who's the one deliverin' crates of liquor to men across the state? The sheriff's gonna look at what you've done an' hang a guilty sign around your neck just as quick as a wink." He shook his head, cackling. "Boy, you ain't got a chance."

Sid's mind raced. As much as he hated to admit it, his actions could be read as helping Asa establish a gambling and drinking hall. He gritted his teeth, stifling a groan at his own ignorance. How could he have gotten Sadie into such a mess?

"Another thing . . ." Asa grabbed Sid's arm and dragged him into the bowels of the barn, well away from the sunlight-splashed opening. "That sheriff's gotten mighty snoopy. I think he might be spyin' on Sadie. He tried to court her."

Sid's heart caught. What all had gone on while he was on the road, unknowingly delivering Asa's home-brewed liquor?

"Havin' her as his intended would sure make it easy to pry information out of her. Somethin' needs to be done about that man afore he up an' arrests the whole lot of us."

Sid shook loose of Asa's grip. "What're you sayin'?"

"I'm sayin' we're all in danger of bein' thrown in the clink. You an' me bein' men, we'd probably come out of it unscathed, but what about Sadie? Little gal like her—bein' all shut up behind iron bars would just about kill her, I'd think. Like cagin' a wild bird."

Fear created a foul flavor on Sid's tongue.

"You wanna protect your cousin, don't you?" Asa's wheedling tone took on a hint of desperation that matched the feeling constricting Sid's chest. Sid nodded, and Asa flicked a glance over his shoulder, then advanced at Sid again. His hot breath touched Sid's face as he said, "Only one way to make sure we all stay safe. Gotta get rid of that sheriff."

30

Thad slid the crate holding his food stores from the shelf above his bed and peeked inside. A single can rolled around in the bottom of the crate. He plucked it out, grimaced, and threw it back in. No way could he make himself eat peaches right now. After jamming the crate into its spot on the shelf, he sank onto the lumpy mattress and let his head hang low.

The street was finally quiet. The echoing footsteps on the boardwalk—folks heading to the mercantile to attend the Friday night opera house performance—had nearly driven him to distraction earlier that evening. A part of him longed to join the townspeople, to listen to Sadie's lilting voice bring the songs to life. He'd listened to other good singers in his lifetime, but not until Sadie had he heard the songs with his heart. She sang with her soul, not just her voice— a rare gift. And she'd squandered it on a bawdy tune. Then she'd spurned him.

Jolting to his feet, Thad stomped to the front window and looked out across the empty street. The lonely view became representative of the hole in the center of his being. Why had she turned him away? From their first moments together, he'd felt a kinship with Sadie. She made him laugh. Made him feel strong and important. She wanted the same things he wanted. Something had changed her, and Thad needed to know what. He needed to know, so he could understand.

Lord, let me understand, because until I understand, I can't get her out of my heart.

In the meantime, he had a job to do. The mayor and the town council of Goldtree weren't paying him to moon over Sadie. He'd best catch their bootlegger and bring the man to justice. His gun and holster hung on a peg in his living quarters. Thad retrieved them and fastened the wide leather belt around his hips, the weight of the pistol heavy against his thigh. The weight of responsibility lay just as heavily on his shoulders.

So far his daytime observations hadn't turned up anyone traipsing out to the cave. Now he would watch the opening at night. He wouldn't be needed in town, not with nearly everyone enjoying Sadie's performance. Kimbrough had said he could borrow Thunder anytime, so he'd just saddle the horse, ride out, and camp at the cave. Maybe he'd finally catch whoever was responsible for those stills. And after he'd turned the perpetrator over to the mayor, he'd pack his bags and leave Goldtree. He didn't know where he'd go, but somewhere. Away from Sadie and the frustration of her rejection.

He plopped his hat on his head, wrinkling his nose at the slight aroma of skunk caught in the hat's fabric, and headed outside. He paused for a moment, angling his ear toward the mercantile. Sadie should be in the middle of her performance right now, but not a single note carried on the evening breeze. Asa had built those walls extra thick, making sure the sound stayed in the sing-ing room. Nobody'd be able to steal a listen—you had to pay your fifty cents to enjoy the show.

His toes tried to inch in the direction of the mercantile, but he got firm with them and pointed his feet toward the livery stable instead. *You got a job to do, McKane, just like Roscoe Hanaman's always telling you. So get to it.*

He saddled Thunder, then started to lift his foot to the stirrup. But he spotted a lantern hanging from a nail on a nearby upright post. He might need it. He grabbed it, slipped the wire handle over the saddle's horn, and then climbed aboard. "Let's go, Thunder." Minutes later, he and Thunder had left the town behind.

Two days of blazing sunshine had dried out the road after Wednesday's rain shower, but wagon wheels had sunk when the ground was wet, leaving deep ruts just wide enough to trap a horse's hoof. Thad didn't push the horse into a gallop—as much as he wanted to reach the cave before the sun slunk below the horizon, he wouldn't act rashly and injure a borrowed horse. Besides, the leisurely ride with the sky streaked a soft peachy-pink and a breeze carrying the scent of refreshed earth and budding plants did him some good. He felt the tension of the past days melt away the farther he got from town.

Thunder released a few snorts as they neared the spot where they'd encountered the skunk, but Thad bounced his heels on the horse's side and encouraged him to continue onward. He angled the animal off the road and through a break in the thick, scrubby trees and bushes. The brush slowed their passage, and Thad had to duck to avoid losing his hat to low-slung branches. His trousers got snagged more than once on prickly brush, but he pushed Thunder onward until he was only a few feet from the cave's opening.

"Whoa there, boy." Thad swung down and, after a quick perusal of the area, led Thunder behind a cluster of pin oak saplings. He tied the reins tightly to the trunk of one small tree, tested them to make sure they'd hold in case the horse got another start, then grabbed the lantern. He gave the animal's neck a pat before moving stealthily toward the cave.

Outside the black yawning mouth, he paused and lit the lantern. He'd extinguish it once he'd found a good hiding spot inside, but he needed to see to get in. He used his bootheel to strike a match, and the warm glow of the lantern promised Thad a well-lit path. Holding the lantern well away from his body, he ducked inside the cave.

He stifled a sneeze at the dank odor that greeted his nose. He moved past the first chamber and entered the second one, which was the largest of the three. Raising the lantern, he turned slowly, examining every detail of the space. On his last visit, he'd taken note of a stack of empty crates on the far wall and dozens of waiting jugs surrounding the still. Now the floor was empty of jugs, and the crates had been rearranged—lined up along the wall, two high. He peeked inside one crate and let out a whistle. Six jugs nestled inside the crate, each sealed with a fat tan cork.

Setting the lantern aside, Thad hooked his finger in a jug's handle and pulled it out. He squeaked the cork from the mouth and stuck his nose over the opening. The scent of a stout beer assaulted him. Crunching his face in distaste, he slapped the cork in place and examined the jug. Someone had glued on a paper label that proclaimed "High-Quality Molasses." Thad snorted.

He returned the jug to the crate, then moved

back into the opening chamber of the cave. He stepped past the quiet still, its coiling tubes cool to the touch, and focused on a hulking shape covered by a canvas in the farthest corner of the misshapen room. A peek under the heavy cover revealed a tower of empty crates. Crates intended to carry liquor to buyers. Liquor that would change men from docile to angry, from sensible to foolish, from men dedicated to family to men bent only on satisfying self.

Hot anger filled Thad's chest. It stung his pride to have this operation set up so close to the town where he served as lawman. He should batter the stills to bits. He snatched up one crate and held it over his head, ready to fling it at the still. His muscles straining to toss the crate with all his might, he paused. If he destroyed the stills, he wouldn't have evidence to show to a judge. Besides, a verse in the seventh chapter of Ecclesiastes advised that patience is better than pride.

Slowly, he lowered the crate and put it back on the stack. Then he tucked the canvas over the pile just as he'd found it. Drawing in a calming breath, he slipped into the narrow gap between the tall stack of crates and the damp wall. He blew into the lantern's globe, watching the flame flicker and die. Darkness surrounded him. He shivered as a feeling of aloneness fell over him. So many times as a boy, he'd huddled in his bed in a dark room, all alone, wishing his father would come home. And then, when Pa finally staggered into the room, he'd wished to be alone again.

He gave his head a shake, sending the memories far away. He wriggled into a more comfortable position. Black nothingness greeted his eyes. A muffled *brrrip-bip, brrrip-bip*—water droplets, probably from an underground stream—echoed from the deepest chamber. The wind whispered through the brush outside the cave's opening. Gentle sounds. Comforting sounds.

Let him show, his thoughts begged, reminding him of his oft-murmured boyhood prayer. *Let the bootlegger show,* he amended. Closing his hand over the gun's handle, he rested his head on the cold, smooth cave wall and sighed. He allowed his eyes to slide shut. Now he'd practice patience and wait.

Thad awakened with a jolt. His head bounced against something hard and immovable, and pain exploded in his temple. Rubbing his head, he opened his eyes and blinked into murky gray, disoriented. Where was he? Then the dank odor brought recognition. He stifled a groan as he realized he'd fallen asleep in the cave.

Carefully, he slid his hand across the ground until he located the lantern. A small tin of matches waited in his shirt pocket. He withdrew one matchstick and flicked it against his bootheel.

The flare of the match made him wince, but he squinted his eyes and touched the lantern's wick. Golden light filled the chamber. Thad unfolded himself, his muscles stiff, and stepped around the pile of crates.

The first room appeared the same as it had when he'd entered earlier, but he sensed something was different. His hips complained as he picked up the lantern and aimed it at the second chamber's jagged opening. A surprised exclamation left his lips. He stumbled forward, his gaze darting everywhere. At least a dozen of the crates containing jugs of beer were gone.

Thad stared, disgusted with himself. The bootlegger had come, and he'd slept right through it! He charged out of the cave and looked around, his eyes watering at the soft glow of early morning. Apparently, he'd slept all night. He rubbed his aching temple, chastising himself silently. Small wonder he'd fallen asleep. He hadn't rested for several nights. Not since Sadie had made clear she wouldn't accept his courtship. But even so, how could he have been careless enough to allow the bootlegger to take the goods from right under his nose?

He extinguished the lantern and trotted to the spot where he'd left Thunder tied. To his relief, the horse remained firmly tethered, saddle in place. Thad rubbed the beast's velvety nose. "I'm sorry, boy. Sure am glad no wildcat or bear came along. You'd have been helpless against an attack."

Guilt over his irresponsible behavior bowed Thad's shoulders. Some lawman he'd turned out to be, endangering a borrowed horse and sleeping on duty. Mayor Hanaman might take away his badge, and Thad wouldn't blame him. He had no excuse for letting the bootlegger get the slip.

"Well, time to 'fess up," he told Thunder. He started to heave himself into the saddle, but something caught his attention. The edge of a sheet of paper poked out from underneath the saddle's seat. Thad pulled it loose and unfolded it. A scrawled message greeted his eyes.

Hey sheruff. Or are you Rip Van Winkel. Ha. Ha. Hope you had Plessant Dreams.

Thad wadded the note and crammed it into his trouser pocket. *Ha. Ha.* A sneering laugh rang in his imagination. He clenched his jaw so hard his teeth hurt. With pounding steps, he marched to the cave and dragged the remaining jugs into the sunshine. One by one, he hefted the jugs over his head and flung them against a trio of boulders outside the cave entrance. His satisfaction grew along with the pile of shattered pottery. Pale golden liquid soaked into the ground, its stench permeating the entire area.

Only one jug remained, but instead of throwing it onto the ground with others, Thad tied it to the saddle horn. Then he marched inside the cave and yanked the tubing loose from all three stills. He kept one piece separate and twisted the remaining lengths of tubing into a snarl that would take years to unwind. He wrapped the remaining piece around the only undamaged jug. He'd give the items to the mayor when he returned to Goldtree.

Poking his boot toe into the stirrup, he pulled himself into the saddle and aimed Thunder for the road back to town. The lump of paper inside his pocket seemed to burn a hole through his pants. He pressed his palm to the offending note, the muscles in his shoulders tightening. The bootlegger probably thought he'd won. But he thought wrong.

It bruised Thad's pride to be caught sleeping, but he wouldn't slink away in shame. Not when somebody was breaking the law and making liquor available. And he knew what to look for now—jugs bearing a molasses label. He'd check every wagon coming into or leaving Goldtree. That bootlegger better not relax his guard. Thad wasn't finished yet—not by a long shot.

"I might have to concede on this battle," he said to the clear sky overhead, "but, God, as You are my witness, I will win the war."

31

"You have yourself a good day with Sid." Miss Melva stood on the boardwalk, grinning up at Sadie.

"I will." Sadie forced a bright tone, determined to assure her employer she'd be just fine. The Baxter sisters had done too much worrying over Sadie already.

Sid settled himself on the springed wagon seat beside Sadie as Miss Shelva sidled up beside her sister. "Stop somewheres purty along the road an' enjoy the things in that basket." Miss Shelva's lips curved into an exact replica of the smile gracing Miss Melva's face.

"Oooh, a picnic." Miss Melva hunched her skinny shoulders and giggled. "Just the thing to lift a gal's spirits."

Miss Shelva shook her head and clicked her teeth. "An' how would you know about that, Sister? You ever been on a picnic with a fella?"

Pink tinged Miss Melva's cheeks. "Well . . . no. But I come close that one time, remember? Harry Eugene asked me? Only you come down with the grippe an' Mama was a-feared I'd get it, too, so she made me stay home, an' he took Shirley Taylor instead."

"Oh, so I s'pose it's my fault you didn't never go on a picnic with Harry Eugene, is that what you're sayin'?"

Before the twins could launch into an all-out argument, Sadie called from her perch on the wagon seat, "Are you sure you won't need me today? I don't have to accompany Sid to Macyville." She ignored Sid's grunt of protest. "I can stay here and work."

"No, no," they chorused, flapping their hands at her in perfect unison. Miss Melva said, "You ain't took a Saturday off since you started workin' for us. Time you had yourself a break."

"An' Macyville's close enough you'll be back in time for the singin' tonight," Miss Shelva added. "Not many o' Sid's trips are quick ones, so you'd best go while you can."

As much as she looked forward to some time away from Goldtree—an entire day of not having to worry about encountering Thad on the board-walk—Sadie battled guilt about leaving the two women shorthanded. "If you're sure . . ."

"We're for certain sure," Miss Shelva insisted.

"Get along now—you'uns have a good day." Miss Melva linked arms with Miss Shelva and the pair backed up beneath the porch's over-hanging roof.

"You have a good day, too," Sid called, then snapped down the reins. He shot Sadie a happy grin as the wagon rolled toward the edge of town. "Never thought I'd get to take you along on one of my deliveries. It'll be nice to have company. Gets kinda lonely on the road all by myself."

Sympathy swelled in Sadie's breast. "I would imagine so."

Although she'd initially balked at taking the day off—she'd come to Goldtree to work, not lazily travel across the countryside on a freight wagon—now she was glad she'd agreed to the Baxter twins' instructions to enjoy a day of leisure. She'd had very little time with Sid lately, and their long-time friendship had suffered for it. Perhaps today they could recapture their easy camaraderie. And while she had him to herself, she could satisfy her curiosity.

After Sid had talked with Mr. Baxter on Thursday evening, he'd indicated she needn't worry—he'd take care of things. But he hadn't told her what had transpired between the two of them. Away from town and curious ears, she could ask the questions that burned in her mind. She opened her mouth to speak, but Sid nudged her lightly with his elbow and bobbed his head toward the wagon's bed.

"Look behind the seat, Sadie. Next to the picnic basket Misses Melva an' Shelva packed. There's a little somethin' back there for you."

Sadie offered him a curious look, but he just grinned. She twisted around in the seat, jouncing a bit as the wagon rolled over a rut, and spotted what appeared to be a small hatbox. Stretching her arms into the bed, she retrieved the box and set it in her lap. "What is it?"

"Open it an' see." Excitement lit Sid's face, but he shrugged—an apparent attempt to appear nonchalant. "Just a little somethin' I found in Beloit."

Sadie remembered him promising to bring her a gift. Although only a week had passed, so much had happened in the interim the promise seemed a lifetime ago. She hugged the box tight against her ribs. "Sid, you don't have to buy me presents. Save your money to get things for yourself."

He angled his head to look directly into her face. Tenderness crept across his features. "Aw, Sadie, you oughtta know by now anything I have, I wanna share with you." His cheeks mottled red. " 'Cause I love you, Sadie."

Although the words were dear, Sadie couldn't help but wonder why he looked so embarrassed while uttering them. Shouldn't a man proclaim love for a woman boldly rather than hesitantly with cheeks aglow? Thad wouldn't flush pink and stammer out his love for her—he'd pull her close, speak plainly, and then validate his statement with a kiss. But she'd sent Thad away. She ducked her head to hide the sudden welling of tears.

Sid gave her another gentle nudge. "Go ahead. Open it. I wanna see if you like it."

Sniffing to banish her sadness, Sadie lifted the

lid on the box. She pushed aside a wad of cotton batting, then gasped. Her gaze jerked to Sid's smiling face and then back to the contents of the box. With trembling fingers, she lifted out a delicate glass figurine of a bluebird. She held the bird securely with one hand and traced the line of the pointed black beak with her finger, allowing her fingertip to trail over its blue head and then under its chin to the pale peach throat. Even though the bird was formed of glass, she imagined the softness of feathers beneath her touch. Tears stung again. "Oh, Sid . . . it's lovely."

"I knew you'd like it." His chest puffed, and he gave the reins a little flick. "Thought about gettin' you—" More red splashed his cheeks. "Well, never mind. Just figured you'd like this little bird a heap better. For now."

"I love it." Very carefully she returned the bird to the box and then tipped sideways to deposit a sisterly kiss on Sid's jaw. "Thank you so much! You know how much I adore songbirds."

"Yep. I know." If Sid's chest expanded any farther, he'd pop his shirt buttons. He heaved a huge sigh and sent her a sidelong glance, his brows low. "I know pret' near everything about you, Sadie. I know how you love listenin' to birds singin' in the trees. I know how you love peaches but don't like sweet potatoes. I know how you'd rather read than pick green beans—"

Sadie stifled a laugh, remembering the day

they'd been scolded for sneaking behind the barn to read a storybook when they'd been sent to gather beans for supper.

"—an' that pink is your favorite color. I know you love to sing, an' you love to laugh, an' pleasin' your family means more to you than seekin' your own happiness."

Sadie's chest ached, listening to Sid's simple recital. He meant so much to her—her favorite cousin, her best playmate. Why couldn't she love him the way he loved her? It would make things so much simpler.

"I know all that 'cause since I was nine years old, you're the only girl I cared about." Sid's voice turned husky with emotion. "I want us to be more than cousins or friends, Sadie. I want us to be . . ." The red in his cheeks streaked down his neck. "Man an' wife."

Sadie sat in silence. Her heart ached with loneliness. Having a beau would fill that empty hole. As he'd indicated previously, they weren't blood relatives—it wouldn't be improper for them to court. Her mother knew Sid and trusted him or she wouldn't have agreed to Sadie traveling all the way to Goldtree at his beckoning. She was comfortable with Sid. She genuinely liked him. They'd been friends since they were small children and had always gotten along well. Would it be so wrong to accept his attentions?

She caressed the top of the box in her lap,

envisioning the sweet figurine inside. His thoughtfulness touched her. He wanted her to be happy. Surely if she agreed to keep company with him as more than friends, they'd find happiness together. "Sid, I—"

Pounding hoofbeats and a stern voice intruded. "Hold up there!"

Sadie jerked toward the voice. A rider barreled toward them—a man with a silver star shining on the chest of his leather vest. Her heart caught. Thad!

Sid pulled back on the reins, intoning, "Whoa, Hec an' Rudy. Whoa there . . ."

Thad reined in on Sid's side of the wagon. He flicked an unsmiling look across the pair of them before turning his attention to Sid. "Doing inspections on cargo. Set that brake an' hop down."

Sid held tight to the reins as if battling the urge to slap them onto the horses' backs and escape. "What're you lookin' for?"

Thad snapped, "Just do as I said."

Sadie had never seen Thad so forceful and unfriendly. Her stomach whirled at the hard expression on his face. What had happened to the tender, considerate man who'd stolen her heart? She leaned forward slightly, the little box cutting into the underside of her rib cage. "We've got to hurry, Th—Sheriff. Sid is due in Macyville by noon."

Thad didn't even glance at her. "Set that brake, I said."

Sid's hand shook as he slipped the brake into place. He clambered down and followed Thad to the back of the wagon. "Just makin' a delivery for Asa Baxter," Sid said. His voice sounded unnaturally high.

Fear suddenly gripped Sadie. Sid had told her not to worry, and she'd assumed he meant Asa had released them from involvement in his illegal activities. She'd seen the labels on the jugs—Miss Melva had lifted one out and chuckled about how her brother could make just about anything he had a mind to, including molasses. So there was no reason to worry. But looking into Sid's colorless face made anxiety nibble at the fringes of her heart anyway.

Thad yanked a jug from a crate at the rear of the wagon bed and examined the paper label, his brows pulled into a scowl.

Sadie called, "It says 'High-Quality Molasses.' They're all the same."

Thad shot her an impatient frown. "I can read. I know what it *says*." He sent a glowering look in Sid's direction. "But labels can be deceiving."

Sid hung his head, his fists clenching and unclenching.

Sadie looked from man to man. Thad's brusque behavior left her troubled. And a little angry. Just because she'd refused his courtship didn't mean he should run roughshod over Sid. With a huff of aggravation, she set the box containing her bird figurine aside and climbed down. She marched to the rear of the wagon and tugged the jug from Thad's hands. The weight took her by surprise, and she nearly dropped it. But she regained her hold and turned the jug so the label faced Thad.

"See? Right there it says 'Molasses.' " She grasped the cork and worked it loose, grunting with the effort. "Put your finger inside and take a little taste." She disliked this version of Thad who'd been transformed from courteous to curt. The sooner she could leave his presence, the happier she'd be.

Thad grabbed the jug, but instead of taking a taste, as she'd suggested, he pointed the spout at her face. "Take a whiff of that, Miss Sadie."

With her lips pursed, Sadie leaned over the jug. Then she reared back, her eyes widening in shock. "Th-that's not molasses!"

Thad shook his head, his green eyes so dark they almost appeared black. "No, ma'am, it sure isn't." He smacked the cork back into the opening and plopped the jug in the wagon bed with a resounding thud. "An' the two of you are now under arrest." For a moment, something akin to pain flickered in Thad's eyes. But then he closed them briefly, and when he looked at her again the hard edge had returned.

He spun on Sid. "Climb up an' turn the wagon around. We're going back to Goldtree."

Sid caught Sadie's arm and gave her a gentle push. "Get in the wagon, Sadie. I need to talk to the sheriff."

Sadie's mouth went dry at the grim expression on his face. "W-why?"

"Do as I say." He faced Thad, his former cowering pose replaced by a square-shouldered bravado. "Can we step over there a ways? I need to talk to you, but . . ." He sent a quick glance in Sadie's direction.

Thad's eyes zipped toward Sadie briefly, and he gave a brusque nod. "All right."

The men walked side by side several yards down the road. Sid pointed into the thick brush. His lips moved, Thad's shoulders rose and fell in a sigh, and then the pair disappeared into the brush. Her heart pounding with trepidation, Sadie inched alongside the wagon toward the front. But she didn't climb in. Wind teased her hair, tossing strands across her cheeks, but she pushed the tendrils aside and stared at the spot where Thad and Sid had been swallowed by a cluster of scruffy bushes. Questions crowded her mind. What was Sid telling Thad? Why couldn't he say it in front of Sadie? When would they come back?

Suddenly a shot rang out—one sharp blast of a gun. Sadie let out a yelp of shock, and the horses shied in their traces. She took two stumbling steps in the direction of the noise, then halted, fear freezing her in place. Sid burst from the brush and sprinted toward her. Hardly slowing, he grabbed her arm and propelled her to the wagon.

"Get in!" he barked.

But her trembling legs turned clumsy and refused to lift her. With a grunt of impatience, Sid grasped her around the middle and lifted her, nearly throwing her onto the seat. She fell forward and her hand hit the box he'd given her. It bounced from the seat onto the wagon's floor-board. The lid popped loose, sending the glass bird onto the wooden floor. Sadie gasped in alarm as the little bird broke into two jagged halves. She reached for the pieces, but Sid clambered up and stepped over her, forcing her to lean out of his way. To Sadie's dismay, his bootheel crushed the bluebird's head and chest.

He dropped into the seat and released the brake, then snapped the reins. "Hah! Hah!"

The wagon jolted. Sadie grabbed the seat, fearful she'd be thrown as Sid urged the horses into a gallop that bounced the jugs together. She clung hard, her face aimed backward, watching —hoping—for Thad to emerge from the brush. But he didn't. Her throat ached with the desire to cry, but she held it all inside, fearful of Sid's reaction.

The wagon rolled around a slight bend, and Sadie slowly turned forward. Her gaze fell on the broken shards of blue and peach glass dancing across the floorboards. Poor little bird. Poor, beautiful little bird, broken and battered beyond repair. Tears welled and spilled down her cheeks. She looked at Sid. He sat in stony-faced silence, his gaze straight ahead and his mouth set in a forbidding line. What had he done? Oh, Lord in Heaven, what had he done? She swallowed the gorge that filled her throat.

She feared her heart was broken into more pieces than the little bird at her feet.

32

"Don't be askin' any questions, Sadie," Sid commanded through clenched teeth. The less she knew, the better. Then nobody could hold her responsible for anything Asa or Sid had done.

Her horrified expression pierced his heart, but he steeled himself and barked, "All right?"

Very slowly, she nodded. She held her lower lip between her teeth and didn't make a sound, but tears ran down her pale cheeks. Sid stifled a groan. How he hated hurting her, but what choice did he have? Asa had made a mess, and Sid was wallowing in the midst of it. He refused to get Sadie in any deeper than she already was.

Pulling back on the reins slightly, he drew the horses from an all-out gallop to a gentle trot. The deafening rumble of pounding hooves and wheels on hard ground quieted. Sid pulled in a long breath and held it, then released it bit by bit. With the last little expulsion, he shifted the reins to one hand and reached for Sadie with the other. He found her hand and squeezed. Her fingers lay limp and unresponsive within his grip. "Sadie?"

She looked straight ahead, her chin quivering and her cheeks moist with endlessly trailing tears. Had she even heard him? He squeezed her hand again, hoping his touch offered some reassurance. "We'll be in Macyville in about an hour. They got a nice little park area with a pergola. We can have us our picnic there."

Her head jerked so quickly, he wondered how her neck managed to stay connected to her shoulders. She fixed a disbelieving stare on him. "W-what?"

"Picnic," he repeated, his gaze whisking back and forth from Sadie's stunned face to the road. "I reckon you'll be hungry by the time we get there, so—"

"I can't eat!" Her voice sounded shrill. She yanked her hand from his and stacked her palms over her chest. "How can you act so . . . so normal? Sid, you—"

He shook his head hard. "Don't say nothin'." With a firm pull on the reins, he brought the team to a stop. Sid tipped his head for a moment, listening. Wind whistled across the rolling grassland that stretched in both directions. Somewhere in the scrubby brush, a bird chirped a cheerful song. The horses bobbed their heads, releasing soft snorts. All of the sounds were good sounds —comforting sounds. No hoofbeats pounded in pursuit. They were safe.

Slipping his arm behind Sadie, he curled his hand over her shoulder. Her muscles tightened at his touch, but he didn't release his grip. "I gotta act normal. You do, too. When we get to Macyville an' leave off these jugs, nobody can suspect we know what's really inside 'em. We gotta act like it's any other delivery."

He looked into Sadie's tortured face, and his heart banged against the walls of his chest. She'd ruin everything if she wasn't careful. He wished he'd left her at the mercantile, but wishing wouldn't change things now. She was on the wagon seat with him, caught up in Asa's crimes, and she'd have to play it through. He curved his hand around the back of her neck—a gentle touch. "Sadie, I know this is hard, but you gotta relax. Just trust me."

She didn't respond, and Sid let out a heavy sigh. He repeated, "Just trust me." Then he shifted to take hold of the reins again. His boot sole scuffed on something, and he glanced at the floorboard. Sadie's little glass bird lay crushed beneath his feet. Deep regret smacked him. "I'm sorry, Sadie." And he was. Sorry for so many things. "First chance I get, I'll go back to Beloit an' get you another bluebird."

She shook her head wildly. "No. I don't want another one. It will remind me of—" She turned her face away from him, and her shoulders shook with silent sobs.

Sid hung his head. Leaning forward, he picked up the larger pieces of colored glass and tossed them over the edge of the wagon. Then he gave the reins a little flick that put the horses in motion again. The wagon rolled on, leaving behind the evidence of the broken figurine, but it would take a heap more effort to fix what had broken in his relationship with Sadie. He could only pray she'd one day understand. And forgive him.

Thad wished he'd stopped to pack a sack of grub before setting out for Clay Centre. But he'd wanted to get to the county marshal's office as quickly as possible. If the liquor-making and gambling operation was as big as Sid Wagner had described it, he'd need more guns than his own to bring it all down. He hoped the marshal had a passel of deputies he'd be willing to loan out. Sid had promised not to let Asa know the law was on to him, so Asa'd be home, smug and unmindful, when Thad and the deputies returned to Goldtree.

He patted Thunder's thick neck, grateful the horse hadn't bolted when he'd fired that shot at a badger growling from the bushes. If he'd had to chase down his mount, it would have delayed his leave-taking. "Soon as we get to Clay Centre, I'll find a livery stable an' set you up with some oats, big fella. Who knows how long it'll take to get things organized?"

The hunger surprised him. After Sadie had jilted him, he hadn't felt much like eating. Maybe knowing the end of the conflict was near helped drive out the heaviness weighing in his middle. He hoped so. He was ready to move on from Goldtree and pursue his dreams of becoming a preacher.

"Lord, go ahead of me an' prepare the marshal's ears for what I have to say," he prayed aloud. "And if there's any way to keep Sadie from facin' a jail cell, I'd like to do it."

Was it wrong to want Sadie to escape punishment? Even though Sid said she was an innocent party, Thad suspected Sid would say just about anything—even an untruth—to protect his cousin. It only made sense that she knew what was going on in the cellar room. Besides, he'd heard her practicing that song—a song she hadn't shared with the Friday or Saturday night audiences. So if she had a special program planned for the gambling nights, she had to know about the illegal activities.

His heart caught. If the marshal ordered it, Thad would arrest her along with Asa Baxter and Sid Wagner. He'd have to—he was paid to enforce the law. A person couldn't pick and choose where to apply justice.

Then again, every man stood before God as a sinner, but God chose grace. Might a judge look at Sadie and choose grace rather than condemnation? Even though she'd done wrong—and even though she'd hurt him—prayers for grace rang through Thad's heart the remainder of his ride to Clay Centre.

He reached the town as the sun slunk toward the horizon. He aimed Thunder for the marshal's office, determined to speak with the man before turning in. But when he entered the office, he found only a deputy marshal on duty.

"Marshal Abbott's gone into Glasco to pick up a horse thief," the deputy said, looking Thad up and down. "Can I help you?"

The deputy didn't have the authority Thad needed, so he shook his head. "When will he be back?"

"He left Thursday, so I figure he'll be back tomorrow. 'Less he decides not to travel on Sunday. Then it'll be Monday."

Thad stifled a groan. Now more than ever he wished he'd packed some clean clothes, his razor, and a few food stores. He hadn't intended to be gone so long. "All right, then. I'll check by tomorrow," Thad said. "Where's the nearest livery? I need a place to bed my horse."

The deputy wordlessly pointed north before closing himself back in the marshal's office. Thad heaved his weary body into the saddle. He hoped the livery stable wasn't too far outside of town. He and Thunder were ready for a rest.

Thad reined in beneath an arched sign bearing the name Hines Livery & Feed Stable. The green paint on the sign was peeling, and the livery building, with its weatherworn timber construction and plain square front, wasn't nearly as nice as some he'd seen in other cities, but he didn't need anything fancy. It would do.

He swung down, his muscles complaining. A man wasn't meant to straddle a saddle for the better part of a day. The wide doors stood open, and lanterns glowed from within the large barn. Somebody must be at work. Thad caught Thunder's reins and guided the horse inside, his stiff hips giving him an awkward gait. "Hello? Anybody here?"

A tall, wiry man with sparse gray hair sticking up in wispy tufts on his age-spotted head emerged from a small room at the back. "Howdy. Need to board your horse?" He gave Thunder's nose a friendly rub.

"Both of us need boarding," Thad said, stifling a yawn. "Can I bed down somewhere, too?" He'd spotted a fine-looking hotel as he'd entered town, but he suspected he wouldn't have enough money in his pocket to afford a night at the Dispatch. Besides, the hay in the stalls smelled fresh—he'd slept in worse places.

The man laughed. "Well, now, mister, a barn's suitable for critters, but I'd never expect one of our state's lawmen to sleep in the hay. You can bunk at my place tonight, if you've a mind to. Got an extra room behind the kitchen—nothin' fancy, but from the looks of ya you're tuckered enough to sleep on a pile of rocks."

Despite the tension-filled day, Thad released a chuckle. The man's open affability put him at ease. "Reckon you're right there. You sure you don't mind?"

"Not at all. My Faye's used to me bringin' folks home. Got some good hotels in town, but even so, our back room does a boomin' business." The man took the reins and drew Thunder into a nearby stall strewn with clean hay. "I'll unsaddle your mount an' get him settled in. There's a trough out back if you'd like to splash a little water on your face—chase off some of that trail dust."

"Thanks. I'll do that." Thad left Thunder to the livery owner's care and made his way out a side door to a cleared space behind the barn. He located the trough set beside a tall pump. A few thrusts of the handle resulted in a rush of fresh water. He tossed his hat aside and leaned into the stream, dousing his head and neck. His shirt got splattered, too, but he didn't mind. Maybe it would serve as a wash of sorts.

He stood upright and ran his hands down his cheeks, removing the last droplets. His face was already prickly from the day's growth of whiskers. By morning they'd be even thicker, and he didn't have a razor. He preferred to be clean-shaven when he faced the marshal, but there wasn't any fix for that now. The local merchants were all closed down for the night. Besides, he didn't want to spend his limited funds. He might need to pay for another night's lodging and feed for Thunder if the marshal didn't return until Monday.

He snatched up his hat and plopped it over his damp hair. From now on, he'd make sure he had a saddlebag of necessities packed before he set off for a day's work. A lawman ought to be better prepared. Of course, he reminded himself as he turned toward the barn to check on Thunder, once he brought Asa Baxter and his cohorts to justice, he intended to turn in his badge and take up his Bible instead.

His feet slowed as an odd feeling crept over him. After Thad reflected for a moment, he identified the feeling as regret. Almost against his will, his hand rose and touched one point on the silver star pinned to his chest. It wouldn't be as easy to let loose of his title of sheriff as he'd once thought. He glanced quickly upward, taking in the flickering stars appearing across the dusky

sky. "But you know I'm meant to be a preacher, God . . ." Before he had a chance to fully examine the odd feelings, the livery owner stumped out into the yard and shot Thad a grin.

"Your horse's all settled in. Let's you an' me head to my place now." He pointed to a small square house on the opposite side of the narrow corral next to the barn. "Faye'll have supper warm on the stove. After you've et, I'll show you the sleepin' room."

Thad ambled alongside the older man. He slipped his hand in his pocket and fingered his meager supply of coins. "I appreciate your hospitality. What do I owe you?" He prayed he'd have sufficient funds.

With a deep chuckle, the man shook his gray head. "No charge, mister. Faye'd have my hide if I took your money." Another grin creased his thin, tanned cheek. "You know what the Good Book says—'whatsoever ye do for the least of these.' Let me an' Faye add a couple of jewels to our crowns. It's more'n enough pay." He opened the planked door to the house and ushered Thad inside. "Faye! Got some company!"

A sweet-faced woman with a white braid coiled around her head turned from the stove. A swirl of steam lifted from a large black pot, carrying with it a wonderful aroma. She set aside the wooden spoon she'd been using to stir the pot's contents, wiped her hands on her apron, and reached toward a shelf on the wall. "Well, then, seems I better put another plate on the table."

A scarred table and four chairs sat on a braided rug in the middle of the room—the only place to sit. The livery owner gave Thad a little push toward the closest chair. "Have a seat there, mister." He scowled. "I ain't even asked your name."

"McKane," Thad provided, removing his hat and sliding into the offered chair. "Thad McKane."

The older man held out his hand. "An' I'm Estel Hines. Good to meet'cha."

As Thad shook the man's hand, Faye bustled over and plopped a plate, cup, and silverware in front of Thad. "Welcome, Mr. McKane." Her tone, soft and kind, let Thad know he wasn't an intrusion. She took his hat and hung it on a peg by the door, then hurried back to the stove. "You look like a man in need of a cup of coffee." She used her apron to protect her hand from the pot's hot handle and poured dark brew into Thad's waiting cup. "Don't have cream, but can I fetch ya some sugar?"

Looking at the humble dwelling, Thad surmised sugar was an extravagance—one he could easily forego. "No, ma'am. This is fine." He took a sip, allowing the strong coffee to revive him. "Mmm, good."

Faye bestowed a crinkling smile of thanks on Thad, then aimed a teasing look at her husband.

"Soon as Estel washes the barn from his hands, we'll have our supper."

Estel chuckled and crossed to a washstand in the corner while Faye removed a pan of golden corn bread from the oven. Within minutes, the pair joined Thad at the table. They clasped their hands beneath their chins and closed their eyes, and Thad followed suit. Estel offered a short but heartfelt prayer of gratitude for the meal and the opportunity to share with a stranger in need. "Amen," the two chorused, and Faye ladled up hearty servings of beans, ham, and onions swimming in a rich broth. The simple meal filled Thad's stomach, and the pleasant company fed his soul.

After supper, Faye showed him to a little lean-to tucked behind the kitchen. "Ain't much," she said, bouncing her gaze around the simple space, "but it's better'n sleepin' in the barn. You have a good rest now, young man." She departed quickly, closing the door behind her with a click.

A square, uncovered window set high on the wall above the bed allowed in a faint shaft of moonlight. Thad shimmied down to his long johns and stretched out on the creaky rope bed. The straw-filled mattress caressed his tired body, and he sighed in contentment. Despite his reason for being in Clay Centre, despite his weariness and aching heart, the kindnesses exhibited by Estel and Faye Hines soothed like a healing balm.

Thank You, Lord, for the reminder that good people are walking around in this world, doing Your work.

For some reason, he didn't add his familiar request that the Lord make easy the way to Thad becoming a preacher.

33

Sadie lay in her bed, staring through the menacing shadows. Exhaustion plagued her, but her body refused sleep. Too many images cluttered her mind—ugly images that stole her ability to relax.

When Sid had dropped her off at the mercantile after their return from Macyville, she'd gone immediately to Thad's office. But the office had been empty, and she turned away, distraught that her prayers to find him there, whole and hale, went unanswered.

As she'd left the office to hurry to the mercantile and change for the evening's performance, the blacksmith, Mr. Kimbrough, had stepped onto the boardwalk and said, "Howdy, Miss Sadie. You seen the sheriff?"

Sadie's conscience had panged to ignore the question, but Sid had cautioned her to silence. After her cousin had shot Thad and left him lying beside the road, she feared crossing him—he might be capable of anything. So she'd chosen a careful reply. "I was looking for him, too. He isn't here."

The man scratched his chin. "Neither's my horse. I told him he could borrow Thunder anytime, but I forgot to tell him the horse's got a loose shoe. I was wantin' to git that fixed up." He lifted his beefy shoulders in a shrug. "Guess it'll have to wait. Just hope McKane ain't running that animal all over the countryside. Could do some damage." He ambled back toward his shop.

Sadie had considered calling after the man, instructing him to ride toward Macyville and look for Thunder. The animal was probably tied to a sapling, unable to make his way home again. And then maybe Mr. Kimbrough would find Thad. Because certainly he lay dead or he would've returned to Goldtree.

She crunched her eyes closed, willing the remembrances away. But glimpses of the day continued to play behind her eyelids—the shattered bluebird, Sid's grim face, the spot in the bushes where Thad and Sid had disappeared but Sid had emerged alone—as well as one alarming picture purely from conjecture. She shuddered. *God, make it go away!* If only she could ignore the horrible image of Thad's lifeless body lying in the brush. She feared it would haunt her forever.

Restless, she rose and tugged on her robe. She

crept through the hallway, down the stairs, and into the mercantile. As always, the silence of the store at night sent shivers down her spine. How a place so bright and bustling during the day could feel ominous and eerie at night, she couldn't understand. Tonight the looming gray shapes seemed even more threatening. But she knew only her vivid imagination gave the inanimate objects power. The real threat lay within her—a secret that could damage her soul if she didn't allow it release.

Without conscious thought, she lit a lantern and unlatched the door leading to the cellar. Moving on tiptoes to avoid waking Miss Melva and Miss Shelva, she made her way to the singing room. As she walked up the center aisle, the lantern light bounced off the polished wood paneling and sent a soft glow over the velvet cushions on the chairs. Such a beautiful, beautiful room . . . A place where she had fulfilled some of her fondest, lifelong hopes and dreams.

She crossed to the stage and stepped between the pillars. Only a few hours ago she'd stood at this same spot and sung her favorite hymns. How had she managed to bring forth song with her chest weighted by grief and guilt? She looked across the rows of now-empty seats. Applause and cries of admiration rang in her mind. Tears stung, and she spun away from the seats. If those people knew what she'd done—who she was underneath the surface—they wouldn't have cheered for her.

Mr. Baxter had caught her afterward and hissed a warning in her ear. "You didn't give your best tonight, girlie. Might've fooled them others, but I can tell—you was holdin' back. Don't you think about holdin' back come Tuesday. I don't pay a full wage for half a performance, you hear me?"

Even now, hours later, the malice in his tone made her cringe. How she wished she could go upstairs, pack her bag, and return to Indiana, where she'd feel safe again. She turned a slow circle, taking in the ostentation of the room once more. Its beauty hadn't changed, but Sadie had. She was now tainted—tainted by what she'd seen, by what she'd done, by what she knew.

Tonight, as she faced her audience and sang sweet hymns meant to show God's power and majesty, she'd felt every bit the hypocrite. Oh, how she'd tried to lose herself in the music. But she'd failed. The music was lost to her. And she knew the only way she would ever get it back was to rid her conscience of the darkness it now carried.

But how?

"I have to talk to Sid." Her raspy whisper echoed eerily in the empty room, bouncing from the ceiling and returning to her ears. It was late, it was dark, it might be foolhardy to go out on the streets at this hour, but she had to convince him to turn himself in. And she'd divulge her part— knowingly entertaining men who partook of illegal beverages—as well. How wonderful it would feel to unburden herself.

Grabbing the hem of her robe, she scampered toward the stairs. But as her foot landed on the first riser, she froze. If she told, would she be sent to jail? What would Mama and the children do if she were imprisoned?

With a groan, she turned and sank onto the stairs. The damp of the stairway seeped through her nightclothes, chilling her. She hugged herself, the dark hallway becoming a cell that closed in around her. Sid had told her to keep silent. It seemed sound advice, considering the consequences. But, no! She was finished being a party to illegal dealings. No more singing to the raucous crowd. Mr. Baxter would bluster and threaten, but she would stand firm. Somehow Mama and the children would have to make do with only her mercantile salary.

She jerked to her feet and began once more to climb the stairs. But then she changed direction and returned to the singing room. Pausing in the doorway, she sent one more slow, deliberate look across the beautifully decorated room. From left to right her gaze roved until she reached the row of seats mounted on the short platform along the south wall. Her eyes lingered on the seat Mr. Baxter had assigned to Thad. *I'm so sorry, Thad.*

Tears spurted into her eyes, and the chair swam. Pressing her fist to her lips, she held back the cry that longed for release. Her chest ached so badly, drawing a breath became torture. So much had been stolen in the past days—the joy her music had once brought, her peace of mind, and Thad. Perhaps, with time and distance, she might one day experience peace again. Perhaps, someday, she might even rediscover the joy of music. But Thad was lost to her forever. And Sid would be, too, if anyone discovered Sid had killed Thad.

She couldn't save Thad. But she could still save Sid. If they stayed in Goldtree, they'd never be free of guilt. They had to leave—both of them. Away from here, they could forget everything that had happened. Away from here, she would forget about Thad and how special he'd been to her.

Yes, they must go. Now. Before morning light flooded the town and illuminated their wrong-doings. To her sleep-deprived mind the plan made perfect sense. Holding tight to the lantern, Sadie raced up the stairs and to her room. She dressed quickly and started to pack. But how would she carry her trunks down the stairs? Her things weren't nearly as important as her cousin. She could abandon her belongings for Sid.

On stealthy feet, she sneaked out the back door and across the darkened yard, running as quickly as the feeble light from the moon would allow. She reached Sid's little house, breathless and panting. Slumping against the doorjamb, she banged her fist on the door. She waited, watching the window for a glow that would mean Sid had awakened and lit a lantern. But no glow came.

She knocked again, harder, cringing as the thumps echoed through the sleeping neighborhood. Several houses down, a dog began to bark, but no sound came from within Sid's house. With a little huff of frustration, she rounded the house to its rear and stopped beneath the window where Sid's bedroom resided. She tapped on the glass and tipped her head, listening. Wind rustled in the trees, the dog's bark became more insistent, but the house remained silent.

Sadie shifted slightly, leaning against the wood siding and peering through the deep shadows. Where could Sid be? Had Asa Baxter sent him on a nighttime delivery? She couldn't wait here all night—she should go back to the mercantile. Once more, the urge to escape washed over her, but she quelled the desire. As long as they were gone before Tuesday, when Mr. Baxter would expect her to sing again, it would be soon enough.

Hugging herself, she scuffed her way back toward the front of the house. The dog, thankfully, ceased its clamor, but an owl took up a nighttime hoot and a second one answered. The forlorn calls of *whoo-whoo* increased Sadie's loneliness. How she wished Sid had been home.

Her head low, watching the progress of her feet as she slowly retraced her steps back to the mercantile, she didn't see anyone approach. But the crunch of footsteps reached her ears. She came to a halt, her skin breaking out with gooseflesh. She spun around, and a cry of alarm rose in her throat as someone stepped out of shadows. Then she recognized the man's face in the moon's glow.

Sid hustled close and took hold of her arm, searching her face. "What're you doing out here in the middle of the night?"

"I came to talk to you." She pulled loose, examining him from head to toe. Even in the muted light, she could see something was amiss. She brushed dirt and bits of grass from his sleeve. "You're filthy. What have you been doing?"

He jerked backward, his face pinching in a fierce scowl. "You ask too many questions."

Suddenly, she knew. She backed away, gorge filling her throat. "Were you—were you burying . . . something?"

He turned his face from her. "I told you . . . don't ask."

"Oh, Sid!"

"It had to be done!" He grabbed her upper arms and shook her. "Sadie, I told you earlier, you can't tell anybody. You just have to trust me."

His hands tightened painfully on her arms, but she welcomed the discomfort. It distracted her from the agonizing pain in her heart. "B-but . . ."

"Think back, Sadie." Sid's voice, so low it was nearly a growl, turned pleading. "All the years you've known me, have I given you reason to distrust me? I've always been there for you, haven't I? Defendin' you, protectin' you." He shook her again, and she released a whimpering agreement. "Then believe me when I say I'm still protectin' you."

He let go of her, and she almost fell. But his arm coiled out, catching her around the waist. He propelled her into the empty street. "C'mon. I'm takin' you back. You get on up to bed. Go to church in the mornin' an' pray."

Her feet moved automatically in step with his, her skirts rustling with the rapid pace. "Will you be there, too?"

"No. I can't. But—" He stopped and grabbed her arms again. Leaning close, he peered directly into her face and whispered, "But you go, an' you pray, Sadie. You pray for me. An' for you. If we're gonna come outta this mess unharmed, it'll take angels workin' on our side. So you pray *hard*. Will you?"

Sadie nodded, too afraid to do otherwise. She cringed as Sid leaned in, but he only planted a kiss on her forehead. When he pulled back, she glimpsed genuine fear shining in his dark eyes.

"Whatever happens, Sadie, know I'm sorry I got you involved in this. Know I didn't mean it. An' remember . . . I love you."

He turned and strode away. Moments later, shadows swallowed his form and Sadie was all alone.

• • •

The smell of frying bacon awakened Thad, and he sat up, his mouth watering. He snatched his pants and shirt from the end of the bed and scrambled into them, wrinkling his nose at the musty odor emanating from the rumpled fabric.

He opened the lean-to door and stepped into the kitchen. "Good morning, ma'am."

Faye aimed a bright smile in his direction. Her hair was neatly wound around her head in the shining white braid, and she'd tied an apron over her dark blue dress. Compared to him, even in her homey clothes, she looked as if she'd stepped out of a bandbox. "Well, good morning, Mr. McKane. Did'ja sleep well?"

Thad took a deep draw of the wonderful bacon smell. "I did, thank you. But please—call me Thad."

She bobbed her head toward the washstand in the corner. "Left Estel's razor and soap out for you. He already sharpened it up good. So go ahead an' use it."

Thad didn't hesitate. Getting his face cleared of the scraggly black whiskers made him feel clean all over, even though he still sorely needed a bath and a change of clothes. He finished shaving and cleaned the razor on a length of toweling, then inched toward the peg where his hat waited.

Faye flipped a thick strip of meat. A sizzle rose from the pan. "Where you goin'? No need to check on your horse—Estel's already gone over to the stable. So just pour yourself some coffee an' set yourself down. Breakfast'll be ready afore you can down your first cup."

Flapjacks browned in a separate pan, their sweet aroma mingling with the rich scent of the bacon. Thad swallowed. Temptation moved him toward the table. But then his conscience pricked. "That's very kind of you, ma'am, but I shouldn't be eatin' up all your food. Besides, I have some business to tend to."

A brief scowl pursed her brow. "On Sunday?" Her expression cleared. "Oh, of course—you bein' a lawman, you probably don't get to quit workin' just 'cause it's the Lord's day. But business or no, you shouldn't be tryin' to work on an empty stomach." She lifted two slices of bacon from the pan and laid them on a waiting plate. With smooth movements, she flipped a flapjack next to the bacon and held out the plate to him. "I might not be able to offer you a feast, but it'd please me to see you make this here sidemeat an' flatcake disappear." Her smile turned teasing. "You wouldn't want to disappoint an old lady now, would'ja?"

Thad stifled a chuckle. He rubbed his finger over his mustache. "No, ma'am, I surely wouldn't."

She slid the plate onto the table and pointed to the chair. "Then have a seat."

Thad decided not to argue. He sat and bowed his head to pray. When he thanked God for the food, he also asked a blessing on Estel and Faye. He ventured a guess there wasn't a pair of purer souls in all of Clay Centre. When he opened his eyes, he found Faye waiting with the coffeepot in hand, ready to pour his coffee. He accepted the cup gratefully.

"Good to see a young man like yourself givin' thanks where it's due," she said as she returned to the stove. "Too bad you got business this mornin'. Me an' Estel'd be plumb tickled to have you go to service with us at the chapel. 'Less we're sick or the barn's on fire, we never miss."

Thad chopped free a good-sized chunk of his flapjack and put it in his mouth. Even without butter or syrup, the flaky cake melted on his tongue. Faye's flapjacks rivaled Cora's. He picked up a piece of bacon and blew on it. "When I'm home, I don't miss, either. But today . . ." As he thought about all he needed to do, his appetite disappeared. He dropped the bacon without tasting it.

"Somethin' wrong?" Faye asked.

Thad sighed. "A whole lot. But—"

The front door burst open and Estel stepped through. "Mr. McKane, I'm afeared I got some bad news for you."

34

For the first time she could remember, Sadie didn't attend church services on Sunday morning. She was awake—she hadn't slept all night—but when Miss Shelva tapped on her door and asked if she was ready for breakfast, Sadie called through the closed door, "I'm not feeling well. Please let me rest."

The twins stood in the hallway and argued for several minutes about whether or not they should enter the room and check on their clerk or leave her in peace, but to Sadie's relief they finally headed to their own church and left her alone. The moment they departed, she jumped up, pulled one of her trunks from the corner, and began packing. Tears stung behind her nose as she layered her photographs between items of clothing, hiding her family's faces from view. They seemed to stare at her in reproach from their little frames. She deserved their censure. She'd certainly let them down.

Before covering the family portrait, she took a moment to gaze into Papa's face. Then, with a flick of her wrist, she flipped the skirt of one of her dresses over the photograph and slapped down the lid of the trunk. Turning and sitting on the chest, she let her head hang low. Papa had done his best to teach her right from wrong. He'd be heartsick to know how far she'd strayed from the moral values he'd instilled in her.

His final letter sat on her desk, where a shaft of sunlight lit her name written in his hand. She reached over and picked it up, finding comfort in holding the piece of paper and envelope that Papa had held. For long moments she sat with the envelope pressed to her chest, loneliness for her stepfather creating an ache in her stomach. Needing a stronger connection to the man who had raised her, she started to open the envelope and reread the letter.

But then another idea struck. *The Bible*. Papa gained his strength, his wisdom, his creed by which to live from God's holy word. She searched her memory, trying to recall the last passage she'd heard him read aloud before she moved to Goldtree. She believed it was in Hebrews.

Eager to revisit the words, she dashed to her bedside table and snatched up her Bible. Her fingers moved nimbly, easily locating the book of Hebrews. She lay the open Bible across her lap and scanned the words until she reached chapter ten. Then recognition bloomed in her memory —yes, this was the last passage she'd heard in Papa's voice.

Leaning over the pages, she read slowly,

carefully, drawing the deep timbre of her step-father's tone from the recesses of her mind. She read straight through, and when she reached the twenty-sixth verse, she gasped. Her stomach trembled, and she read the Scripture aloud. " 'For if we sin wilfully after that we have received the knowledge of the truth, there remaineth no more sacrifice for sins, but a certain fearful looking for of judgment and fiery indignation, which shall devour the adversaries.' "

She sat upright, her heart pounding. She knew breaking the law was wrong—drinking liquor for the sake of intoxication, tempting men with provocative lyrics, murder . . . All of these things were wrong. Yet she'd unwittingly become a party to each of these sins. And now certain judgment awaited. Even if she escaped Goldtree and started over in a different town, in a place where the people had no knowledge of her former sins, God would know. God would always know. Hadn't Mama advised, "Be sure your sins will find you out"? Better to be discovered and punished than to carry the weight of guilt or to ignore one's conscience until it no longer spoke truth to one's heart.

Sadie set aside the Bible and paced the room. "What should I do, God?" Although no audible answer came, she knew. She must face the conse-quences of her choices. But first, she needed to seek forgiveness.

Sinking to her knees beside the bed, she folded her hands and closed her eyes. "Dear God, I've done wrong. I sang songs that didn't honor You. I lied to Thad. I did it because I wanted to take care of Mama and Effie and the boys, but—" Realization struck like a lightning bolt from the blue. Her eyes flew open and she stared straight ahead, shamed by the worst of her offenses.

Tears rolled down her cheeks as she bent over her clasped hands once more. "And all of it was because I didn't trust You. You made it possible for me to come to Goldtree. Papa and Mama both believed it was Your will. But I lost sight of that and took it all on myself. I was wrong to think I had to do wrong things to see to my family's needs. I needed to do right, to honor You, and trust You to meet our needs. I'm sorry, God. Please forgive me for not trusting You enough. Let me trust You now."

She remained in her bent-low pose, alternately crying and praying, until a hesitant peace crept over her being. Then, sniffling, she whispered, "Amen." She shifted to sit on the edge of the bed, and her eyes fell on the open Bible. The twenty-second verse seemed to pulsate beneath her tear-distorted gaze. She blinked and read the verse aloud. " 'Let us draw near with a true heart in full assurance of faith, having our hearts sprinkled from an evil conscience, and our bodies washed with pure water.' "

A genuine smile formed on Sadie's face, and more tears ran. But not tears of sorrow or remorse—tears of joy. God had removed her blotch of wrong, washing her clean once more. Her faith had been restored. She didn't know what would happen next. She might lose her job. She might even have to go to jail. But she would lean on her heavenly Father with the full assurance of faith Papa had taught her.

She stood up and stated firmly, "I choose to trust." Then her mouth widened in a yawn. Tiredness collapsed her bones. She curled in the bed with Papa's letter in one hand and her Bible cradled against her ribs. Within minutes, she fell into a deep, restful sleep.

Thad knelt beside Thunder and cradled the big horse's foot in his lap. Thunder snorted, blowing air down the back of Thad's neck, apparently unconcerned about the swelling in his leg. But Thad was concerned. And so was Estel.

"I can fix that shoe," the older man said, scratching his head and making his hair stand up. "That's not a problem. But I'm not sure you oughtta be ridin' him for a few days. That leg of his needs to rest up. Leastways 'til the swellin' goes down."

Thad released Thunder's foot and stood. He rubbed the animal's jaw, self-recrimination bringing a rise of remorse. How could he have been blind to the horse's discomfort? He'd been so focused on reaching Clay Centre—on bringing an end to his own problem—that he'd created a harmful situation for Thunder. "I'm sorry, big boy," he whispered.

Estel curled his hand over Thad's shoulder and gave a comforting squeeze. "Don't be feelin' bad now. Important thing is we caught it. An' I'll get him fixed up. So don't you worry."

Thad followed the older man to the house where Faye waited, apron gone and a flowered bonnet covering her braided coronet. Estel told her about Thunder's sore leg, and she listened, nodding, her face creased with concern. When Estel finished, he bustled into a side room and shut the door.

Faye turned to Thad. "I'll say a prayer for your horse, Mr. McKane. An' since it appears you won't be goin' no place quick, I reckon that means you don't need to see to your business today. How 'bout you come to church with us?"

Thad gestured to his dust-encrusted shirt and trousers. "Like this?"

Faye gave him a quick perusal, then pointed one finger at him. "Wait here." She bustled to the door where Estel had disappeared and slipped inside the room. She returned moments later with a white cambric shirt and a rumpled black ribbon tie. "Can't help with the britches—Estel's as skinny as a tomato stake an' none of his would fit ya, even though you ain't exactly a portly man—

but I reckon you can make do with one of his shirts. Go give it a try."

Thad considered arguing, but how could he refuse in the face of such generosity? He slipped into the lean-to and exchanged shirts. The shirt was plenty tight across his shoulders and the top button pinched, but he managed to get into it. He emerged to find the Hineses waiting. Faye held a well-worn Bible in the crook of her arm. Her face lit when she spotted him.

"Well, now, that makes all the difference. You look fine, Thad. Mighty fine."

Thad tried to work his finger beneath the collar to loosen it. He felt mighty pinched. But he wouldn't complain. "Thank you, ma'am. But I hope nobody'll be offended by the sight of these britches. They're just about stiff enough to stand on their own." He sniffed, grimacing. "An' I don't smell too fresh."

The woman laughed merrily. "Now, Thad, you oughtta know by now the Lord ain't too concerned about what we put on our outsides. He's one to look upon a man's heart. An' unless I'm a poor judge of character, your heart gives your Maker a heap of pleasure."

Thad fidgeted under Faye's praise. He hoped her judgment was correct. He didn't want to think of God being disappointed in him.

"Let's get goin'." Estel opened the door and gestured his wife through. "Just a short walk to the chapel, but I'm not wantin' to arrive late an' disrupt the service."

The "short walk" turned out to be eight city blocks, but Thad didn't mind. The morning was pleasant, and it gave him a chance to work all the stiff kinks out of his legs from yesterday's long ride. They reached the shady yard of a white-painted clapboard building. Inside, rows of scarred benches served as pews. From the moment Thad entered, he experienced a welcome. The minister's straightforward teaching ministered to his troubled soul, and by the closing benediction, he was grateful he'd had the chance to worship with Faye, Estel, and their congregation.

The sun had found its way to the top of the sky by the time they headed home, but trees lined the street, offering shade. They walked three abreast, Faye in the middle, with her hand tucked in the curve of Estel's bony elbow. Their ease reminded Thad of the days he and Sadie had walked together, but he pushed the remembrances away. No sense in spoiling a good day.

Halfway back, Faye suddenly asked, "Thad? Afore Estel came in this mornin' a-hollerin' about bad news, you told me there was lots of things wrong." She touched his arm. "Anything we can do to help?"

Can you turn back the clock and keep Sadie from partnering herself with a bootlegging gambler? The question quivered on the tip of his tongue. Helplessness tangled his stomach in knots. He tugged the tie from around his neck and released the top button on the shirt, giving him room to swallow. "It's kind of you to ask, but there's not a whole lot anybody can do."

"Got anything to do with the business that brought you to town?" Estel asked, leaning forward to peek past his wife.

"Yes, sir." Thad kicked a rock, sending it skittering far ahead. "I'm gonna be depending on the marshal to help me know how to proceed." He released a rueful chuckle. "I'm pretty new to sheriffing. Not always sure of what's right."

"You read the Bible, don'tcha?" Faye's eyes crinkled as she squinted up at Thad. She waited until he nodded. "Well, then, of course you know what's right. You just do what's written in God's book. Long as you follow His teachin', everything'll come out just fine."

Thad searched his memory for verses that would help him know how to handle the situation with Sadie. Several crowded his mind—Scriptures on granting mercy competing with those avowing justice. But which was appropriate? "I reckon I better just talk to the marshal."

"But—" Faye started.

"Now, Faye." Estel cut her off with a gentle admonition. "We don't know the whole story, an' it appears Thad here wants to keep it to hisself. So don't be pushin' at him. Let him be."

Faye's wrinkled cheeks turned rosy. She flicked a penitent glance at Thad. "I apologize if I seemed nosy. Just hate to see a nice young man like yourself so befuddled." She patted his arm. "You talk to the marshal, Thad. I'm sure he'll give you all the help you need." The stable loomed just ahead, and Faye hurried her steps. "I need to get our lunch on the table. I reckon you'll want to go check your horse. While you're doin' that, I'll be sayin' a prayer for you an' for the marshal, that whatever you decide'll be the most God-honorin' way of handlin' the problem. Whatever the problem is."

35

Thad propped his ankle on his opposite knee and hooked his elbow over the back of the spindled chair. The marshal had ridden into Clay Centre Sunday afternoon, prisoner in tow, but he'd asked Thad to wait until Monday morning to discuss the situation in Goldtree. Thad had agreed, but he'd shown up at the office first thing, eager to seek the more experienced lawman's advice.

Bless Faye's heart, thought Thad as he pondered how she'd broken her usual practice of resting on the Lord's day and laundered his clothes Sunday afternoon while he hunkered, embarrassed, in Estel's tattered robe so he could meet the county marshal without feeling ashamed of his appearance. Taking in the marshal's crisp suit and polished boots, Thad sent up another prayer of gratitude for the Hineses' generosity.

"So you're saying this man's making beer and wine in a cave, and shipping it all over Kansas?" Marshal Abbot's eyes glinted with anger.

Although the marshal was brusque, Thad felt at ease with the man. They had a common goal— bringing an end to illegal operations. "That's right. I found the beer-brewing equipment myself, but his worker told me about the wine." Sid's remorseful face flashed in Thad's memory. "He also told me there's gambling going on one night a week in the opera house—seems there's a tunnel leadin' from Baxter's barn to the cellar under the mercantile, where the gambling takes place." Thad winced, thinking about Sadie entertaining the gamblers. He hadn't yet mentioned Sadie's involvement. He was half scared what the marshal would say.

"Well, Sheriff McKane, sounds like you've got enough evidence to bring Asa Baxter to trial. I'll send a couple of my deputies to hide out at the Baxter place tomorrow evening and round up the men who try to make use of that tunnel. But you don't need to wait for them—head on back to Goldtree and take Baxter into custody."

Thad sucked in a breath. "What about those who've helped him?"

"Them too." Marshal Abbot spoke forcefully. "A judge might not see 'em all as equally responsible—especially the one who turn-coated and let you know what was happening—but it's not for us to decide. So round 'em all up."

Thad's chest constricted. "Yes, sir."

Marshal Abbot frowned. "You have a jail over there?"

"Of sorts. Just a little cellar under my living quarters. But I can lock the door on it, so if I put them down there, they'll be secure."

"Fine." The marshal opened the middle drawer on his desk and withdrew a pencil and paper. "I'll get a wire sent today to the circuit judge, telling him the situation and asking him to contact you to set up a trial date."

Thad didn't like to think of Sadie holed up in that dreary cellar for a long period of time. "When do you think that might be?"

"Depends on what else he has to tend to," Marshal Abbot said, scribbling on the paper. "Might be a week. Might be a month. But he'll get there in due time—he'll be eager to see these perpetrators brought to justice." The man sent a wry grin across the desk. "Judge Bradley worked hard to bring prohibition to Kansas. He'll be banging his gavel with zeal at this trial."

Although Thad knew he should celebrate

seeing justice served, his heart felt heavy as he left the marshal's office and scuffed back to the livery. A judge who'd battled for prohibition would be bent on vengeance rather than mercy. Sadie was doomed.

Thad heard a ringing clang as he approached the livery. When he entered the barn, he spotted Estel bent over his anvil, bringing down the hammer on a fiery red horseshoe. Thad watched the man plunge the horseshoe into a nearby water bucket. Steam billowed and a sizzling *sssssh!* sounded. As soon as the noise died away, Thad called Estel's name.

The man turned. "Thad!" He held the tongs with the horseshoe pinched in its grip aloft. "Workin' on that shoe for Thunder. Just about got it ready to fit."

Thad ambled closer, examining the bent piece of iron. "That's good, 'cause I'm needin' to get back to Goldtree quick as possible."

Estel pulled his lips into a grimace. "Well, now, Thad, just 'cause the shoe is pret' near ready don't mean Thunder's ready." He tapped the bow of the horseshoe with the tip of his gloved finger as if testing it. "The swellin' in his leg is down a heap this mornin', thank the Lord, but I wouldn't be making him go trottin' back to Goldtree 'til it's completely gone."

"How long?" Thad hadn't meant to bark, but his question came out sharp.

Estel shrugged. "Hard to know." He spun and marched toward the stall where Thunder contentedly munched from the feed box. "Not today, though. I'd say tomorrow at the earliest."

Thad jammed his hands deep into his trouser pockets and stifled a growl. Without a word, he turned and left the barn. He'd already been gone from Goldtree for three days. What if Asa knew Thad was on to him? The man could be in Nebraska by now.

He reached the Hineses' house and knocked on the door. Faye's cheerful voice called for him to come on in. He entered and marched past the woman, who sat at the table with a pile of mending in her lap. Yanking up the pot and a cup from the stove, he poured himself some coffee, then took a big gulp. The liquid nearly scalded his tongue. He let out a hiss of surprise.

Faye's soft chuckle sounded. "Careful there. That pot's been boilin' for near an hour."

Thad smacked the cup down, sloshing black brew across the stove's surface. He should clean up the mess, but instead he paced to the single window and looked out across the sparse grass yard to the street. A groan left his throat.

"Your dealin' with the marshal not go well?"

Faye's sympathetic voice cut through Thad's irritation. He turned to face the older woman. "My dealings with the marshal went fine. I know what I gotta do." A band of regret wound itself around his chest, squeezing the wind from his lungs. It wouldn't be easy, but he'd do it. It was his job.

"Then why so glum?"

Thad tromped to the table and sat, propping his elbows on his knees. " 'Cause I have to wait." Seemed he was always waiting. Waiting for his pa to quit his drinking ways and become a loving father. Waiting for his chance to step behind a pulpit and preach. Waiting for a lame horse to heal so he could arrest Asa Baxter and fulfill his obligation to Mayor Hanaman. Waiting for his heart to stop pining for Sadie . . .

"Y'know, Thad," Faye offered softly, working her needle in and out of the shirt in her hands, "waitin' serves a purpose. Patience is a virtue, but we don't learn it no other way than havin' to practice it."

Thad grunted.

The woman laughed. "I've lived a heap longer'n you. Sometimes bein' older means bein' wiser. You could tell me what's wrong. Might be I could offer some advice."

Thad examined Faye's face. Although many womenfolk he'd encountered seemed eager for details so they could gossip, he believed she genuinely wanted to help. And he could use advice. With a nod, he opened up and shared everything. Except how he'd fallen in love with a young woman who would soon be arrested and brought to trial. He didn't want to talk about that.

Faye's hands had fallen idle while he talked. Now she sat back and gazed at him, wide-eyed. "Why, Thad, you been called into the ministry of the Lord?"

Thad blinked twice, startled by the question. *Called?* "Well . . . yes. I reckon so."

Her brow puckered. "You reckon or you know?"

Did it matter? Doing good was doing good, no matter the reason. Thad shrugged.

Faye shook her head. "Thad, you gotta *know*. If you ain't been called to a service, you won't be happy doin' it. It'll be a trial rather than a blessin'. An' it'll keep you from doin' what the good Lord planned for you."

Thad threw his arms wide. "But I have to preach."

"*Have* to, huh?" She tucked her chin low, sending him a puzzled look. "Why?"

Thad looked away, fiddling with the star pinned to his vest. "I got a lot of sins to make up for." But he didn't want to explain those sins. His father's illicit behavior would shock this dear woman.

Faye clicked her tongue on her teeth, shaking her head slowly. Lantern glow gave her white hair the appearance of a halo. "Thad, Thad, Thad . . . didn't you tell me you're a believer?"

Thad nodded.

"Well, then, whatever happened in the past is gone." She pointed to a narrow shelf across the room. "Fetch me my Bible. Lemme show you somethin'."

Thad followed her direction, and she carefully turned whisper-thin pages. Her face lit. "Ahh, here it is. In Titus, chapter three, the fifth verse." Her finger underlined the words as she read. " 'Not by works of righteousness which we have done, but according to his mercy he saved us.' " She pinned Thad in place with a fervent look. "Our lovin' Father washes away every stain. There ain't one thing you can do to make up for past wrongs . . . an' you don't have to, 'cause Jesus already took care of it when He hung on the cross." A tender smile graced her lined face. "But you got to let go of those past wrongs, too, or they'll forever keep you bound up." She reached across the table and cupped Thad's hand. "Sometimes, Thad, before we can find freedom, we gotta forgive ourselves."

A snippet of a conversation he'd had with Sadie winged through his memory—she'd asked if it were possible to make amends for someone else's sins. And suddenly he realized the answer was no. Why hadn't he seen the truth before now? He'd chosen the ministry for all the wrong reasons.

Forgive me, Lord, for being so shortsighted.

He turned his hand to give the woman's fingers a gentle squeeze. "Faye, you are a heap wiser than me."

She laughed, squeezed his hand back, and pulled loose. "Nice to know these white hairs on my head are more'n window dressin'. Now . . ." She set aside the mending and pushed to her feet. "I best be puttin' some lunch on the table. Estel'll be in soon, an' he's always hungry as a bear after a mornin' of labor in the stable."

Thad rose, too. After his churlish behavior, he owed the livery owner an apology. "I reckon I'll go over an' see if he needs any help."

Faye waved her hand in reply, and Thad quick-stepped across the yard. The clear sky of early morning had changed during his time talking with Faye. A hot wind pushed billowing puffs of white across the blue expanse. Thad paused for a moment to examine the sky, wondering if the wind would send the clouds on or let them stay long enough to drop some rain. He didn't look forward to a wet ride, but the farmers could use the moisture.

Estel was in the stall with Thunder, the horse's foot resting on the man's knees. As Thad approached, he dropped the horse's foot to the floor and straightened, one hand pressed to his lower back. He turned and gave Thad a relieved grin. "Fits fine. Just fine." He patted Thunder's flank. "An' the swellin' looks even better now than it did this mornin'. I'm gonna put some burlap soaked in cold water on his leg to speed things up."

"So I can maybe ride out tomorrow, then?" Thad asked hopefully.

"Nope."

Thad jolted. "Nope?"

Estel rocked back on his heels, a teasing grin twitching on his grizzled face. "You can ride out today." He scratched his head, his expression turning sheepish. "Shoulda thought of it earlier. I was so caught up in seein' to your horse . . . but if you're wantin' to, you can borrow one of my horses an' ride it to Goldtree."

Thad had noticed the three horses in stalls on the other side of the stable, but he'd assumed Estel was boarding the animals. He wished he'd known they were for borrowing—he could be long gone by now. But if he'd left earlier, he wouldn't have had his moments of time with Faye. Her words of wisdom, accompanied by truths from God's word, had begun a healing deep within his soul. He wanted to examine the Scripture again and do some praying, but he believed he'd soon have answers to questions that had burned unanswered far too long.

He flung his arm around Estel's thin shoulders. "Estel, you and your sweet wife are angels on earth. There's a lot of work waiting for me in Goldtree, so I'll borrow one of those horses." A lump filled his throat. "Thank you for everything you've done for me."

36

Asa flung himself from Percival's saddle so fast he almost fell on his rump. With a muffled curse, he caught his balance and then stormed into the mercantile. The bell over the door clanged wildly, piercing his ears, but he hollered over the clamor. "You seen that no-good, lowdown, worthless piece of nothin' I call my drayman?"

Two customers dropped their baskets and scooted out the door, inching around him as if they thought he might bite. He stifled a snarl. They just might be right.

Both of his sisters scuttled from different corners in the store, their long-fingered hands stirring the air and their faces wearing identical scowls of worry. Melva reached him first. "Asa, what's got you all a-dither?" Shelva fluttered to his other side. The two of them patted him the way womenfolk tried to soothe a colicky babe.

He lunged away from their useless ministrations and flung an angry look around the store. "Where's your clerk?"

The blanket covering the storeroom door waggled, and Miss Wagner poked her head out. "D-did you want me, Mr. Baxter?"

Asa pointed to the spot of floor in front of him. "C'mere, girl."

Her face white, the girl scurried toward him.

Both Melva and Shelva clucked, shaking their heads in dismay. "Asa, Asa," Shelva said, "mind your manners."

Melva added, "Don't know what's got into you, speakin' in such a way to a lady."

Asa swung on his sisters. He'd never been one to holler—being soft and quiet had always served him well. But his lungs demanded exercise. "Go about your business an' leave us be!"

With startled squawks, the pair bustled behind the counter and put their heads together, whispering and shooting flustered looks in his direction. Asa snorted—blame fool women, anyway. He grabbed Miss Wagner's arm and dragged her to the hallway leading to the back door. Once out of sight of his sisters, he gave her a rough shove.

"Where's your cousin?"

She rubbed her arm, tears glinting in her blue eyes. "I . . . I haven't seen him today."

Asa leaned close, squinting. "You sure? 'Cause if you're lyin' to me, I'll—"

She shrank back. "I'm not lying! I saw him last on Saturday night. I . . . I'm worried about him."

Asa balled his hands into fists. "You oughtta be worried. When I get my hands on him . . ." Clutching the hair at his temples, he growled. It had to have been Sid who'd dismantled his stills, smashed his jugs of beer, and tore apart his wine-making equipment. Nobody else knew about it. Except that sheriff. But the sheriff wouldn't have destroyed everything. He'd want to use it as evidence.

Catching hold of Miss Wagner's arm again, he gave her a vicious shake. "That cousin of yours shows his face around here, you tell him I'm huntin' him. An' you tell him he best come see me right away. Longer it takes, madder I'm gonna get. An', girlie, when I lose my temper . . ." He clamped his jaws on the threat forming in his mind. He shook her again, then let loose. "You tell him."

He turned and stormed through the mercantile. Melva and Shelva remained behind the counter, their long, skinny arms wrapped around one another. He shot them a murderous glare as he charged for the door, earning a round of confused whimpers. Just as he reached the screen door, it flew open and Mayor Hanaman stepped inside.

"Asa . . ." He yanked his hat from his graying head and glanced around the store. His eyes lit on the twins, and he nodded. "Ladies, I'm hoping you can help me. I've been asking up and down the street, but nobody's seen him."

Asa scowled. "You huntin' Sid, too?"

The mayor looked confused. "Sid? No. I'm trying to find McKane. Cora said he set off on one of Kimbrough's horses right after breakfast Saturday morning. But nobody's seen him since."

Asa wanted to leave, but the big man blocked his way. So he stood twitching in place while his sisters emitted little flustered exclamations of concern.

"M-Mr. Hanaman?" Miss Wagner's hesitant voice carried from behind Asa.

He looked over his shoulder to see her slowly approaching, her hands pressed tight against her stomach as if she might be sick at any minute. She shot him a wary glance, then focused on the mayor.

"I . . . I know where you can find Th—Sheriff McKane."

Hanaman leaned in, his jowls blotching. "Where?"

"Unless wild animals have . . . have disturbed his body, he'll be lying in some brush about a mile east of town."

Asa's startled yelp was covered by his sisters' shrill cry. Melva and Shelva raced around the counter to loom over Miss Wagner.

Mayor Hanaman's jaw dropped. "Are you telling me the sheriff is . . . is *dead?*"

Miss Wagner nodded. Tears slid down her white face. "I believe so, sir. He stopped Sid and me when we were making a delivery to Macyville. And Sid . . ." She gulped. Her body quivered worse than a penny on a railroad track when the train was approaching. "Sid shot him."

The mayor, Melva, and Shelva surrounded Miss Wagner, their combined voices creating a bigger commotion than a fox in a henhouse. Asa eased around the group and stumbled onto the boardwalk. He clutched his chest when the rapid *bumpity-bump* of his heart tried to bruise the inside of his ribs.

Sid had shot the sheriff. Asa'd told him something had to be done, and the boy had up and done it. A gleeful laugh formed in Asa's throat, but he held it inside. With the sheriff gone, and everybody focused on the murderer, nobody'd be paying any mind to him. He could rebuild his stills. With luck, he might be able to produce enough liquor to satisfy his buyers before they decided to go to somebody else.

He clambered onto Percival's back, grunting with the effort. No need to keep hunting Sid. If the boy was smart, he'd be in the next state by now. Asa had more important things to do.

"I suppose it's possible animals drug him off."

Sadie cringed on the buggy seat, wishing she hadn't overheard the mayor's statement. The mayor and two other men had borrowed one of Mr. Kimbrough's buggies and asked her to lead them to the place where she'd seen Sid and Thad slip into the brush. The beautifully fringed buggy with its twin tufted seats and silver trim often served as transport for grieving relatives on the way to the town cemetery. Sadie hadn't wanted to climb into it, but the men had insisted she go along. While Sadie remained in the buggy, the men searched the bushes. But after more than half an hour, they hadn't found so much as a piece of torn fabric to prove Sadie's statement.

Mr. Rahn turned a scowl on Sadie. "You sure this is the spot?"

Sadie leaned sideways a bit, making the leather seat squeak. "Yes, sir. Or very close to it." She would forever carry an image of that break in the bushes. "You . . . you haven't found anything?"

Mr. Easterberg stepped onto the road, shaking his head. "Not unless our sheriff suddenly grew a fur coat. All I found was the remains of a critter—a badger from the looks of it. But something tore into it good. Not much left."

Mr. Hanaman and Mr. Rahn both joined Mr. Easterberg, their fine suits bearing bits of dried leaves and dust from their romp in the brush. Mr. Rahn rubbed his nose. "Well, Roscoe, as you said, animals might've dragged him off. But there'd be something left behind—animals wouldn't eat his clothes or his bones."

Sadie shuddered at the picture the man's words painted. The fact that the men hadn't discovered any evidence of Thad's remains should have comforted her, but instead it proved her suspicion that Sid had buried Thad to hide his crime.

How she hated turning in her cousin, but she couldn't cover for him. She'd told God she would speak the truth and trust Him. Now she must keep her promise.

Drawing a deep breath, Sadie gathered her courage. "M-Mr. Hanaman, there's something else to look for. . . ."

The three men all looked at her expectantly.

"You might seek what appears to be a grave."

Mr. Rahn's eyebrows rose while the other two exchanged a startled look. "You have reason to believe he might've been buried?"

Miserably, Sadie nodded. "I . . . I saw Sid very early Sunday morning. He was filthy—covered with dirt—and he admitted he'd been digging."

The men shook their heads, muttering to one another. Sadie's heart ached, but at the same time a bit of her burden lifted. Secrets lost their power when exposed to the light of the sun, she realized. If only sharing the secret hadn't condemned Sid . . .

"Gentlemen," Mr. Hanaman said, his voice low and stern, "I think we should cease our search for the sheriff and begin a search for Sid Wagner. He's the only one who will be able to tell us where to find McKane's body."

Mr. Rahn and Mr. Easterberg expressed their agreement. The men joined Sadie, and Mr. Hanaman turned the horses, aiming the buggy for town.

Sadie gazed at each of the men and took a deep breath, ready to reveal the rest of her story. "I haven't told you everything yet."

Mr. Hanaman, his hands on the reins, jerked his chin in Sadie's direction. "What else has Sid done?"

"Not just Sid, Mayor." Sadie swallowed. "Sid, and Asa Baxter, and . . . and me." Her shoulders felt lighter as the weight of her lies finally fell free. No matter the consequences, she would divulge every bit of the deceit, and trust God with the outcome.

Sadie huddled in the dirt-walled cellar beneath Thad's living quarters. The mayor had given her a blanket to wrap around herself, but not even the thick wool could stave off the chill of the underground room. A tiny cot filled one whole wall, leaving a narrow space where she could pace back and forth. A peg pounded into the wall held a lantern, which provided a welcome glow. But it also cast light on the abundance of spider webs decorating the dingy room. Sadie tried to ignore them. She hated spiders.

Before climbing back up the ladder and locking the door behind him, the mayor had slipped a chamber pot into the corner and deposited a small basket of crackers, cheese, dried peaches, and a jar of water on the end of the cot. He'd seemed embarrassed, not even looking at her as he put the things in place, and then he'd offered gruffly,

"I'll be looking for somewhere else to put you. We won't want you down here with Baxter and Wagner, once we find them. But for now . . ."

Sadie had thanked him, and he'd departed, leaving her alone. She glanced at the door overhead. Not even a sliver of light showed around its edges. It had been suppertime when she'd come down, but she had no idea how much time had passed since then. It felt like ages but might have been only minutes. The silence was nearly unbearable.

She wriggled around on the cot, trying to get comfortable. She wished she'd asked to bring a book down with her. She longed for her Bible. Papa had always said, *"Whatever you need, Sadie-girl, God will provide."* How she needed the comfort available in the pages of God's book. Closing her eyes, she sent her mind through the Scripture she'd memorized over the years.

The verses in the third chapter of John came easily, and a small spiral of warmth touched her when she recalled God hadn't sent Jesus into the world to condemn it, but to save it. A verse from Second Corinthians about having sufficiency in all things so that believers could abound in good work made her heart ache with the desire to serve her God more fervently.

Something tickled her cheek, and she swatted at it. She opened her eyes and saw a black spider scrambling across the plaid cover on the cot.

She let out a shriek and moved away from it, bringing up her knees beneath her chin.

As much as she wanted to believe God was with her and be brave, her heart pounded in fear. She clung to the blanket, fighting the urge to climb the ladder and claw her way through the door to freedom. She couldn't bear being locked up all alone this way with no window, no means of determining time, with spiders crawling on her skin. She'd told the truth—she'd followed her conscience—and this was her reward?

"Choices bear consequences, Sadie-girl—both good an' bad." Papa's voice from long ago whispered through Sadie's memory. Very rarely had Papa raised his hand to his children, but she remembered him applying the rod of correction to her backside when she'd blatantly disobeyed Mama. Afterward, he'd dried her tears and held her tight, assuring her he still loved her.

Recalling Papa's strong arms wrapped around her, the comforting beat of his heart in her ear, Sadie once again experienced a wash of peace. Just because she must face the consequences of her actions didn't mean God had abandoned her. Didn't she have the promises from His word? He'd also promised she could do all things through Christ, who strengthened her.

Clasping her hands, she murmured, "If I must face a jail cell, I will do it, trusting in Your strength to see me through."

The moment she completed the prayer, a song wound its way through her heart. Sadie sat up, lifting her face to the ceiling. Instead of seeing floor joists and a sturdy door, she imagined a blue sky, a bank of white clouds, and bright white beams bursting from the cloud's belly. She opened her mouth and began to sing. "A mighty fortress is our God . . ."

37

Crickets chirped a welcome as Thad drew his borrowed horse to a stop right outside his office. He tied the reins, then gave the white stripe running down the horse's nose a scratch. "Rest for a few minutes, boy. Before we head out again, I'll take you to the blacksmith's stable an' find you something to eat. I don't think Kimbrough'll mind sharing some of his oats an' hay with a visiting beast."

Digging in his pocket, he withdrew his key and unlocked the door. He stepped over the threshold and paused, his gaze drifting slowly around the humble room. Not much to look at, he acknowledged. Unplastered walls, scuffed plank floor, hand-me-down furnishings—but it was his. He couldn't deny a feeling of satisfaction as he moved on into the room.

On his ride from Clay Centre, he'd had plenty of time to think. To talk to God. To sort things through. Thanks to his time with Faye Hines and the prayers she and Estel had offered on his behalf before he'd left at noon, he had a clear vision of what he was meant to do. "I won't be preaching," he said as he hooked his hat on its waiting peg, "but I'll be serving. Right here in Goldtree, if the fine folks decide to keep me." If Mayor Hanaman decided his service here was done once he brought Asa Baxter, Sid, and Sadie to justice, then he'd seek another position as a lawman.

Thad smiled, his chest expanding with gratitude. God had certainly guided him to the Hineses. They'd been His ministering angels, His messengers. Thad might not know what would happen with Sadie, but he knew God was in control. The evidence of God's hand during the past few days convinced him he had nothing to fear.

But he had a lot of work to do. He needed to locate and arrest Asa, Sid, and Sadie. He'd better see Mayor Hanaman first thing in the morning about feeding the prisoners—who knew how long they'd sit in the cellar room before the circuit judge arrived to hear the case against them and make his judgment.

He moved through the office toward his sleeping quarters. As he opened the door, a melody, carried by a sweet, lilting voice, reached his ears. He froze in place, holding his breath. With his head tipped, he strained to catch the words of the song.

"Be still, my soul: thy God doth undertake to guide the future as he has the past. Thy hope, thy confidence let nothing shake; all now mysteries shall be bright at last . . ."

The song continued, but Thad's rushing pulse covered the words. The music seemed to rise from the shadows and confirm the very conclusions he'd drawn on his ride home. Eager to hear more, he stumbled forward two steps, and his heels scuffed the floor. Abruptly the song stopped. Then a tentative query wavered: "Is someone there?"

Thad recognized the voice. He spun in a circle, his gaze seeking. "Sadie?"

Long seconds of silence fell. Then he heard her again. "Thad . . . is that you?" Her voice held a note of disbelief.

She was calling from beneath his feet. He dropped to his knees and tugged at the cellar door. But a padlock held it tight. Leaning close to the crack in the door, he called, "Sadie, what are you doing down there?"

"The mayor put me in here after I confessed I'd been entertaining gamblers."

She was crying—her voice broke with sobs. Thad thought his heart might break. Even though he'd made the decision to lock her up himself, the reality of the situation crushed him. He pressed his palms to the wooden planks, wishing he could hold her. "I'm sorry, Sadie."

More sobs rose. "Oh, Thad, you're alive! You're alive!"

Alive? What on earth had Hanaman told her? The sound of her distress tore him in two. He had to see her—to hold her and assure her. "Sadie, hang on—I'm gonna get the key for this padlock. I'll be right back."

He didn't wait for a reply but raced out of the office and around the corner to the mayor's house. His frantic pounding on the door brought a grumbling command. "I'm coming, I'm coming. Don't break down the door."

The door opened, revealing the drowsy mayor topped by a striped sleeping hat that matched his nightshirt. His mouth was stretched in a yawn as he opened the door. "Who's out—" He spotted Thad and gave a strangled yelp that almost knocked him backward.

Thad held out his hand. "I need the key for the padlock on my cellar door."

The mayor shook his head, the tassel on his hat swinging like a pendulum. "W-w-what?"

"The key," Thad repeated. "I need to open the cellar door."

Hanaman looked right and left, his face cloudy with confusion. "Where'd you come from?"

"Clay Centre. Now . . . the key? I'm gonna need it if I'm to lock Baxter down there."

"You caught Baxter?"

Thad blew out a short breath. "Not yet. I'll be going after him soon as I have a way of locking him up."

Hanaman finally seemed to come out of his stupor. "Oh! The key! Yes, yes, wait here. I'll get it." He scurried off, and Thad tapped his boot toe, impatiently waiting. Finally Hanaman returned. "Group of us rode out to Baxter's house late this afternoon, but he wasn't there. We think he might have hightailed it out of the county."

"Don't worry. I'll find him," Thad vowed. He held out his hand.

The mayor dropped the key into Thad's waiting palm. His ruddy face glowed with wonder. "Good to see you, Sheriff. We all thought—"

Thad already knew what they all thought. He just didn't know why. But he wanted to hear the story from Sadie rather than the mayor. He turned and bounded off the porch, then ran the distance to his office. His feet skidded on the floor as he rounded the corner, and he dropped to his knees to release the padlock. "I'm back! Sadie, I'm here!" His trembling fingers gave him some trouble, but he finally managed to pull the padlock free. Thad yanked the door open. "I'm coming down!"

He used only two rungs of the ladder, jumping the remaining distance. The moment he turned, Sadie dove into his arms. He held her close, just like he had the day she'd learned of her

415

stepfather's death. Now, as then, her tears soaked his shirt. But last time she'd wept in sorrow. He sensed these tears were ones of relief and joy. Feeling her shoulders heave and listening to her deep sobs, however, made tears prick in his own eyes. He rubbed her back, murmuring, "Shh, now. Everything'll be all right. Shh, Sadie."

"You're alive. I can't believe it. I thought . . ."

He guided her to the cot and sat, pulling her down beside him. His arm curled around her waist, and she nestled her head on his shoulder. Her soft yellow hair, shining in the lantern light, caught in his whiskers, but she made no move to pull away.

"Sadie, how'd everybody get the idea I was dead?"

Tears continued to rain down her cheeks as she shared about hearing a shot, Sid's lone return, and then the other clues that had led to her belief that Sid had killed him and buried him.

Finally, she hiccupped, sucking in several breaths. "I'm so relieved Sid didn't . . . I'm so relieved you're alive."

He embraced her again, kissing her hair. How he lamented the pain she'd borne, thinking him killed at the hands of her beloved cousin, but he couldn't begrudge his time in Clay Centre. He'd needed that growing time.

"Here now, sit up." He gently pushed her upright, then removed his handkerchief from his pocket and wiped her face. She sat trustingly beneath his touch, her blue eyes locked on his as if she couldn't get enough of him. He understood. He wanted to sit here holding her forever, but he couldn't. He had a job to do. But as sheriff, he had the power to make a slight change.

"As you can see, I'm alive and well." She rewarded him with a wobbly smile, and he went on. "And the first thing I'm gonna do is get you out of here."

She drew back, alarm on her face. "No, Thad! I did wrong, and I have to pay for it."

He crushed her to his chest. "Sadie, I know you gotta pay for it." *Oh, God, let the judge be merciful to her, please. . . .* "But I can't leave you down here in this hole."

He rose, drawing her up with him and urging her toward the ladder. "I trust you not to run off. I'm taking you to the mercantile. While we wait for the circuit judge, you can keep working for Miss Melva and Miss Shelva."

She paused at the bottom of her ladder, uncertainty marring her face. "Are you sure? I don't want to get you in trouble with the town council."

"Town council's gonna have to learn to trust my judgment." He gave her a little nudge. "Go ahead now, get up there." He waited until she started up the ladder before adding, "Besides, there's somebody else who's gonna need to take up residence here. Soon as I get you settled in your room, I'm aiming to bring him in."

Asa tightened the last bolt, taking care not to crimp the copper tubing. Then he stepped back to admire his work. It had taken him most of the day, but he'd finally repaired all three stills. By morning, he'd be ready to start filling jugs again.

He turned toward the back chamber of the cave for one more look at the biggest still, snorting softly. He didn't have any jugs to fill, thanks to Sid's rampage. But he had barrels in his barn. He'd bring them over after he'd gotten some sleep. He could fill barrels, then transfer the beer to jugs when he'd gotten a new shipment.

That was something else he had to do—find somebody to operate his freight wagon. He cursed again, tweaking the coil on the still so it lay just so. Might not be easy to find somebody as easy to fool as that dumb kid from Indiana, but he'd manage. He always managed. He was like a cat—always landed on his feet.

He yawned, a mouselike squeak escaping his throat. It was late. Time to go home and get some sleep. Ambling toward the front chamber of the cave, he inwardly rejoiced at how well everything was working out. Sid was long gone, no doubt hiding after doing away with the meddlesome sheriff. The little singer gal was too scared to tell what she knew.

He grabbed a burlap bag and dropped in the tools he'd used to repair the stills. The metal tools clanked together in the bottom of the bag, echoing through the chamber. A spooky sound. Asa gave himself a little shake. No need to be acting like his goosey sisters, afraid of underground places. He slung the bag onto his back and headed through the opening into the star-speckled night.

A coyote howled, his lonely voice carrying on the light breeze. Asa hurried out of the cave. He had a gun strapped to his hip, but he didn't care to use it. A gun blast at night carried for miles and would surely rouse somebody. He entered the clearing where he'd left his horse and wagon and came to a startled halt. He looked around in confusion, the bag's weighted bottom bouncing against the backs of his knees. "Where'n tarnation is my wagon?"

"I moved it."

Asa yelped in shock as someone stepped out of the shadows and directly into his pathway. He squinted through the murky light. Then he let out a grunt of irritation. "Sid Wagner! What're you doin' sneakin' around here? I figured you were nigh on into Oklahoma Territory by now."

Sid stopped within several feet of Asa. His unsmiling face glowed white in the muted light of the moon. "I've been around. Watchin' you. Makin' sure you didn't skedaddle."

Asa let out a bold laugh. "Why would I need to skedaddle? I got no reason to run."

"Yes, you do. 'Cause I'm aimin' to turn you in."

Asa dropped the bag and balled his fists. He sneered at the boy. "You forget you're in as deep as me. Deeper now."

Sid's brow furrowed momentarily, then cleared. "You're right, I'm in deep. I been busy—collapsin' your tunnel to the gamblin' room—"

"You *what?*"

"—an' stealin' your bottles. But I did all that to keep you from doin' more wrong."

Fury boiled in Asa's middle. He tasted bitter acid on the back of his tongue. "Why you miserable, ungrateful cur. After all I done for you, givin' you a good job an' bringin' your cousin in? This is how you repay me?"

Sid went on calmly, as if Asa hadn't spoken. "I already told the sheriff what you've been doin'. Now I'm willin' to turn myself in. Take my licks."

The boy's final statement made no sense. "Sheriff? What sheriff? He's dead an' buried!"

Sid drew back, his jaw flopping like a fish gulping air. Color drained from his face. "McKane . . . is dead?"

Asa snorted. Had the boy gone loco? "Sadie told us—you put him in the ground yourself!"

"That's where everyone's mistaken."

The voice came from behind Asa. He spun around. His boot caught in the discarded bag at

420

his feet, tripping him. The fall took hide off the heels of his hands. He rolled over, cradling his hurting palms against his middle, and stared, wide-eyed, as a tall man topped by a cowboy hat stepped from the trees. Moonlight shone on the silver star pinned to his chest.

Asa gasped. "McKane! You ain't dead?"

"That's right, Baxter. I'm not dead. And I'm here to take you in."

38

"Finding you guilty of knowingly and deliberately producing illicit alcoholic beverages for the purpose of sale and profit, and for knowingly and deliberately providing the opportunity to indulge in games of chance, I seize for Five Creek Township all of your assets including your home, your businesses, and your personal belongings. I also sentence you to ten years of hard labor in the Kansas Penitentiary in Lansing."

Two men bearing deputy badges took hold of Mr. Baxter's arms and ushered the blubbering man out of Thad's office. Behind Sadie, Miss Shelva and Miss Melva broke into wails of anguish. Sadie's heart ached. She wished she could comfort her dear employers—they loved their brother so much. His punishment would no doubt hurt them as much as it did Asa. But she couldn't leave her chair, where she'd been placed at the beginning of the trial as a defendant.

The circuit judge, seated at Thad's table in lieu of a bench, glared at the twins. He brought down his gavel with a resounding bang. "Silence!"

With strangled gulps, the women obeyed the judge's command, and the murmurs from the gathered townsfolk also abruptly ceased. Sadie's pulse tripped faster and faster, making her feel lightheaded. The man's lack of compassion heightened her fear. She clutched her hands together and stared at the judge, hardly daring to breathe. Would Sid's and her sentences be as harsh as the one given to Mr. Baxter?

The judge turned his dark gaze on Sid. "Sidney Wagner."

Sid bolted to his feet, his shoulders square and chin high. "Yes, sir."

"And Sadie Wagner."

Sadie clumsily rose. She tried to stand as proudly as her cousin, but her knees quivered. She licked her lips and rasped, "Y-yes, your honor."

The judge's dark brows formed an intimidating V. "It is within my power to hold both of you accountable for your association with Asa Baxter and his illegal practices and bring a judgment of imprisonment."

Sadie's fingers tightened painfully on her own

palms. She wished she could cling to Thad. *" 'When thou passest through the waters, I will be with thee . . .' "* The promise from God's word whispered through Sadie's heart. Peace washed over her. She aimed her unwavering gaze at the judge and placed herself in her Father's hands.

The judge cleared his throat. "However, taking into account Mr. Wagner's willingness to make known the unlawful dealings to the authorities, and having heard testimony pertaining to Miss Wagner's initial innocence concerning her participation, I find myself leaning toward leniency."

Sid's shoulders sagged, and from behind Sadie, a chorus of exhaled breaths told her how many people found relief in the judge's statement.

"I sentence both of you to one year's supervision by Goldtree's sheriff, Thaddeus McKane. If, at the conclusion of the year, he can verify you have conducted yourselves as upstanding, law-abiding citizens, then there will be no further penalty." The judge brought down his gavel. "Court is adjourned." He snatched up his belongings and hustled out the door to his waiting carriage.

The townsfolk, mumbling loudly, filed out after the judge. Those fortunate enough to hear the judge's verdict with their own ears would spread the news to those who'd been forced to wait on the street, outside of hearing. Only Sadie, Thad, Mayor Hanaman, Miss Melva, Miss

Shelva, and Sid remained in the small office.

Sid turned to Sadie, relief etched on his features. But before his arms could reach her, she found herself swept into a hug by someone else. She didn't need to see to know who'd captured her—the familiar essence that spoke *Thad* filled her senses. She clung, happy tears raining down her face.

"He chose mercy, Thad," she whispered, her face pressed to Thad's neck. "He chose mercy."

Thad set her down and cupped her face in his broad, warm palms, smiling at her through a shimmer of tears. "Thank God for His mercy." Somehow she knew they both acknowledged God's mercy rather than that offered by the earthly judge.

A hesitant *harrumph* reached her ears, and she turned to Sid, who stood sheepishly to the side. He held out one hand to her. "Sadie, guess this means we're both out of a job. I'm sorry."

Sadie clasped his hand between hers. "It's not your fault, Sid. You couldn't know we'd be caught up in all this. I'm just glad"—she whisked a smile over her shoulder at Thad—"the truth came out. Now we needn't hide our faces in shame."

"Well, I'm surely feelin' shameful." Miss Melva sniffled, holding tight to her sister's hand.

Miss Shelva added, "How can we show our faces in town now, knowin' what Asa done? Nobody'll look at us the same again."

"We gotta make it right somehow," Miss Melva declared.

Thad stepped forward and embraced the pair. "You've done no wrong." Emotion deepened his tone. His warm-eyed gaze found Sadie's and held her as securely as his arms now held the Baxter twins. "Asa must make atonement for his own sins. You aren't accountable for your brother's choices."

Sadie's heart fluttered within her chest. In Thad's eyes she glimpsed freedom. Her soul rejoiced at the release of his long-held burden. Gliding forward, she curled her arms around the twins' waists, forming a circle with the three people who meant so much to her. "Let's make a pact—no more regrets over yesterday."

Her eyes locked with Thad's. The warm tenderness reflected in his green eyes nearly melted her. He offered a slow nod, granting his agreement. With difficulty, she tore her focus from Thad to the twins.

"Miss Melva? Miss Shelva?"

Their shoulders rose in unison, and matching sighs whooshed from their lips. Then, as if in one accord, their heads bobbed in synchronized nods. "No more regrets," they chorused.

Then Miss Melva released a soft titter. " 'Cept for one."

Miss Shelva frowned. "What's that?"

Miss Melva's thick eyebrows waggled. "Our

givin' up our fear o' down-under places."

"That's right. We done it, didn't we, Sister?"

"That we did." The pair chortled together.

Sadie sent Thad a puzzled look, and he smiled. "Miss Melva and Miss Shelva visited Asa every day. While he was in the cellar room."

Sadie gawked at the twins, who gazed back, satisfaction shining in their eyes. She shook her head, amazed. "But you said you never went into hidey-holes—not even if a twister was coming!"

The pair hunched their shoulders and tittered again. They stepped aside, exchanging a knowing look. "Reckon fears are overcome," Miss Melva began.

"—when love goes deeper than the fear," Miss Shelva finished.

" 'Perfect love casteth out fear,' " Thad quoted, and Sadie's heart lifted. He'd make a wonderful minister someday. Except the judge had given Thad responsibility for overseeing Sid's and her sentence. He wouldn't be able to set aside his badge for at least a year. Had Thad realized that yet?

"Sister, we got a mercantile to run," Miss Melva said.

"Then let's go," Miss Shelva said. The twins coiled their arms around each other's waists and ambled out of the office.

At their departure, Mayor Hanaman stepped forward, propelling Sid along with him. "Sheriff, this young man's going to have to remain in Goldtree under your supervision, but it seems he lost his job with Baxter."

Thad slipped one hand into his trouser pocket, assuming the casual pose that was as familiar as breathing to Sadie. "I have a suggestion." He stroked his finger over his mustache. "Since the judge also gave all of Baxter's holdings to Five Creek Township, somebody is going to have to be in charge of maintaining his rental houses an' taking care of his house an' land outside of town until the council decides what to do with it. What do you think of making Sid the foreman of those properties?"

The mayor gave Thad a hearty clap on the back. "Why, that's grand thinking, Sheriff!" He turned to Sid and aimed a finger at him. "You're already familiar with Baxter's holdings, so you shouldn't have any trouble handling those duties, will you, Sid?"

Sid looked dumbstruck, but he bounced his head in a jerky nod. "Not at all. I'm glad to do it."

"Good, good." The mayor threw his arm around Sid's shoulders. "Come to the bank with me, and we'll get the details of your new position squared away." They started out, but then Mr. Hanaman turned back and fixed Sadie with a serious look. "Miss Wagner? There's something of importance I need to discuss with you. Soon as you're"—he cleared his throat, a sly smile creeping up his cheek—"finished here with the sheriff, come on over and see me."

Sadie nodded in reply, and the mayor and Sid left. The moment they departed, Thad pulled her snug against his length. She nestled, the feeling of homecoming sweeping over her once again. She would have been content to remain there in his arms for the rest of her life, but she needed to tell him something, and she wouldn't hide against his chest as she said it.

Pulling back slightly, she peered into his dear face. "Thad, about my sentence . . . I'm so sorry you'll be forced to remain as sheriff for another year."

His low chuckle rumbled. "I'm not." He drew her close again, resting his chin lightly against her temple. "You see, God's been doing some speaking to my heart, an' He let me know my wanting to be a preacher wasn't for Him—it was all for me." His hands moved up and down her spine, the touch warm and welcome. "I've been praying for Him to show me how I'm meant to serve, so the judge putting me in charge of you an' Sid for the next year gave me my answer. I'm to be a lawman, Sadie. I'm meant to serve the town of Goldtree."

Her fears about preventing him from achieving his intended purpose melted away beneath a wash of gratitude. "Oh, I'm so glad . . ."

"Me too. As for you . . ." His hands curled around her upper arms, moving her aside.

She blinked twice beneath his unsmiling gaze. "Y-yes?"

"You're to sing." His mild scowl dissolved, a gentle smile appearing on his face. "In the opera house."

With Asa Baxter locked away, the opera house was no more. "But Mr. Baxter—"

"Not in the singing room under the mercantile, Sadie." Thad's mustache twitched, excitement glittering in his eyes. "In a *real* opera house."

"But . . . but . . ." She couldn't rein in her confusion to adequately voice the questions crowding her mind.

"Shh." Thad touched her lips with one finger. "Just listen. The town council met last week, and after seeing how many people came to your performances, they've decided having an opera house would be a real benefit to the town. Since Asa won't be building one, they've taken it upon themselves to erect one in the open lot south of the Congregationalist church. Mr. Hanaman owns the property, and he's donated it for the town's use.

"Miss Melva and Miss Shelva gave permission to have all the chairs and light fixtures removed from the cellar singing room and placed in the new building. Roscoe Hanaman has already ordered lumber and stone to build the opera house, and he hopes to have construction completed in time for a special Christmas performance."

Sadie listened, enthralled. She'd spent the three weeks of her time under arrest working at the mercantile or holed up in her room, per Thad's instruction. The Baxter twins had to have been aware of the plans, yet they hadn't uttered a word of it to her. "Are you sure Mr. Hanaman means for me to sing? After I . . . I . . ." She gulped.

Thad's expression softened. He gently cupped her jaw. "Mr. Hanaman, as well as the entire town, has been given a view of your soul through your music. They know your involvement in the illegal happenings wasn't intentional. They're willing to forgive an' forget." His voice dropped to a husky whisper. "So now you must forgive yourself."

Sadie tipped her head, pressing her cheek more fully into the sweet pressure of his palm. Her eyes slipped closed as she absorbed his steady presence, his tender touch. Her soul ached to agree to singing in the new opera house, but there was something she must do first. Opening her eyes, she looked into Thad's dear face. "I want to sing, Thad—you know how much I want to sing. But I need to pray about it, to make sure it's what God wills for me." She swallowed happy tears, experiencing complete peace in waiting. "I want to sing for Him, not to please myself."

The approval shining in Thad's eyes told her he understood.

She drew in a deep breath. Now that the weeks of tension—of wondering what the judge would deem appropriate—were past, tiredness claimed her. She hid a yawn behind her hand. "Oh my . . . I don't suppose Miss Melva and Miss Shelva would allow me the afternoon to nap."

Thad chuckled. "You don't have time for a nap just yet. You need to talk to Mr. Hanaman, remember?" He caught her hand and raised it to his lips, brushing a kiss across her knuckles. The soft tickle of his mustache sent tremors up her arm. He placed her hand in the bend of his elbow. "Let me escort you to the bank, and when you're finished talking with him about the new opera house, I'll return you to Miss Melva and Miss Shelva. Give them a yawn like you just gave me, and they'll be the ones to suggest a nap."

Sadie giggled as Thad led her onto the boardwalk. He was right—the twins cared about her. They'd assumed a motherly role toward her, and even though they were sometimes brusque, she didn't doubt their affection.

When they were halfway across the street, someone called Sadie's name. Mr. Rahn trotted toward them, waving a piece of paper. He panted to a halt and pressed the paper into Sadie's hand. "This here telegram just arrived. Figured you'd want to see it right away." He touched Sadie's shoulder. "Me an' the missus are awful happy you aren't headin' to jail, Miss Sadie. 'Specially now that—" He backed up, waving his hands. "Well, never you mind. Read it for yourself." He spun and trotted off.

Sadie watched him go, the telegram fluttering in the light August breeze. His words of congratulations touched her. She hoped the rest of the town would be as accepting.

Thad gave her a gentle nudge. "Aren't you going to read your telegram?"

Sadie hunched her shoulders, releasing a self-conscious giggle. "Of course." She unfolded the paper and read the brief message: CHILDREN AND I COMING TO GOLDTREE STOP WILL ARRIVE FIRST OF SEPTEMBER STOP CAN'T WAIT TO HEAR YOU SING ON STAGE STOP ALL MY LOVE MAMA.

For a moment, Sadie stared at the paper in confusion. Mama moving the family to Kansas? Then she gave herself a little shake. Why shouldn't she move? With Papa gone, nothing held them in Indiana. And coming here would give them all a fresh start—a chance to be together again.

Mama would get to hear her sing on the stage of a real opera house. A bubble of laughter formed in Sadie's throat, and her eyes slipped closed. *Thank You, God, for new beginnings and fresh chances.*

Thad's soft voice intruded in her thoughts. "Sadie? Everything all right?"

Sadie let out a whoop and threw her arms around Thad's neck, knocking his cowboy hat askew. "My mama and sister and brothers are coming here, to Goldtree!"

"What?"

She laughed anew at his startled expression. She showed him the telegram while laughter continued to roll from her lips. Such heartfelt joy had to find release.

Thad grabbed her in another hug, rocking her, his chuckles combining with hers in a sweet harmony of delight. Then he pulled back, an impish grin twitching his mustache. "It's a good thing she's coming, too. 'Cause you'll want her here to witness our nuptials."

Sadie gaped at him, her laughter ending with a startled gasp. "W-what?"

"That is," he said, dropping to one knee right there in the middle of dusty Main Street, "if you'll have me."

His image swam with the spurt of tears. She reached out, catching his hands. "Yes, Thad. Oh yes!"

He rose, scooping her into his embrace. His lips found hers—warm, soft, and moist with happy tears. Locked in his arms, her lips captured by his, she thought she imagined applause. But then Thad lifted his head, looking beyond her. Red splashed his cheeks. She twisted around to look, too. All along the boardwalk townsfolk stood, faces wreathed in smiles, clapping in approval. She hid her flaming face in Thad's chest. Thad joggled her loose, encouraging her to acknowledge the gathered crowd. She did so, her lips quavering in an embarrassed-yet-pleased grin.

Mr. Hanaman called from his spot by the bank doors, "Sheriff, are you making an arrest, or can we assume somebody's gone and captured you?" Laughter rang up and down the street.

Thad rubbed his finger over his mustache in a self-conscious gesture that made Sadie giggle.

Then another voice called out—one that made Sadie's heart turn over. "If he don't go willingly, he's a plumb fool." Sid's teasing comment offered his blessing on Sadie's choice.

Sadie sent him a grateful smile, which he returned with an almost indiscernible bob of his head.

Slowly, the townspeople turned and began ambling toward their places of business or waiting wagons. Mr. Hanaman and Sid disappeared inside the bank. A mockingbird swooped from a treetop, trilling a song he'd learned from a cardinal. His cheerful tune, not of his own making, reflected Sadie's desire to sing the songs given to her by her Father. *For You, dear Lord. Always, only for You . . .*

Sadie and Thad stood in the middle of the street, watching and waving until everyone had dispersed. Then Thad curved his arm around Sadie's waist and deposited a kiss on her forehead.

"C'mon, Miss Sadie. Time to move on."

Yes, Sadie agreed, her stride aligning perfectly with Thad's, time to move on. Into her God-kissed future. She smiled upward, her heart thrilling at Thad's tender smile in reply. Serving together, their lives would create a melody of God's merciful faithfulness.

Acknowledgments

Mom and Daddy, Don, and my girls—thank you for walking this pathway with me.

Critique Group—thank you for your encouragement, your support, your listening ears, and your splashes of humor right when I need them most.

My soul sister, *Kathy*—thank you for that afternoon in Paxico, where the seed blossomed into story. Another memory . . .

Judy Miller—thank you for lending me the book from Jim's "to be read" pile—it helped bring the setting to life for me. Your friendship is one I treasure.

Shelva, a woman I met at a book signing in Ohio, and *Melva,* my choir buddy—thank you for letting me borrow your names. The high-strung characters in the book in no way reflect *your* characters!

Charlene and the staff at Bethany House—thank you for all you do to help me bring the people residing in my heart to life. I appreciate you!

Finally, and most importantly, *God*—thank You for the melody of grace that rings through my soul. May any praise or glory be reflected directly back to You.

About the Author

KIM VOGEL SAWYER is the bestselling author of more than twenty novels. Her books have won the Carol Award, the Gayle Wilson Award of Excellence, and the Inspirational Readers Choice Award. Kim is active in her church, where she leads women's fellowship and participates in both voice and bell choirs. In her spare time, she enjoys drama, quilting, and calligraphy. Kim and her husband, Don, reside in Central Kansas and have three daughters and nine grandchildren.

www.kimvogelsawyer.com
writespassage.blogspot.com

Center Point Large Print
600 Brooks Road / PO Box 1
Thorndike ME 04986-0001 USA

(207) 568-3717

US & Canada:
1 800 929-9108
www.centerpointlargeprint.com